THE HUNTER
TARA CRESCENT

THE
HUNTER

Text copyright © 2024 Tara Crescent
All Rights Reserved

No part of this book may be reproduced in any form or by any electronic or mechanical means including information storage and retrieval systems, without permission in writing from the author. The only exception is by a reviewer, who may quote short excerpts in a review.

This book is a work of fiction. Names, characters, places, and incidents either are products of the author's imagination or are used fictitiously. Any resemblance to actual persons, living or dead, events, or locales is entirely coincidental.

Editing by Molly Whitman at Novel Mechanic, www.novelmechanic.com

Cover Design by Bookin It Designs, www.bookinitdesigns.com

Model Cover Photography Michelle Lancaster, www.michellelancaster.com

v. 20240125

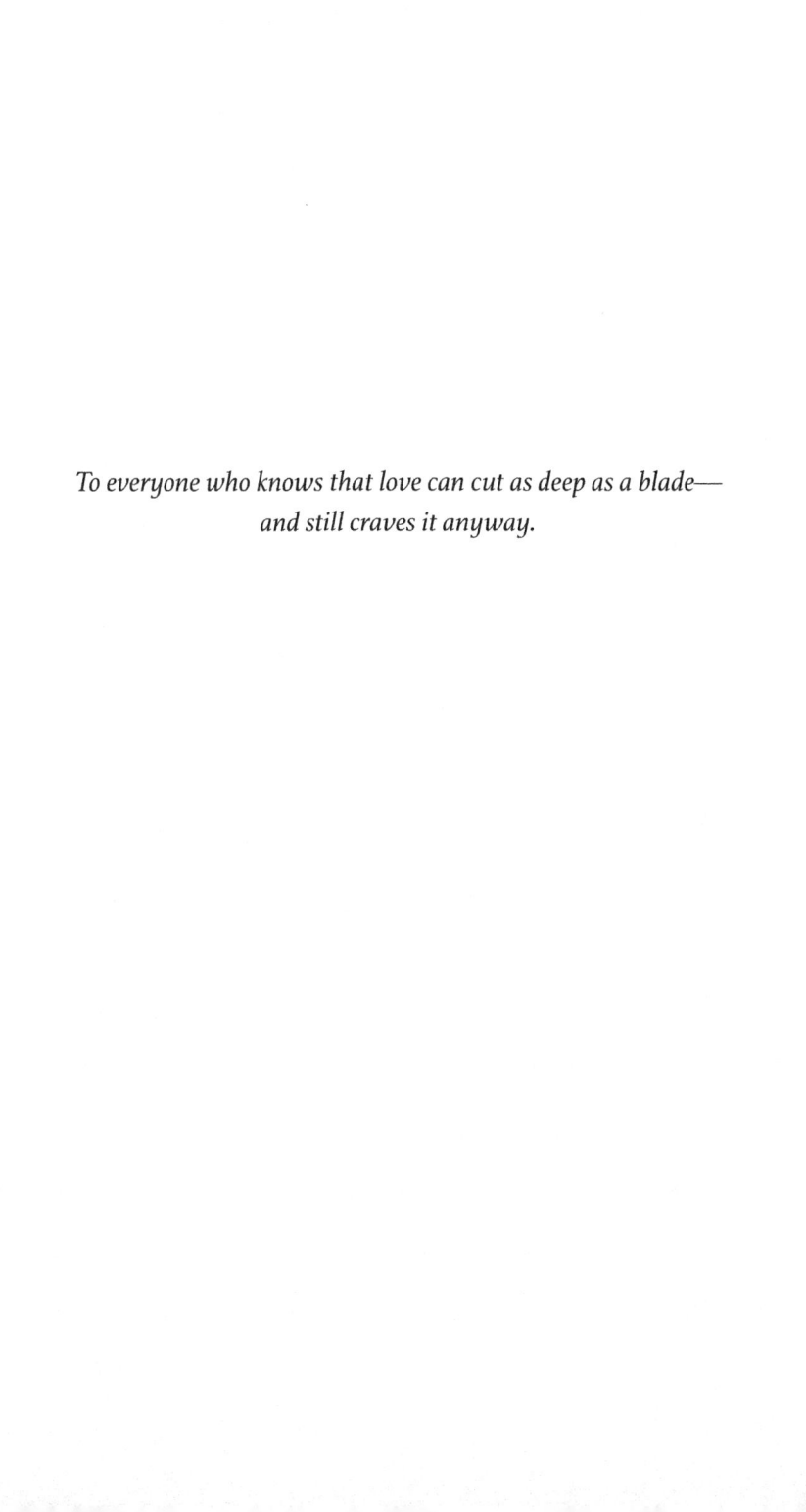

*To everyone who knows that love can cut as deep as a blade—
and still craves it anyway.*

CONTENT NOTE

The Hunter contains explicit sex, violence, attempted murder, murder, death of a child during childbirth, and violence toward children, both off and on-page. But rest assured, everyone that hurts a child dies in *very* painful ways.

1
STEFI

A man is on the ground, cowering before me, trying to crawl away, tears streaming down his eyes. "Please," he begs. "Please... I don't know who you are, and I don't know what you want, but please don't shoot me."

I should be moved by his fear, but I haven't been able to feel anything for a long time. No sadness, no joy, nothing. I'm numb inside and out.

"Do you remember me?" I lift my gun and aim it at him. "I was just a child, and I didn't understand what was happening to me. I begged you for help, and you looked at me as if I was dirt on your shoe. And then you said, 'Stop crying and pay attention. I don't care about your tears.' Remember that?"

His eyes widen in horror. Oh yeah. He knows who I am now.

"You knew we were trafficked," I say. "You knew Bach acquired us from all around the world, and you didn't care. You just cared about your paycheck."

"Please," he whispers. "Have mercy."

"Stop crying and pay attention," I tell him. "I don't care about your tears."

Then I shoot him in the head.

I HAVE A HIT LIST.

When I started it seven years ago, it had thirty-nine names. Since then, I've narrowed it down considerably, and there are only four entries left.

Varek Zaworski and Pavel Dachev, two bounty hunters who worked for Bach and hunted down anyone foolish enough to run away from his control.

Antonio Moretti, the Venice crime lord, who's been funding Bach's operations for the last five years.

And finally, the man himself. My former trainer, the man who molded me into a killer. Henrik Bach.

Four rich, powerful, dangerous men, and I'm determined to kill them all.

2
JOAO

I'm sitting on my yellow couch with a beer, my black cat Mimi on my lap, trying to find something to watch on TV, when I get a summons from Antonio Moretti to meet him at Casanova.

That's *unusual*. I saw the padrino at headquarters earlier today when I delivered a report on our smuggling operations. He was in a good mood, joking about his wife's pregnancy cravings. "Her checkup went well, and the nausea is easing, thank heavens." He made a face. "Never get someone you love pregnant, Joao. It's hell watching Lucia suffer and knowing there's nothing I can do to prevent it."

Casanova is a sex club. Why are we meeting there, of all the places?

My boss doesn't like to be kept waiting, so I grab a jacket and head out. It's an unusually warm October evening and Venice bustles with tourists. No surprise there. I live in Giudecca, which is typically a little quieter than the mainland, but not by much. Every year, the island gets more crowded as people discover its charms. The art galleries are thrilled by this, as are the restaurateurs.

Me, not so much. There are too many people and too many threats, and I know from experience that an attack could come from anywhere.

My senses tingle as I walk to the boat launch, threading past the clusters of tourists dining al fresco, lingering over their dessert and coffee.

I was kidnapped from my home as a child and trained to be an assassin. In one particularly memorable training exercise when I was ten, my team was set loose in a simulated city square to find our target, and a member of the opposing team nearly knifed me. In those days, I still foolishly trusted kindly authority figures, and she'd been dressed as a nun.

Stefi had rescued me by throwing a brick at the nun's head. And it was a hard throw. The nun went down, and even as I blinked in confusion, this girl with red hair in two fat pigtails darted over to me and grabbed my hand. "Come on," she said, her green eyes flashing impatiently. "She won't stay down long. Let's get out of here."

Stefi's been dead for eight long years, but even now, I only have to close my eyes, and she's there. As real to me as when she was alive and we were together, her eyes laughing, her long hair mussed on a pillow. My wife loved warm nights in October. If we were between jobs, we would sneak away to Prague or Valencia or Dubrovnik, and she'd drag me to a square where we would drink cold beer or cheap wine in a small cafe. "This weather is a gift from the summer gods," she would say, throwing out her arms expansively. "We can't reject their gift."

Henrik Bach, the man who took us from our homes when we were children and molded us into killers, never liked for his trainees to get too friendly with each other. If we banded together, we would become a threat to his authority. If he knew we got married in secret, he would have killed us both.

Despite the risks, whenever Stefi called, I would be there. I could never say no to her. *I never wanted to.*

I push those memories down, jump into my speedboat, and cross the lagoon. Enough time has passed that I should be able to remember the happy times without an influx of pain. But even now, even after all these years, every time I think about Stefi, it feels like someone is shoving a red-hot poker into my heart.

It hurts less to keep the memories buried.

Less than thirty minutes after I received the padrino's text message, I walk into Casanova.

Antonio is in a private room, his wife Lucia snuggled next to him on a couch littered with throw pillows. My eyebrows creep up when I see her there. "This is awkward," I quip. It's weird enough that he wanted to meet me at a sex club, but why is his wife here? Something is going on, and my first response is to make a joke about it. "The padrino said something about strange cravings earlier, but I thought he was talking about food. I'm flattered, of course, Signora Moretti, but—"

Antonio's face draws into a frown. Lucia snort-laughs and throws a pillow at me. I catch it in mid-air, set it back down on the couch, and give my irritated boss a placating smile. "You know people are going to gossip."

Antonio Moretti is the most powerful man in the city, and every move he makes is thoroughly scrutinized. Even though Casanova has rules about maintaining the anonymity of their guests, by tomorrow morning, everyone who is anyone will believe that the padrino and his wife had an intimate rendezvous with an unknown man.

"It can't be helped. If Lucia wasn't here, people would gossip that I was cheating on my pregnant wife, and I will not have that." He gestures to a chair, and I lower myself into it. "I wanted to talk to you privately, and this is one of the most secure places in the city. Drink?"

"No, thank you." What does he have to say that we couldn't discuss at headquarters? It can't be a job—if it were, Lucia wouldn't be here. The padrino doesn't keep secrets from his wife, but especially now, he's careful not to upset her.

I study him as he pours Lucia a glass of sparkling water with a lime wedge. He smiles at his wife as he hands her the drink, but his eyes stay hooded.

Something's bothering him. The look he's giving me. . . It's almost as if he's afraid of me. No, not afraid—Lucia wouldn't be here if he was—but he's definitely wary.

He settles back on the couch and fixes me with a hard stare. "When you joined my organization, Joao, we made a deal," he says. "Every time I asked you to kill, you had the right to ask why, and you had the right to say no. And in exchange, I wanted the truth. Complete honesty about your past."

The Hunter

"I remember."

"Cecilia d'Este sent me this." He pushes a large brown envelope across the coffee table, keeping his eyes on my face. "This is a file on Gemma, the woman who came after Tomas's fiancée."

Tomas is our money guy, and Alina is his fiancée. A couple of weeks ago, her estranged father hired a professional to abduct her from Venice. Gemma, or whatever her name really is, walked into Alina's gym and befriended her. She took her out to dinner, drugged her during that meal, and left Ali on a deserted dock for two petty criminals to pick up.

Thankfully, Tomas intercepted the men before they could remove Ali from Venice. Less ideally, he killed them before I could question them. An understandable reaction but a strategic mistake because we still haven't been able to track down this *Gemma*. She's hidden her tracks very well, and while there are cameras in Ali's gym, every time Gemma was there, she kept her head down. She even paid the men in cash, so there's no paper trail to follow.

She came to Venice to abduct Ali, and *she almost succeeded*. I should have guessed the padrino wouldn't let it go.

She walked into Venice and threatened one of us.

A response must be made.

And now Antonio seems to have a lead on her. Anticipation sharpens my focus as I open the envelope in front of me. *Gemma* is going to discover it was a very bad idea to cross us.

A photo falls out of a woman with honey-blonde hair.

I take one look at it, and shock ricochets through me.

Her hair is a different color now, blonde instead of a red as warm as fire. Her eyes are brown in this picture, not a green so bright it reminded me of a forest. Her nose is different. She's smiling in this picture, but the dimple in her chin, the one I kissed a thousand times, is gone.

But Stefi is etched deep into my soul, and I'd know her anywhere.

"The woman who almost abducted Alina is an assassin who goes by the name of Stefania Freitas," Antonio says, his voice hard. "And, according to Cici, she's your wife. Is there anything you'd like to tell me, Joao?"

3

STEFI

I'm having the best dream.

I'm living in Venice with my husband Joao, our son Christopher, and our black cat, Mimi. It's Christmas morning, and I've just woken up to the delicious aroma of chocolate wafting through the house, and when I go downstairs, Joao greets me with a kiss and a steaming cup of coffee.

Then, a shrill ring cuts through the haze.

For a disorienting moment, I don't know what's happening, and then my alarm rings again. I roll over in bed and look at the cheap clock on the bedside table. Eight minutes after nine. Oh crap, I slept in. I should have logged into the company website eight minutes ago, and I didn't. My supervisor, Lynda, doesn't need an excuse to bitch at me, but now she has a perfect one.

I throw back the covers and make myself get up. I stumble my way into the kitchen and make some coffee. I need the caffeine to shake the black mood that I'm in. I dream of Joao often, and it always hurts, but it's not often that our son appears in my dreams. It's almost like my mind's drawn a curtain over his death to protect me from my grief.

Once the coffee is done brewing, I pour myself a cup and start to take a sip when my phone beeps with a news alert. I glance at it, and my system floods with shock at the headline that flashes on my screen.

'Henrik Bach, Austrian businessman and philanthropist, killed in tragic road accident.'

No. It can't be. I feverishly pull up the website of the news station that broke the story and skim the details. According to the reporter on the scene, sometime between three and four a.m. this morning, Henrik Bach was driving home to his estate just outside Vienna when he fell asleep at the wheel, swerved off the road, and collided with a tree.

Death was instantaneous.

My stomach churning with disbelief, I read the brief story again, slower this time.

For seven years, I've dreamed of killing Bach. For seven years, my goal of putting a bullet between his eyes has been the only thing that's kept me going.

I haven't let myself live, and I haven't let myself feel. Not since Joao.

Three months is the longest I've ever stayed in one place. I live a solitary life, moving from city to city to avoid detection.

All because of my former captor.

And now he's dead. In a car accident, of all the

fucking things. Fate has a cruel sense of humor. If there's ever been anyone who doesn't deserve a quick death, it's Henrik Bach.

My hand trembles, causing coffee to spill to the floor. Before I can clean up the mess, one of my burner phones rings. I hurry into my bedroom to pick it up. "Marcus," I say, keeping my voice level with effort. "What's up?"

Marcus O'Shea is the only person who has this number. He's a former assassin who now functions as an intermediary between contract killers and the people looking to hire them. Marcus is useful, but I don't trust him enough to give him my real name. He only knows me as Nina Lalami, a former soldier who occasionally acts as a contract killer to supplement the money she earns as a data analyst.

"Nina," Marcus booms. "A contract just went up. I thought you might be interested in the target."

"Who?"

"Varek Zaworski."

Zaworski. I hear that name, and fresh memories sweep me under.

A group of teenagers huddled near a cliff. Zaworski strides up to us with a self-satisfied smirk on his face and throws a large black bag on the ground. Henrik speaks, his voice as cold as ice. "Open it," he says, pointing his gun at me. My fingers shake as I undo the drawstrings. I already know who I'm going to find in the bag: my friend Michaela, who wanted away from Bach so badly that she was willing to risk death for her freedom.

I already know how this is going to end. *We all do.*

She's still alive. Her forehead is bleeding from a cut,

her lips are split, and she's badly bruised, and when she sees us, fear fills her face. "Please," she begs, tears welling up in her eyes. "Please have mercy."

Bach doesn't respond to her. "Don't turn away," he orders us. "I want you to watch. All of you. I want you to see what happens if you try to leave."

And then he shoots her in the head. I'm still kneeling next to Michaela, close enough that I can see the exact moment she realizes she's going to die. Close enough that her blood splatters on my face, wet and coppery and so, so warm.

"Good job finding her, Varek. Take care of the body, will you?"

"Nina," Marcus O'Shea says, his voice on the phone dragging me back to the present. "Are you interested?"

Seven years ago, when I clawed myself out of a psychiatric ward in Istanbul, I made a promise.

I wouldn't let myself rest until I dismantled every last bit of Bach's sick, twisted network.

The people who found orphans for him to train as assassins.

The people who financed his operation.

The people who hired him knowing full well how he acquired us.

I vowed that I would go after *every single one of them.*

Bach is dead, but it changes nothing. I still have targets on my list who are very much alive. Targets like Zaworski, who carelessly kicked Michaela's lifeless body over a cliff.

"Yes," I respond, my voice hard. "I want the job."

4

JOAO

My fingers tremble as I pick up the photo of Stefi. "This is not possible," I whisper in disbelief, my head spinning. "She's dead. She died eight years ago." I take a deep breath and try to gather my thoughts as best as I can. "When was this picture taken?"

"A month ago, in Bucharest. Stefania and her date went to a bar to watch a football game. Somehow, they ended up in a brawl, and the man she was with was stabbed. He died the next day. When the police went to question your wife, they couldn't find her. She was gone."

I barely register his words. I'm staring at Stefi, drinking her in.

She's... *alive.*

How?

I thought she was killed eight years ago in a house fire, but I was wrong *because she's here.* I trace the outline of her face and can almost feel her softness on my fingers. I inhale and swear I can smell her jasmine-scented skin.

She must have faked her own death.

The realization hits me like a blow to the chest. It's the only possible explanation. Eight years ago, Stefi robbed a morgue, put the wedding ring I slipped on her finger on the corpse, and set fire to the guest house she was staying at.

And then she disappeared.

Joy that she's still alive wars with a growing sense of betrayal. We were married, Stefi and I. When she made her plans, she would have known I would mourn her, but that didn't deter her. She knew that her death would shatter my heart, and she let me suffer *anyway*.

Why?

I loved her. I thought she loved me. We'd never spoken about leaving our indentured servitude—even dreaming about escape was dangerous. Bach's network was extensive, and runaways were always found, brought back, and killed.

So why run? And if she was determined to leave, why didn't she ask me to join her? Why didn't she trust me with the truth?

Antonio clears his throat, and I snap my attention back to him. "You didn't know she was still alive? This begins to explain why I had no idea you were married." He comes to the same conclusion I did. "She faked her own death? Why?"

I wish I knew. "Same reason I did, probably," I reply. "Bach owned us. Death was the only way out."

"She was one of his trainees?" he asks sharply. "That's how you met?"

"Yes." From the day she saved my life, I knew I found

my person. My soulmate. "Why does Cecelia d'Este have a file on Stefi?"

He ignores my question to ask one of his own. "Is she a good assassin?"

"She's excellent," I reply, pushing down my turmoil to answer his question. "She's always prepared. She does her homework and doesn't miss the details. And Stefi never loses her head in the heat of the moment. She's brave, but never to the point of recklessness." My throat tightens. The reality seems impossible, but somehow, despite the odds, she's still alive.

"And you're married to her. Wonderful." Antonio exchanges a look with Lucia, his voice resigned. "As to why Cici has this file, I'm not sure, but I have a theory. This file has information on each person Stefania Freitas allegedly killed. One of those people is Andrei Sidorov's father-in-law."

Fuck. Andrei Sidorov is the pakhan of one of Russia's largest bratvas, and his ruthlessness is legendary. A couple of months ago, a rival family made the unwise decision to torture and kill Sidorov's sister's boyfriend, and even more stupidly, they sent her the footage. Sixty days later, that family's leadership is gone. The pakhan, his heir, and half a dozen others—all dead.

"It's a testament to Stefania Freitas's skill that Andrei hasn't found her yet," Antonio continues. "But make no mistake, he will." He leans forward, his fingers steepled, an intent, focused look on his face. "I want her first. And that's where you come in."

I tense immediately, and the padrino's gaze drops to the photo. I realize that my fingers have been tracing

Stefi's cheeks, and I snatch my hand back, but it's too late. I've given myself away.

So be it. Might as well put my cards on the table.

"I won't kill her," I say flatly. I'm feeling a lot of conflicting emotions—happiness that Stefi is alive, intense betrayal about her decision to leave, anger that she didn't tell me what she was planning—but one thing is clear.

I don't have it in me to kill my wife. I cannot target the woman who has always been the missing piece of my soul.

And if that's what Antonio is asking me to do. . .

"I told you this would be his reaction," Lucia says, a smile playing about her lips. "Pay up."

Antonio gives his wife a wry look and passes her a hundred euro note. His dark eyes study me for a long moment. "So much loyalty, Joao," he says. "Is she worth it?"

"She's my *wife*."

"She let you believe that she was dead for *eight years*," he counters. "She came into Venice to abduct a civilian, the fiancée of one of your best friends."

Doubt trickles down my spine.

"Eight years is a long time, and people change," he continues. "God knows I've done plenty of things in the past that I'm not proud of. Your faith in her is commendable, but Stefania might not be the girl you remember."

I keep stubbornly silent. Antonio stares at me, then leans back with a sigh. "Very well," he says. "You've been loyal to me, and loyalty goes both ways. I give you my word that she's in no danger from me." His voice hardens.

"But she came into my city and tried to abduct someone under my protection. She owes me answers. Find her and bring her to Venice."

I open my mouth to refuse, but the padrino holds up his hand. "Before you tell me you'd rather quit than hunt down your ex-wife, consider this. Sidorov's people will kill Stefania. If anyone can find her before she ends up in a body bag, it's you."

He's promised Stefi safety, and I trust Antonio to keep his word. "Okay." I take a deep breath and get to my feet. "I'll do it."

Assassins in movies always have cool nicknames. Copperhead. Cottonmouth. Black Mamba. In real life, that kind of nonsense will get you killed. If you want to live, you keep a low profile and don't make waves.

But when my wife went missing eight years ago, I went to Mexico to try to find her. And during that bloody search, I acquired a nickname.

The Hunter.

For almost a decade, my wife let me believe she was dead. I want answers, and I'm going to get them.

The Hunter is going on the hunt.

I RETURN HOME, my head reeling, feed an indignant Mimi, and start on Cecelia d'Este's file. There's a USB key in the envelope the padrino handed me, so I pull out an old laptop that isn't connected to the Internet, insert the key, and pull up the contents.

Eight years, two months, and five days. That's how long it's been since she failed to check in after her hit in Puerto Vallarta. That's how long I've believed she's been dead; that's how long I've mourned her.

You shouldn't have run from me, little fox.

There are seventy-three folders, each one detailing a person who died under suspicious circumstances. If this intel is to be believed, Stefi killed all these people.

I should go through each of them to see if there's something I can use to find my wife, but instead, I stare at her photo, a thousand memories swirling through my mind. She'd been sent to kill Peng Wu when she disappeared. Peng, the emissary of a Chinese triad based in Shanghai, was in Mexico to make alliances with the dominant cartels in Guadalajara and Sinola, and Bach's client didn't want that to go through.

They said she was killed in a house fire. A body was recovered at the scene wearing the wedding ring I slipped on Stefi's finger. Everyone else was satisfied it was her, everyone except me. The body was too badly burned for a DNA test, and absent a positive match, nothing was going to convince me she was dead. She couldn't be; I wouldn't allow it. I couldn't imagine a world without Stefi in it.

I walked off a job of my own and flew to Mexico the day after she failed to check-in. Peng went underground shortly after she disappeared, but I hunted him down in Mazatlan. He refused to answer my questions, so I chopped off one finger at a time until he talked.

The Hunter

But he knew nothing.

I expanded the search. Unable to accept that she was dead, I went on a single-minded quest to find her, leaving a trail of blood, bodies, and broken bones in my wake. I don't even remember half of what I did—I was driven by frantic desperation.

For months, I searched high and low for answers. I stalked the crime scene. I investigated the local morgues to see if a body had been stolen from any of them. I interrogated the guest house owner, the detectives in charge of the case, the insurers paying out the claim. *Everyone.*

Three months after she went missing, Henrik paid me a visit. "Enough," he said. "She's dead. It's unfortunate, but people die in our line of work. It's time to accept it and move on."

Thinking of Henrik always leaves a sour taste in my mouth. I pour myself a Scotch to banish it and return my attention to the laptop in front of me. If I can find out what connects all these deaths, then I can predict the next one and intercept my murderous wife before she has a chance to kill yet again.

It's almost four in the morning when I finally have a breakthrough. Last year, Reyhan Benita, an Algerian smuggler, died in a cafe in London. The autopsy listed the cause of death as a heart attack, but the pathologist noted two strange things: Benita's nails were unusually brittle, and his blood had an elevated level of potassium in it.

Brittle nails and potassium. Why does this ring a bell?

I search my memory until it comes to me. Twenty years ago, an assassin going by the unoriginal nickname of Black Death had achieved some notoriety by poisoning his victims. Marcus O'Shea had a Ph.D. in chemistry and swore his proprietary poisons were undetectable, no matter how thorough the autopsy.

O'Shea is retired now. He lives in Dublin and runs a new-age apothecary in Temple Bar, where he sells overpriced incense and lotions to unsuspecting tourists.

I'm almost positive he had nothing to do with Benita's death.

But if I'm not mistaken, somebody used one of his signature poisons to murder the smuggler.

I'm looking for answers, and Dublin is a good place to start.

I lean back in my chair and shut my eyes. Stefi was the only light in my life, and she was taken from me far too early.

For eight years, I haven't been able to forget her, and I haven't been able to move on. I live in Venice because it was her favorite city. I have a black cat because she always wanted one. My entire life is a shrine to the girl I lost.

And then to find out she's still alive? I'm not angry. No, anger is far too simple a description for the cocktail of emotions churning through me.

I'm feeling *betrayed*.

My wife is alive, and I will move heaven and earth to find her. This time, I won't give up. If finding her takes up the rest of my years, then I'll consider it a life well spent.

She owes me answers, and I intend to get them.

5

STEFI

According to Marcus, Zaworski is dining with a business associate in a fondue restaurant on the outskirts of Zurich on Thursday.

The morning of the meeting, I fly into Zurich and take a train to Sihlwald. I leave my rental car in the parking lot of the train station, two kilometers away, and hike to my destination. Partly so that no one can get a photo of my license plate but also to steady my nerves.

Zaworski has been one of my most difficult targets. I've been trying to get at him for years, but I've never found an opening. The former bounty hunter is retired now. He lives in a tiny village an hour north of Krakow and rarely leaves. Even if my Polish were fluent enough to pass me off as a native—which it isn't—the small, insular village is the kind of place where a stranger will instantly be noticed.

Which makes this rendezvous at the fondue restaurant a once-in-a-lifetime opportunity to cross him off my list.

As much as I've been trained to be detached on a job, restless anticipation buzzes through me. I don't know most of the people I've taken out over the years, but I do know Varek, and this hit is *personal.*

So personal that my heart is racing, and my palms are damp with sweat.

The trail is quiet. It's a Thursday evening in October, and I don't encounter too many people on my walk, just a couple of old men with binoculars around their necks who nod at me in greeting but don't stop to engage in conversation.

The forest is lush and green, with tall pine trees towering on either side of the trail. Peaceful. There's been an acute shortage of peace in my life, and I soak in the atmosphere as I hike toward my destination. It rained a few hours ago, and the smell of petrichor fills my nostrils.

Petrichor.

The moment that word flashes through my mind, memories of Joao follow. My husband was delighted by odd words. Petrichor—the earthy scent after a rainfall— was one of his favorites. Defenestrate was another.

Every time I think of Joao, a stab of pain goes through my heart. Today is no exception. For a moment, it hurts to breathe, and I stop walking and slump against a tree, waiting for it to pass.

He's been dead for seven years, but the pain of his loss has never faded. Every Internet article I read promises me that time is supposed to soften the grief, but they all lie. The wound is as raw as ever.

I breathe, long and deep, and count backward from ten in my head. *You can mourn him for the duration,* I promise myself. *But when you get to one, you need to walk again.*

I count down slowly, feeling the warmth of his body against mine and hearing the sound of his laughter in my ears. I hold him in my heart for as long as possible, and then I let him go and start to move again.

The trail comes to an end twenty minutes later, and my footsteps slow as I near my destination. I've wanted to kill Zaworski for a very long time, and the moment is finally within reach.

I take a deep breath, cross the street, and make my way to the fondue restaurant. The sign in the pothole-filled parking lot proclaims in three languages that Frau Augsburger is the home of the best fondue in all of Switzerland. Somehow, I doubt that's true. There is an air of neglect about the place. The windows are dusty, the paint is peeling, and it very much looks like its glory days are in the past.

Four cars are parked in the lot, but none of them are the black Audi that Zaworski drives. There are no lights in the windows either.

Something's not right here.

I approach the front door, my senses on high alert.

According to Google, the restaurant is open today. It's ten after five, and the dinner rush should just be beginning. It's maybe a little early to eat by Swiss standards, but Sihlwald is a tourist destination, and this restaurant, serving fondue and rosti in the foothills of one of Zurich's mountains, is a tourist trap. Even on a random Thursday in October, there should be some signs of life. Music, the noise of conversation, the banging of pots and pans in the kitchen.

But there isn't.

It's as quiet as a tomb.

This is a bad idea, my intuition whispers.

This is the best chance of getting Zaworski, my heart counters. *Nobody knows who you are. You're dressed like a tourist—jeans, long-sleeved black T-shirt, hiking boots—and you have Google Maps on your phone screen. Nobody will suspect you of anything. This is as easy as it gets.*

My heart wins the argument. The doorknob turns in my hand as I push open the door.

And freeze.

The smell hits me immediately, a sharp, coppery tang that I am all too familiar with. My eyes take a few seconds to adjust to the dimness, and then I see blood everywhere. Blood splattered on the walls. Blood dripping down photos of celebrities posing with the proprietors, blood staining the mirror behind the bar.

What the fuck happened here?

Then there are the bodies. Slumped over tables and draped over the bar, pools of blood spreading from under them. I count instinctively. There are six dead and dying people, all dressed in black.

It's such a shockingly unexpected sight that, for a split second, I have no idea how to respond.

Then, before I can make myself run, I hear the click of a gun being cocked.

A tall man glides out of the shadows, the barrel of his weapon pointed straight at my head. His shoulders are broad, and his waist is narrow. He takes another step forward, and light from the setting sun falls on his face.

I suck in a breath.

High cheekbones, full, sensual lips, and vividly blue eyes. I'm staring at a face that was once as familiar to me as my own.

"Hello, Stefi," my dead husband says. "Fancy meeting you here."

Am I hallucinating?

The room swims around me. It can't be Joao—I'm seeing a ghost. Joao died seven and a half years ago. He drowned just off the coast of Marseilles, and when I found out, I lost my mind. I'd already been teetering on the edge of madness, and his death pushed me over, the triggering event that led to me being locked up in a psych ward for five months.

But here he is, standing right in front of me, menace radiating from him in icy waves.

My brain tries desperately to make sense of what I'm seeing and fails.

"How can you be here?" I ask in a shocked whisper, my heart hammering in my chest. "You died."

His lips tilt into a smile that does not meet his eyes. The gun barrel never wavers. "Surprise, little fox," he says. "I'm still alive. And so are you. Turns out you didn't die in that house fire in Mexico after all." An edge creeps into his voice. "You faked your own death, even though you knew it would wreck me."

I swallow hard. I knew that Joao would hate me for what I did, but I didn't realize how hard it would be to see him staring at me with loathing in his eyes. He's never looked at me this way.

The Joao I knew was in love with me.

This man looks like he wants me dead.

"I'm sorry," I force out through numb lips. "I had to. . ."

He doesn't let me finish. His jaw tightens, and his knuckles whiten around the gun. There's a flicker of emotion in his eyes, but it's gone almost instantly, replaced by a mask of ice. "Nicely done, Stefi," he sneers. "Just the right amount of emotion, the right amount of regret in your voice. But I'm not buying your act."

"What act?" My brain is struggling to comprehend Joao's presence here, but one thing is clear: this version of Joao isn't the boy I married. My Joao—the love of my life—would never, ever point a gun at me. Not in a million years. *My* Joao would die before he hurt me.

"Let me guess why you ran," he says mockingly. "You didn't want to be an assassin any longer; you never wanted to be one in the first place. And the only way to escape Henrik was to fake your own death."

I wish it had been that simple, but the truth is far, *far* more painful than that. "Yes." Tears fill my eyes. "We both know—"

"Oh, come on. Drop it. I've seen your record, Stef; I know the truth. I know you've been killing people for the last eight years, ever since you left. Even worse, you're a mercenary, someone who murders people for the right price." His face twists in disgust. "Take off your clothes."

I can't have heard him right. "What?"

A muscle ticks in his jaw. "You heard me," he snaps. "I

The Hunter

know how you operate, remember? There's the gun tucked in the small of your back, but that's not your only weapon. You came prepared to take out Zaworski. What else do you have?" His eyes run over my body. "Throwing knives strapped to your ankles, lengths of wire to garrote your hapless victims, and probably some kind of explosive to cover your getaway."

His finger moves to the trigger. "I'd be a fool not to search you, Stef. And my days of being a fool for you are long over." He gestures with the gun. "You heard me the first time. Strip."

6

STEFI

My heart hammers in my chest. I reach behind my back for my gun, never taking my eyes off Joao's face, and slowly, *carefully* place it on the floor. I learned to be an assassin through training and long hours of practice. Joao, on the other hand, was a natural. He was the best shot of our class, his bullets traveling with a sniper's deadly precision.

I can't afford to take any chances.

"Good girl," he says. The words are approving, but his tone is flat. "Kick it over to me."

I do as he orders. He picks it up, his aim never wavering from my forehead. "Now the rest."

My mouth is dry. I wet my lower lip with my tongue, and his gaze locks onto it. A moment passes before I risk a question. "How did you find me?"

"Marcus O'Shea. You used one of his bespoke poisons in—"

"London." I curse myself for my stupidity. Reyhan Benita was a rush job, and I used one of Marcus's vials as a shortcut. A moment of impulsiveness has resulted in a breadcrumb trail that's led Joao straight to me. "Is O'Shea still alive?"

His face darkens. "He shouldn't be," he growls. "But he is. Unlike you, Stefi, I only kill when I have to."

He looks. . . different. Harder. The boy I knew has grown up to be a man with frost-blue eyes that radiate power and menace. His shoulders are broader than I remember, and his face is leaner and more angular, no trace of softness left in its lines.

There's a narrow scar just under his lower lip. There was a time when I knew every inch of Joao's body as well as my own.

But this scar is new. I don't know it.

I don't know *him*.

"What the hell is that supposed to mean?" I demand, keeping the shakiness out of my voice with ruthless effort. Bending down, I unbuckle the ankle band holding my half-dozen sharp throwing knives and kick it his way as well.

"I haven't killed seventy-three people in the last six years. It's an impressive body count, I admit, but a little too high for my tastes."

His contempt stings. "You should talk," I throw back, looking at the slumped bodies on the floor. "Or are these people merely injured, the way Marcus O'Shea is?" Then his words sink in. "Seventy-three? No, I've only killed thirty-five."

And I shouldn't have said that. I've given too much away, and I need to go on the offensive before he registers what I said. Joao's sudden reappearance has me dangerously off-balance. He's someone I loved with all my heart, and he's looking at me as if I'm his enemy. My stomach churns and my head spins at the disgust in his voice and the disdain in his eyes. "Who do you work for, Joao? Who hired you to take me out?"

A thin, humorless smile stretches his lips. "I'm not here to kill you, sweetness. If I wanted you dead, I'd have shot you the moment you stepped inside, the way these guys were going to." He nudges one of the bodies with his foot. "This was a trap. Someone went to a great deal of effort to lure you here."

It should be reassuring that he doesn't want to kill me, but it isn't. There are too many unknowns here. My thoughts are still chaotic, my equilibrium dangerously disturbed. I kick off my boots, unbutton my jeans, and push the waistband down my hips. More weapons follow. The garrote taped to my ankle, the blades worn against my skin.

"Who?" I ask, forcing myself to push Joao's reappearance to the background and work out the possibilities. Who set the trap? O'Shea is the most likely possibility, but why? The reward had to be pretty great; he, better than most, knows that in our line of work, betrayal usually results in death.

Joao's eyes move over my body slowly as my bare skin comes into view. His aim, however, doesn't waver. The gun stays fixed on my forehead. "I'll tell you if you answer one question. Why did you leave, Stefi? Why did you let me believe you were dead?" For the first time, his voice cracks. "Do you have any idea what it feels like to stare down at a badly burned body, thinking that it's your dead wife? I searched for you for *months*. I visited every morgue in Jalisco and Nayarit, looking for missing corpses because I couldn't accept the truth."

I suck in a breath.

"You faked your own death," he continues. "You put your wedding ring on that corpse's finger, and you walked away without a backward glance. For eight years, you let me mourn you. *Tell me why.*"

Every word is an accusation slicing into my heart. I hear the pain in Joao's voice, and I can't bear it. I can't bear knowing I was the cause of his anguish.

I had to do what I did. It broke my heart, but there was no other choice open to me. None at all.

And I knew it would hurt Joao. It was the only way, but I *knew* I was stabbing my husband, the love of my life, in the heart.

But I desperately hoped he would recover. *He'll move on,* I told myself. *Give it a couple of years, and you'll be a memory. He'll forget you and find someone else.*

But I was lying to myself to make my choice bearable. He hasn't forgotten me at all. The way he's staring at me. . . The hurt in his voice. . . If I've been in hell for the last eight years, *so has he.*

"Nothing to say?"

I could try to explain, but there's *nothing* I can say that will erase what I put him through. And the truth—*the whole and complete truth*—would wreck him.

And I don't have it in me to hurt him more than I already have.

"Is there anything I can tell you that would change

the past?" I ask quietly. "Is there anything I can say that would make it okay?"

He stares at me for what seems like an eternity, then takes a deep breath and shakes his head. "No," he replies. "There isn't. Just tell me this one thing. I thought we were in love. Was that a lie, too?"

My chest is tight. It feels like his fist is wrapped around my heart, squeezing. The break in his voice is bringing back the past I thought I left behind. The shell I built around my heart is cracking open, all of the caged emotions are tearing free, and I'm once again a scared girl in an airport bathroom, staring down at the two lines on the—

He can't see me cry. *I won't let that happen.*

"No," I whisper. "That wasn't a lie. Leaving you behind was the hardest thing I've ever done in my life." I swallow back the lump in my throat and remind myself that Joao isn't the same person he used to be. I have only to look at him to see that. The Joao I knew lived in T-shirts and jeans, but this grown-up version is wearing a bespoke navy-blue linen suit and a watch that costs a hundred thousand euros.

The boy I loved is gone forever, and the man in front of me now is holding a gun to my head.

Be careful, Stefi. Be very, very careful.

I nudge my jeans toward him with my toe. I need answers—I have to ask. "You went missing off the coast of Marseilles a year after I died; Bach thought you'd drowned in the Mediterranean. What happened?"

"How did you know that?"

Because I almost contacted him.

I regretted my decision to fake my own death the moment the guest house went up in flames, but I forced myself to stay the course. Joao and I used to communicate through a secret chat room in an obscure corner of the Internet so that Bach wouldn't find out about our relationship, and as many times as I wanted to log on to talk to Joao, I didn't let myself. For so many months, I made myself stay away. Too much was at stake, and I couldn't take any risk that might lead Bach or his minions to my door.

But then, after everything fell apart and I wept alone in a darkened hospital room, I called Bach's intermediary. Pretending to be a client looking for a hitman, I asked Tommy Power if I could hire Joao.

And Power told me that the man I loved more than life itself was dead. "That assassin is unavailable," he said. "He was killed on a job. Unfortunate, but not entirely unexpected, to tell you the truth. He fell to pieces when the woman he loved was killed, and it was only a matter of time before he made a fatal mistake."

I was already deeply wounded, but hearing that Joao was dead, and that it was *my fault,* shattered me. It fractured my mind so badly that it took me years to glue myself back together.

"Nothing to say again, Stefi?" Joao asks mockingly. "I don't think you understand how conversations work. Quid pro quo, honey. You give me answers, and I'll do the same." He shrugs his shoulders and answers me anyway. "Working for Henrik—I couldn't stand it any longer. I had to get out. And then, once I did, I didn't know what I was supposed to do with myself." His lips twist in a wry smile. "You know how it is. All our lives, we were raised to be killers. I didn't know what else I could be. I bummed around the world for eighteen months. Spent some time in Japan meditating and making soy sauce—"

Despite the current circumstances, I feel myself start to smile. "Seriously? You, meditating?"

His lips twitch. "Almost a whole year, if you can believe it. Then I realized that I didn't leave Henrik only to lock myself away from the world. I needed to do all the things we used to dream about. So, I got a job I loved, working for a boss I respect, and I made friends—" The smile wipes off his face. "Why am I telling you all of this? Keep stripping."

For a moment, it almost felt like old times. But he's still got a gun aimed at me. I'm still in danger.

I start to lift my T-shirt over my head, and he inhales sharply. I freeze. The scar has faded to almost nothing, and he shouldn't be able to see it at this distance—

"Who did that to you?" he demands, his voice strained.

Did what? I follow his gaze to my ribcage, where an angry red line extends from just below my right breast to my left hip. Oh right. I was so focused on the scar just below my bikini line that I forgot about my most recent souvenir.

"Why do you care? You're holding a gun to my head."

"Who, Stefi?" His voice promises murder for my assailant, and it sends a thrill through me. The ice-cold version of him I might not recognize, but this hot rage? *This* is the Joao I knew, who lived life with laughter and passion. "Tell me who hurt you."

"Save your rage—he's dead. I took care of it." He's given me an opening, and I'm going to use it. I drop my T-shirt on the floor and take off my bra. His eyes flare with heat, his look so intense that it sends a shiver through me.

I take a step toward him. My emotions are all over the place, and I feel dangerously off-balance. Maybe I'm testing him. Maybe I want him to feel the same turmoil I'm feeling. But I can't reconcile the memories Joao—my Joao—to this man threatening me with a weapon.

"Would you really shoot me if I tried to run?" I ask softly. "Could you?"

The barrel wavers.

I recklessly step even closer, close enough to lift my hand and cup his cheek. "I can't believe you're still alive," I whisper. "I can't believe you're here. I've missed you so much, Joao. And now Henrik Bach is dead, and I—"

"Bach is dead?" he cuts in.

I nod. For a moment, shock and disbelief shows on his face before he wipes his expression clean.

"Stefi." He clenches his eyes shut. "Fuck. I've dreamed about this moment for eight fucking years. I've wanted. . ." His voice trails off, and he takes a deep, shuddering breath. Turning on the safety, he tucks the gun into his waistband. "Fuck it. Come back with me to Venice and—"

I freeze and jerk back. "You live in Venice?" The hope building inside me bursts like an overfilled balloon, and every nerve in my body screams in warning. If Joao is here, then it means. . . "Who do you work for, Joao? *Who sent you here for me?*"

He frowns. "Antonio Moretti. Why?" He takes in my stricken expression. "Is this about Alina? The padrino isn't thrilled about your abduction attempt, but it's okay. He's a really good guy. He's my boss, yes, but he's also my friend. I talked to him and—"

I inch a step back and then another. "You work for Antonio Moretti." My voice is shrill and high. There is a trap, but it's not O'Shea who lured me here. No, it's the King of Venice himself, one of the hardest targets on my hit list. "Why, Joao? Of all the people in the world, why him?"

"What's wrong with him?" His expression turns concerned. "You've turned deathly pale, little fox. Are you okay? Come here, let me—"

"No." No, I'm not okay. For a second there, I dared to dream. I became hopeful. There was a chasm between us, one that I created eight years ago when I made the decision to disappear, but for one brief, shining instant, I thought that maybe it could be bridged.

But hope is for other people. Every time I start believing that my future holds something other than misery and pain, something happens to remind me otherwise.

Seven years ago, I made a promise in a graveyard in Istanbul to kill every single person in Bach's network.

And Antonio Moretti, padrino of the Venice Mafia, a man that Joao considers his *friend,* is pretty damn close to the top of my list.

Sirens sound in the distance, getting rapidly closer. *Finally.* Joao hears them, too. He turns his head toward the window, and in that brief second of distraction, I dart forward and grab my gun.

His head snaps back to me. "You had someone call

the police?" he asks, ignoring the weapon I'm now pointing at him. He nods in reluctant appreciation. "Nicely done."

His praise warms me from the inside out. But my heart is breaking because, once again, I have to let Joao go. "You know me," I say lightly. Keeping my eyes on him, I grab my T-shirt and jeans. "I always like to have an exit plan."

"Oh, I know," he says, his voice coated with bitterness. "Puerto Vallarta taught me that." He could probably wrestle the gun from me if he was really determined, *but he doesn't*. Instead, he pushes a tendril of hair away from my face with calloused fingers, his touch unexpectedly tender. "I can't stop you from leaving here, not without hurting you," he says. "But I'm going to find you again. I'll be seeing you around, Stefi."

7

JOAO

I've known for four days that my wife is still alive, ever since Antonio called me into Casanova to ask me about her. But there's a difference between knowing that something is true and *believing* it, and I don't think I really, truly believed that Stefi wasn't dead until I saw her framed in the doorway of Frau Augsburger.

Maybe that explains why I was such a fool.

Maybe that explains why, instead of searching her, tying her up, and driving her back to Venice, I got distracted and let her grab her gun.

Stupid, stupid, stupid.

I let Stefi get under my skin. One look at her, and the past evaporated, the last eight years of anguish and misery gone in a flash. One look into those beautiful forest-green eyes, and I was once again the guy who was so crazily in love with his wife that he would do anything for her.

She refused to answer any of my questions. She

wouldn't tell me why she decided to leave without a single word of explanation, she was cagey about what she's been doing for the last eight years, and she wouldn't even discuss what drove her to abduct Alina.

The very mention of Venice seemed to make her distraught, and I have no idea why.

And yet... Despite all of that, one look at her, and I'd been ready to take her back. No answers, no explanations, *nothing*. The moment I saw her again, I was ready to abandon my hard-fought peace of mind and let her into my life. It took everything in me to fight the urge to slam her against the nearest wall and fuck away the pain of the last eight years.

My reaction isn't healthy, not even a little, nor is it romantic. This is toxic as fuck. Even knowing how bad Stefi is for me, there's a secret, shameful part of my heart that would abandon everything for her. My coworkers, my friends, my home—I would walk away from it all for my wife.

I curse as I jog back to my car. Stefi wrecked my life when she disappeared, and the pain of her death has never gone away. But I cannot be that guy again. I just cannot. I cannot race to Zurich because my wife is walking into a trap, and I cannot kill half a dozen of Andrei Sidorov's people just to keep her alive.

Except I already did.

I should know better than to get sucked back in.

Strip, I ordered, and she complied. And when she whipped her T-shirt over her head, for one brief second, anxiety flickered in her eyes. The moment of vulnerability was gone before I could blink, but I saw it, and it made my heart hurt.

As if the scars on her body could ever diminish her loveliness.

I reach my car, unlock the door, and get in. Daniel calls just as I merge onto the highway. "According to Valentina," he says, "you're in a forest reserve south of Zurich, and a dozen cop cars are rapidly converging on your location. Have you caused an international incident, and if so, do you need a lawyer?"

Daniel Rossi is Antonio's go-to lawyer. The man is a shark—smart, ruthless, and competent. I should have guessed that he'd call, and I should have also guessed that Valentina Colonna, our hacker, would be tracking me. "Did the padrino tell you to keep an eye on me?" I ask, maneuvering around a slow-moving Toyota. I'm not speeding—that'll draw too much attention—but there's no need to be stuck behind someone who's driving slower than Daniel's ninety-year-old grandmother.

"Obviously," he replies. "And you didn't answer my question."

"No."

"Is that no, I didn't create an international incident, or no, I don't need a lawyer?"

"No, I don't need a lawyer."

"What happened?" Daniel asks. "Did you find your wife? Incidentally, I had no idea you were married. I didn't have you pegged as the secretive type, Joao, but you kept that very quiet. It's all anyone can talk about."

I'm not secretive by nature. But some wounds run so deep that they're never going to heal, and what's the point of talking about them? It's only going to make the people around me worry. It's better to act as if everything is okay—to laugh and joke and sing karaoke and pretend to flirt—than to let someone look inside and realize how deeply broken I really am.

"I'm glad I've given you something to gossip about," I say dryly. "I traced Stefi to a restaurant called Frau Augsburger. She was there to take out a bounty hunter, Varek Zaworski."

"You saw her? Is she with you now?"

"Yes, I saw her. No, she's not with me."

Daniel makes a noise of frustration. "Joao, are you going to answer all my questions in monosyllables, for fuck's sake? You were supposed to bring her back to Venice. What happened? Did she manage to get away from you?"

"Yes." I had a gun pointed at Stefi. But when I saw the scar across her chest, I'd been so blinded by rage at the thought of somebody hurting her that I couldn't think straight.

I gave her an opening, and she took it. Ignoring the gun in my hand, she walked right up to me. *"Would you really shoot me if I tried to run?"* she whispered, cupping my cheek. *"Could you?"*

Her jasmine scent overwhelmed my senses, and the softness in her voice left me weak in the knees.

Fool.

I can sense Daniel's irritation on the other end of the line, and I can't say I blame him. He's trying to help me, and I'm not cooperating. I'm still reacting to seeing Stefi again, still off-balance at her reappearance in my life.

The Hunter

I take a deep breath to calm myself. "Forget Stefi for the moment," I tell him. "I'll find her again. I have more pressing things on my mind. First, she told me that Henrik Bach is dead. Is he?"

"Yes."

"When? How?"

"A couple of days ago. Car accident."

I exhale slowly. The tormentor of my childhood, the man who shaped my life into its present form, the man responsible for snatching me from a loving home and throwing me into the hellfire that was his training academy, is finally dead. I almost don't believe it.

Daniel clears his throat. "Are you okay?"

He sounds acutely uncomfortable. Last year, he took on a pro bono case that had nothing to do with the mafia. A single mother and her baby were getting acutely sick from the mold in her apartment, and the company that owned the building was gaslighting her into thinking she was imagining it. Daniel absolutely destroyed the company in court, but he ran away when Olivia tried to thank him. The lawyer isn't good with emotions.

"I'm fine. Second thing. Someone set a trap for Stefi. When I got to the restaurant, her target was nowhere to be seen, but there were a half dozen people there, sent to take her out."

"Andrei Sidorov's people, you think? There's going to be hell to pay if you killed six members of the Sidorov Bratva." He swears under his breath. "Okay, I'll start doing some damage control—"

"I don't think they were bratva," I say, cutting him off. "They weren't even Russian."

"How can you tell? Did you interrogate them?"

"I killed two of them before they realized I was there. The third one turned toward me, and he swore out loud when he saw me. In French."

"Okay?" Daniel sounds confused. "I'm not getting the significance of this."

"No matter how well trained you are, when you see your life flash before your eyes, your training breaks. The guy spoke French at the moment of his death. He's not Russian. None of them were."

"That's dark," Daniel responds. "Hang on, I'm hooked into the police scanners. Everyone in the restaurant is dead? Did you kill the kitchen staff? The other patrons?"

"There were no other patrons—the restaurant was closed for a private event. And no, of course I didn't kill the staff."

"Can they identify you?"

I roll my eyes. Does the lawyer think I started doing this yesterday? I've been a killer all my life. "No, Daniel, they cannot. Stop worrying; nothing can tie me to the crime scene."

"If you say so. Back to the hit team. If they're not Sidorov's people, who are they? Mercenaries?"

"Maybe," I say doubtfully. "But the one guy I left alive bit down on a suicide pill before he could talk. Mercenaries don't typically kill themselves to avoid being questioned. Money doesn't usually buy that kind of loyalty. Unless they were more afraid of what Sidorov would do if they talked. Anyway, I took pictures of them. Can you ask Valentina to ID them?"

"Will do. Who called the cops? The staff?"

I can't help the smile that lifts up the corners of my lips. "No, that was Stefi." The sirens took me by surprise, but I should have guessed that she'd have a way out. My wife is always prepared.

"Why?"

"Exit plan," I explain. "You always leave yourself a way out, just in case things turn messy. If I know Stefi, the call to the cops would have been placed if she didn't check in by a certain time. She didn't give herself too long to take care of Zaworski, but then again, she wouldn't have needed it."

Daniel clears his throat. "It sounds like there's a conflict of interest here. Do I have to remind you she almost succeeded in abducting Alina?"

"I'm aware, yes." My words come out clipped. Daniel's not wrong to point out what my wife did, but at the same time, his tone rankles. There's no need to jump to conclusions—none of us know why Stefi acted the way she did.

He hears the edge in my voice and wisely lets it go. "Okay. What happens now? Are you coming home?"

"No, there's a lead I'm going to chase down."

I made a mistake today. I let Stefi see that she still affected me, and it gave her the opening she needed to escape. But I wasn't the only one making mistakes. She touched my cheek and whispered, "I miss you so much."

And yes, it was partly a calculated strategy to play on my emotions.

But I looked into her eyes, and the regret in them was real. I'm absolutely sure of it.

Which means I'm not the only one tantalized by the

possibility of a second chance. I'm not the only one who wants to roll back time.

Sooner or later, Stefi is going to reach out to me. She's going to log back into our secret chat room, and when she does, I'll be there, waiting for her.

I'm going to find my wife again. And this time, I'm going to take her back to Venice.

My little fox might not care that she almost walked into a trap, but I do. I thought I lost her once, and it nearly destroyed me. I will not let that happen again.

8

STEFI

I managed to grab my T-shirt, bra, and jeans, but no panties. I discover that unpleasant fact when I get dressed behind the restaurant, hidden by the dumpsters, but there's nothing I can do about it. The sirens are nearer now, and going back into the restaurant is an act of sheer folly.

I put on a pair of gloves before I entered Frau Augsburger so the authorities wouldn't be able to lift prints off my weapons.

But panties mean DNA. *Damn it.*

There might be a match for my DNA in the system. Hospitals in Europe aren't supposed to store the genetic data of their patients, and they're definitely not allowed to share it with the police. But six people are dead in a Swiss restaurant, and there's going to be a lot of pressure to find the killer.

Seven and a half years ago, I was forced to go to a hospital in Istanbul. I used an assumed identity, of course, but if they've kept my DNA on file...

Stop worrying about things you can't control. Just get to the train station.

The trail is busier now. Families are out for an evening stroll, and young people are taking their dogs out for a walk. I force myself to move at a leisurely pace. My Swiss German isn't good enough that I would pass as a native, so I stick to my identity as a tourist. I take dozens of photos of the nature reserve, coo over dogs, and exchange pleasantries with their owners.

Forty minutes later, I'm at the station. I was a little afraid that the police would be here, but they're nowhere to be seen. I hop on the train into the city. An hour later, I arrive at Zurich HB, and two hours after that, I'm on an overnight train back to Paris.

It's only after I sink into my seat that I finally allow myself to break the chokehold I've kept on my thoughts.

Joao is alive.

The weight of that realization crashes over me like a tidal wave. I thought he was dead; I thought I lost him forever.

Eight years. Eight years of long, lonely nights. Eight years of missing his laugh, his touch, his voice. Joao left me a voicemail once on a burner phone. It was the briefest of messages before leaving for a job. *Sweet little fox, I'll see you in Prague on Monday,* was all he said. But as short as it was, I used to listen to it over and over again, my heart shattering each time at the magnitude of my loss.

But he's alive.

"Surprise, little fox," he said accusingly, his voice as cold as a glacier. "I'm still alive. *And so are you.*"

Little fox. I remember the day Joao came up with that nickname. I was thirteen years old, and Bach had just forced me to kill my first person. Afterward, I wept on Joao's shoulder, my heart breaking for my victim's family and loved ones. "You have a heart as soft as a baby bird," he said as he comforted me.

"I'm not a baby bird," I replied, stung that he saw me as something that weak. Joao had a growth spurt that summer. For years, we used to be the same height, but then he shot up, and now I barely reached his shoulder. "I'm tougher than that." My mind searched around for a suitable animal until I landed on one. "I'm a fox."

His eyes laughed at me, and he rested his chin on the top of my head. "A little fox."

I stare out of the window at the speeding countryside. Why had I never entertained the possibility that he might have faked his own death the way I had? Why had I never considered that he might also want to escape Bach's clutches? When Tommy Power told me that Joao drowned in the Mediterranean, I believed him. Maybe because Joao always seemed to like being an assassin, or maybe because my heart couldn't bear to hold onto hope.

I ache thinking of the time we lost.

Focus on the mission, Bach's voice whispers in my ear. His presence is unwelcome, but the advice is sound. Getting distracted will get me killed.

With effort, I make myself stop thinking about Joao and pull out my phone. News about the attack should be breaking now. I scroll to a Swiss news site, and sure enough, it's headline news. A video is playing of a news anchor breathlessly reporting on the gruesome discovery.

I plug in my headphones and turn up the volume just as they cut away to the local police chief's news conference.

"There's not much I can reveal," he says, looking harried as a dozen jostling reporters shove microphones under his face. "Our investigation is in the preliminary stage."

Phew. He says nothing about having a suspect in custody. Joao got away; of course he did. When it comes to raw talent, my husband is off the scales. He's not going to get caught.

He'll remain in Zurich tonight. The protocol that Bach drilled into us dictates that he spends the night in a busy hotel in the heart of the city. He'll make no efforts to avoid detection. If he's pretending to be a tourist, he'll take a lake cruise tomorrow or sign up for a wine and cheese tasting. If he's masquerading as a businessman, then he'll make sure he's in meetings all day.

"How many victims did you find?" a reporter demands. "Have you identified them?"

The police chief looks like he wants to be anywhere but there. "There were six homicides. We have not been able to identify them yet."

"What about the restaurant staff? Is it true they're all alive?"

He starts to answer, but just as he does, the broadcast cuts back to the anchor. "This just in, our reporter at the scene, Lisa Keller, is interviewing Frau Augsburger, the proprietor of the fondue restaurant. Let's jump to Lisa."

"Thank you, Elijah. I'm standing here with Frau Claudia Augsburger. Frau Augsburger, what can you tell us about today's tragic events? Did you see the killer?"

The Hunter

Claudia Augsburger is a buxom blonde woman in her late thirties. She's holding it together better than most people would. She's undoubtedly had a very bad day, but she's got a fresh coat of makeup on her face and is giving interviews to the media.

"I did not, Lisa," she replies. "I have no idea what happened. A group had rented the restaurant for a private event. I had just finished serving the appetizers and headed back to the kitchen, where Leonie and Ava were cooking the main courses. One moment, I remember telling them to hurry, and the next moment, I'm lying on the kitchen floor." Her face crumples. "And there were six dead bodies in the front room."

"You didn't see anything?"

"No, nothing."

"You were unconscious during the entire incident? Do you think the killer drugged you?"

Not drugs. Despite what the TV shows would have you think, no drug causes instant unconsciousness. Joao would have simply applied pressure on their carotid arteries until they passed out.

"I must have been," Frau Augsburger replies. "When I woke up, Leonie and Ava were still on the ground. My first thought was the risk of fire, but thank God, all the stoves were turned off. If he hadn't done that, we might have gone up in flames."

Lisa, the reporter, opens her eyes very wide. "You're saying that you think the killer turned off the stoves?"

"I'm saying it wasn't one of us. And that's not the only gentlemanly thing he did. When I woke up, there was a cushion under my head."

A sudden, unexpected, hot surge of jealousy goes through me. How considerate of Joao to put a cushion under the busty Frau's head. God forbid she gets a crick in her neck.

I turn off my phone, lean back in my seat, and shut my eyes. What a tangled mess. There's almost a Shakespearean quality to it all. For eight years, Joao thought that I died in a fire in Mexico, and for almost as long, I believed he drowned off the coast of France.

Yet here we are, both still alive.

Romeo and Juliet have nothing on us.

For one brief moment at the restaurant, I thought—hoped—we could get past the missing years, but that dream had shattered almost before it formed. Yes, Joao is still alive, but he lives in Venice and works for Antonio Moretti.

And when he spoke about the man, there was more than respect in his voice. *There was affection.*

But Moretti is one of the people who've bankrolled Bach's operation. Five years ago, Henrik made a series of bad financial decisions and was on the verge of total collapse when Antonio Moretti invested three million euros into his business.

Bach's academy would have shut down, but Moretti's money kept it alive. As far as I'm concerned, Antonio Moretti bears just as much culpability for Bach's crimes as my former trainer.

Even if Joao could forgive me for faking my death, he won't be able to forgive what I'm planning to do. He's built a full and complete life in Venice, and I am going to take a wrecking ball to it when I target his boss.

The Hunter

No happy endings in my future.

A tear trickles down my cheek, and then another. Before I know it, I'm full-on weeping. The kind-faced middle-aged woman in a black headscarf sitting across from me gives me several concerned looks before tentatively asking, "Is everything okay, my dear?"

"My boyfriend just broke up with me." It's not the exact truth, but it's close enough.

A look of sympathy flashes over her face. She digs in her bag for a packet of Kleenex and offers me one. "I'm so sorry," she says. "I remember how sharp the loss of love can feel." Her smile is gentle. "You're young. You might not believe me when I tell you it gets better, but it does. In two years, he will be nothing but a distant memory. You'll look back to this moment and wonder why you were so upset."

Her words are kind, and she means well, so I smile back at her. "Thank you."

I'm twenty-seven. That's objectively young, I guess, especially from where she's sitting. But I had no childhood to speak of, and I feel old beyond my years. And as much as I wish that what she was saying was true, I know it isn't.

It's been eight years, and the pain of leaving Joao hasn't faded, not even a little bit. The heartache still lingers, agonizingly sharp and naggingly sore, as if no time as passed at all.

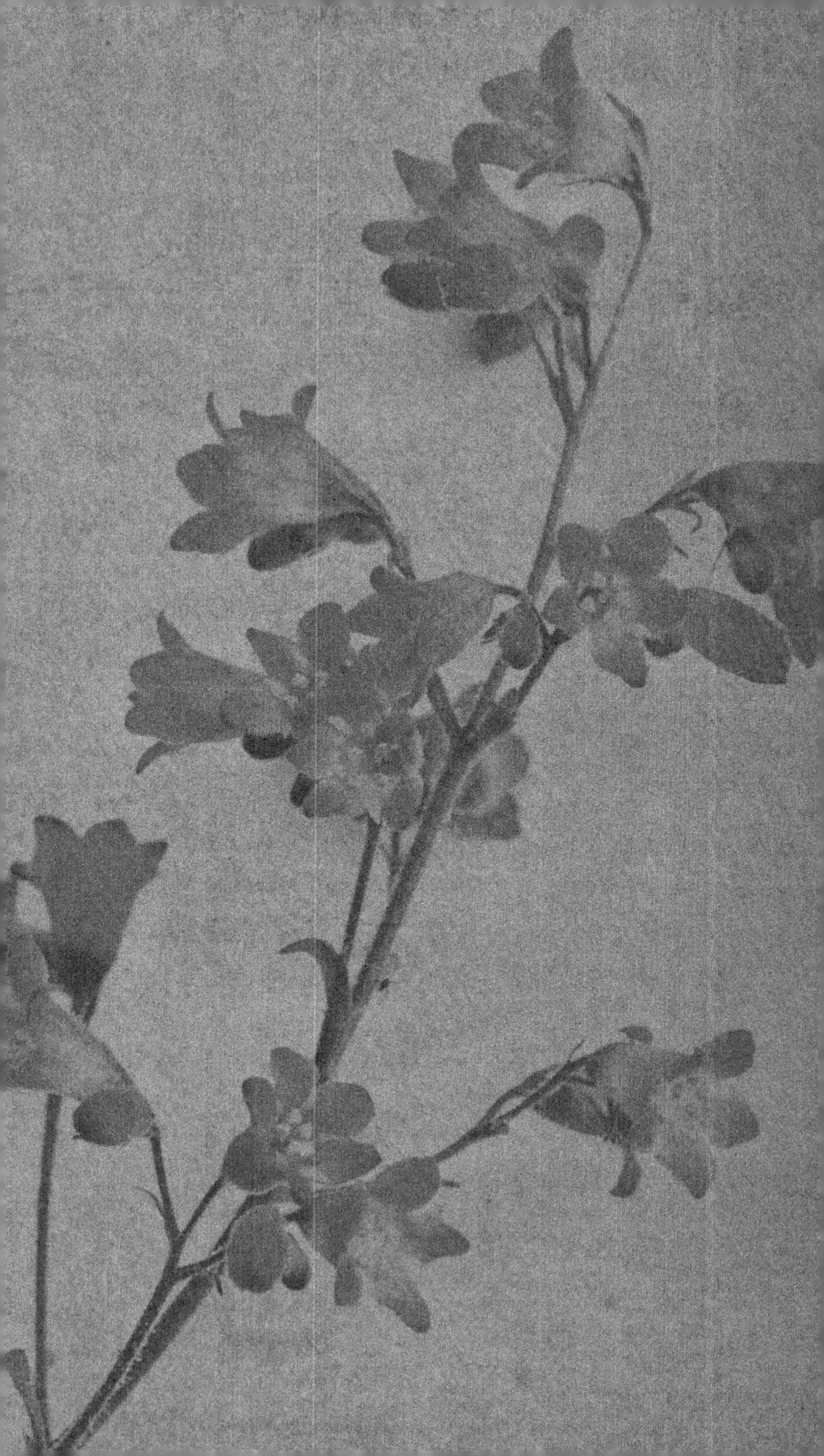

9

STEFI

My travel companion, Fatima, and I part ways at Basel, where I change trains. It's almost ten in the morning by the time I reach my apartment in Paris.

A cheery voice greets me the moment I open the door. "Good morning," Charlotte Bellegarde says in French, holding up a cup. "I made coffee." She grins wickedly. "I also logged into your work so Lynda wouldn't bitch at you. You're welcome."

Ah, yes. My unwanted teenage house guest, the reason I was forced to go to Venice and abduct Alina Zuccaro.

Three months ago, I arrived in Paris to kill René Vannier. I broke into his apartment and found the sixty-year-old former prosecutor in bed with a seventeen-year-old girl. I told her to get the hell out and shot Vannier in the head, but to my surprise, she didn't bolt. "Take me with you," she begged. "Please. If you leave me here, my stepfather will just pimp me out to someone else."

I should have walked away. But seventeen-year-old Charlotte had been failed by every adult in her life, from the stepfather who first raped her when she was thirteen and pimped her out to his wealthy connections to the mother who refused to hear the truth about her husband and pretended nothing was happening.

So, I took her with me. The only way to prevent her stepfather from coming after her was to take him out. Unfortunately, he was a high-ranking soldier of the Cosa Nostra, and to get to him, I needed Vidone Laurenti's help.

But Laurenti was a scumbag who wanted me to abduct his adult daughter from Venice and bring her to Sicily.

His daughter, Alina Zuccaro.

I didn't want to do it. I balked when I found out what the job was. Alina hadn't done anything to deserve this. Even worse, to get access to her, I had to pretend to be her friend, and Ali was nice to me. She showed me around her gym and made me feel welcome, and when I gave her some bullshit story about my mother dying to get closer to her, she was genuinely kind.

In a different life, I would have liked to be friends with her.

Assassins don't form friendships, a voice inside my head says, a voice that once again sounds very much like Bach. *They can't afford to.*

I hate my sadistic ex-trainer with every fiber of my being, but he was right about this. Attachments are weaknesses, and weakness will get you killed.

"Gotta say," Charlie says, her voice dragging me back

to the present, "I'm surprised by how easy it was to get into your computer." She smirks. "Newsflash, Stefi. abc123 isn't the most secure password in the world."

"It's not meant to be." My French used to be rusty, but spending time with a native speaker has brought most of it back. "The online help desk job is a cover, and my real laptop is encrypted." Suppressing a sigh, I take the coffee from Charlie. "For the hundredth time, you don't need to wait on me. I can make my own coffee."

"I don't mind," she responds brightly. "Are you hungry?" She doesn't wait for me to respond. "I didn't know what time you'd be back, so I made chicken stew. It reheats better than roast chicken, you know? Do you want some? Or if that's too odd for breakfast, there's some bread left over from yesterday."

"The stew is fine," I say tersely, cutting her off. "It's after nine. Weren't you supposed to meet someone about a place to live this morning?"

Her smile falters. "I didn't feel good." Her gaze slides away from me. "So I canceled."

Bullshit, I want to say, but I keep my mouth shut. Charlotte is clinging to me in an effort to feel safe, and after everything she's been through, I can't really blame her for it. But the sooner she learns that I'm not her sanctuary, the better. "I have this apartment for the rest of the month," I tell her. "That's it. I'm leaving Paris after that."

Her face falls. I feel like a jerk, but there's no helping it. I shouldn't have gotten involved in her life in the first place. When you're an assassin, you don't form friendships, and you certainly don't have relationships.

"Where will you go next?" she asks. "Once you leave Paris, I mean."

She's staring at me with puppy dog eyes, and it's obvious that she wants to come with me. I square my shoulders and set down my mug on the counter. "Stop making me out to be some kind of angel," I tell her bluntly. "I'm an assassin. Hang out with me, and you're going to get killed."

Her mouth sets in a stubborn line. "I don't care. You killed René. You killed my stepfather. My mother is searching for me, I know she is, but she doesn't give a shit about me. Please don't make me—" She stops talking abruptly, her eyes running over my face. "Stefi, what's wrong?"

Damn it. Charlie is too observant for her own good. "Nothing."

"Your eyes are red. Have you been crying? What happened? Did you get hurt?"

She's staring at me with so much concern that a lump rises in my throat. I've always told myself that my quest is worth the cost. It's the right thing to do. But the road I've chosen is a lonely one, and being in the right doesn't keep me warm at night.

I stay away from people. No one has worried about me for a very long time. Not since...

"I saw someone," I whisper. I shouldn't burden this teenager with my problems, especially when she has so many of her own, but I can't seem to stop the words from spilling loose. "Someone from my past. Someone I thought was dead."

The Hunter

"Who?"

"My husband."

Her mouth falls open. "You're married?"

"I was. I guess I still am." Are you still married if you're declared dead but turn out to be very much alive? I have no idea. It doesn't really matter what the legalities are—in every way that matters, Joao will always be my husband.

"Was he your target? Did you have to kill him?"

"What?" Okay, that's not entirely a crazy question—I *am* an assassin. "No. He's an assassin, too."

"And he was there for the same target?"

I shake my head. "He said he was there to protect me."

"That's so romantic," Charlie says wistfully. She catches sight of my expression. "What? It *is* romantic. Do you still love him?"

I don't know how to answer that question. "I thought he was dead, Charlie."

Her reply is practical in a way that only the French can be. "Well," she says. "He's not. Are you still in love with him?"

It's so simple to view the world through a seventeen-year-old lens. "I haven't seen him in eight years. I don't know who he is anymore."

Charlie heads to the kitchen and bustles around to heat up the stew. "That's not actually an answer to my question," she points out. "Why don't you call him and catch up? After all, you're not dating anyone right now, are you?"

Dating. That's hilarious. "No."

She places a steaming bowl in front of me. "And have you dated anyone in the last eight years?"

"No," I say again.

She gives me a triumphant smile. "Because you're still in love with your husband."

Enough. This isn't a fairytale. I give my teenage houseguest an exasperated look. "I'm an assassin," I tell her. "I don't form ties."

"Fair enough. If you didn't want a relationship, you could've gone on the Internet for anonymous sex. Did you do that?"

"No."

"Why not?" she asks smugly. Charlie obviously thinks that's a gotcha question. Everything she's hearing from me supports her theory that I'm still in love with Joao. But it's not quite that straightforward. Nothing is. I haven't slept with anyone else because it would have felt like a betrayal of my marriage vows.

And I've betrayed Joao enough.

"Hang on," Charlie says slowly, looking as if she's just realizing something. "If you didn't date and you didn't hook up, does that mean. . ." Her mouth falls open. "Don't you miss sex?"

And that's quite enough of this interrogation. I lift my head up from the delicious stew and fix her with a stern look. "Don't you have somewhere to be?" I demand. "Don't you need to look for a place to live?"

"Okay, okay, sheesh," Charlie says. "No need to bite my head off; I was just curious." She looks at my empty bowl. "You want more food?"

"Yes, please. I'll get it." I head to the kitchen and

spoon more stew into my bowl. It really is good, swimming with tomatoes, herbs, and olives. "Where did you learn to cook?"

"Mama and I used to cook together," she responds. "Before..."

Before her stepfather moved in. Her voice trails off, and I curse myself for my thoughtlessness. I'm not the only one who doesn't want to talk about the past. "Have you ever thought about being a chef?"

She looks up, startled. "A chef? No, I couldn't. I'll have to go to school for that. It takes years to get certified. I'll be almost thirty by the time I'm done."

Ah, teenagers. Charlie is acting as if turning thirty is the most horrific thing in the world. Joao and I used to fantasize about that milestone. Less than ten percent of Henrik Bach's trainees made it to thirty, and we were determined to beat the odds.

"Would it hurt to try? The years are going to pass anyway." I finish my stew and wash the bowl. "You might as well spend the time doing something you love."

I HAVE three hours before I have to get up for work, so I head into my bedroom for a nap. Stripping naked, I get under the covers, but sleep is maddeningly elusive. Charlie's question plays in my mind. *Don't you miss sex?*

A complicated question. I don't miss sex exactly. Most

things are easily taken care of with a vibrator. But I miss *intimacy*.

Why don't you call him and catch up?

It's a tempting thought. As if the chasm that divides us can be crossed by a simple phone call, but of course, that's not possible. I don't even know Joao's phone number—like me, he probably goes through burner phones like candy. Even if I was brave enough to reach out, I have no way of getting hold of him.

What about the chat room? My subconscious prompts. *You could try contacting him there.*

He's not going to remember the chat room, I counter.

Would it hurt to try?

Damn it, it sucks when you lose an argument with yourself. I pull out my personal laptop, navigate to that dusty corner of the Internet, and log in, the username and password still as familiar to me as my own name.

Then my heart stops.

I haven't logged on in a very long time. I wanted to, so many times, but I couldn't risk it. If Joao found out I visited the chat room, he'd know I was alive. And if he knew that, he would come for me. I knew that with absolute certainty. He would have moved heaven and earth to find me, *and he would have gotten himself killed.*

But Joao *has* logged in, and he's left me messages, so many of them. They started the day he learned about the fire that supposedly killed me.

I can't believe you're gone, I won't. I refuse to imagine the existence of a world that doesn't have you in it, Stefi, because if I do, *I will drown.* I refuse to face the fact that our kiss before you left was the last one ever. That our stolen trip to Prague was the end. No more carafes of cheap wine, no more extravagant toasts to the Summer Gods. That the message you sent me last week, the one where you yelled at me for taking stupid risks, is the last message you'll ever send me.

Living without you isn't life. It isn't heartache—I can't feel heartache without a heart, and you've always had mine in your keeping. No, this is terrifying emptiness, this is a deathly void, this is madness. Tell me I've been in a coma, and I've hallucinated your loss. Tell me it's a lie. Tell me I'll hear you laugh again and promise me you'll whisper my name into my ear once more. Tell me this is a sick, twisted nightmare, and wake me up, little fox, I beg you. Tell me anything except this.

There are more notes in the weeks that follow, desperately sad notes that wreck my heart. Messages on what would have been our first wedding anniversary. My birthday. The anniversary of the day he proposed by forming a twist tie into an impromptu engagement ring. "I'll get you a real one soon," he promised.

But there hadn't been time.

And then the messages abruptly cease at the same time as Joao supposedly drowned off the coast of Marseilles. Turns out I'm not the only one who stopped visiting this chat room after I faked my death. Joao did the same.

I wipe the tears from my cheeks. How can I reach out to him and catch up as if nothing's happened? It's impossible. He's never going to forgive me for what I did.

There's been too much pain, too much hurt—it's all laid out here in one heart-wrenching message after another—and there's no coming back from that.

My laptop beeps. On the screen, words appear.

> Hello again, little fox. I've been waiting for you.

10

JOAO

Have I been up all night waiting for Stefi to show up? Not really. Sure, I logged into our secret chat room as soon as I got back to my hotel room, and yes, I stayed up far too late to see if she'd show up. And *okay fine,* I might have fallen asleep in my clothes with the laptop on my pillow.

But it's not because I'm waiting for her; that's ridiculous. It's *not* because I want to talk to her again. I'm here because of the mission, *that's all,* and because, as furious as I am with her, I don't want to see her killed by Andrei Sidorov.

Then my laptop beeps to tell me that someone's logged in. I instantly come fully awake and sit up. *Hello again, little fox,* I type, anticipation jolting up my spine. This is better than caffeine. *I've been waiting for you.*

She responds after a long pause.

STEFI

Joao. Where are you?

> Zurich. You?

Ha, nice try. Why would I tell you where I am? So, you can show up and point another gun at my head?

> Call me.

Why?

> I want to hear your voice. Call me.

I type in my phone number and wait, my heart pounding in my chest. Will she call, or will she bail? The old Stefi would have taken me up on my challenge, no questions asked, but then the old Stefi trusted me.

Did she really? Or were you just fooling yourself?

The phone rings. I look at the display, and the number is blocked. No surprise there. "Hello, Stefi."

"Joao." Her voice is soft and a little breathless, at once familiar and not.

Don't get sucked in.

"Are you calling me from Geneva," I ask lightly. "Or are you hiding your location?"

"You already traced me? Impressive."

I laugh. As if she'd be stupid enough to call me on an open line. "Oh, come on, Stefi. I already know you're not in Switzerland."

"Really?" she asks pertly. "How can you tell?"

"Geneva is three and a half hours away from Zurich. If you were there, you'd have logged into our chat room much sooner. You're further away. You don't like to drive at night, so I'm guessing you took the train. You're going to base yourself in a big city because it's easier to stay anonymous in them. So where are you?" I look at a map of Europe and find her likely stops. "Paris? Brussels? Frankfurt?"

She doesn't answer, not that I think she's going to. Her silence is telling enough. One of my guesses is right. Which one?

"What's your goal, Joao?" she asks after a long pause. "What do you want with me? Why were you really in Zurich?"

"I told you already. I found out you were alive, and I came to warn you. Zurich was a trap, Stefi. The head of the Sidorov Bratva wants you dead, and he's sending his people—"

"Hang on," she interrupts. "You didn't tell me any of that."

"I didn't?"

"No," she says. "You just told me to strip."

I replay our conversation in my head, and, fuck me, she's right. Making sure she was unarmed wasn't a bad idea, but the moment she took off her clothes, all thought fled my brain. I didn't just let her go; I failed to tell her about Sidorov in the first place.

God, I'm a fool. *A fool for her.*

"Can you blame me?" I ask, as casually as I can manage. "I always lost my mind when you got naked, and that hasn't changed. You're beautiful."

We grew up together, and Stefi was my best friend,

but I never thought of her as a *girl*. That changed the summer we turned sixteen. I'd gone on a training exercise in Ethiopia, and when I returned to Bach's compound in Latvia, the first person I saw was Stefi, laughing at something her friend Michaela was saying.

And I realized that without me noticing, my best friend had blossomed into a beautiful young woman.

I wanted her with an all-consuming intensity. I barely spoke two words to her that summer, in the grips of a crush that was more painful than any of Henrik's little tortures.

She sucks in a breath at my words, and that sound brings me back to the present. "There are dozens of people who want to kill me," she says flippantly. "But the Sidorov Bratva isn't on that list. I don't even know who they are." There's the smallest hint of shakiness in her voice. "Why should I believe you?"

"Why would I lie?" I counter. "Four years ago, you were hired to kill Aldo Caruso. The name ring any bells?"

I can hear typing on the other end of the line. She's not looking up Caruso—I know for a fact that Stefi remembers every single kill. As a teenager, she would cry after every job, and I'd wrap her in my arms and do my best to comfort her. She's searching for information on the Sidorov Bratva. "Yes," she says finally. "I remember."

"Aldo's daughter Mira is married to Andrei Sidorov, the pakhan. You went after his family, Stef. He's going to hunt you down. He almost succeeded yesterday." If I hadn't reached the restaurant in time. . . My blood runs cold. "Antonio's ordered me to bring you in, and he's willing to offer you protection. Come back with me to Venice, Stefi. It's the only way to keep you safe."

"I'm going to pass on that offer, thanks," she replies coolly. "I can take care of myself."

"If I hadn't been there, they would have killed you yesterday. The threat is real. Stop being so stubborn—"

"Drop it, Joao."

She's on the verge of hanging up, and I don't want her to do that, so I change the topic. "Can I ask you something? Why did you come for Alina? The Stefi I knew would have never done that."

She exhales in a long breath. "I didn't want to," she admits finally. "Three months ago, I broke into a target's apartment to take him out and found him in bed with a seventeen-year-old girl. Her name is Charlie. Her stepfather pimped her out to my target, and her mother turned a blind eye to what was happening."

I hate all rapists, but there's a special place in hell reserved for men who prey on children. If it had been me in Stefi's shoes, I would have taken my time killing the stepfather. I'd have started by chopping his dick off. I don't enjoy torture, but a quick and painless death is a mercy that not everyone deserves. "You killed the stepfather." I don't ask it as a question because I already know the answer. I know what my wife would have done.

"I did, but it wasn't straightforward. He worked for the Cosa Nostra. I couldn't take him out in Sicily—that would have been a suicide mission. I needed to wait for him to leave Italy, but finding out when and where he'd be traveling was difficult. Vidone Laurenti offered to sell me that information."

"In exchange for Alina Zuccaro's capture."

"Yes," she says, sounding deeply troubled. "I *hate* that I got her involved, but I had to protect Charlie." She hesitates. "Do you know if she's okay?"

"You haven't checked?" I ask, surprised.

"I haven't been able to bring myself to look her up."

"She's fine. Tomas reached her before your goons showed up." Something's been nagging at me ever since I found out that Stefi drugged Alina. The whole attempt was so uncharacteristically sloppy, and that's not at all like my wife. "Hang on," I say slowly. "You took her to an out-of-the-way spot along the canal. You could have gotten her out on a boat by yourself, but instead of doing that, you hired a couple of low-level criminals to finish the job. Why?"

"I was careless," she murmurs evasively.

Stefi is *never* careless. "That's not the only thing that doesn't make sense," I continue. "You drugged Alina but got the dosage wrong. She regained consciousness before your guys could get her on the boat. Even more importantly, you left her with her phone." The pieces fall into place with a click. "You *wanted* her to wake up and call for help."

She doesn't respond.

"You're not answering my question."

"You didn't ask me one. What do you want me to say, Joao? I was in a rush to save Charlie, and I got sloppy."

"No, I don't think so. You forget I know you, Stefi. You don't make mistakes." My voice softens. "Ali's phone was transmitting her location; there's no way you'd forget to destroy it. You left Tomas a trail to

The Hunter

follow and made sure there'd be enough time for him to get to her. Faced with an impossible choice, you did everything you could do to protect her. Why won't you admit it?"

Her voice, when she replies, is shaky. "I'm not the person you think I am."

I frown. What is she hiding from me? "I'm not going to stop hunting you," I growl, a threat and a promise rolled into one. "I'm not going to let go. I will chase you to the end of the earth."

"And then what?" she snarls. "You'll take me to Venice? You'll have to find me first."

This isn't the first time we've clashed, and it won't be the last. I can picture her in my head, face tilted up to me, green eyes spitting fire, hands clenched into fists. I can picture cupping her chin in my hand, tugging her close, my lips finding her soft ones, feeling her anger melting into pure sweetness as she kisses me back.

My cock hardens at the image. Where is she right now? Is she in bed, too, naked under the covers? Is our clash turning her on? Once we started dating, our fights always ended in bed in an explosion of raw passion. Does she remember?

"I'll find you." My voice dips lower. "I'm going to keep you safe, whether you like it or not." I finger the scrap of silk next to me. "You left your panties behind. They're very pretty."

"You took them?"

"Of course I did. You can't leave DNA behind in a crime scene. Send me your address, and I'll mail them to you."

She chuckles, the sound rich and warm against my ear. "You really think I'm going to fall for that?"

"Then I guess I'll just have to keep them."

This conversation reminds me of all the times we used to call each other on jobs. We'd talk for hours about everything under the sun, and invariably, because we were horny teenagers who couldn't keep our hands off each other, we'd end up having phone sex.

Some madness prompts me to bring that up. "Remember our phone calls? Are you going to think about me when you masturbate tonight, little fox? When you come, will it be with my name on your lips?"

She sucks in a breath. "You're delusional."

She's trying to sound defiant, but once again, she sounds a little breathless. I hear the hitch in her voice, and intense satisfaction surges through me. Stefi's not as unaffected by me as she's pretending to be. *She's my wife.* I know exactly what buttons to push, and I'm enough of an asshole to push them.

"I'll be thinking of you tonight," I continue. It's a lie: I'm not planning to wait until tonight. I *cannot*. I only have to close my eyes and she's here, standing in front of me, dressed in this scrap of black silk and nothing else. "Thinking about how hot and tight you felt when I thrust into you. You remember how you'd rake your nails down my back? Because I do. I'm going to fist myself with your panties wrapped around my cock, Stefi. And when I come, it'll be you I'm thinking of."

"Joao," she whispers. "Please..."

What. The. Fuck.

I snap out of my trance at the sound of her soft plea.

The Hunter

For the second time in twenty-four hours, my assignment is nowhere on my mind. Once again, I've lost sight of the mission, and I'm burning for Stefi, ready to drown in her remembered sweetness.

But the past is a lie, and my memories can't be relied on. And if I don't get my head out of my ass and focus on finding Stefi, Andrei Sidorov's men will kill her before I can get her to the safety of Venice.

"Talk to you later, Stef," I say tersely. Then, before I can do something stupid again, I hang up.

My fucking cock is hard as a rock. I'm holding her panties in my hands, and the sound of her voice is still in my ears, the scent of her on my fingers, and I can't stop myself. I jerk myself off, stroking hard and fast, my hips bucking, my breathing shallow, the silk sliding on my erection, and I erupt almost instantly, her name on my lips.

Fuck.

The buzz of the orgasm fades, and common sense slowly returns, and with it, bitter self-recrimination. *What the hell am I doing?* One conversation with my wife, and I completely lose focus. It's always been this way, and it looks like nothing's changed in eight years. Stefi's under my skin, tattooed into my heart. Instead of being furious about her long disappearance, I'm fantasizing about her. Instead of planning my next move, I'm jerking off to the sound of her voice.

I head into the shower, stand under freezing cold water, and give myself a stern talking-to. I make myself remember all the reasons that I don't trust Stefi. Vanishing without a trace, letting me believe for eight years that she's dead. Killing thirty-five people even though she escaped Henrik because she couldn't bear to be an assassin anymore.

It's only when I'm toweling myself dry that I realize that during our conversation, she inadvertently gave me a clue.

I know how to find Stefi.

11

JOAO

I wait until ten to call Valentina Colonna, our chief hacker. "Hey Joao," she says. "Hang on while I secure this line, okay?"

"Sure thing."

She comes back after a minute. "You're using the phone I gave you, right?"

"Yes." For the moment, I am, although stopping at an electronics store is pretty high on my to-do list. I don't like the idea of Valentina or anyone else being able to listen in on my conversations with Stefi.

"Good." Her voice softens. "I was just about to call you. I heard the news. How are you doing?"

There's been one giant revelation after another in the last week. What specific piece of news is she talking about? "When you say news, you're referring to...?"

"Henrik Bach's death," she replies. "Daniel said you already knew about it. Are you—"

"I'm fine," I interrupt tersely. I don't like talking about

my feelings, and I'm hoping to cut this conversation off before it gets going, but Valentina doesn't take the hint.

"You don't sound like you're celebrating," she says. "And trust me, I get it. These things are never black and white. Take me, for instance. I have every reason to hate Angelica's biological father, but without him, she wouldn't exist." She takes a deep breath. "What I'm doing a very bad job of saying is that it's okay to feel a little conflicted about his death. After all, it was because of Bach that you were taken from your family, and it was his fault that there are no records about your true parentage. Anyway, I'm here if you need to talk about it."

As a child, I used to fantasize about my parents. In my dreams, they were larger-than-life characters who would show up with flaming swords, kill Henrik, and rescue me from the hell I found myself in.

I gave up on those fantasies a long time ago, accepting that I'll never find them. I've also realized that you don't need to be connected by blood to be family. Venice is my home now, and the men and women of the mafia are the family I've chosen for myself.

It's kind of Valentina to offer her support. "It's not that I don't appreciate your concern, but—"

"Let me guess, you want me to change the topic," she says wryly. "Dante predicted that you wouldn't want to talk about your feelings."

"I don't know what I'm feeling," I admit. I don't want her to think that I don't appreciate her support. "Like you said, it's complicated." It's impossible for Valentina to understand what it was like growing up in Bach's academy. I can only talk about it with somebody who was there. Someone like Stefi. "But thank you for caring."

"Of course I care, Joao," she responds. "You're my friend. You've always made me feel welcome in the organization, and you've never once implied that I couldn't do my job because I'm a woman. This is the least I can do." Her voice turns brisk. "But you didn't call me to talk about Henrik Bach. What can I do for you? If you're calling about an update about the ambush at the restaurant, you're right—they're not Sidorov's people. At least, none that we know about."

It gives me no pleasure to know my instincts were right. But if the people waiting for Stefi weren't bratva, then who are they? Who else wants Stefi dead? "Could they be mercenaries Sidorov hired? Have you identified them?"

"Not yet. I'm working on it, though, and I'll call you as soon as I know."

"Okay." Valentina is the best in the business. I have no doubt she'll figure it out. "I need some information. You maintain files on Cosa Nostra, don't you?"

"Of course. What are you looking for?"

"A name. Someone killed in the last three months."

I hear her typing. "I have twenty-seven matches. Can you narrow it down?"

"Yes. The guy was married with a seventeen-year-old stepdaughter."

"Eighteen of them are married," she replies after a minute. "No matches on a stepdaughter."

Damn it. I was hoping this would be easy, but of course, the asshole would have kept his stepdaughter hidden. Cosa Nostra isn't exactly filled with saints, but even they would have drawn the line at raping a minor.

What else did Stefi say? "He was killed outside Italy."

"Aha. We're down to three. Two drive-by shootings in Spain and one guy stabbed to death in an alleyway in Paris."

"Paris." A drive-by shooting is too impersonal, and Stefi would have wanted to inflict pain. "It's Paris. What's his name?"

"Brando Pignotti. Married to Severine Bellegarde two years ago."

"Severine Bellegarde. That's a French name." The hair on the back of my neck stands up. I'm getting close; I can feel it. "What can you tell me about her?"

"The marriage happened in Paris," she says after a minute. "She moved to Sicily after the wedding. Let me search French records. . . Hang on, Severine has a daughter from a previous relationship. Charlotte Bellegarde."

Yes! This is the Charlie Stefi mentioned.

"I need Severine's phone call log for the last three months."

"Give me a minute." I hear the clicking of her keyboard as she hacks into the telecom company. "Okay, I've just emailed it to you. How is this connected to Stefania?"

"Brando Pignotti has been raping Charlotte since he married her mother. Stefi found out and killed Pignotti. But if I know my wife, that's not all she did. Stefi would feel protective toward the young girl. All I have to do is find Charlotte Bellegarde, and she'll lead me to my wife."

The Hunter

Valentina's quiet for a long minute. Finally, she speaks up. "You realize you called her your wife?" she asks. "Twice in a row. But she isn't just your wife, Joao. This woman is an assassin. If Cecelia d'Este's file is to be believed, she's killed seventy-three people in the last six years."

"The file is wrong. The number's lower."

"Who told you that? *Your wife?* And you believe her?"

Her voice is openly skeptical, and my hackles rise. "I'm not interested in discussing this with you."

"I know," she says unhappily. "I can hear it in your voice, and yes, I know it's none of my business. But I'm not the only one who's concerned, Joao. This woman isn't good for you. Just be careful. Please."

I hang up and push Valentina's words aside. Now's not the time to dwell on them. Sidorov is after Stefi, and he got pretty damn close in Zurich. Right now, my only priority is finding her before she gets killed.

Opening up Severine Bellegarde's call log, I get to work. I go through the entries one by one and cross off the numbers in her contacts. Most of the calls she receives are from her husband, her hairdresser, and her cleaning lady.

When I'm done with my analysis, I have one phone number I can't account for. Severine received a phone call from this number three weeks ago, and it only lasted thirty seconds.

I try and put myself in Charlotte Bellegarde's shoes. Her stepfather—the asshole who raped her and pimped her out to his friends—is dead. Her mother stood by and let it happen, and logically, Charlotte should be furious with her.

But feelings are complicated. I should be furious with Stefi, but instead, I'm doing everything I can to keep her alive.

Would Charlie call her mother? Not to talk, but to hear the sound of her voice? Stefi would never make such a mistake, but Charlotte is seventeen, and teenagers are not noted for their impulse control.

I search for the current location of the phone number and hit paydirt. Paris. 19th Arrondissement. A mid-rise apartment just off the Avenue de Clichy.

I'm coming for you, little fox.

12

STEFI

I get two hours of restless, dream-filled sleep before it's time to wake up. All morning, I sit at the table and work my boring customer service job, ignoring Lynda's passive-aggressive digs with an equanimity that drives her insane.

And while I work, I think about Joao.

I'm still reeling from seeing him yesterday. For more than seven years, I've believed he was gone, and I'm still struggling to absorb that he's alive. The deepest, truest wish of my heart has come true, and I don't know what to do about it.

I shouldn't have talked to him this morning. I was rattled seeing him again and shaken by the messages he left me in our chat room. It was a mistake, and I knew it, but the moment he said, 'I want to hear your voice, little fox,' I started dialing.

I could never resist Joao. Not the first time he kissed me, not when I was eighteen and he proposed with a twist tie, not when we impulsively got married on a weekend trip to Copenhagen.

Then there's Henrik Bach's death. With everything else that's been going on, I've barely processed that the man I've dreamed about killing all my life is now forever beyond my reach.

I haven't felt this dangerously off-balance since Puerto Vallarta.

Stop thinking about Joao. There's a more immediate threat you need to address.

I almost got killed yesterday. When Marcus told me Varek Zaworski was leaving his village to meet a business associate in Switzerland, I'd been unbelievably careless, and instantly accepted the job. I hadn't stopped to think that it might be a trap, and I sure as hell skipped doing any due diligence of my own. I should have double-checked Marcus's intel with my own contacts, but I didn't. I hadn't even asked him who wanted the bounty hunter dead.

I deserved to be killed.

Had it not been for my husband, I would have been.

If Joao is to be believed, Andrei Sidorov, head of the Sidorov Bratva, sent a half dozen people to take me out in Zurich.

Something's been bothering me ever since Joao let that tidbit drop. Somehow, Sidorov figured out that he could reach me through Marcus O'Shea. But how? When I killed Sidorov's father-in-law, I used a different identity, not Nina Lalami.

So how did Sidorov connect me to Marcus O'Shea?

That's not the only problem. Joao said he had a file on

me. It doesn't have the most accurate intel in the world—I haven't killed seventy-three people, for starters—but at least two of the targets are right. Sidorov's father-in-law was in Joao's file, and so was Reyhan Benita.

How are these people gathering intel on me? What am I doing wrong? I've done my best to kill my targets in different ways. Some I've poisoned, some I've stabbed under the cover of a bar fight, and some I've shot in their homes.

Have I revealed something about myself in my approach? Do I have a 'tell'?

It's not you, you idiot. It's your targets.

Shit. I swear out loud, cursing my stupidity and my hubris. Of course, they found me. Every single person I've killed has been a part of Henrik Bach's network. As soon as Sidorov figured that out, he could predict what target to dangle in front of me.

Varek Zaworski was the perfect bait.

For a moment, I allow myself to despair. With Henrik's death, I have just three targets left on my list, but I can't fight this war on two fronts. I can't take down Bach's network *and* avoid Andrei Sidorov's killers. I'm as helpless as I was eight years ago when I faked my own death and disappeared.

Maybe I should take Joao up on his offer of safety and go to Venice.

No. I shake my head violently. Going to Venice with Joao would mean that I'm trading one enemy for another. Taking refuge in Moretti's city isn't safety—it's surrender, and I will never do it. *Never.*

I only have Joao's word that Andrei Sidorov is after

me. I don't think he'd lie to me, but what if he's wrong? What if it's Antonio Moretti who's figured out that I'm killing Bach's known associates? What if he's using Joao to find me, and this is all a ploy to kill me before I can succeed in killing him?

Another wave of despair overtakes me. I love Joao. I've always loved him, but there are too many secrets between us and too many powerful forces intent on keeping us apart. First Bach, now Moretti. Even if Joao could forgive me for disappearing, even if somehow, what happened in Istanbul doesn't wreck him, there's still the fact that his boss is one of my three remaining targets.

The entire fucking city of Venice loves its self-proclaimed king. Even his enemies agree that he's much better than his predecessor. And Joao works for him. I could show him everything I have—the financial records, the shell companies, the trail of money that connects his boss to Henrik Bach—but what if it isn't enough? What happens if he doesn't believe me? What if he refuses to see that his friend isn't who he thinks he is?

Bach trained us to be lone killers, but Joao and I were always two halves of a magnet. When we got married in Copenhagen—when Joao promised to love and cherish me *forever*—it was the happiest day of my life. His love was the salve to my heart that I didn't know I needed.

If he takes Moretti's side against mine, it will wreck me. I will fracture into a thousand broken pieces.

I managed to claw my way out of a prison my mind had built for me once, but it took everything I had to rescue myself. I don't think I have what it takes to do it again.

The Hunter

It's one in the afternoon, and Charlie still hasn't come back home. She left two hours ago to go shopping. "I might check out the youth center, too," she said as she left. "Maybe meet some people my own age. No offense, Stefi."

It's the first time she's shown any interest in making friends, and I should be ecstatic that she's acting like a typical teenager, but I'm twitchy. If Sidorov or someone else wants to get a hold of me, Charlie is a great way in. She's an innocent teenager who's done nothing to deserve the things that have happened to her. If she were in danger, I'd sacrifice myself in a heartbeat to keep her safe.

This is why it's a bad idea to get attached.

I push my worries aside and do my job on autopilot, sipping my apple tea and glancing at the clock every minute or two. Ten minutes go by, then twenty. It's almost two when I hear footsteps come up the stairs and a key scrape in the lock.

My hand closes on the knife taped under the table.

Charlie opens the door. "You wouldn't believe what the butcher was charging for lamb," she says indignantly. "It's robbery, I tell you." She puts her bags of groceries down on the table and registers that I'm on my work laptop. "Lynda still bitching at you?"

"Always. You were gone a while." I don't want her to think I was worrying, so I phrase that as casually as I can.

"Yeah, I stopped by the youth center and got to chatting with the people in charge. They have a track there." She looks a little wistful. "I used to love to run. I've been thinking of starting again."

"Ah." That's a good sign. Charlie is reasserting who

she is, an important step toward recovery from what her stepfather did to her. "That's a good idea. You should buy proper running shoes. I'll give you some money."

She frowns. "I can't keep taking your money."

"Yes, you can," I reply. "Pignotti had a bounty on his head. If you really think about it, that's your money, not mine."

The expression on Charlie's face tells me she's not buying it. "You're the one who killed him, not me. You've earned that money." She starts to put away the groceries. "I'm thinking about getting a job. There was a 'Help Wanted' sign in the window of the grocery store. They don't pay much, but the proprietor, Madame Allard, seems very kind."

I glance up at her. "You know money isn't an issue, right? You don't need to work at the grocery store. I will pay for you to go to culinary school if that's what you want, so don't make any hasty decisions, okay?"

I've accumulated a little nest egg. I'm not a millionaire or anything, but it's enough to put Charlie through school. It'll leave me tight for a while, but I'll figure it out. I'm used to it.

"Okay," Charlie replies. "I promise. I'll think about it."

She sounds like she means it. Good. I don't push anymore; she needs to get there on her own, so I change the subject. "What did you buy?"

"Lamb sausage, cauliflower, some parsley. I thought I'd roast the cauliflower and use the sausage in a pasta sauce."

"You don't have to cook all of our meals. I can make dinner if you'd like."

The Hunter

She gives me a withering look. "Stefi, no offense, but you cannot cook."

"None taken." Food has always been fuel, something that provides me with enough calories for me to function. It's never been something to be savored.

Except when I was with Joao. We'd seize moments away from Bach and spend hours eating bread and cheese, drinking cheap wine, and talking about everything under the sun. And even though it was just bread and cheese, it tasted better than anything I'd ever eaten.

Sudden, unexpected footsteps come up the stairs, and I frown. This doesn't sound like Monsieur Didier, the piano professor who lives across the hallway, and it isn't one of his young students—they typically skip up the stairs in an excess of energy.

No, this is someone heavier than our skinny French neighbor. A man, just one, and he's not making any effort to conceal his presence.

"Are you expecting someone?" I demand.

Charlie shakes her head in reply.

"Did you give anyone this address?"

"No, of course not," she says. "I swear I didn't."

The man knocks, and Charlie looks at me, her eyes wide and scared. "What should I do?"

I grab the knife from under the table.

"Answer it," I say tensely. I incline my head toward my bedroom. "I'll be right behind the door."

The knock sounds once again, polite yet insistent. "One moment," Charlie says, her voice shaking a little.

"I'm right here," I mouth to her, grabbing my laptop

and disappearing into my bedroom, out of sight of the front door.

She moves to open it. "Oui?" she asks. "Est-ce que je peux vous aider?"

"Bonjour," Joao says in fluent, unaccented French. "You must be Charlotte. I'm looking for Stefania."

Shit, shit, shit. *How did he find me?*

"My name is Joao Carvalho," he continues. "I'm her husband."

13

STEFI

I run.

I'm not proud of myself for bolting, and under normal circumstances, I would *never* abandon Charlie to a stranger at the door. If it had been anybody but Joao, I'd have dealt with the threat.

But I cannot face Joao. *I just cannot.* I cannot feast my eyes on his achingly familiar face. I don't trust myself not to trace the scar on his lip with my fingertips. Every muscle in my body is tugging me toward him, and I have to resist.

"Oh. My. God," Charlie exclaims. "You're Stefi's husband? The one she thought was dead?" I can hear animation and interest in her voice. No fear, none at all. My teenage ward thinks she's in the middle of a rom-com. "Come on in."

If she sounded afraid, I'd show myself to Joao, let him take me, and find a different way of escaping.

But she's not.

And I know with complete, utter certainty that Joao would never hurt her to get to me.

That's got to be good enough.

When I rented this apartment, I made sure there were two exits in case I needed to make a quick getaway. The fire escape is just to the left of my bedroom, and there's a door in the apartment that leads straight to it. But if I try to get to it, Joao will see me.

So I'm going to have to do this the hard way.

Grabbing my backpack as quietly as I can, I sling it over my shoulder, open my bedroom window, step out on the ledge, and jump toward the fire escape.

For a harrowing minute, I think I've missed the railing. An image of me plummeting to my death pops into my mind before my fingers grip the cold iron step, and I pull myself up. I've never had a head for heights. During training exercises, Joao would swing around like he was Tarzan, and everyone else thought he was showing off. I was the only person who knew he was doing it to take the attention off my struggles.

I race down the fire escape as fast as I can, hoping Charlie's buying me some time. There's no one waiting for me at the base of the stairs. Joao came alone. Muttering a silent prayer of thanks under my breath, I race through the garbage-filled back alley, vault the fence that separates our building from its neighbor, and run toward the subway station at full speed.

Charlie hasn't managed to distract Joao for long. I barely get to the corner before I hear his running footsteps behind me. "Stefi," he shouts as he vaults the fence. "Wait."

I double my speed, my heart pounding. How did he get to Paris? What did I reveal that led him to my door? What did I inadvertently give away? This is why I shouldn't have talked to him this morning; this is my fault for being unable to resist him.

Idiot, idiot, idiot. You knew that forming attachments was dangerous, and you did it anyway. You knew talking to Joao was a mistake, but you couldn't stay away. And now everything's a disaster.

I'm never going to be able to go back to my apartment—it's too risky. I've abandoned Charlie after promising her I wouldn't. Joao's not a fool. He'll watch the building and put a tail on her. Even talking to her on a burner phone is risky.

I take the stairs to the underground train station at full speed. It's a little after two, and the platform is almost empty. My heart sinks. I was hoping to lose Joao in the crowds, but that's not possible.

Where can I go, where can I run? How do I get away?

And then fortune favors me. A train pulls into the station, and the doors open. It's a piece of luck I don't deserve, but I take it anyway and dart inside.

Joao skids to a stop on the platform and lurches toward me.

But he's a second too late. The doors slide shut, and the train starts to pull out of the station.

Our gazes lock. My husband doesn't look annoyed that I've managed to escape him. No, his eyes sparkle, and an admiring smile curves his lips. As I watch, he mimes holding a phone to his ear.

"Call me," he mouths.

Then the train gathers speed, and he disappears from sight.

I should be ecstatic that I've eluded Joao's grasp. I have a brief moment of elation, and then it deflates like a balloon.

I've forgotten how good Joao is. Unlike me, he's not working alone. He is backed by the Venice Mafia, a powerful and well-connected organization. Even outside Venice, he'll have the kind of operational support that I can't get. Access to information, phone records, and security cameras.

A shiver of fear trickles down my spine. This was too close, and it's only going to get harder from this point on.

Joao lives for the chase, and I've grown sloppy.

If I want to survive this hunt, I need to up my game.

14

JOAO

I am such a fucking idiot.

When I figured out Stefi's possible location, I should have picked up the phone and called for backup. Leo Cesari, our enforcer, would have sent me a handpicked team, men and women chosen for their competence and ability to get the job done. They would have surrounded Stefi's apartment building, guarding every possible exit so my wife wouldn't be able to get away.

What did I do instead? Acted like a fucking fool, that's what I did. Eager to see Stefi again, I caught the first available flight to Paris from Zurich. I changed my clothes and brushed my hair, as if I were on a first date, not a dangerous hunt, and then I bounded up the five flights of stairs to her apartment.

About the only thing I didn't do was buy her flowers.

Stefi loved orchids. Small blooms, big showy ones, purple, pink, and yellow, she adored them all.

Orchids, for fuck's sake? That's what you're thinking

about? Stay focused. If you don't get your shit together, Andrei Sidorov is going to find her before you do.

I watch the train pull away, taking Stefi further away from me, and then, I admit failure and make my way back up to her apartment. Charlotte Bellegarde opens the front door as soon as I knock. "You chased her away," she says accusingly.

"I didn't mean to," I reply, frustrated as hell. "Sorry."

"She's not coming back, is she?" she asks, her voice small.

I feel like a total prick. Without meaning to, I've turned this young girl's life upside down. "No," I admit reluctantly. "I'm sorry. It would be stupid of her to come back here, and she's better than that. But I'm pretty sure she'll call."

"And then you'll trace my calls, won't you? You'll find Stefi that way."

"No, she'll call you from a burner phone."

"Why are you looking for her anyway?"

"Because some very bad people are after her. If they find her before me, they'll kill her."

"And you want to keep her safe?" She asks this with the skepticism of someone who's seen too much of the ugliness of the world to retain illusions about the purity of my motives.

"I do."

"Why?"

A smile rises unbidden to my lips as I remember a girl with two fat red pigtails and determined eyes. "She saved my life once when I was ten. I owe her." More memories from the past bombard me, but I make myself focus on the teenager in front of me. "Stefi will make sure the rent on this place is paid for as long as you want to stay, but she can't risk sending you money." I pull out my wallet and count out twenty hundred-euro notes. "This should tide you over for a month or two. After that. . ." I scribble a phone number on the back of my business card. "If you need a safe place to stay while you figure out your life, call that number. The woman there will take care of you."

She makes no move to take the money from me. "How can I trust you?"

"You can't. You shouldn't—you don't know me at all. Trust needs to be earned. You trust Stefi, though, yes? Ask yourself this. If she thought I was a danger to you, would she have left you alone with me?"

"Hmm. Good point." She takes the notes from me and tucks them in her back pocket. "You and Stefi are married, right?"

Always and forever. "I guess so."

"What does that mean? Do you have a girlfriend? Are you seeing someone else?"

"No. No girlfriend. No relationship. If you talk to Stefi, would you pass on a message? There's only been one woman in my life who's ever mattered. It's always been her. And if she keeps running from me, she's going to get herself killed."

Am I hoping that Charlie will relay my words to my wife? Of course I am. I'm not above using this teenager to advance my cause.

What cause? What exactly are you hoping to do here, Joao?

Twice now, I've had Stefi in my grasp. Twice, I've been

stupid enough to let her go. Finding her for the third time isn't going to be as easy. Stefi will be on high alert. She won't go anywhere near this apartment. I can trace the ID she used to rent it, but she'd have burned that one by now. Paris has thousands of hotels. Stefi's probably already used another fake ID to check into one.

She's gone underground.

I have no way of finding her again.

Unless. . .

Unless, like me, she can't stay away from the chat room.

After leaving the apartment, I head straight to the airport. There's a six p.m. flight to Venice, and I take it. The plane touches down at eight and the moment it does, I immediately log into the chat room.

But Stefi isn't there; she hasn't logged in all day.

I get home by eight-thirty. Mimi, who doesn't like it when I go away, sulks in my bedroom and barely acknowledges my return, so I buy my way back into her good graces with a handful of treats. I shower, then make myself something to eat, staying away from the chat room as long as possible before checking again.

Stefi still hasn't logged in.

The Hunter

ME

> Avoiding me, little fox? Come on, don't be mad. Don't you want to know how I found you?

There's no answer. My message stays unread all night long.

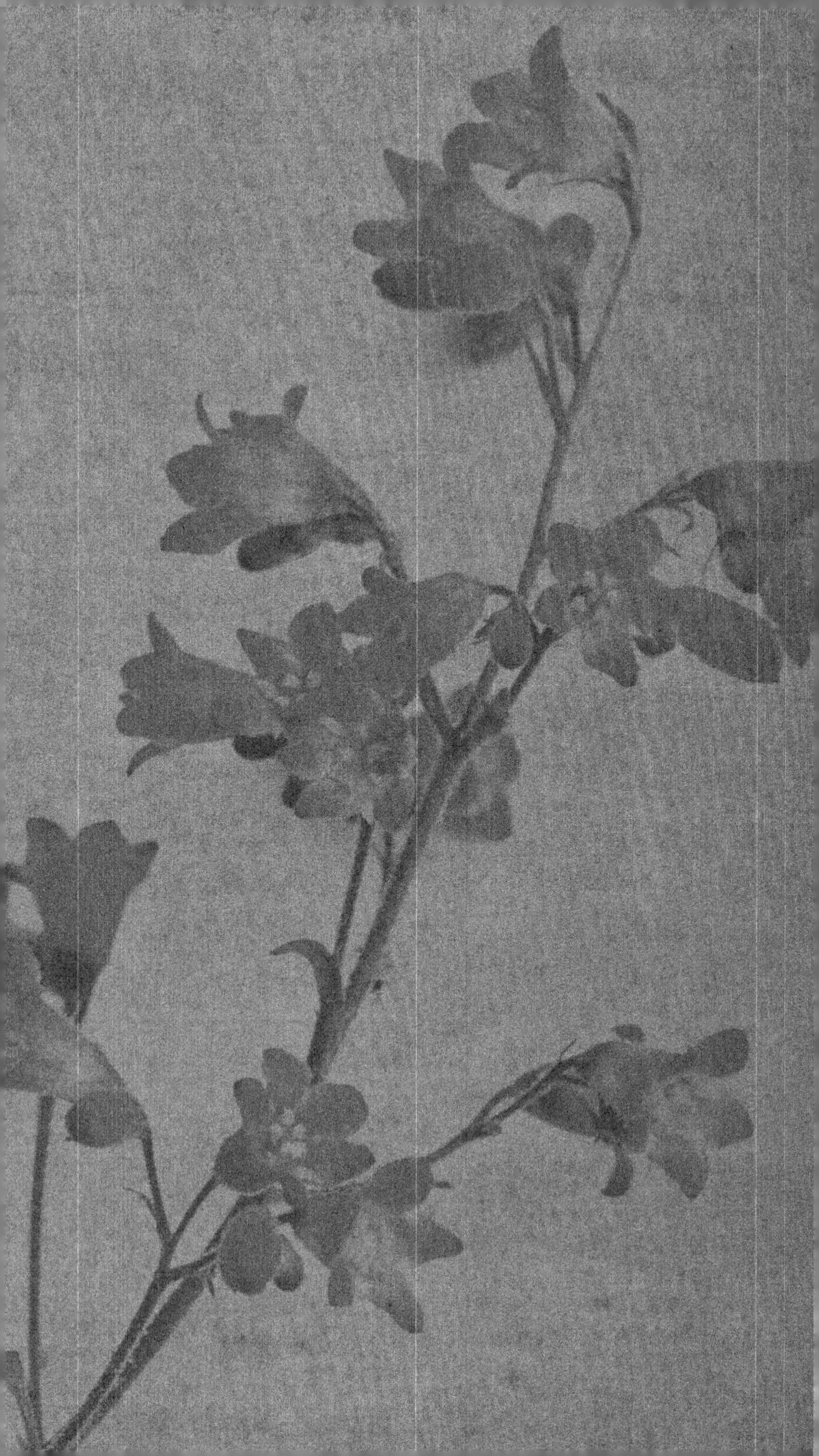

15

STEFI

I stay on the train until the end of the line, get off at the last stop, and then walk fifteen minutes to a nondescript hotel where I check in for the night. It's the sort of place where the staff knows better than to ask too many questions.

The lobby is deserted when I enter, so I ring the bell and wait for the clerk to show up.

It takes him almost five minutes. "Oui?"

"I'd like a room for the night," I say in French.

He gives me a once-over. This is the sort of hotel that's used by junkies, prostitutes, and pimps, and I stick out like a sore thumb. "I need your passport."

"I lost it," I say, slipping a twenty euro note across the counter. "I had to leave in a hurry." I do have spare passports, but good passports that stand up to scrutiny cost money, and I'd prefer not to have to burn another piece of ID. "Can you help me out?"

He gives me another long look. This time, he's wondering if I'm an undercover cop about to bust his business. If I'm going to stay here tonight, I need to soothe his nerves. "My husband was on his way home," I murmur, my voice low. "He's been drinking, and he gets angry and paranoid when he's had too much brandy. I couldn't face another. . ." I let my voice trail off and give him a beseeching look. "I had to get out of there."

His expression softens. He thinks I'm a battered wife running from an abusive husband. Sadly, it's not an uncommon story. "Not a problem," he says, taking the money from me. "I'll handle it." He pulls a passport from under the drawer and writes the details into his register. "Two hundred euros a night. Cash only, no cards."

Two hundred euros will buy me a nice room in a different part of town. Here, it buys me anonymity. "Could I have a room with a deadbolt?"

"That'll cost extra. Another two hundred euros."

My head snaps up. "That's insane."

"Junkies use the deadbolt, lock themselves in, and then overdose," he explains. "I keep having to break the doors down. The two hundred is a deposit. I'll return it when you check out."

I don't have time to argue. I pull the crumpled notes from my back pocket and hand them to him. "Second floor," he says, holding out a key to me. "Stairs are through that door."

I head upstairs. For the first hour, I occupy myself by cleaning the grubby room as best as I can with the threadbare towels in the bathroom. My stomach grumbles as I work, so when I'm done getting the space in decent condition, I cross the street for a döner and take it back up to my room. There are many excellent döner stands in Paris—this isn't one. The meat is greasy, and the pita is stale, but it's food, and I need the fuel, so I scarf it down.

Halfway through the meal, I suddenly realize I left my work laptop behind at the apartment when I fled from Joao. Ah well, it's no loss. It's not like I can show up at that job again. I used the same identity as my apartment rental, which is now irrevocably compromised. *Goodbye, Lynda—I won't miss you.* Maybe Charlie can use that laptop. After all, she needs a computer, but she turned me down every time I offered to buy her one.

Thinking of Charlie makes my heart hurt. I push the pain down deep inside. Joao, Istanbul, and now Charlie... One day, it's going to be too much, and I'm going to explode.

But not today.

I finish my meal, throw the sandwich wrapper in the trash, then sit cross-legged on the bed and pull out my personal laptop.

I stare at it for a very long time. More than anything else, I want to log into our chat room and talk to Joao. But I cannot. *I must not.* I inadvertently disclosed something during our last conversation that led him straight to my door, and I cannot take the risk of repeating that mistake.

Right now, the smartest thing to do is to turn off the lights and make myself fall asleep. I've only had three hours of rest in the last thirty-six, and I'm running on fumes. Sleep deprivation was a routine part of our training, but I never got used to it. If I get less than five hours a night, my brain refuses to function.

I pull the thin blanket over myself and close my eyes.

My emotions have been put through the wringer in the last day and a half, and I'm exhausted. I should fall asleep almost immediately, but I can't make myself relax, and sleep remains elusive.

And when I'm this keyed up, there's one sure-fire remedy to calm me down.

Closing my eyes, I inch my hand lower until my fingertips brush my clit and slip into one of my favorite memories—the first time Joao and I made love.

We were both virgins. The mechanics of sex weren't a mystery to us; we knew what to do. But neither of us had gone further than a few experimental touches. Until. . .

> We're in an abandoned cabin on the far side of the two-hundred-acre compound. Henrik Bach is away; he goes away every summer and returns with a batch of scared five and six-year-old children, and I'm sure this time will be no exception. And when I think of how afraid they're going to be and what he's going to do to them, my stomach heaves and my heart clenches with sadness.
>
> But that's later. Right now, Bach isn't here, and Joao is on the bed next to me, his lean, muscled, *naked* body pressed up against mine. "Hello, little fox," he murmurs, his hands cupping my face and bringing me in for a kiss. "Fancy meeting you here."
>
> I wrap my leg over his hip and kiss him back passionately, acutely aware of his thick erection pressing against my thigh. We've done some above-the-waist stuff before, but this is the first time we've both been fully naked, and my heart is racing with anticipa-

tion. I stroke his length with my fingertips, and he grabs my ass and tugs me closer. "Harder," he rasps. "Stroke it harder." He wraps his hand around mine and coaxes it up and down, showing me how he likes it. "Yes, just like that."

His face is etched with desire, and a shiver rolls down my spine at his reaction. I kiss him again as I stroke him, and he finally pulls away with a groan. "No, not yet."

"Why not?" I prop myself up on an elbow and stare at him. "Was I doing it wrong?"

"No." He pushes me on my back. "It's because I want to do this." He cups my right breast with his hand and lowers his head to my nipple, gently sucking it between his lips. "And this." He strokes my aching pussy. "You feel incredible," he marvels, the tip of his finger slipping inside me. "Hot and tight." He strokes me again. "Tell me how you like it."

Another shiver runs through me. I move his finger until his thumb presses down on my clit. "Right there."

He moves down my body and spreads my legs. His finger finds the exact spot he touched a moment ago, and his tongue follows. Joao was always a fast learner. "Here?" he asks, his voice muffled.

A shudder goes through me at the memories of that day at the cabin. First, Joao made me come with his fingers. Then, with his tongue, and finally, he positioned himself between my legs and pushed deep.

My breathing quickens as I picture him next to me, staring down at me with his ocean-blue eyes.

We were teenagers the last time we slept together. Joao is a man now, big, broad, and powerfully muscled. If it comes to sheer physical strength, I'm no match for him. If he were here now, would he hold me down as he thrust into me? Or would he push me up against the window, cage me in with his body, lock my hands above my head, and take me hard?

Are you going to think about me when you masturbate tonight, Stef? When you come, will it be my name on your lips?

Yes, and yes again.

My fingers circle my clit, fast and hard, and my muscles tighten as my orgasm draws near. My cheeks are flushed, and my thighs tremble as I press down on that sensitive bundle of nerves and arch and cry out as the tidal wave crests and a shock of pleasure explodes through me.

I groan out loud and pummel the pillow next to me. Instead of plotting how to escape him, I'm spending my time fantasizing about my husband.

Damn it. Damn it all to hell.

16

JOAO

The next morning, I drink two cups of coffee, vacuum my already spotless house, and then do something I've been avoiding ever since I found out Stefi was alive. I make myself go talk to Tomas and Alina.

Tomas lives around the corner from me, so I head to his house and knock on the front door. He answers almost immediately. Given that my wife tried to abduct his fiancée, I fully expect him to slam the door in my face.

But when his eyes rest on my face, he opens the door wider. "You look like you need a cup of coffee."

"I've already had two, but why the hell not? Are you offering?"

"Of course," he replies. "Come on in." He leads the way to the kitchen and turns on the coffee maker. "Ali just went for a run. She should be right back."

"I'm back," a voice calls from the front door, and Tomas's fiancée, Alina, enters the kitchen, her face flushed. "It's surprisingly hot out there." She gives me a warm smile. "Hey, Joao. Good to see you."

I doubt it. After what happened, Alina has no reason to like me. "I met the padrino last week," I say bluntly, dispelling the greetings. "You already know what he told me."

"That the woman who drugged Ali is your wife," Tomas responds. He hands Ali a glass of water and pours me a cup of coffee. "I didn't even know you were married."

"How much do you know?"

"Very little," he says. "Just that your wife is an assassin. Are the two of you separated? Is that why I've never heard about her?"

Daniel mentioned that my marriage was the subject of much speculation, and I just assumed everyone already knew all the gory details. But Antonio doesn't gossip, and neither does Lucia. Daniel and Valentina only know about Stefi because they're providing operational support.

"No. We're not separated, and we're not divorced, either. I thought she was dead."

Ali nearly spits out her water. "What?"

Stefi drugged Ali and left her to be kidnapped by a pair of thugs. I've heard her end of the story and know she did it for the best of reasons, but still. If there's anyone who deserves an explanation, it's the two people in front of me.

"I don't really talk about my past," I reply. "But I was trained to be an assassin from when I was a child, and so was Stefi. We used to watch out for each other. She was my only friend. We got married when we turned eighteen. Ten days after her nineteenth birthday, she died in a house fire in Mexico. Or so I thought."

Of course, that's not enough of an explanation. Ali and Tomas have dozens of questions, and I answer them as best as I can. I tell them about the fire in Puerto Vallarta, the search for her body, and my refusal to accept that she was gone.

"But you were *married*," Tomas says when I'm done. "You loved her, and she still let you think she was dead?" He shakes his head in disbelief. "Wow. That's brutal."

If I see the expression of sympathy on his face, I'm going to lose it, so I turn to Ali instead. "I'm sorry about Stefi," I say tersely. "I'll take care of it."

"How? Are you going to look for her?"

"Yes, the padrino asked me to. The search is already underway." I leave out the part where I've already found her twice, and both times, she's managed to slip away.

"Do you know why she targeted me?" Ali asks quietly.

"Yes. She was in a bind." I explain about Charlotte Bellegarde and her rapist stepfather, and Alina's expression turns horrified.

"That's terrible," she exclaims. "The poor girl."

"That doesn't justify what she did," Tomas points out.

"I'm not saying it does," I say tersely. That's a lie: I *am* trying to make Tomas and Ali realize that Stefi had no other options. As stupid as it sounds, I want my friends to *like* my wife. "I'm just telling you what I know."

"But what you're saying is that if your wife truly wanted to abduct me, she'd have succeeded." Alina chews on her lower lip. "She deliberately adjusted the dosage so I'd wake up early. She *chose* to leave me with my phone. Right?"

"Yes. And she asked me to apologize to you. She's really sorry. She never meant to get you involved."

Tomas's face is a thunder cloud. "You know what this sounds like?" he demands. "Like one bullshit excuse after another. For fuck's sake, Joao. Your wife made a choice to come after Alina. If you want to pretend that she's blameless, you do that. Delude yourself if that's what will help you sleep at night. But don't expect me to go along with it." He gets to his feet. "Are you done with your coffee? I think you should go."

Alina takes in Tomas's expression and turns to me. "Thanks for coming by, Joao," she says with a sympathetic smile.

"No worries." I drain my mug in silence and get to my feet.

Tomas and I have been friends for five years, but he won't meet my eyes as I take my leave.

Yeah. That went *great*.

I SENT the padrino a message outlining my progress the moment I touched down in Venice. A couple of hours after my disastrous conversation with Tomas and Ali, I get a message telling me to drop by his house at two.

Goran is on guard duty when I walk up. "Hey, Joao," he says. "How's it going?"

"It's been better. You?"

"Can't complain." He inclines his head toward the house. "You here to see the padrino?" I nod and he adds, "Door's open. Go on in."

Antonio is in the kitchen, stirring something on the stove. "Enzo and Tatiana are coming over for dinner," he says. "And Agnese is away. Give me a minute, will you? Grab a drink if you need."

I get myself a glass of water. "How's Signora Moretti doing?"

"She's good. She and Valentina went shoe shopping or something. Speaking of Valentina, it's been two days, and she still hasn't been able to identify the guys you killed."

"That's odd." Valentina usually has all the answers. "Was she able to get a hold of their fingerprints?"

"Yeah, she hacked into the Swiss police database. Only problem: the prints don't match anything on file." He turns off the stove and wipes his hands dry. "I need to call Andrei. You killed six people who might or might not work for him. There's an etiquette to these things, and I don't want to make Sidorov my enemy."

He leads the way to his office, waves me into a seat, and video calls the Bratva pakhan. Sidorov answers almost immediately. "Antonio," he says. "What can I do for you?"

The padrino doesn't beat around the bush. "We might have a problem," he says. "A couple of days ago, one of my people was on an assignment in Zurich when he was surprised by some of your guys, and he was forced to kill them."

Sidorov frowns. "Zurich? No, we're not doing anything in Switzerland."

I sit up.

"Are you sure?" Antonio asks. "Could this be something Natalya is working on?"

Natalya is Sidorov's sister and the Bratva's second-in-command.

"She's not working on anything. After Vassili's death. . ." Sidorov's voice trails off, and a look of sadness flashes across his face before he wipes it away. "Yes, I'm absolutely sure." He leans forward. "What's going on, Antonio? What was I supposed to be doing in Zurich?"

"Sending a team to take out the assassin who killed your father-in-law."

"But that was years ago." He looks confused. "Besides, Aldo was a prick whose actions repeatedly put my wife in danger. Why would I go after the person responsible? If I knew who they were, I'd send them a fucking Christmas present."

I don't understand. If it's not Sidorov, then who sent the strike team I took out? Who else wants Stefi dead?

Antonio and I exchange a look, and then he asks, "It wasn't your people who compiled a file on Stefania Freitas?"

"Who?" he asks, his expression blank.

He has no idea what we're talking about.

Antonio frowns. "Cici sent me a file on the assassin who supposedly killed Aldo, and I assumed she got it from you. Stefania Freitas is married to one of my people, so I figured she wanted me to take care of my own dirty laundry, so to speak. But if you're not involved—"

"I'm not." His expression turns intrigued. "You haven't been able to identify the dead team?"

"No, Valentina is stumped."

"Send it to me," Sidorov suggests. "I have access to databases that even she can't reach."

"Will do. Any theories of why Cici sent me that file?"

"No," the Sidorov pahkan replies. He seems to gather his thoughts before he speaks again. "Cici is my wife's cousin. She's family. I would trust her with my life, and I believe she would do the same. However, you know the way she grew up as well as I do. There's a very small handful of people that Cici truly confides in, and neither Mira nor I are on that list. If she hasn't already told you why she sent you that file, she's not going to. I'm assuming you've already tried asking her directly and she's refused to answer?"

"Pretty much," the padrino replies tightly. "We're just going to have to proceed in the dark. See you at the next poker game?"

"Sure." Andrei Sidorov grins like a wolf. "I look forward to taking your money."

The screen goes dead. The padrino pushes his monitor out of the way and stares at me. "That call was extremely informative," he says. "I could have sworn that Andrei was after Stefania, and that's why Cici sent me her file, but clearly, I had it wrong." He leans forward, his expression frustrated. "This doesn't make any sense to me, Joao. Why is Cecelia d'Este interested in your wife?"

I'm just as confused. "Could Stefi have killed someone connected to her?"

"Maybe. But Cici is more than capable of taking a lone assassin out without my involvement."

I don't care why; I just want to know who wants Stefi dead. "If Sidorov's not after Stefi, then it means someone else is." Someone whose motives are unclear and whose movements I can't predict. It's my worst nightmare come true. "Venice is still the safest place for her to be."

"It is," he agrees. "And my offer of protection still stands."

"Thank you." I hesitate before my next words. "Stefi freaked out when she found out I work for you. You haven't met her before, have you?"

He shakes his head immediately. "No. If we'd been introduced, I'd remember. I don't forget faces."

Hmm. "Is there any other reason she'd react that way?"

"None that I know."

The padrino is excellent at keeping control of his emotions, but I can usually tell when he's lying. This time, though? I can't get a clear read from Antonio at all.

17

STEFI

The next morning, I turn on my VPN, open an anti-tracking browser, and send Charlie an email telling her I'm fine and will reach out when I'm able to. I want to call her, but it's not safe. Her reply comes almost instantaneously, a paragraph of stream of consciousness liberally punctuated with exclamation marks.

> I'm so glad you're okay!!!! Your husband said you wouldn't be able to contact me, and he gave me some money just in case. Two thousand euros, can you believe it? After you left, I opened your laptop and tried to pretend I was you, but I didn't know how to answer any of the customer support questions, so Lynda fired me. Well, you. Well, me. Anyway, sorry about that. Joao is sooo hot, btw. He wanted me to pass on a message to you. He said, *"she's the only woman in my life who's ever mattered."* Sooo romantic!!! Not gonna lie: I totally swooned. You should call him. Anyway, he also said

that you're going to get yourself killed if you keep running from him, which, you know, would really, really suck, so please don't die.

She's the only woman in my life who's ever mattered.

I stare at those words on my screen for a very long time. I desperately want to believe them, but even if they are true, I don't deserve Joao's love. Not after what I did to him in Mexico, and especially not after what happened in Istanbul.

Even if he means them, when Joao finds out why I ran, it'll change *everything.*

I don't stay in Paris. The next day, I take the train to Lyon. The day after that, I leave France entirely and head to Barcelona.

It's been a few months since I was on the run, and I haven't missed it. The feeling of constantly looking over your shoulder, your senses on high alert. . . I haven't felt this hunted in *years.*

And I constantly fight the urge to reach out to Joao.

I should stay away from the chat room—nothing good will come from my dangerous obsession. The more time I spend with Joao, the more I'm going to want to be with him. And that's *impossible.* Even if Joao could bring himself to forgive me for disappearing eight years ago, it doesn't change the present.

But it only takes three days on the road for my willpower to evaporate. Seventy-two hours of craving Joao, craving the sound of his laughter, the caress in his voice when he calls me 'little fox' before I give in and log into the chat room.

His message comes almost immediately.

JOAO
Call me, little fox.

What number?

Same one as before.

What the hell? I dial it immediately, and as soon as he picks up his phone, I demand, "You gave me your real number? Is that safe?"

He chuckles. "Hello to you too, little fox. Why wouldn't it be safe? Are you planning on killing me?"

His voice is as smooth as a really good whiskey and just as potent. It messes with my senses and makes my head swim. He's always had this effect on me, and the years apart only seem to have made it stronger.

"You're being careless," I accuse.

"And you're worried about me."

"Don't flatter yourself," I scoff. "Why did you give me your real number?"

"I want you to be able to reach me. Day or night, whenever you need me."

I clench my eyes shut. His words unwittingly rub at an old wound. I've always been able to reach Joao when I needed him. *Until that fateful day...*

Joao was on a job, and so was I. We weren't supposed to be in contact at all, but I was freaking out and needed to talk to him. I tried to call him, but his phone was turned off. I logged into the chat room, but he didn't show up there either.

I waited as long as I could, but I couldn't get a hold of him. In the end, I just ran out of time.

Joao's waiting for me to respond, and I'm trying to choke back my swell of emotions. "Oh," I manage. "Thank you." I need to change the topic before he realizes how upset I am. "What name do you go by nowadays?"

"Still Joao," he replies. "Different last name though. It's Carvalho now."

I navigate to a different window and do a search on him. "You kept your first name? Was that a good idea?"

"I thought about changing it," he says. "But I didn't see the point. Joao's a common enough name in Europe. Besides, you kept yours, too."

"I did." I already had to give up Joao—I couldn't bear to give up the name he whispered in my ear as well. "Joao's not a common name in Venice, though."

And I shouldn't have done a search on him. Picture after picture of Joao appears in the results, always laughing, never alone. Joao in a suit, flanked by two beautiful women. Joao at a gala on the dance floor, his arm wrapped possessively around his partner. Joao working out at the gym, Joao playing pool, his eyes focused.

What did you expect him to do, Stefi? Did you expect him to mourn you forever? Did you expect him to stay celibate for eight years?

A seething ball of jealousy roils in my stomach. I do my best to push it down. Women have always flocked to Joao, attracted by his laughing eyes and his devil-may-care attitude. Why would it be any different now?

"True." His voice turns amused. "You sound

distracted. Let me guess. I told you my last name, and now you're searching for me on the Internet."

I jump like a startled cat and immediately shut the browser window, my cheeks hot with embarrassment. "I'm doing no such thing."

"No? I'm not ashamed to admit I looked you up. Interesting persona you've adopted. Cat memes, photos of every meal you've eaten, but never any of you. It's a perfect cover. Nobody would give Stefania Freitas a second glance."

"Maybe I'm just boring nowadays," I say before I can help myself. I feel dull compared to Joao. Call it a self-pity spiral, but Joao is surrounded by people, and I'm watching TV alone, holed up in a nondescript hotel. He's embracing life while I'm hiding away from it.

"You? Never in a million years. What did O'Shea say when you told him Zurich was a trap?"

"I didn't—" I start to say before I clamp my mouth shut. He just slid that question in there, and I almost answered. Joao hides a razor-sharp intellect under his golden retriever exterior. Add in how well he knows me. . . If I'm not careful, he'll find me again within a week. "Damn it, that almost worked. How did you find me in Paris, by the way? I've been wracking my brains, and I can't figure it out."

"What will you give me if I tell you?" he teases. "Will you tell me where you really are? My phone says Lisbon, but I don't believe it."

"Why not? We went there once, remember?" The moment those words leave my mouth, I regret it. What's the point of reminiscing about the past? Even if I could go back in time, I wouldn't change anything. I had to do what I did to protect—

"Mmm," he says. "And you stole my custard tart. Don't think I've forgotten about that."

I laugh as I remember the incident. Joao had gone inside to get me a second cup of coffee and made the mistake of leaving his pastel de nata unattended. I scarfed it down and tried to pretend a seagull stole it, but one look at the outrage on Joao's face, and I couldn't keep a straight face. I started giggling so hard that everyone around us stopped to stare. We'd ended up eating a dozen of them huddled together on the beach, while the ocean threw fine saltwater spray all over us.

"I forgot about that," I admit. "I haven't eaten one in *years*. Can you get them in Venice?"

"I don't know," he replies. "I've never looked. It wouldn't have felt right to eat one without you."

He doesn't want to eat a pastel de nata without me. My heart clenches painfully, and Joao abruptly changes the subject. "You told me about Charlie and let slip that her stepfather was one of the Cosa Nostra. That was enough to figure out her real name. Then I looked at her mother's phone logs, and—"

"She called her mother. Of course she did, damn it."

It was stupid of me not to realize it was a possibility, but I grew up without family. I never had anyone to lean on, so I don't know how it feels. Severine Bellegarde is a terrible parent, but she's the only one Charlie has. I should have predicted she'd call her mother.

And unlike me, Charlie doesn't keep switching

burner phones. The moment Joao found her number, he had her location and, by extension, mine.

Joao's chuckle is warm and sexy against my ear. "Teenagers aren't exactly models of restraint," he says. "Remember us? We couldn't keep our hands off each other. It's a miracle Henrik never found out."

"He would have killed us if he did." Joao was one of Bach's favorite trainees. Even after he killed Michaela in front of us, I don't think Joao truly ever saw how dangerous he really was.

"He would have," he agrees soberly, taking me by surprise. "It took me a while to see who he really was. I was an idiot in those days, a stupid, cocky kid who believed I was indestructible. And Henrik knew how to mold us into his perfect little tools. He made us believe that we were doing what needed to be done, what most of the world was too soft to do." His voice turns reflective. "I bought his spiel, hook, line, and sinker. You never did."

"You're being hard on yourself," I say softly. "You knew Bach was a psychopath; we all did. We didn't have a choice in what we did. If we didn't obey, we died."

"And now he's dead from a car accident," he says grimly. "Daniel sent me the coroner's report. Looks like the bastard died instantly. I don't believe in the concept of heaven and hell, but I'll make an exception for Bach. If there's any justice to be had, he's burning in the hottest of hellfires."

"I'll drink to that."

We both fall silent. Truth is, with everything that's happened in the last week, it hasn't really sunk in that Henrik Bach is dead. Every year, I make a trip back to

Istanbul to Christopher's grave and celebrate the people I've killed that year with a toast. This year, when I drink, it'll be an extra-large pour. I might not have succeeded in killing Bach, but he's dead, and that's all that counts.

Joao's voice jerks me away from my grim thoughts. "You got away from him," he says. "You're the first one who succeeded. It couldn't have been easy."

I think back to the early days of constantly looking over my shoulder, moving hotels every night, and never staying in the same city for longer than a week. "It wasn't." Part of me thinks I should hang up—every word I say to Joao could be a clue that helps him find me—and another, hopeful, yearning part cannot bear the thought of ending this conversation.

"How did you do it? I can guess some of it already. You obviously robbed a morgue for the body that was found in the fire, and you put your wedding ring on her finger."

I was forced to part with my ring, and I feel its absence every single day. "No, I didn't," I interrupt. "I wouldn't rob a morgue—that's really creepy. No, the cartel sent an assassin to greet me. She almost succeeded in taking me out." I'd been distracted by my positive pregnancy test and wasn't really paying attention to my surroundings, and she nearly managed to kill me. "Luckily for me, she was the same height and build as me."

"An assassin?" Joao's voice sharpens. "Henrik said it would be an easy in-and-out."

I laugh bitterly. "He lied. Veronica got chatty before she died. Called me a bitch, told me there were more

The Hunter

cartel soldiers on the way, and advised me to make my peace with God because I was going to die."

And the moment she said that, I knew I had run out of choices. If I stayed, the cartel assassins would kill me. To survive, I had to get the hell out of there.

But we were expected to do whatever it took to take our targets out, even if it meant we died in the attempt. If I returned to the compound without killing Peng Wu, there would be consequences. Severe ones. Bach was perfectly capable of killing me for my failure.

And for the first time in my life, I knew I had to live. I was pregnant with our baby, and the only way for that child to survive was if I quit being an assassin.

I had to disappear, and I had to disappear immediately. Before the cartel assassins showed up, and before Henrik Bach found out I didn't kill Peng Wu.

And the worst thing was that I couldn't tell Joao. I couldn't leave him a message in our chat room because if it got intercepted, I'd be putting our unborn child at risk. And if it didn't get intercepted and Joao came to find me, I knew Bach wouldn't rest until he hunted us down. My disappearance he might be able to ignore, but Joao was the most talented assassin he'd ever had. Bach would stop at nothing to find him.

"Stefi?"

"Yeah." I swallow the lump in my throat. "I'm still here." I take a deep, shaky breath. What were we talking about? Oh, right. How I managed to get away. "Peng Wu brought twenty high-quality diamonds to the cartels as proof of good faith. They were worth three, maybe four million euros. I knew I needed money to stay hidden from Bach, so I stole the gems from his safe."

"How did you find a fence?"

"I got lucky and found a crooked cartel soldier who was willing to take the risk of fencing them in exchange for most of the profits. I ended up with a million." A million euros seems like a lot of money, but it goes quick if you're always on the run. Fake passports, the kind that withstand electronic scrutiny, are expensive. "I made my way to Nicaragua and got on a cargo ship headed to Morocco. From there, Tunisia, then Athens and finally, Istan—" I catch myself.

Once again, I'm revealing too much. But it's always been so easy to talk to Joao. All my life, I've always told him my hopes and dreams and fears, and even though everything is different now, my subconscious is ready to fall back into that old, familiar groove.

"You make an impossible journey sound easy," he says quietly. "But you still haven't told me why, Stef. Why did you leave? Were you hurt? Did you get spooked? Why didn't you call me, little fox? I wasn't anywhere close to Mexico, but I could have helped."

"I did," I say, the words wrenched out of my aching heart. "I tried to call, but I couldn't get a hold of you."

No, no, what am I doing?

Joao cannot find out the truth. He just cannot.

I cannot do that to him.

I cannot buy my own absolution at the cost of his happiness.

If he finds out about our baby, it will wreck him. Not

just emotionally. I know my husband, and he won't rest until he finds and kills the people responsible.

No matter how dangerous it is.

I cannot risk his life. I won't drag him on my path. Eight years ago, I made the choice to put Joao's safety ahead of our happiness, and I'd do it all over again if I had to.

This is my burden and mine alone.

"I have to go," I say abruptly. Then I hang up.

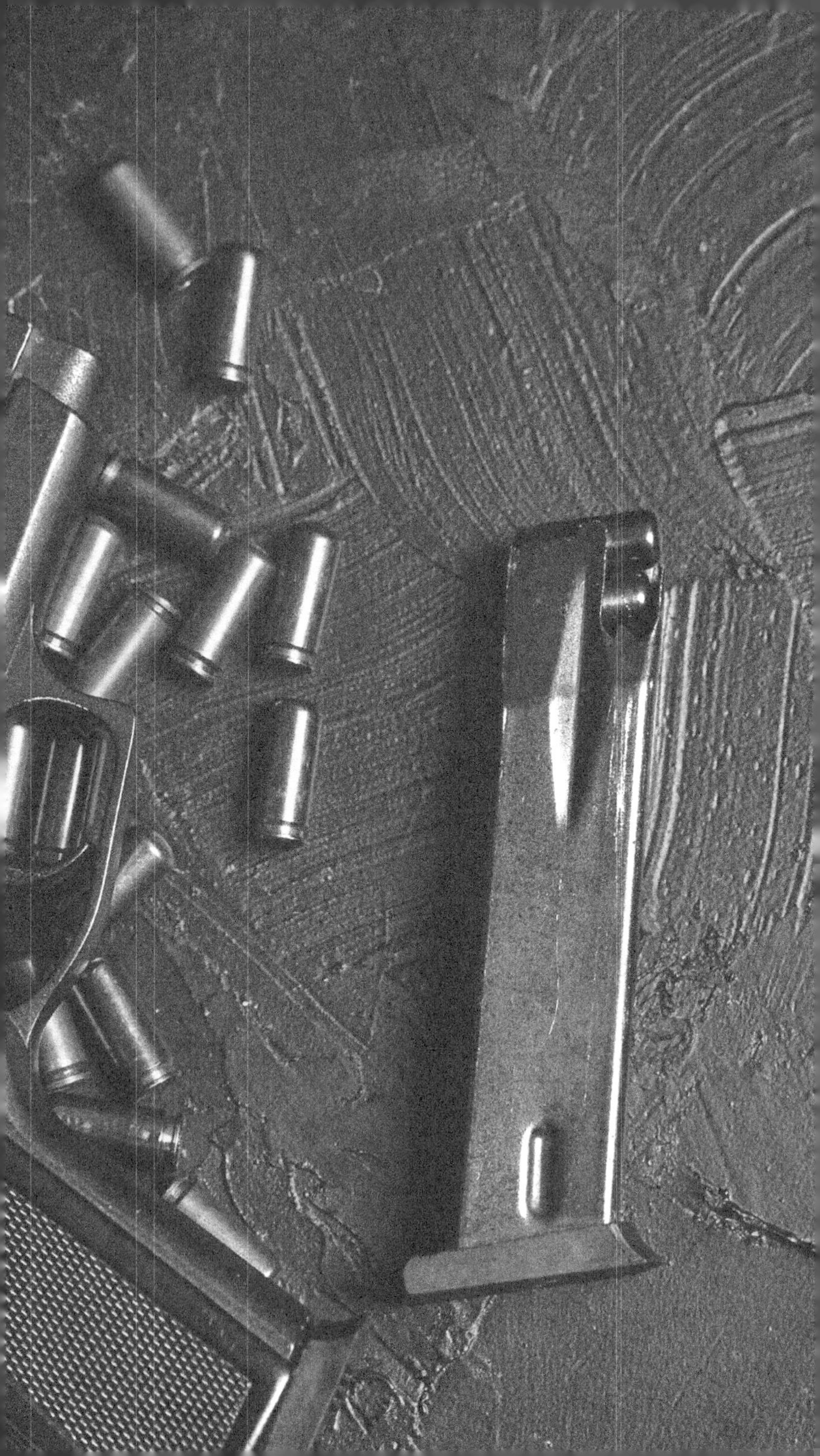

18

JOAO

Once again, I was so distracted by Stefi that I forgot to tell her that it wasn't Sidorov's men I killed in Zurich. And she hung up so abruptly that I didn't get a chance to warn her to be careful.

I go into the chat room, hoping to find her there, but she doesn't show up. I have to tell her, so I leave her a message outlining Antonio's conversation with the Bratva boss.

> It's not Andrei Sidorov who is hunting you —it's someone else. Valentina, our hacker, hasn't been able to identify the team waiting for you in Zurich.

> Which suggests that whoever hired them is extremely powerful.

> Please be careful, little fox. Be cautious and paranoid, and double and triple-check any intel coming your way

> Because it could be another trap.

I can't sit still, my nerves are on edge. Stefi's in danger and I need to find her urgently, before the person who's after her succeeds in taking her out.

If only I knew what she was doing.

Cecelia d'Este's file is the key to unlocking her motive; I'm sure of it. And although I've poured over the file until my eyes glazed over, I still haven't figured it out.

I'm staring at my screen in frustration when Daniel knocks on my door. "I just got back into town," he says. "It's been one hell of a week, and I need a drink. Let's go."

"It's Tuesday."

"Like I said, one hell of a week. Coming?"

"Sure, why not? It's not like I'm getting anywhere staring at this fucking file. Detailed analytical work isn't exactly my strong suit."

"Why don't you ask Valentina for help?"

I make a face. Daniel interprets my expression correctly. "Let me guess; I'm not the only person who warned you to stay away from your ex-wife?"

"The only people who haven't weighed in are Leo and Rosa, who are on their honeymoon, and Dante, who is busy dealing with the fallout from the Spina Sacra affair."

"Show me what you've got."

I step aside so he can enter my house. "I thought you wanted a drink."

"You have beer in your refrigerator, don't you? That'll work. Let's see this file that has you stumped."

"Thanks, Daniel." The mafia lawyer has a mind like a steel trap. The data just looks like noise to me, but if there's a pattern, Daniel will find it. I grab a couple of bottles of beer and lead the way to my study. "Not to look a gift horse in the mouth, but why are you helping me? Aren't you in the 'She's bad for you' camp?"

"I'm reserving judgment until I meet her," he replies. "Besides, my opinion doesn't matter. You're going to do whatever you're going to do, irrespective of what I or anyone else thinks. And you're determined to chase this woman."

He settles himself on the couch in my office and cracks open his beer. Mimi saunters into the room and rubs herself against Daniel's legs, and he picks her up and puts her next to him. "How are you doing, by the way?"

"I've been better."

"No shit," he says. "On the one hand, your ex-wife is still alive, and on the other, Henrik Bach is dead. It's a lot to deal with all at once."

This is the second time he's called Stefi my ex-wife, and I fight the urge to punch him. "I thought you didn't like talking about feelings."

"Unfortunately, my therapist encourages me to do it, so I figure I'll practice on you." He lifts his beer to me. "Let's drink to the death of that asshole."

Stefi should be here. I should be toasting Henrik's death with her, not with Daniel. We went through the wringer together and should be celebrating the end the same way. But to do that, I'd need to know where she is, and it's not like she's going to tell me.

"Burn in hell, you bastard," I say, clinking my bottle against Daniel's.

Bach made me kill my first man when I was thirteen. I didn't want to do it. For a week, I resisted, but I wasn't the first child he broke, and I hadn't been the last. He didn't hurt me—that would have been too easy. He tossed me into the pit and didn't let me sleep for five days. By the time he pulled me out, I was cold, starved, and almost delirious. I would have done anything to end the torture.

Stefi held me afterward. I couldn't talk about it, and she didn't make me. We just clung to each other, and it was enough.

Daniel gives me a searching look. "You barely talk about Bach, but I have some idea what you went through. I have to ask: why didn't you ever try to kill him? After what he did to you, nobody would have blamed you for taking him out."

"I'm not saying the idea didn't occur to me." I gulp down the ice-cold beer. "And I would have if the opportunity presented itself. But I never went looking for him."

"Why not?"

"What's the point?" I ask bitterly. "If I killed him, someone else would take his place. Pavel Dachev has been not-so-patiently waiting in the wings, ready to pick up the reins. The supply of children is never going to dry up, Daniel. Like most of Bach's trainees, I assume I was abducted from a refugee camp. My parents probably spent years looking for me, but nobody else would have cared. Nobody gives a shit about refugees. There are too many wars and too many displaced people. That's how Bach got away with it, over and over again."

I drain the rest of my beer. "In any case, he was already doing a pretty good job fucking up his empire on his own. He made one bad decision after another the last few years. He was going to fail—it was just a matter of time."

Daniel is giving me a peculiar look. "I didn't realize you kept track of his dealings."

"Let's talk about something else."

"Did you find out why your ex-wife tried to kidnap Alina?"

"She's my *wife*," I bite out through gritted teeth. "Stop calling her my ex. We never got divorced. As far as I'm concerned, we're still married."

Daniel stares at me for a long time. "That's how it is?"

"Yes," I say flatly. "That's exactly how it is."

He whistles through his teeth. "The next few months are going to be *interesting*." He shakes his head. "So, did she tell you why she targeted Alina?"

"Yes." I tell him what Stefi told me. "Her story checks out," I finish. "Charlie is real, the stepfather is real, and she really killed him. She didn't take the job for money—she was doing it to save the teenager."

"And now you're wondering if she also had a good reason for faking her own death."

"Am I that obvious?"

"Yes," he replies, not trying to sugarcoat it. "Was she the first one to try to run?"

I shake my head. "No." I try not to think about the others. Eren, Jonathan, Dalia, and Michaela. "Bach always sent bounty hunters after the runaways. Zaworski and Pavel Dachev—he was Henrik's other bounty hunter—were well paid to find anyone who got away, but it wasn't just the money. Both men got a sick pleasure from hunting us down. And when they were brought back to the compound, Bach would kill them."

And he'd make us watch.

"If Stefania told you she wanted to get out, what would you have done?"

"Left with her," I reply promptly. Stefi was the one bright, shining star in my life. I would have followed her to the end of the Earth.

"It's harder for two people to stay hidden than one, isn't it?"

"Am I being cross-examined, Daniel?"

"Are you avoiding answering my question, Joao?"

Touché. "Yes, it is."

"Maybe that's your answer. Maybe she was trying to keep you safe."

I exhale in frustration. "Yes, but why? Why run at all and so suddenly? Escaping wasn't on her radar—I know it wasn't. She was still shaken up from what happened to her friend Michaela."

"What happened to her friend?"

"Bach killed her. Stefi had to. . ." Michaela had begged for her life, but Bach wasn't the merciful sort. He ordered us to gather in a circle, and he blew her brains out. Stefi had been close enough that her friend's blood landed on her face. "The details don't matter. What matters is that I'm sure she wasn't planning to make a break for it."

"Okay. Then it stands to reason that something happened to change her mind."

I'd come to the same conclusion. "I don't know what it is, though." Only Stefi does, and she refuses to talk about

The Hunter

it. So far, she's shut down every attempt I've made to bring it up.

"I went to see Ali and Tomas," I confess.

"And?"

"Tomas is furious. He thinks I'm making excuses for Stefi."

Daniel looks unperturbed. "Give him time," he advises. "Under his stoic facade, Tomas feels very deeply. Alina is the love of his life, and the kidnapping attempt freaked him out. He needs to believe she's safe again. Until that happens, he's not going to react well to anything you're going to say."

He gets up to get another beer. "Okay," he says. "Let's tackle this file. Give me your laptop?"

"Sure." I hand it to him. "Here's the problem I'm wrestling with. There are seventy-three folders here, one for each of Stefi's supposed victims. However, she told me that the real number was thirty-five. I'm trying to narrow it down to the people she actually killed, but I'm getting nowhere."

Daniel pulls a notepad from my desk. "Let's start with what we know. We know who she was targeting in Zurich."

"Varek Zaworski," I growl. "He's the one who hunted down Michaela and brought her back to Bach's compound."

He writes the name down on his pad. "Then there's the guy she killed in Paris. Not the rapist stepfather, the guy she found in bed with the child. Do you know his name?"

I'd forgotten about him. I replay our conversation in

my head. "No, but she said she broke into his apartment to take him out. Hang on, that's not all. She gave me a timeframe. She said she killed her target three months ago." Charlotte Bellegarde is French, and she's a minor. Unless Stefi got her a new passport, she wouldn't have been able to take her out of the country without alerting the authorities. Which means. . . "The guy she killed is in France."

"Let's find him."

It takes us half an hour to get a name. "René Vannier," I say aloud. "His name isn't even in Stefi's file, damn it."

"Maybe because the murder was too recent." Daniel has a frown on his face. "Why do I know his name?" He stares into space, then snaps his fingers. "That's it. It was in a file Valentina put together on Henrik Bach."

"Why does Valentina have a file on Henrik Bach?"

"Because of you, Joao," he replies, not looking at me. "Obviously."

Something doesn't ring true about his explanation. Before I can call him on it, he continues, "Vannier was a retired prosecutor. A year ago, his department was going to bring up charges against Bach, but then he abruptly decided not to prosecute."

"Henrik paid him off to look the other way." I wish I were surprised.

"Money talks." He writes Vannier's name down on his notepad. "You know what this is looking like, don't you?"

"Yes."

A dark foreboding fills me. Stefi's targeting Henrik Bach's network. One by one, she's taking out the people who worked for him and the people who shielded him from consequences. She's killing everyone who stood by and watched as Henrik Bach took defenseless children and molded them into killers.

No matter how rich, powerful, and well-connected they are.

My heart starts to race.

This is a suicide mission.

And she used to call me reckless.

Stefi is on a dangerous, *dangerous* path. Now more than ever, I need to find her before she gets herself killed.

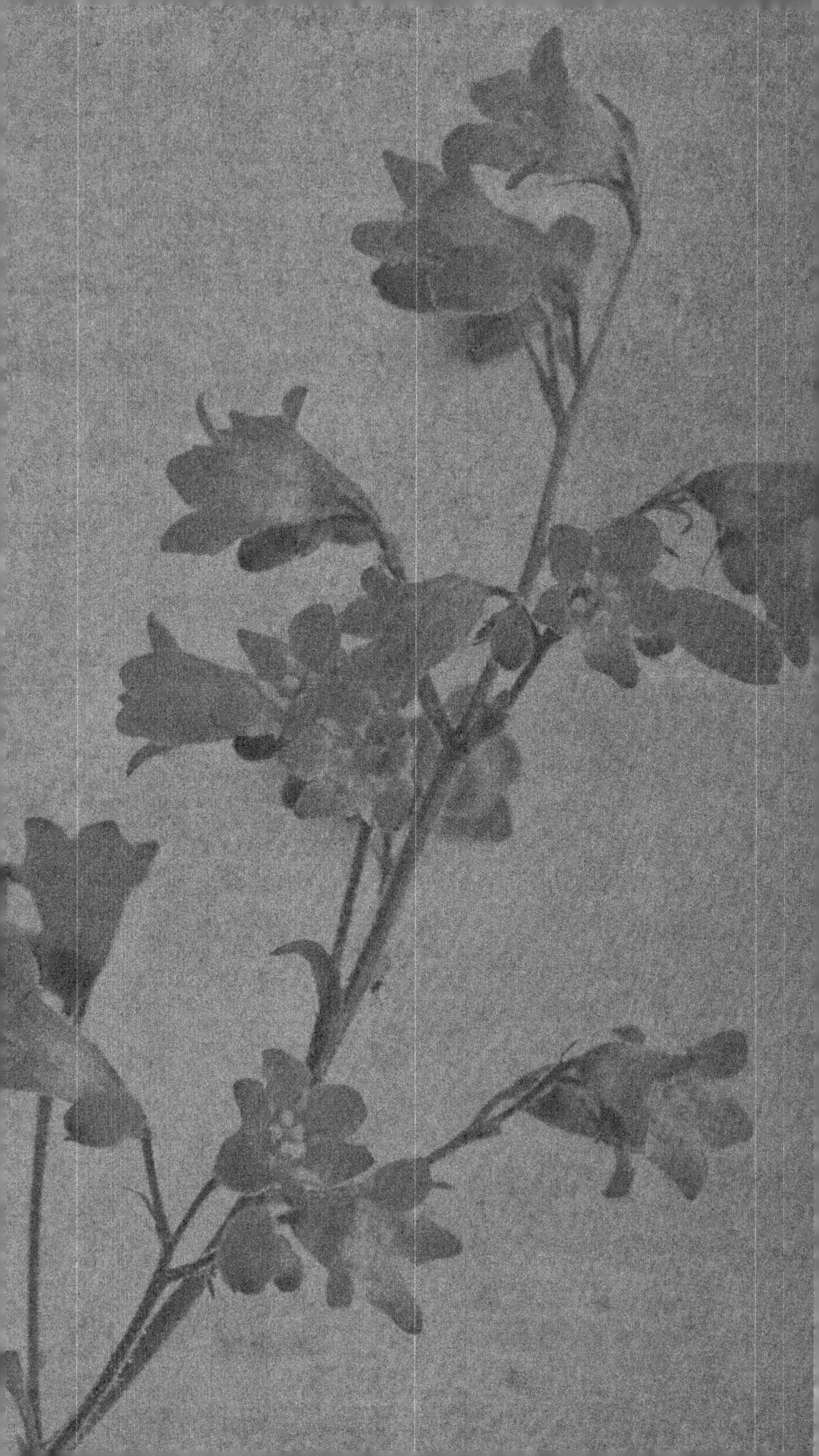

19

STEFI

I never wanted to be an assassin.

In the early days after I faked my own death and fled, I kept my head down. I moved from town to town, traveling on fake passports that Ramon, the crooked cartel soldier, helped me get.

From Mexico, I took a harrowing overland trip to Nicaragua, armed only with the knife Joao gave me as a wedding present. I talked my way on a boat heading to Northern Africa, then bounced between the countries lining the Mediterranean Sea.

In the middle of my second trimester, I ended up in Istanbul. Turkey was the perfect place to stay hidden. Henrik Bach had pissed off enough people there that if he set foot in the country, his life would be forfeit. My Turkish was fluent, and I was able to blend right in.

I wanted a quiet, peaceful life for my child, the kind I never had a chance to have. I got a job at a restaurant and rented a room near the Galata Bridge from the owner's mother.

I worked there for three months. Three months looking over my shoulder, wondering if staying in one place for too long was risky and fretting about whether Bach was going to find me. I was heartsick about losing Joao, and my hormones were all over the place. I held it together at work, but then I'd get home and weep for hours on end. The only thing that offered a glimmer of hope was the child growing inside me.

Our child—Joao's and mine.

But then Pavel Dachev found me...

I shake the memories loose before they can tug me under.

It's been a week since I last talked to Joao. I've ended up in Hamburg, in a small aparthotel on the outskirts of the city. I want to reach out, of course I do, but so far, I've resisted the clawing urge to call him. I have to stay away. I came too close to telling him everything the last time we talked, and I don't trust myself not to blurt out the truth.

My laptop beeps. I click on the notification to find a message from Q waiting for me.

> Q
>
> Are you still looking for Varek Zaworski?

When I first started hunting the people in Bach's network, I quickly hit a block. The support I'd taken for granted—fake identities, passports that would withstand scrutiny, access to weapons, intel on my target—all fell away.

The hardest part was the intel. It's not like there's a convenient database of men and women I need to kill.

The Hunter

My targets took great pains to conceal their involvement in Bach's horrifying little scheme.

I started hanging out in the dark and unsavory corners of the Internet, and over the years, I found a couple of informants who gave me what I needed.

Q is one of them. I know nothing about them. I don't know their gender, where they live, or who they work for. As best as I can guess, they're either one of Henrik Bach's disgruntled former employees or, like me, they're an assassin who managed to escape his clutches.

Joao's warning rings in my mind. *Be cautious and paranoid, and double and triple-check any intel coming your way because it could be another trap.*

It's a little unusual that Zaworski's name has come up again so quickly after Zurich. A coincidence that should cause me to pause. But Q has proven themselves many times over as a reliable source of information, and my usual caution evaporates in the face of an opportunity to get at the former bounty hunter.

> Yes.

> He's celebrating his fiftieth birthday party at a club in Warsaw.

My heart starts to race. I know Zaworski rarely leaves his village—it's one of the reasons I hurried to Zurich without double-checking Marcus O'Shea's information.

But O'Shea's intel led me to a trap. What if Q does the same?

I hesitate over the keyboard, conflicted. Yes, it's suspicious that Q's reaching out with a tip about Varek

Zaworski, but at the same time, I've been able to eliminate dozens of targets because of their tips. I have no reason not to trust them.

Besides, trap or not, a real chance to take out the bounty hunter doesn't come along every day.

I reach a decision.

> Tell me more.

Q sends me the details. This weekend, Varek Zaworski will be traveling from his village in the south of Poland all the way to the capital to celebrate his fiftieth birthday. It looks like it's going to be one hell of a bash. Zaworski has rented out Warsaw's fanciest nightclub, and the guest list has over two hundred and fifty carefully vetted people on it, flying in from all over the world.

I have four days. It's not enough time to prepare, not nearly enough.

> This weekend? You couldn't let me know more in advance?

> I have other priorities. You're not my only client.

I can't let this opportunity slip through my fingers. I just cannot. I owe it to Michaela. Her death has haunted me for years. I feel her warm blood splatter across my face in my nightmares and hear the crunch of Zaworski's boot as he pushes her lifeless body over the cliff.

> I need the guest list.

The Hunter

> It'll cost you. Fifty. Okay?

Fifty thousand dollars. What the hell. That's much higher than Q's usual prices. It's a lot of money, more than I want to pay, but if it gets me a way in, it's worth it.

> Yes. We have a deal.

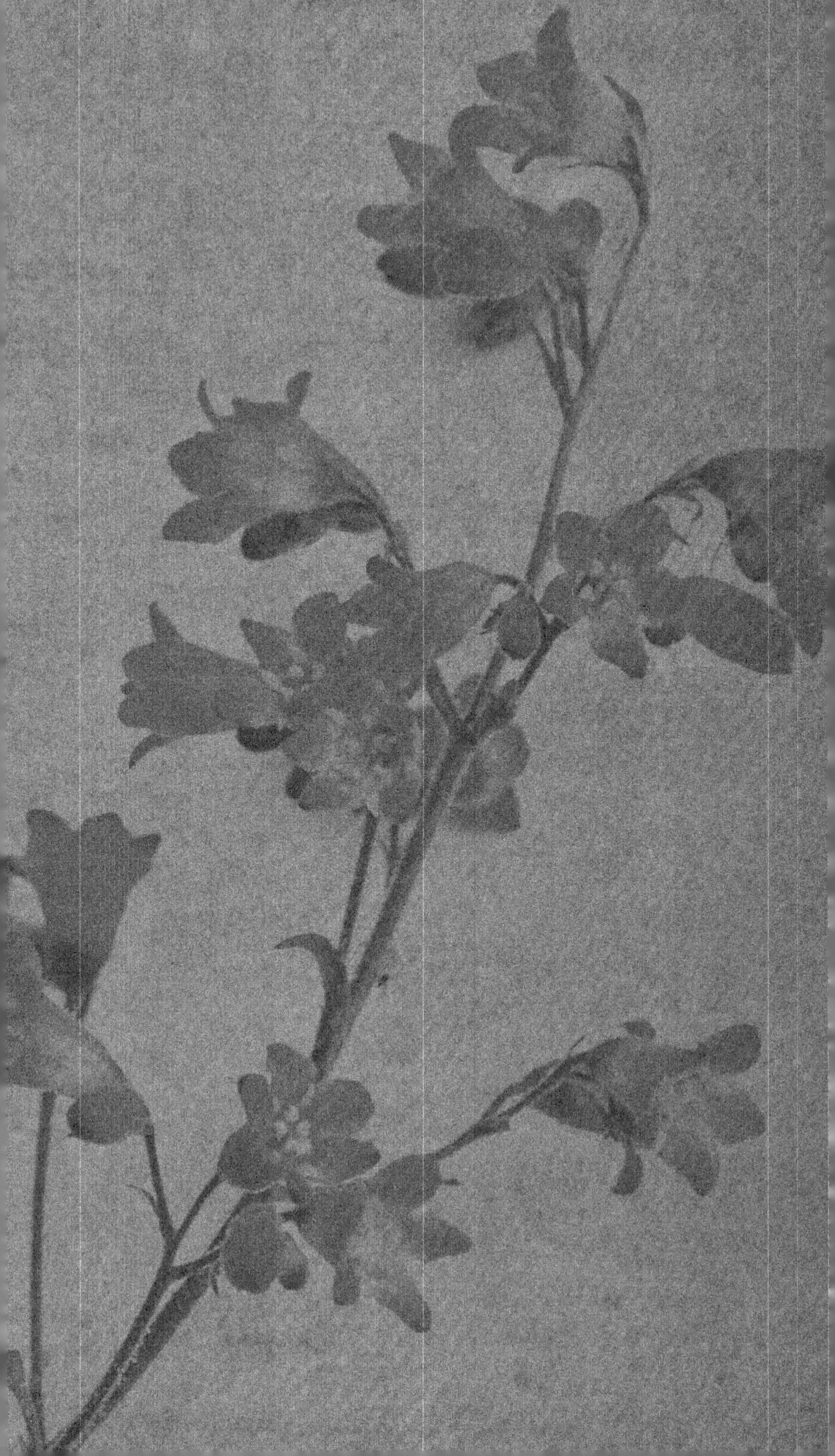

20

STEFI

True to their word, Q comes through with the guest list in record time. I look through it and quickly home in on the weakest link.

Borys Kawka.

Kawka is married to Zaworski's sister, Klara, but their marriage is on its last legs. They've recently separated, and a bitter and contentious divorce is imminent.

Normally, Kawka wouldn't be invited to the party, but unfortunately, Zaworski and his brother-in-law are in business together, so leaving him off the guest list isn't an option.

Luckily for me, Kawka is also in the grip of a full-on midlife crisis. Last week, he brought an escort to his fourteen-year-old son's birthday party. According to Klara's best friend's Facebook post, the scantily clad woman draped herself all over him and embarrassed his long-suffering wife. Klara promptly retaliated by taking up with a twenty-one-year-old bodybuilder.

Words were said, insults were traded, and from the

hints both of them are dropping on social media, Zaworski's party is going to be the next battleground in the couple's acrimonious split.

Long story short: Kawka is most probably going to hire another escort for this party, and my best way in is to be that woman.

I spend the afternoon painstakingly studying Kawka's social media history. He has a thing for supermodels—redheads in particular. I can't be tall and skinny, but the hair I can manage.

I fly to Warsaw the day after my conversation with Q. Once I land, I check into the hotel that houses the nightclub where the party is going to take place. From there, I go straight to a busy fast-food restaurant in the heart of the city and walk into the washroom, where I change into a tight, faded T-shirt and a cheap pair of jeans and don the long red wig I bought in Germany.

Once I'm sure I look the part, I head to the escort agency Kawka uses to apply for a job.

The two-storied building is painted a nondescript gray in color. There are no signs on the outside, nothing that indicates what happens inside the premises. I ring the doorbell and a buzzer sounds, letting me in.

Two women greet me in the lobby. They're both in their late forties or early fifties, carefully made-up and dressed as if they stepped out of the cover of a fashion magazine. I introduce myself and tell them I want to be an escort, and they look me over critically. "My name is Ivana," the skinny blonde one says. "And this is my sister, Magda. Tell me why you want to work here."

I've worked carefully on my cover story, that of a

The Hunter

down-on-her-luck former escort who needs to get back in the game to be able to afford rent. "I was an escort three years ago, and then I met a guy," I reply. "He wanted me to quit. But now he's—"

"Let me guess," Magda cuts in, her expression knowing. "Once you became dependent on him, he broke things off with you."

"Something like that." I give her an appealing look. "I could really use the work."

"Hmm." She circles me, her eyes taking me in, and I do my best not to squirm under her pointed gaze. I feel like a piece of meat. "What color is your hair under that wig?"

"It's red," I reply truthfully. "Just shorter. I'm just wearing the wig to grow out a bad haircut."

The two women exchange looks. "Okay. Leave us your number. We'll call if we need you."

They call the very next day and ask me to come back to the agency. "Wear something sexy and revealing," Ivana orders on the phone. "You'll be meeting a client."

I show up in a mini-skirt and a low-cut top that leaves very little to the imagination.

Ivana greets me in the lobby. It's just her today—Magda is nowhere to be seen. "Adequate," she says, giving me a thorough once-over. "You'll be auditioning for a VIP client. Do I have to explain what that means?"

"Let him do whatever he wants," I reply, making my voice sound bored and jaded. "I know how this works."

"Good," she says, mollified. "Under normal circumstances, you'd have to work for us for six months before I even show you to our VIP clients, but Mr. Kawka is bored of our regular girls." She rolls her eyes. "He says he's never fucked a true redhead. Come."

Yes! My strategy seems to have worked. Thank heavens for social media.

She drags me into a room where a half-dozen girls are waiting to be paraded in front of Boris Kawka. When it's my turn, I sashay in front of the leering man and give him my best sultry look, the one I've been practicing in my hotel room.

I'm rewarded when he points at me. "This one," he says. "She's new, isn't she? I'll take her."

All of Zaworski's security measures, undone by one careless man who can't keep it in his pants.

"She is," Ivana confirms with an obsequious bow. "Excellent choice, Sir."

"She needs a gown. Something tight and low-cut."

"I'll arrange it."

"Good." He comes up behind me and spanks my bottom. "I love redheads." He presses his crotch into my ass. Ugh. "Nice and tight," he says approvingly. "See you Saturday."

My entry secured, I turn my attention to the next part of my plan—how to kill Zaworski and get away with it. After pouring over the blueprints of the building, I decide on smoke bombs. I'll set them to explode when the party is in full swing and be able to stab Zaworski in the resulting confusion.

On Friday night, I make it a point to attend the club and 'accidentally' leave my phone there. Saturday morning, I show up at the door right after Zaworski's security team has completed a sweep of the premises. The venue is deserted apart from the solitary guard blocking the door.

"I'm so sorry," I say, batting my eyelashes at him. "I lost my phone last night, and I think I might have left it here. Would you mind if I take a quick look?" I put my hand on his arm. "Please?"

He lets me in without searching my bag. Mistake. It only takes me a minute to unscrew the grill over the women's bathroom vent and stash my knife there. Another minute to hide the smoke bombs inside the planters that hold the lush tropical plants dotting the room, then I retrieve the phone I hid in one of the stalls and make my way out again.

I take the elevator down to my room, my heart racing in anticipation. The bombs are in place, and tomorrow, once I get inside the party, I'll be able to retrieve my knife. That's all the advance prep I can do.

With any luck, it'll be enough.

Two hours before I'm supposed to meet Kawka, I show up at the escort agency to get ready for the event. When I arrive, Ivana hands me a surprisingly nice red dress. It's skimpy, of course, and reveals an astonishing amount of cleavage, but it fits perfectly, and the silk feels amazing against my skin. "It's a loaner," Ivana says when I admire it. "If you damage it, I'll take it out of your pay."

I'm getting the hell out of Poland the instant I kill Zaworski, so I'm not going to get a chance to return it. But then again, Ivana won't have to pay me for tonight. I figure that's a fair trade. "I'll be careful," I promise her.

"You better."

She hands me a pair of red shoes next. The heels are high—stupidly so. Making a face, I slip into them and take a few experimental steps. It's not good. My feet slide around in them, and I'm not going to be able to run without risking breaking my ankle. "They're too big," I complain.

"I don't care," she retorts. "Stuff tissues into them if you need to." She stares at my face, her expression thoughtful. "Bright red lip," she says aloud, handing me a tube of lipstick. "Smoky eye. Can you do your own makeup?"

"Yes, ma'am."

I don't know if she believes me. "I want every man's eye on you tonight," she warns. "But you cling to Borys, do you understand? He wants to make his wife jealous, and I pride myself on giving the customer everything he wants." She fixes me with a long, pointed look. "Are we clear, girl?"

"Yes, ma'am," I say once again.

I'll follow instructions. Until I'm within sight of Varek Zaworski.

The Hunter

After that, all bets are off.

At eight, I walk into the party on Borys Kawka's arm. We're fashionably late, and judging from the poisonous look Klara sends us, it's intentional.

Borys smirks at her. "Come on," he says to me. "Let's get a drink."

"I have to go to the bathroom," I murmur. "I'll just be a second." I detach myself from Kawka's grip and slip away into the restroom, wait for it to empty, and retrieve my knife. I strap it on my thigh and immediately feel safer.

I rejoin an impatient-looking Borys, drape myself all over him, and ignore the fact that he's pinching my ass. As we weave through the crowds to get to the bar, I scan the room as discreetly as I can.

Where is Zaworski? It's his party; he should be here by now. I can detonate the smoke bombs with a remote trigger, but they're also outfitted with an automatic timer. One way or another, I have less than twenty minutes before they blow.

That's when I feel a gaze sear into me, as hot as fire. The room seems to hush, the noise of the party receding into the background. I look up and meet Joao's gaze. He's staring at the proprietary arm Borys Kawka has around my waist, and his eyes snap back to me...

And he's furious.

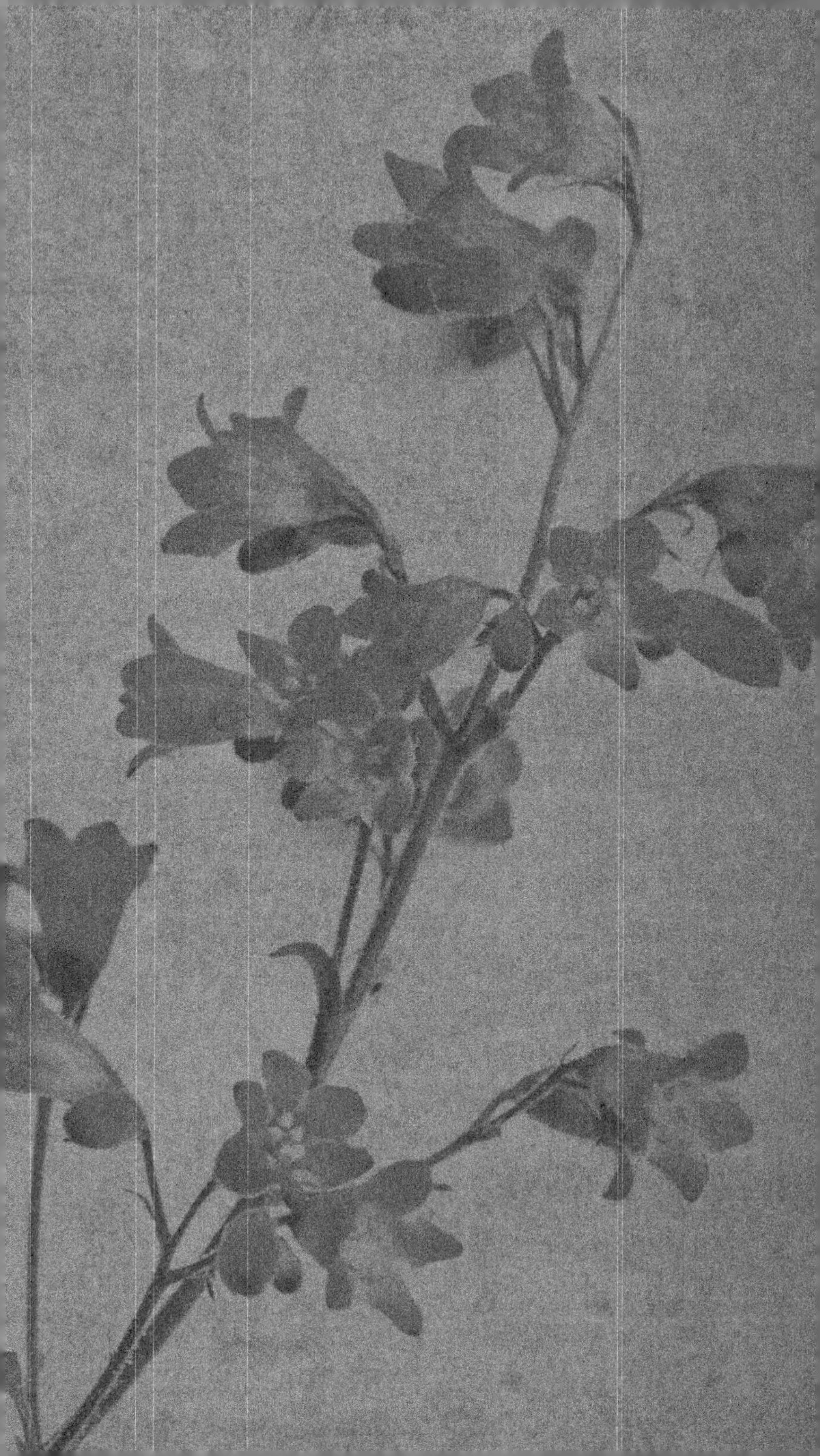

21

STEFI

Joao is looking at me with murder in his eyes, and I need to act *now* before he blows my cover. I pull free of the handsy Borys Kawka. "I'll be right back."

"Again? What the—?" He frowns in displeasure and draws up to his full height. "I'll be telling Ivana about this," he huffs as I leave his side.

Whatever. I move toward the doors leading to the washroom again, but before I get there, Joao intercepts me and drags me to a hidden alcove. "Hello, little fox," he says grimly. "I thought I'd see you here."

His eyes study me, moving slowly from head to toe, taking in the red of my wig and the green of my eyes. No colored contacts today. I look, as much as still possible, like the girl who loved the man in front of her with all the fervor of a youthful heart.

"Joao. How did you—"

"Stop talking." He pushes me against the wall. "I don't want to hear it. I fly halfway across the continent because you're marching into a suicide mission, and when I get here, what do I find? You dressed in *this*—" His eyes rake over me in burning fury, taking in the red of my lips and the swell of my breasts. "Letting some random man paw you."

I wet my lips with my tongue and drink him in. He's wearing a tuxedo, but he hasn't bothered to shave for the occasion. His cheeks and jaw are covered in stubble, his hair is tousled, as if he's dragged his hands through them, and the blue of his eyes is an ocean I could drown in. "He's a way in, nothing more. I'm here for Varek—"

"I don't care." He steps closer, close enough to sense the desire burning through my body, and strokes my lower lip with his thumb.

I inhale sharply at his touch, breathing in the scent of him, the sandalwood of his soap layered with something that's purely Joao. He's so familiar to me—the faint lines around his eyes, the dark sooty sweep of his eyelashes, the tempting fullness of his lips—so familiar, yet somehow new and tantalizing.

It's intoxicating, this pull between us, heavy and undeniable. It feels like the ground at my feet has shifted to draw me closer to him. My heart pounds, my breath catches, and for a moment, the world narrows to the space between us.

I want Joao. *I ache for him.* I want to beg him to kiss me. I need him to mark my skin, to hurt me, to yank my hair until a million cruel pinpricks assault my scalp. I'm making no effort to hide the emotions I'm feeling, and I see the precise moment he realizes the depth of my need because his grip tightens over me, and he yanks me against his body.

"You're *my wife,* Stefi," he growls into my ear. "It appears that you need a reminder of that."

And then his lips crash down on mine.

Have I wandered through the desert for eight years, thirsting for the feel of his possessive touch on my body? *Yes.* Have I ached for this heat that burns through my core, all those lonely nights? *Yes, I have.*

But I didn't realize how much I missed Joao's touch until his mouth moves over mine, demanding, devouring, all-consuming. I hadn't realized how much of a void he left until his fingers thread through my hair, tugging just hard enough to straddle the knife edge of pleasure and pain.

He cups my cheek in his callused hand, the shock of his touch jolting through me. His tongue slides along the seam of my mouth, coaxing it open, and then he kisses me as if he owns me, and I'm being punished for forgetting it.

I can't pull away. I'm trapped, not by him, but by my own memories, my own longing. I lean into his touch, desire surging through my body like a tidal wave, and I kiss him back, laying myself bare for him.

My body has been waiting eight years for this moment. Eight long, lonely years. My nipples tighten. I'm not wearing a bra, and if he looks down, I know he'll see them through the thin silk of my dress. Anyone could round the corner and see us, but I cling to him, uncaring, discretion abandoned, all thoughts of Varek Zaworski fleeing my mind.

This is the only thing that matters.

His hand moves to my hair. "Red again," he says, running his fingers through the loose spiral curls. I want his grip to hurt, punishment and penance rolled into one. "I like it." He pushes his knee between my thighs and stares into my eyes. "Yes?"

Yes. Yes, to him. Yes, always. Yes, forever.

I don't say that out loud, though. I have to remember that this Joao is a different person than the boy I knew, loved, and married. And it's not just the lost years that have created a chasm between us—it's also the secrets I keep.

Instead, I nod wordlessly.

It's as if he's been holding back his need with iron control, but my consent breaks the floodgates. His tongue pushes inside, and he explores me—not with urgency, but slowly and thoroughly—as if I'm a gift laid out for his pleasure. He cups the back of my neck with a firm grip and pulls my hair to tilt my head up, biting my lower lip hard enough to make me gasp.

And when he hears that sound, I feel his feral smile of satisfaction against my skin.

He squeezes my breast through my dress. "Still yes?" His tone is almost mocking. He's daring me to run away, to disappear again without a word, and there's a warning there that I should heed if I'm being smart.

But I was never smart about Joao.

"I don't remember saying no," I taunt. "Maybe you're hesitating because it's you who wants to stop."

"Is that the way we're playing it?" His hand closes over

The Hunter

my throat, his grip punishingly firm. "You want me to pull away, you know what to do."

A surge of heat runs through my body, weakening my knees and leaving me breathless. Eight years ago, Joao's body was as familiar to me as my own, but this darkness is new. His cock is hard, his erection straining against his trousers, and he's staring at me with barely concealed menace. Warning klaxons should be blaring in my mind, but instead of scaring me away, the prospect of an angry Joao just adds to the thrill.

Maybe because he's never rage-fucked me.

And maybe I want—need—to know what that feels like.

"Don't stop."

He bites my lower lip in response. "If I want you to talk, I'll tell you to. The only words I want to hear from your mouth are yes, please, and harder." He eases his grip on my throat. "Are we clear, little fox?"

"Yes," I whisper. "Please." He squeezes my silk-covered breast, and I add, "harder."

He laughs, a dark, low sound in his throat. "Spread your legs," he orders. "Show me you want this."

I part my thighs obediently. He slides his hand up my skin and stops when he finds my knife holster. His lips curve into an amused smile as he pulls the blade free. "I should have guessed the weapons check at the door wouldn't stop you."

"You didn't come in here unarmed either."

His eyes narrow. "Did I give you permission to speak, little fox?" He holds up the blade, and when he sees the handle, shock shows on his face. It's there only for a second before his expression turns neutral again.

"You kept it," he says flatly.

The knife was a wedding present from Joao. It's a beauty of a blade—eight inches, straight edge, with a thick, ridged handle that feels perfect in my hand. Joao had it custom-made for me in Japan and had the maker carve a fox into the base of the blade.

I never go anywhere without it.

I use one of my three allowed words. "Yes."

"How very sentimental," he says harshly. "Open your mouth."

I part my lips, and he slides his fingers inside, pressing down on my tongue deep enough to make me gag. "Suck."

I do. I suck on them, exhilarating in the look of dark heat in his eyes. I suck as he pushes my legs open wider, yanks my panties down to my knees, and shoves the handle of the knife hard into my pussy.

As wet as I am, it still feels like a fist punched into me.

I exhale in a shocked hiss around his fingers. His eyes rest on me—serious, darkly aroused, waiting for me to say no. To tell him I don't want this. To tell him to back off.

'No' isn't what tumbles from my lips.

"Joao," I whisper.

"That's not one of your allowed words, little fox." He pulls the handle out and plunges it back inside. My pussy clamps down, and I throw my head back as hot pleasure twists through me.

This isn't nice.

The Hunter

This isn't kind.

This is dark and dangerous and twisted.

And I love it.

I've never thought of myself as the masochistic type. But it's not the idea of being fucked by a knife handle that's turning me on. It's the man doing it.

My husband.

His face is closed off, the fingers of his left hand pushed into my mouth to keep me quiet, the fist of the right wrapped around the blade. He's fucking me with ruthless purpose, all his attention and focus directed on me, and it's a heady, addictive feeling, one I can't get enough of.

Forgotten is the mission. Forgotten is the man I used to infiltrate this party, and forgotten is my target, the one I've spent years trying to find. All of that is wiped clean as I whimper around Joao's fingers, my climax rocketing toward me with the deadly speed of a tornado.

He hasn't even touched my clit.

"Look at that," he murmurs cruelly. "So needy. So wet. So close to the edge already, aren't you, wife? Your body remembers who it belongs to." He pushes the handle so deep that it hits my cervix with a shock. "If you want to come, then beg for it. Beg me to give you permission."

I keep silent. I'm not being stubborn—any minute now, I'm going to give in and plead. But as greedy as I am for my orgasm, I don't want this moment to end. I would willingly stay in this dark alcove for the rest of my life, with Joao's ice-blue eyes drinking in my pleasure.

But his words only serve to push me closer to the edge, and I tip past the point of no return, and there's no holding back my climax. "I'm going to come," I mumble around his fingers. "Joao, I can't stop. . . Please, may I come. . . I need. . ."

"Is that what you call begging? I think you can do better than that."

"Joao." It's a plea and a whimper rolled into one. "Please. . . I want—need —to be undone by you. I can't hold on, I'm begging you—"

"That's an improvement." He sounds coolly disinterested. He knows I'm only seconds away, and he's making me wait, all because he can, and somehow, it just makes me hotter. *Wetter.*

"Very well, little fox," he rasps into my ear. "Come for me."

His words push me over the edge. I shudder as I come, my teeth sinking into Joao's fingers as I force myself not to cry out. My hips thrust forward, and my muscles clench around the knife handle, tight and hard. I'm drowning and floating at the same time, riding wave after wave of sheer bliss.

Joao never takes his eyes off my face.

He doesn't stop fucking me. He wrings every last bit of pleasure out of my shattered body, then finally, when the word 'stop' is quivering on my lips, he pulls his fingers from my mouth and wrenches the handle from my cunt.

The entire interlude couldn't have taken more than ten minutes.

But I will never be the same again.

22

JOAO

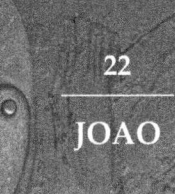

Stefi's normal sharp alertness fades into blissful pleasure when she orgasms. She leans back against the wall, and her eyes flutter shut. Her breathing evens, and her muscles turn relaxed. The shell of the killer fractures for a moment, and what peeks through is the real woman.

Watching Stefi's face as she comes is *transcendent*. I've killed more people than I care to remember, and this is close to heaven as an assassin like me is going to get.

Awareness slowly returns to her eyes. Her gaze locks onto my erection, and for a heartbeat, I want to stay here forever, just her and I, like it's always been. Us against the world. But the noises of the party raging around us intrude into our oasis, and Stefi sharpens into focus.

"What time is it?" she asks. She fumbles for her purse and pulls out a cheap burner phone. "Shit."

"Do you have some place to be?"

"The smoke bombs are going to blow in ten. I've got to get to Zaworski."

"Smoke bombs, that's your plan? The fire alarms will go off, the sprinklers will come on, and as everyone stampedes to the exits, you're going to stab him in the resulting confusion?"

It's not a bad plan. Simple and efficient, it's a variation of her approach in Bucharest. But this isn't just any old bar, and this isn't some random guy. The security here is tighter, and her plan is not without risks.

I fight the urge to protectively hustle her out of the bar. I want to; God knows I do. But Stefi will never forgive me if I stop her from taking out Zaworski. The other hits might have been routine, but this one is personal.

"Pretty much." She holds her hand out for the knife I just fucked her with. The handle is still sticky with her juices. "Why are you here, Joao?" Her voice is cool, but the tremor in her fingers gives her away. She's not unaffected by what just happened.

"I've already answered that question. You're just not listening to me." My fear, kept tightly contained for the last week, spills out. "Going after Bach's network? What the fuck, Stefi? This is a suicide mission."

"How did you find out?" she demands and then shakes her head. "Never mind. I don't have time for this. Give me the knife and stay out of my way."

"That's not going to happen," I growl. "You might not care that what you're doing is suicidal, but I do." I hand her the blade. "I'm going to be right next to you."

She takes the knife from me and notices the blood on it. "Did you get cut?"

"It's not important."

The Hunter

I keep my hand in a fist so she can't see the cut, but she grabs my wrist. "Show me."

I open my palm. Blood wells from where the knife blade sliced into me when I was fucking her, and I see the precise moment she puts it together. "You idiot," she hisses. "You were holding the blade? This is your right hand. How could you be so careless? How deep is it?"

She tugs my hand closer so she can better see the wound in the dim light. I resist. "It's not a big deal."

"Yes, it is. Stop trivializing—"

"I'm fine." I clench my hand into a fist again and stare into her luminous green eyes. "Do you think I give a fuck about this cut?" My throat feels like sandpaper. Her touch is gentle and careful, and it's that softness that undoes me. Her obvious concern makes long-buried emotions rise to the surface. I've been holding the words back for days, *weeks,* but I can't anymore. It hurts too goddamn much. "I mourned you for *eight fucking years.* Eight years, two months, and five days—that's how long I believed you were dead. And for all that time, my heart bled. I walked around like a zombie, feeling hollow and incomplete. Day after day, I woke up alone, wishing you were in bed next to me. I would have given everything for one more night with you." I hold up my hand and watch the blood drip down my wrist, staining the white cotton of my shirt a bright, vivid crimson. "This is *nothing* compared to that. This is just skin and flesh—it will knit itself back together. *This cut will heal.*"

She freezes like a deer caught in headlights. For a long moment, she says nothing. The weight of everything

I lost feels like an anchor tugging me under, but Stefi's fingers are still locked around my wrist, and her touch keeps me from drowning.

"Joao," she whispers. "I'm so sorry." She swallows hard. "I know there's nothing I can say to erase those lost years. Nothing I can do—"

I tug her forward so our foreheads touch. "You can tell me why."

"I can't," she whispers, tears welling in her eyes. "I don't want to remember. Ask me anything else, please, but don't ask me this."

The evening Antonio told me that Stefi was still alive, he asked me if she was worth it. Right after the incident in Zurich, Daniel reminded me that Stefi came into Venice and abducted one of our own. Valentina warned me that she was an assassin. Tomas pointed out that even though we were married, even though I loved Stefi, she let me think she was dead.

Standing in a secluded alcove in a nightclub in Warsaw, I finally find my answer. Standing next to Stefi, our foreheads touching, so close that our breaths mingle with each exhale, *something clicks into place.*

I know my wife. She is not fickle, and she's not flighty. I don't know what she's hiding or why, but I know with absolute certainty that she left for a good reason.

And for the moment, *that's enough.*

"I thought you were dead, but you're alive." A tear rolls down her cheek and I brush it away. "And I don't care about anything else. Run from me if you need, little fox. But know this. I will always find you. If I spend the rest of my life searching for you, it will be a life well-lived."

"Joao," she says. "I can't... You can't..."

"Not now, little fox." I pull my hand free from her grasp. "We're running out of time. Your smoke bombs are going to blow in two minutes. It's time for you to kill Varek Zaworski."

"Just like that?" she asks, her voice trembling. "You're not going to try to stop me?"

"No. But after this job, we're going to Venice, where you will be safe. And if you still want to go after Bach's associates, we do it *together.*"

The moment she hears the word Venice, her expression changes. "I'm not going to Venice with you."

"What the fuck is it about Venice? You've been dreaming about living there ever since you were a little girl. Why are you so resistant now?"

Her chin comes up. "I have my reasons."

"And, let me guess, you're not going to tell me what they are. Well, I don't care. You have an unknown enemy, and you should be in hiding until you figure out who they are and why they're after you, but instead, you're here in Warsaw in the middle of a roomful of killers. So yes, we're going to Venice after this. Whether you like it or not, I'm going to keep you safe."

"You don't control me. You can't stop what I'm doing."

"I'll be happy to have that discussion with you. *In Venice,* over a glass of wine, at this great cafe I know across from the Palazzo Ducale."

She glares at me, but there's no yield in my expression, and she knows it. She abandons the fight for the time being. Grabbing the hem of her dress, she wipes the knife clean of my blood so that no trace of my DNA will come up when the coroners do an autopsy on Zaworski. *Clever girl.* Then she laces her arm in mine and gives me a sweet smile. "Shall we?"

Before I can respond, gunshots ring out. "Everybody, down on the floor," a man's voice yells. "Now."

23

JOAO

What. The. Fuck.

Motioning Stef to stay back, I inch forward just enough to be able to see what's going on. What I see gives me chills. The partygoers are huddled all to one side, and three masked men dressed in black are standing in front of them, holding machine guns with relaxed ease and looking like they mean business.

They could be here for anybody, starting with the guest of honor, Varek Zaworski himself. So why does a sense of foreboding run through me when I see them?

I scan the club. Apart from the three men corralling the guests, there's also a guy guarding the front door and one at the fire exit. There's another exit through the kitchen that might be our way out, but I'm willing to bet there's a guard there, too. These guys don't look like amateurs.

Sure enough, the next words out of the leader's mouth confirm my suspicions. "Ladies and gentlemen," he says in fluent Polish. "We don't mean you any harm. If you cooperate, nobody will get hurt."

"You're here to rob us?" a gray-haired man in an expensive suit demands. "I don't know who you are, but if you think you're going to get away with this—"

"Yes, yes. You're Fabian Walczyk, the president's fixer, and you're going to spare no expense to find us and make us pay." The leader sounds bored. "Your threats will keep me up at night. However, as a point of clarification, we're not here to rob you. We're looking for someone. Please pull out your identification documents. Passports, identity cards, driver's licenses. Gustaw and Hugo will be checking them."

Fuck. They're here for Stefi.

Two guys separate themselves from the cluster. "Come forward, one at a time," the leader continues. "And please, don't try anything. Both Hugo and Gustaw are trained hand-to-hand specialists, and I would hate for anyone to get hurt."

At my side, Stefi's shoulders tense. "They're checking ID," she murmurs. "They're looking for one of us."

"They're looking for you," I correct. My wife has a leak she needs to plug because this is the second time someone apart from me has been able to predict her movements. "Whoever told you about Zaworski sold you out to these men."

"That's not possible."

"It's the only explanation." She starts to argue, and I hold up my hand. "We don't have time for this discussion right now."

She nods, a thoughtful look on her face. "If they're

The Hunter

checking ID, they don't know what I look like. What do you think? Stick to the plan and get out when the smoke bombs blow?"

"Sounds good." As serious as the situation is, I can't help but smile. *I've missed this.* Stefi and I weren't just lovers, and we weren't just married. We were two pieces of a whole. When we did practice missions together, we were always seamlessly in step. My recklessness was tempered by her caution, her tendency toward over-analysis curbed by my desire to get it done already.

"Kamil, search the washrooms."

That's our cue. I round the corner with my hands held above my head, and Stefi follows, a step behind. The leader doesn't react, just waves us into the crowd. That's a relief. Stef's right; these guys, whoever they are, don't have a picture of her. They're groping in the dark, trying to find someone who isn't who they appear to be. Gustaw and Hugo are both holding handheld scanners, and one of them also has a flashlight in his hand, tilting the identity card he's holding under the light to check for flaws in the hologram.

How good is Stefi's fake ID? If she gets pulled aside before the smoke bombs have a chance to blow, will it hold up?

I look around the room again. Zaworski looks apoplectic with rage. His party had a no-weapons rule—not even his bodyguards are armed—and I bet he regrets that right now. I have zero fucks to give for him. The bounty hunter has spent a lifetime preying on people weaker than himself, and he's getting what he deserves.

Standing next to him, looking even angrier, is Borys

Kawka. But Zaworski's brother-in-law isn't glaring at the gunmen. No, his rage is reserved for the woman next to me. That's right, asshole. *She's mine.* Her lipstick is smudged because of me, and her hair is tousled because my fingers ran through the strands. It's *my* name she moaned when she came.

One of the guys is getting closer. I exchange a glance with Stefi. If we have to fight our way out, the odds aren't great. I have a gun tucked into the small of my back and Stefi has a knife, but we're no match for a team of at least six, all armed with machine guns. If her ID doesn't stand up to scrutiny, how do I arrange it so I get taken along with her?

She winks at me. "Relax," she mouths. "Trust the plan."

Then the bombs blow.

Chaos erupts immediately. Thick smoke fills the room, and Zaworski's guests scream in panic. The fire alarms go off, their shrill sirens adding to the confusion. Gunmen forgotten, the crowd stampedes toward the exits, bodies jostling and pushing as they flee down the stairs.

I stick close to my wife. She doesn't want to go to Venice, and I have no doubt that she's hoping to get away from me in the confusion. But I'm not going to let that happen again. Especially now. These gunmen are professionals. If they're mercenaries, they didn't come cheap. Whoever Stefi's adversary is, he or she is powerful and well-connected.

Stefi's scanning the room, looking for Zaworski. I look too and see a familiar figure in a tuxedo push through the crowds in a bid to get out. "He's almost at the exit," I tell her.

"I see him." Stefi sets out determinedly, weaving through the crowd with the grace of a predator, slipping between panicked guests too busy to notice the knife in her hand, and I follow, my senses on high alert. Someone tries to grab her, and I break their wrist before their grip can tighten. They yelp in agony, but the noise is lost among the sirens and the screams.

My little fox catches up with the bounty hunter at the door. With a movement as fluid as water, she slides the knife I just fucked her with between his fifth and sixth ribs on the left side. It's beautiful to watch, deadly poetry in motion, and I want to applaud. Zaworski crumbles to the ground, and without even breaking stride, she steps over him and joins the people streaming down the stairs.

It's perfect.

Almost.

There's only one problem. She—we—didn't account for Borys Kawka. The man hasn't been able to take his eyes off my wife all evening, and even though everyone's fleeing for their lives, he's still watching her.

He's only a step behind Zaworski, in perfect position to see the glint of Stefi's knife.

In perfect position to see the blade slice into his brother-in-law's chest.

For a moment, he can't process what he's seeing. Varek falls to the ground, clutching his heart, his breath coming in shallow gasps, blood bubbling from his mouth, and finally, Kawka's brain catches up with his eyes.

"You stabbed him!" he roars in fury. "You fucking stabbed him."

His voice is loud enough to penetrate the noise of the fire alarm, loud enough that one of the gunmen hears his accusation, looks up, and determinedly starts pushing his way toward Stefi.

Kawka isn't done. "You fucking bitch," he spits out, grabbing my wife by the arm. "You killed Varek."

The moment he touches her, I snap. This fucker had his hands all over my wife, and it's taken all of my self-control not to break every bone in his body. I finally get what Leo was thinking when he broke Simon Groff's wrists last month. I step up and let my fist swing, and it makes contact with Kawka's face with a deeply satisfying crunch.

He goes down.

But the mercenary gunman is still making his way toward us, and even worse, he's raising his weapon.

"Come on," I say tersely to Stefi, grabbing her hand. "We need to get the fuck out of here."

24

STEFI

The smoke bombs have done their trick. The scene is chaotic. People are screaming, rushing toward the exits in a blind panic. The sprinklers finally come on, and the spray of the water sets more people shrieking.

If it weren't for the masked gunman determinedly threading his way through the crowd toward me, everything would have gone exactly as planned.

"Come on," Joao urges, tugging me toward him. "We need to get the fuck out of here."

I hike the skirt of my dress up, duck low in a futile attempt to get lost in the crowds, and race down the stairs. I make it two levels before disaster strikes. My left foot slides awkwardly inside my borrowed stiletto, and sharp pain flares through my ankle like a hot poker. I suck in a breath, my eyes watering from the shock, and Joao stops immediately.

"I'm fine," I tell him before he asks, then try an experimental step and nearly collapse. *Crap.* The gunman is only a level above us. He's not shooting—there are too many people in the stairwell for him to open fire—but he's catching up.

Any moment now, we're going to be trapped.

"Go," I say to Joao through clenched teeth. "Get the hell out of here."

He doesn't dignify that with a response. Instead, he sweeps me into his arms so quickly that I don't even have time to yelp. Then he's rushing down the stairs again, shouldering people out of the way with ruthless focus.

I don't think I've broken my ankle. It's probably just a bad twist. But it hurts so much. Fleeing partygoers collide with my leg, and each time, it sends a fresh jolt of pain through me. Every step Joao takes leaves me dizzy and light-headed, almost nauseous. In many ways, I'm a good assassin, but I've never had any pain tolerance.

I grit my teeth, refusing to cry out, and do my best to keep my eyes on the guy chasing us. The crowd is thinning, and Joao picks up speed, his steps quick and sure.

For a moment, I think we're going to make it...

Then a sharp crack splits the air...

And Joao turns a corner, staggers against the railing, and almost drops me.

"What—?" I start to ask, and then I see blood blooming against his jacket. Gunshot. My heart slams against my ribs, and my mouth goes dry with fear. "Joao, are you—"

His jaw clenches as he forces himself upright. "I'm fine. Just a graze."

Focus, Stef. I can't panic. Joao's making himself move again, but we're sitting ducks in this stairwell. The

The Hunter

gunman's already lining up for another shot, and our lives depend on what happens in the next minute. "Where's your gun?"

"Holster behind my back."

I knew he'd be armed. I grab his weapon in one fluid movement, sight the gunman, and pull the trigger. The bullet whizzes over his shoulder and buries itself into the concrete wall next to him. I correct my aim and shoot again.

This time, my bullet takes him in the head.

Joao turns the corner as the man chasing us goes down. Someone screams, a shrill, ugly sound of total fear. Another woman joins her. Joao ignores them as he continues down the stairs. "Nice shot," he says, as maddeningly calm as always. He gives me an appreciative look. "You've been practicing, little fox."

"He shot you," I say flatly. "Nobody gets to shoot my husband and live." His praise usually makes me feel all warm and fuzzy. Not now; I'm too worried about the rapidly spreading blood on his shoulder. "How bad is it?"

"I already told you, it's just a scratch. Shoot out this lock, will you? This is our floor."

I do, and he pushes the door open. We're in a long hotel corridor. "Where are we going?"

"We need to get to the service elevator," he says. He's alarmingly pale. "It'll take us down to the garage. I have a car waiting."

"The fire alarm's gone off. The elevators won't work."

"And I have an override code," he says with a wink. "You're not the only one who prepped for this mission."

He got shot, he looks like he's going to pass out at any

moment, and *he's winking at me.* Resisting the urge to punch him in his wounded shoulder, I keep my eye on the door we burst through, just in case anyone is following us. But it looks like we're in the clear, at least for now. Everyone's busy panicking in the stairwell, but so far, nobody has had the presence of mind to follow us.

Joao staggers to the service elevator, sweat beading on his forehead. I smash the button, and the doors open immediately. He carries me inside. "There's a key in my back pocket," he says. "Could you get it out?" He grins down at me. "Try to resist the urge to pinch my ass."

"You got shot," I burst out. "I'm trying not to freak out. One more joke, and I'm going to knee you in the groin."

"Promises, promises." He takes the key I hand him and inserts it into the control slot, and the elevator starts to move. Phew.

I try to wriggle out of his hold. "I can stand."

"You were going to fall on the stairs." His eyes fall to my feet. "Your shoes are a couple of sizes too large. Were you trying to break your leg?"

"An expert on women's shoes now, are you?" He gives me an exasperated look, and I sigh in resignation. "Yeah, yeah, you're right. They didn't fit right, and I was going to take them off when I ran for it, but in my defense, I was a little distracted." First by my orgasm and then by the gunmen blasting into the room.

"Is your ankle broken?"

"I don't think so. It's just a twist." At least, I hope it is. Judging by the amount of pain, it's bad. This conversation with Joao is the only thing that's keeping me from screaming in agony. "You should have left me back there." If he hadn't been carrying me, he would have never gotten hurt. "Next time, if I go down, you get the hell out of there, understand?"

"Don't be ridiculous, Stefi," he says, looking down at me with a smile in his eyes. "We're a team, you and me. I'm never going to leave you behind."

Before I can react to that, the elevator lurches to a halt, and the doors slide open. We've reached the underground garage. Rows of cars are parked in neat rows, illuminated by bright overhead lights. I listen for voices, and tentatively point the gun out in front of us, my finger on the trigger, but all is silent, and there are no gunmen in sight.

"Why isn't there anyone here?"

"I might have hacked into the hotel security system and remotely locked all the garage doors," Joao replies with a smirk. "We still need to hurry. They won't stay that way for very long."

His words suggest urgency, but his voice is even, and his heartbeat is steady. Joao doesn't panic; he never has. His calm would be infuriating if he wasn't on my side. "How's your shoulder?"

"Still fine. Stop worrying." He walks down the corridor and opens the door to the underground parking garage. "I'm going to put you down for a second while I get my car, okay? Can you keep your weight off the injured leg?"

"Yes," I reply. He sets me down gently. I kick off my shoes, wincing as a fresh wave of pain surges through my ankle, and lean against the wall. I watch Joao walk up to a black Audi, and it's not until he's about to open the door that my brain starts working again.

"Stop!"

He looks at me. "What's the matter?"

"I'm not getting into your car. We can take mine."

"What? Why?"

"Those guys knew I'd be there." He thinks Q is responsible, but I'm not buying it. "There's a leak in your organization."

A look of outrage passes over his face. "My organization?" he demands. "Absolutely not. The leak's on your end, not mine."

I lift my chin in the air. "You might be sure of that, but I'm not. If you want me to come with you, then we're taking my car."

He stares at me with exasperation for a long moment. "God, you can be so fucking stubborn sometimes," he murmurs. "Fine, not my car. But we're not taking yours either."

He walks up and down the rows of cars, looking for one he can steal. I want to go over and help him, but when I put an experimental foot on the ground, agony explodes up my ankle. "Don't take anything with electronics," I call out. "They can be tracked."

"It's not my first day on the job, Stef," he responds. He disappears out of sight, and then I hear a car start up. Joao drives up to me in a rusted-out Peugeot that's got to be at least twenty years old and gets out of the driver's seat with a grin. "Your chariot awaits, my lady."

He picks me up and puts me in the passenger seat. In the distance, I hear shouts and gunfire getting closer. Joao does too. "We need to go," he says, getting into the driver's seat and buckling up.

I hold out my hand. "Your phone. You need to destroy it."

He rolls his eyes. "Oh, for fuck's sake. Yours too, then. Hand me the gun."

I hand my phone to him and then the gun, feeling naked and vulnerable as I give up the weapon. This has all gone to shit. Varek Zaworski was incredibly well-connected, and Borys Kawka saw me stab him. Ivana from the escort company has my phone number, and her office had security cameras. Any moment now, the Polish police are going to start hunting me, and they'll have my photo.

And my money is in my hotel room, as are my fake passports.

A hotel room I can't get to without risking getting shot.

I'm entirely without resources. All this, and a badly twisted ankle. I'm screwed, and I'd be even more fucked if it wasn't for Joao.

Some of what I'm feeling must be visible on my face because Joao reaches over and squeezes my hand. "Hey, hey, none of that," he says. "We're still alive. Let's focus on keeping it that way."

He opens his door and throws both phones on the concrete. Then he aims his gun at them and fires. "And now nobody can track us. Happy?"

He's insane. I start to giggle, my ears ringing from the sound of the gunshots. "Delighted."

He grins and puts the car into drive just as the door

closest to us bursts open and three gunmen pour out of it. "Put your seatbelt on," he says. "This is going to be a wild ride."

THREE HOURS LATER, we've switched cars twice and finally have time to catch our breath. I make Joao pull over at the side of the road. "We're not going anywhere until I look at your shoulder."

"It's fine."

"Take off your shirt."

He chuckles. "Ah, I see how it is. You just want me naked."

I roll my eyes as he shrugs out of his jacket and then his shirt, and I examine his wound. It's definitely more than a graze, but luckily for Joao, the bullet missed the brachial artery, the humerus, and the cluster of nerves in his upper shoulder. It looks like a clean, in-and-out flesh wound.

I exhale in relief. "It's not bad," I admit.

"Thanks, I've been working out."

"I'm not talking about your muscles."

"So, you did look," he teases.

Once again, I resist the urge to punch him in the arm. "Will you be serious for a second?" I demand. "We're in big trouble. Kawka saw me stab Zaworski. The authorities are going to be looking for me. By now, they'll have my photo. And, if that's not bad enough, I don't have a passport on me, and without one, I can't leave Poland."

He starts up the car again and merges back on the road. "I have a passport for you," he replies. "And money. Unfortunately, if you're right about the leak being in Venice, we can't use it. Not unless we're out of options." He takes his eyes off the road and runs his gaze over me, slow and through. "You look like you're about to pass out. We can make plans tomorrow. Right now, we need rest, and I need to look at that ankle."

"It's fine."

"I'll be the judge of that." He gets on the freeway, headed west toward Poznan and Berlin.

"Berlin?"

"I have a contact there, one who's unaffiliated with the Venice Mafia. She can get us passports."

"She?"

"Are you jealous?" He shoots me an amused smile. "You have no reason to be."

"Not according to Google," I reply tartly, regretting the words the moment they leave my mouth. "You've got dozens of beautiful women hanging onto you, staring adoringly in your direction."

"And you found these pictures on the Internet? When we get our hands on a computer, you must show me these search results." He smiles at me. "I missed this. Running away together, shooting people together. I missed hanging out with you."

"Me too."

I know he wants to know why I ran. It's the question on the tip of his tongue, but he doesn't ask. Maybe it's because he knows I'm feeling increasingly nauseous. Every time the car goes over a pothole, a shock goes through my ankle. Or maybe he's just tired of asking me that question and not getting an answer.

Either case, he holds his tongue and puts his hand over mine.

I look down at our entwined fingers. "Your palm is bleeding." With everything that's happened in the last couple of hours, I'd almost forgotten about his insane knife blade stunt. "The cut's opened up again."

He glances down. "Yeah, it started to clot, but it reopened when I punched Kawka. Totally worth it." He strokes my cheek with bloody fingers, and I lean into his touch. "We're going to be on the road for a couple of hours," he says quietly. "I want to get well away from Warsaw before we stop for the night. Go to sleep, little fox. You need the rest."

"I'm fine," I say automatically. "I'm wide awake."

But it's a lie. Sitting in the car with Joao, I feel truly safe for the first time in eight years. Lulled by the dark and the movement of the car, with my husband holding my hand, I relax back in the passenger seat, and before I know it, I've fallen asleep.

25

STEFI

I wake up with a start. I'm still in the car, but we've stopped moving, and it's pitch-black outside.

"Where are we?"

"Outside an abandoned farmhouse," he says. "A few kilometers outside Zielona Gora. How's the leg?"

I flex my ankle experimentally, and pain shoots up my thigh. "It's not great," I admit.

I start to open the passenger door, and Joao growls in his throat. I bite back my smile. "Are you communicating in growls and grunts now?"

"When you do dumb shit, yes. Your ankle could be broken. Stay where you are; I'll carry you inside."

He comes around the passenger side, opens the door, and hoists me into his arms. "You were out like a light," he says. "I pulled up and went to check out the farmhouse, and you slept through it all. You must have been exhausted."

I wasn't tired; I felt *safe*. After years of constantly

looking over my shoulder for any hint of Bach or his bounty hunters, it's not a feeling I take for granted.

"How do you know it's abandoned? What if the people who live there are just away on vacation or something?"

"There's a giant hole in the roof, the upstairs bedroom has a tree sticking through it, and there are mouse droppings everywhere." He takes in my look of horror, and his lips twitch. "Don't worry, I found a broom and swept out a room." He grins. "Your palace awaits, my lady."

"Thank you, kind sir."

Bantering with him feels slightly unreal. It's been less than two weeks since I found out that Joao is alive, and it still hasn't fully sunk in.

Then there was today. Joao came to Warsaw to support me. He had a getaway car ready and waiting and a fake passport for me.

He lost his shit when Kawka pawed me. He called me *his wife,* told me I needed a reminder that I was married to him, and fucked me with the hilt of a knife until the world disappeared and only we were left.

That was only a few hours ago. Given everything that's happened, our back and forth seems wrong somehow.

But right now, I can't handle anything more serious than that.

The more time I spend with Joao, the more I realize that I need to do the right thing and tell him everything. He deserves the truth; he deserves to know what happened.

But not tonight.

Tonight, I'm going to pretend like there aren't eight lost years between us. Maybe that makes me a coward, but after all this time, Joao and I are together in the same mouse-dropping covered room.

I just want to savor it.

Joao carries me inside the farmhouse and sets me down on a blanket. I give it a dubious look. "Where did this come from? I draw the line at bedding soaked in mouse pee."

"What a princess," he teases. "We got lucky. The owner of the last car we stole was well-prepared for winter. Apart from the blanket, which only smells a little like wet dog, there are matches, bottles of water and some dried jerky. Even better, the farmhouse residents forgot to empty out their cellar before they left." He holds up a dusty bottle. "Behold."

"What is it?"

He pops the cork and takes an experimental sip. "Mead, I think." He offers it to me. "Try some. It's good."

I take the bottle from him and give it a suspicious sniff. "Botulism, here we come," I say dubiously.

He laughs. "Live a little, Stefi. You okay by yourself for a few minutes? I'm going to bring in some firewood."

"You're going to light a fire? Is that a good idea? What if someone sees the smoke?"

"There's no one around," he responds. "It's dark for miles in every direction. And even if someone sees it, so what? They'll just assume we're squatters. We wouldn't be the first—I swept up some empty food cans." He gives the bottle in my hand a pointed look. "Are you going to drink it, or are you just going to keep smelling it suspiciously?"

He knows me a little too well. "Fine, I'll drink it." I take a small sip, and a tart yet sweet taste fills my mouth. Huh. It's actually good. "It's not bad," I admit grudgingly.

"Finish the bottle."

"Are you trying to get me drunk?"

"Yes," he says. "Once I get a fire going, I'm going to have to look at your ankle, and the alcohol will help with the pain."

He's not wrong about that. It's an exceedingly dumb idea to use booze to numb pain, and yet every one of Bach's assassins has done it more than once. He never gave us enough time to heal, and it was often the only way forward.

Ten minutes later, a cheery fire blazes in the fireplace. I lean against the wall and sip my mead, letting warmth wash over me. Joao bustles around, exploring the premises. "There's no electricity or running water," he announces. "But I found a well in the yard." He hangs a steel pail on a hook over the fireplace. "Behold. Hot water."

"My hero," I say, and mean it. It's one of those crisp, clear November nights, and the air is chilly. By some miracle, the glass panes in the room we're in aren't broken, but they're not airtight either. I'll take all the warmth I can get. And more importantly, hot water is going to be necessary to clean Joao's wound.

"A compliment from my wife. Your leg must really be bothering you." He drops to his knees in front of me and

The Hunter

picks up my left leg with light fingers. As gentle as he's being, I still wince as he conducts his examination.

"Well?" I ask when he's done.

"Good news: it's not broken. Bad news: it's badly sprained. You need to keep your weight off the leg for a week."

"A week?" I say, aghast. "We can't be here for a week." I look up at him. "You don't have to stay with me. This is my mess, caused by my carelessness. I knew the shoes were too big, and I shouldn't have forgotten to take them off before I started running."

"You were distracted," he responds with a smirk. "Who knew I had the ability to make you lose focus so completely? Obviously, this situation is my fault." His hands tighten on my gown. "I hope you're not attached to your dress," he says, the only warning I get before he rips a strip off the hem to bind my ankle. He taps the bottle. "Drink up. Tomorrow morning, I'll find some painkillers."

I feel like such a wimp. It's a sprained ankle, and I'm acting like someone put a bullet in my knee. As opposed to Joao, who literally got shot and is treating his wound with about as much concern as he would a mosquito bite.

"You're going around with a sliced palm and a bleeding shoulder," I murmur. "You should drink some of this wine, not give it all to me. My pain tolerance is embarrassing."

"So what? We're not the same person." He kisses me on my forehead, soft and tender. "We make a good team, though. Nice shooting."

"Thank you." He finishes binding my ankle and starts

to sit back, but I stop him. "Get me the hot water. I need to deal with your shoulder."

"It's fine."

"Joao," I say flatly. "I'm not taking no for an answer."

"I'd forgotten how bossy you could be," he complains.

He continues to grumble as I dress his wound and bind his shoulder, and he bitches as I tie a piece of silk around the cut on his palm. I welcome his complaining because I need the distraction. I'm an assassin, and I'm used to blood, but it's entirely different when it belongs to Joao.

By the time I'm done, I'm feeling more than a little faint. My hands tremble as I wipe the last smear of blood from his skin, and the reality of what just happened crashes into me. This isn't just another mission. This is Joao—his blood, his pain– and I'm all too aware that he could have died today, shot to death on a stairwell because he was helping me escape. I swallow hard, fighting the urge to throw up.

His palm looks worse than his shoulder. Every time he flexes his hand, the cut reopens. He needs stitches, but there's no first-aid kit here and nothing I can use to sew the wound shut, so I clean it as best as I can and resolve to find medical supplies first thing in the morning.

We sit side by side in silence when I'm done, taking turns drinking from the bottle.

"Let's make a toast," Joao says finally. "Varek Zaworski, you twisted, evil bastard. May you burn in hell."

His words take a while to sink in. Even when they do, I can hardly believe it. It's finally done—after years of trying and failing to target him, Varek Zaworski is finally dead.

I take a long sip. "Rest in peace, Michaela," I whisper. "Sorry it took so long to avenge your death."

I start to shiver, tears filling my eyes and falling down my cheeks. It's partly the delayed shock and partly the unexpected victory after so many years of futile effort. I try to turn my head so Joao can't see me cry, but he notices.

"Come here," he says softly, wrapping his arms around me and drawing me close. "Let go, Stefi. I've got you." He kisses the top of my head. "I've got you," he says again. "Everything is going to be okay."

His comfort bursts the dam keeping my emotions bottled, and it all comes raging out. I sob harder. "I don't even know why I'm weeping," I hiccup, pressing my head into his uninjured shoulder. "This makes no sense. I'm not sad Zaworski's dead. I'm happy I killed the bastard. So why am I crying?"

"This one's personal." He repositions me so I lean against him, my back to his chest, and wraps his arms around me. "Like you said, you've waited a very long time to avenge Michaela."

I soak in the comfort of his touch, greedy like a sponge, and stare at the crackling fire, warmth flickering over me. "Thank you," I whisper. "You didn't have to help me tonight, but you did. I couldn't have made it without you. You saved my life." Without Joao's help, I wouldn't have even made it down the stairs.

"You don't have to thank me, little fox." I feel the smile

in his voice. "And besides, you saved me first. Remember the fake nun?"

"You've repaid that favor many times over."

"I don't want to keep score, Stef." He kisses my forehead, and then my neck. "You're my wife. I'm always going to be there for you."

We sit together in the quiet, watching the flames flicker in the fireplace. Gradually, my eyes start to close, and I'm too tired to fight it. Leaning on Joao's shoulder, I let the darkness draw me under.

26

STEFI

It's still dark when I wake up. I start to grope for my phone to see what time it is, but then I remember I don't have one. The room is silent, and the only illumination comes from the faint, flickering light thrown from the fire. My ankle throbs and my back hurts from sleeping on the ground. The parts of my body that are in contact with Joao are burning up, and everything else is a little chilly.

"Can't sleep?" Joao asks.

"No," I admit. "My ankle's bothering me a little. I guess the mead wore off. I didn't realize you were awake."

"You sound cold." He wraps his arm around me and tucks me against his body. I become gradually aware of his erection pressing against my ass. I wriggle against it experimentally, and he groans. "Ignore it," he says. "When it comes to you, my cock only has two settings. Aroused and *painfully* aroused. You're exhausted, hurt, and a little drunk. I'm not making a move on you tonight; I'm not that much of an asshole."

I turn in his arms and run my palm over his thick erection. "Can I change your mind?"

"Stef," he rasps. "Don't. I'm hanging on by a thread here, little fox."

"You wouldn't be an asshole if you made a move," I say, stroking his cock through his trousers. "I can't sleep, and if you remember, sex always helped me relax."

"You're in shock. You'll regret it in the morning."

"I've never regretted sleeping with you."

His grip on me tightens. "If you say things like that, my self-control will snap."

He tells me he's about to lose control, and I want to see it happen. "I'm counting on it," I whisper, tilting my head and kissing him on the lips. "What if I ask very nicely?"

"If you ask very nicely," he replies, staring at me with his sky-blue eyes. "Then I'm going to say yes."

And then his lips find mine.

He kissed me at the club, but that kiss felt angry and rushed. This one feels different. It's softer. *Sweeter.* He kisses me as if he has all the time in the world. As if we didn't just get attacked, as if we weren't on the run. He kisses me as if we're in a pocket of time outside reality, and nothing will be allowed to intrude into our domain.

He swipes his tongue along my lip, and I part them. His stubble rasps against my skin, and it sends a hot shiver through me. Earlier at the club, his tongue thrust inside my mouth with demand. Now, it slips inside, sliding against my own in a wicked invitation, and it's an invitation I'm happy to accept.

Ignoring the pain in my ankle, I push him down on

the blanket and straddle him. In this position, I can feel his hard cock against my pussy, and I want more. I grind my hips in a slow, deliberate circle, and he shakes his head and holds me steady.

"What's the hurry, little fox?"

"Eight years," I reply pointedly.

He's unimpressed by my logic. "If we've waited eight years, then we can wait a few more minutes," he says with ruthless determination. "I don't want to rush this. I want to savor every single moment."

His hands stroke the sides of my breasts, his thumbs flicking against my nipples. I gasp and he does it again, this time harder. My nipples are erect from the cold and very, *very* sensitive, and every time he flicks them, it feels like a shock of pure electricity.

I can't get enough of it.

"Come here," he says, his voice rough, pulling me closer. "Let me taste you." He sucks my nipples into his mouth, nipping them with his teeth, and glorious sensation explodes through me. I gasp. Joao was my first and only lover, and when I let myself remember the feeling of a man's touch on my body, it's always Joao I'm thinking about.

But I don't remember it feeling this good. This... *overwhelming.* "I like the teeth," I gasp as he bites my nipple just hard enough to send a hot wave of pleasure through me. "It's nice."

"Nice?" he asks, his voice outraged.

He increases the pressure by a fraction, and I throw my head back. "Okay, nice might be the wrong word. The teeth are *hot*. You have new moves now."

He laughs under his breath and lifts his head up. "I watched a fuckton of porn in the last eight years, Stef."

A warm glow fills me up. "Me too," I admit sheepishly.

"I learn something new about you every day." He shifts me so I'm lying on my back. "I've been dying for a taste of you," he says in a growl. "For six hours, I've been consumed by jealousy, envious of a fucking knife hilt." He slides his hand between my legs, and I part my thighs to give him easier access. "I would have licked it clean if you hadn't snatched it away from me."

"I didn't snatch—" I start to say, and then his fingers part my folds, and I can't speak.

He strokes me, his touch light, and a shiver rolls through me. "Such a pretty pussy," he murmurs, parting my lips and staring until my entire body is flushed, his voice thick with desire. "All pink and wet and slick."

He dips his dark head between my thighs. I hold my breath in anticipation, but rather than tongue my clit like I expect him to, he kisses my inner thighs, soft and reverent. Once again, his stubble scraps against my skin, and it feels the way his teeth did on my nipples earlier, a pain just sharp enough to send pleasure curling through me.

"Joao," I whimper. "I need—"

His tongue flicks wickedly over my clit, and I forget to breathe. "Oh God," I moan disbelievingly. How can this be so good? My body starts to tremble as he circles it with the tip of his tongue, over and over again, as if he can't get enough.

"The taste of you. . ." He grabs my hips and pulls me closer, his mouth hungry. "I thought I remembered, but the memory is only a faint copy of the real thing. . . " He slides his hands under my ass to hold me in place, and he feasts.

My muscles tighten and twist. My ankle twinges, but I don't care. All that matters are the warm, wicked curl of his tongue and the hot, prickling pressure building up inside me.

Is it possible to die from too much pleasure? Because I'm there. I can't take much more of this—it feels too good, too right.

Too damn perfect.

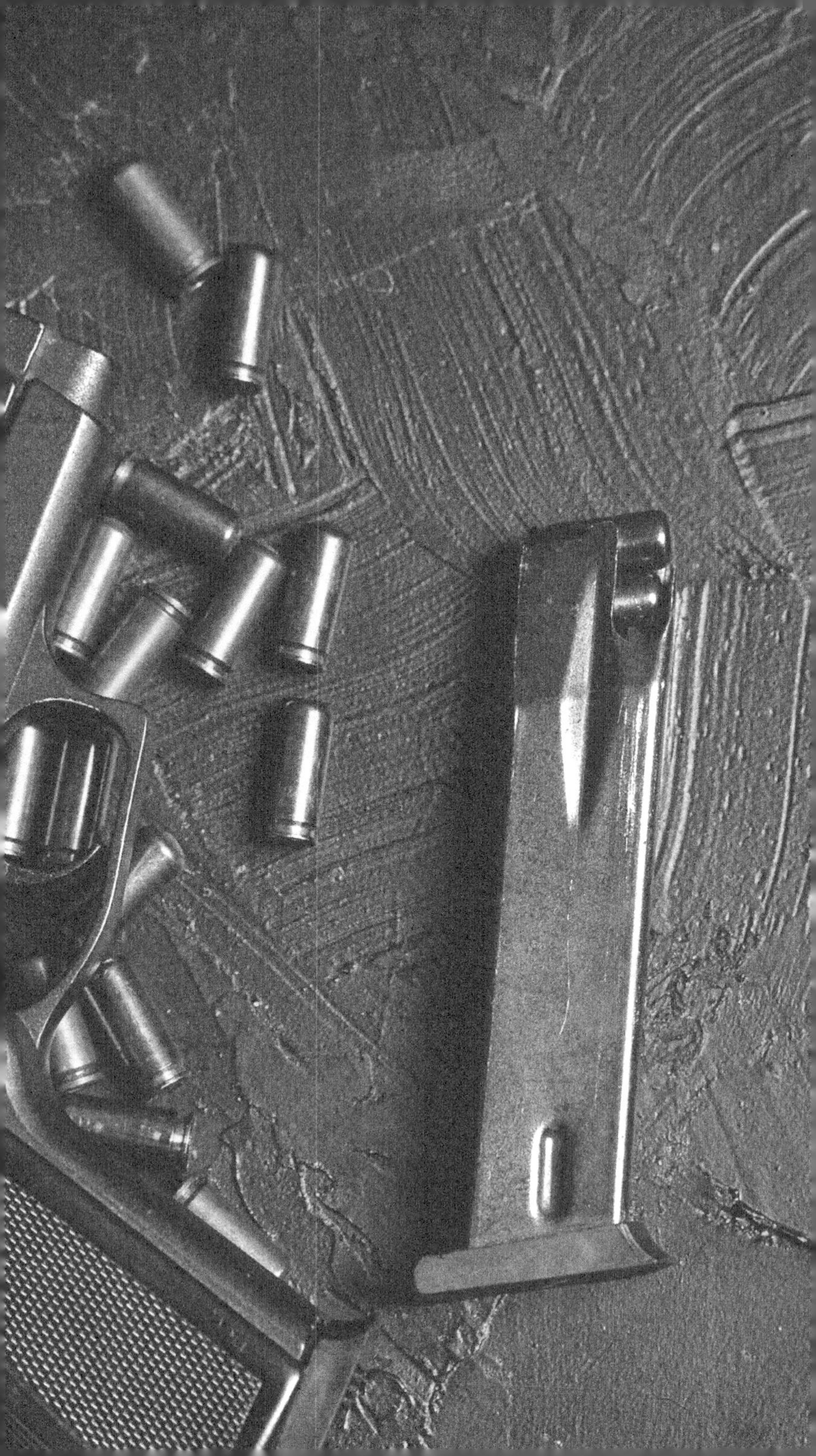

27

JOAO

The feel of her, the taste of her, is indescribable. Stefi holds her breath as I lavish her clit with attention, circling it over and over again like I remember she liked. Her fingers clench in the blanket, alternately tightening and loosening. She's forgetting to breathe, letting it out in one swoosh, and then forgetting again, and fuck, that's one hell of an aphrodisiac.

She's irresistible.

If I tell you I've been dreaming about this moment for the last eight years, it would be a lie. To dream is to hope, and I didn't have any. Hope was impossible when I believed that the love of my life was dead. To fantasize about her would have been like rubbing salt in an open wound, and I've never been that much of a masochist.

Instead, I drifted through life, interacting with everything on a superficial level.

But the core of me—my soul—was numb.

But now...

I devour her, making up for eight years of hunger with one delicious feast.

Eight years ago, her body was more familiar to me than my own. I knew precisely how hard to pinch her nipples, how she liked her clit stroked, how she loved it when I used my fingers and my mouth at the same time.

And now? I ache to rediscover every inch of her body. I burn to discover what she likes, what turns her on. Does she like it harder now, or softer? Does she want to be tied up and spanked or massaged with warm oil and kissed all over her body? I can't wait to find out.

Whatever it is, I'm game for it.

I slide my ring finger inside her, and the feeling of her hot, wet cunt nearly makes me lose it. I grit my teeth and ignore my aching cock for the moment, savoring the indescribable feel of her. I add another finger, and she throws her head back and hisses, "Oh, fuck yes," and my cock jumps again.

I tease her clit, licking and sucking on it a little and then backing off before I start it all over again. Her muscles grip my fingers like a vise. "So tight," I say hoarsely, sweat breaking out on my skin. "Are you going to be able to take my cock, little fox? Are you going to take me like a good girl?"

Her muscles spasm hard. "Yes," she pants. "I will. Oh God, please—"

"No gods here, Stefi. Just me." I flick her clit from left to right with the tip of my tongue and then up and down. "You're so beautiful. A goddess. When I saw your naked body in Zurich, I nearly came in my pants like a horny teenager." I pinch her nipples. "You knew the effect you

The Hunter

were having on me, bad girl. I should punish you for it. I should feed you my cock, inch by inch, until you take it all the way down your throat."

She writhes and quivers. "Oh fuck, Joao, I'm so close. . . I'm going to come. . ."

"Ask for permission." I don't need to control her orgasms, but it's exhilarating watching her balance at that knife edge, struggling not to tip over into an intense, all-consuming climax.

Her knuckles are white, her grip on the blanket tight. I add a third finger to her cunt, and she clamps down on me. I look up at her face, and her expression is one of raw, clawing need.

She looks the way I feel. Undone by pleasure, unraveled by it.

"Joao, please. . ." she begs, biting her lower lip between her even white teeth. "I can't, I need. . ."

I twist my fingers inside her until I find her G-spot. I press down on it and lick her swollen clit, my brain a haze of lust. She writhes and groans, her body shuddering on the edge of release, and I want it. I want her to come for me.

She's my good girl, *my precious wife*, my little fox, always and forever. My atoms are tearing apart, rearranging themselves with Stefi in the center. I breathe her in, her scent and softness filling my nostrils and my mouth and my soul, and I whisper, "come for me, love."

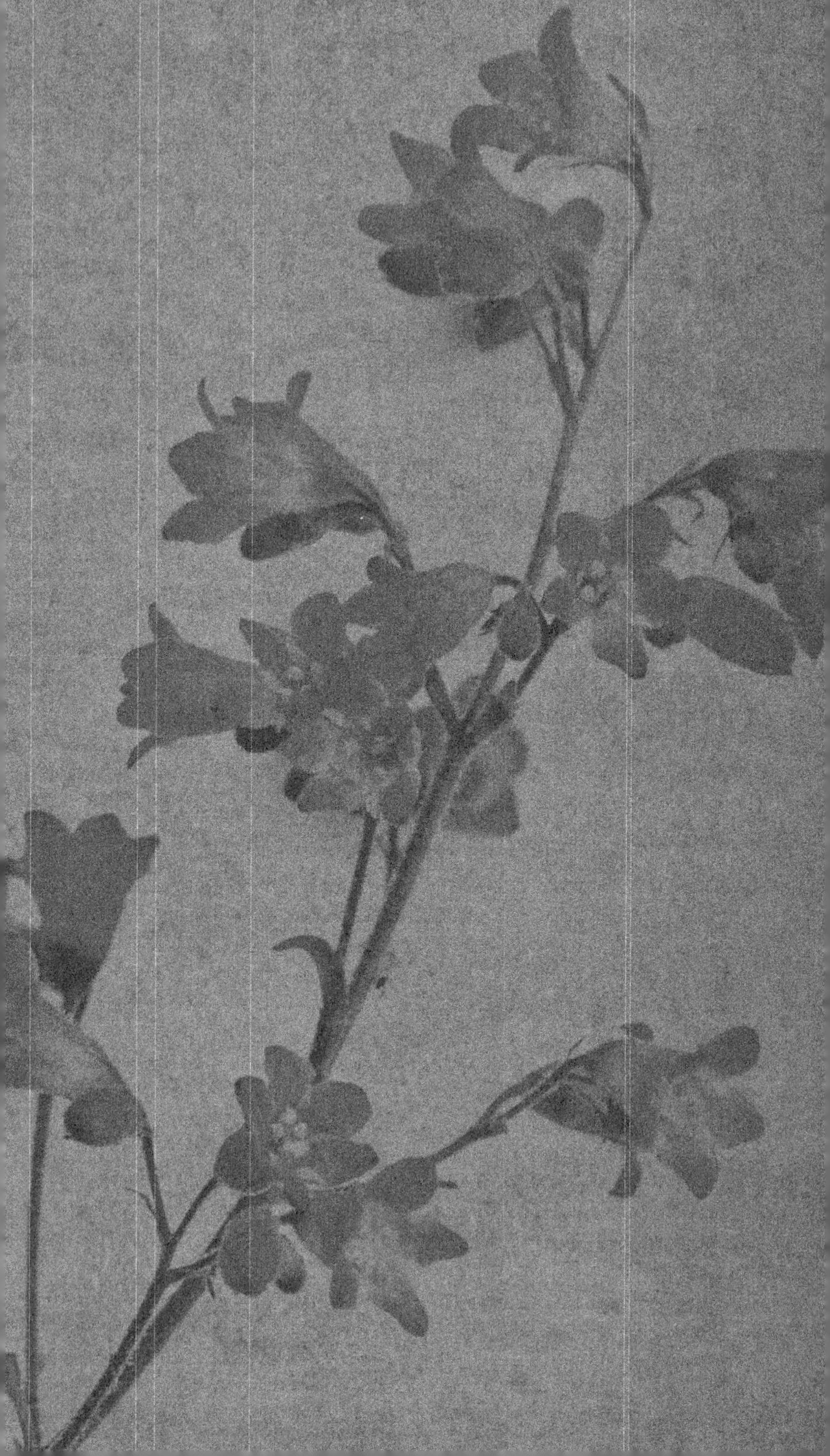

28

STEFI

I come all over his face.

I thought it was hot when he fucked me with the hilt of my knife. And I thought I came harder than I've ever come in my life.

But that orgasm was wrenched out of me. As hot as it was, there is something so much more intimate about making love in this farmhouse, in the darkness, lit only by the flickering embers of the fire.

It's just Joao and me here. No props, no games. None of that is necessary.

He continues to lick me through every last tremor. It's only when I start to push him away does he lift up his head. "Had enough?" he asks, his gaze hungry.

Never. "Not even close," I reply, reaching for him. "Come here."

He obliges, lying next to me and pulling me close, the heat of his skin warming my body. His mouth falls on mine again, devouring my lips, and even though I just came, a fresh burst of heat ignites in my core.

I run my hands greedily over him, skating over his defined abs and down to his hard cock. I squeeze it gently, and he groans. "Stef," he says. "I've been half erect for the last six or seven hours. You are *killing* me here."

I smile in the dark. "So you don't want me to do this?" I skate my thumb over his engorged head, and he growls deep in his throat.

"Tease," he says, pushing me on my back. As raw and ragged as the movement is, he still remembers to be careful with my ankle. Better than me. I've totally forgotten about the pain, distracted by the intense pleasure swirling through my bloodstream. "I'm going to fuck you now, Stefi."

I thought he'd never ask. "Yes, please."

He positions himself between my legs and slides inside, slowly, so slowly. His thick length enters me inch by excruciating inch. Sweat breaks out on my skin as my muscles adjust to his girth. "You're so tight," he groans, squeezing his eyes shut as he pushes inside.

I wrap my uninjured leg around his hip and pull him closer. The burning stretch is intense, and it's just fanning the flames of my arousal. "More," I whisper. "Harder."

He thrusts the rest of the way inside.

Oh. My. God. My nails dig into his back as an intense, overwhelming, tidal wave of pleasure washes over me. "Please," I sob. He's inside me, hard and hot and perfect. My muscles grip him tight and refuse to let go. Blood pounds in my head, and aching need claws through me. I need...

He thrusts into me again. His strokes are deep yet unhurried. He pinches my nipples and squeezes my breasts, and his mouth finds mine again. He draws back to look at me, his gaze possessive and a little bit predatory. "Look at you," he says. "Naked. Wet. Hot and desperate. All for me."

A shiver races down my spine.

"Isn't that right, little fox?"

"Yes," I whimper. He's playing my body like an instrument, and I love every minute of it.

"That's right." He strokes my clit with his thumb, and I clench around him. "Every whimper, every moan, every sigh, every quiver. It's all for me."

The note of possessiveness in his voice sends another wave of heat through me. He thrusts deep, his eyes on my face. Again and again, he pounds into me. I lock my leg around his hips and raise mine to meet each of his thrusts.

I'm going to come again. "Joao," I moan, feeling feverish, *delirious.* I'm right there, right at the edge all over again, my swollen clit so sensitive from my earlier orgasm that if he so much as breathes on it, I will lose control. "Joao—"

"Stefi," he growls, slamming into me. "Oh fuck, yes."

I arch my back, silently urging him to go faster, deeper, harder. His pace picks up, his face contorted with arousal. His fingers dig into my hips, and then he explodes. His cock jerks inside me, and he comes hard, his release setting mine off. My muscles tighten, and I shatter, every nerve in my body exploding with pleasure.

We lie next to each other in the dark. We just made love. This feels momentous; at least, it does for me. We should probably discuss what it means, but I wasn't lying when I said that sex would help me to relax. I barely have time to snuggle against Joao, and then I'm asleep.

29
JOAO

When I wake up, it's daylight outside, and Stefi's nowhere to be seen. I jump to my feet and rush outside, and the car is gone too.

Fuck.

She's run away. *Again*.

I slump against the front door, trying not to take her disappearance personally. After yesterday, I thought. . . I hoped. . .

Damn it. We slept together, for fuck's sake. I thought it meant something. If nothing else, I hoped it would mean she'd stop seeing me as the enemy. That she'd stick around.

I'm such a fool. Three times I've had Stefi in my grasp now. Zurich, then Paris, and now in the Polish countryside, and all three times, she's gotten away. By now, you think I'd have learned my lesson.

Her left ankle is hurt. It won't stop her from driving, but how far can she get without a passport?

I go back into the farmhouse and look through my stuff, and the fake ID I made for her is still there. Where is she going? She's not going to be able to cross the border into Germany, and it's insane for her to stay in Poland. Zaworski was well-connected, Kawka even more so. They're going to be looking for her.

What is she hoping to accomplish, alone, on a twisted ankle, without a working passport?

The sound of a car's engine makes me look up. A Toyota Corolla, the last car we stole yesterday, comes up the laneway. Stefi parks in front of the farmhouse, opens the driver's side door, and gets out, keeping her weight off her left leg as much as possible.

Before she can take a hobbling step forward, I'm there, bracing my shoulder under hers so she can lean on me. "Where have you been?" I demand.

"I woke up early and couldn't fall back asleep, so I went to get supplies."

And I was sleeping so soundly that I didn't even hear her leave. I can't decide if I want to kiss my wife or strangle her. "You're supposed to be resting your ankle," I say pointedly. "I could have handled it when I got up."

"You could have," she agrees. "But if I told you to make sure you got sutures for the cut on your palm, would you have stopped for a first aid kit, or would you have pretended that it was nothing and told me not to worry?"

Definitely the latter, and she knows it. "Exactly," she says with a smirk, pulling out a tin with a red cross on it. "That's what I figured. Let me see your hand."

I fix my gaze on the first-aid kit. "Where did you get

that from?" I ask, mildly aghast. "Did you go to a hospital?"

Stefi gives me an offended look. "Is this my first day on the job?" she demands. "Of course, I didn't break into a hospital. Too many cameras. I robbed an animal clinic." She lifts her chin in a way that makes me want to kiss her. "I figured it was more appropriate since you got that cut on your palm by being an *ass.*"

I snort. She looks a little too pleased with herself. "Been practicing that line, little fox?"

"The entire drive back," she admits. She makes a face. "I also felt bad about breaking the clinic's window, so I left them some money to replace it."

"Of course you did."

I notice she's looking pale again, so I sweep her into my arms, ignoring her protests, and carry her across the threshold. "Call it what you want, but I got cut watching you come after eight years of just having it as a memory. It was totally worth it."

"Like I said, you got cut being an ass," she retorts before changing the subject. "Can you heat some water up?"

I set her down on the blanket, noticing the wince she tries to hide from me.

"Next time, when I tell you to keep your weight off your ankle," I scold, "listen to me. Or I might be tempted to tie you up."

"You should try that." She winks at me, the little minx. "I think I'd enjoy it."

"Would you now? Why does that make me suspicious?" I refill the pail and stoke the fire as we banter. "Have you gotten good at getting out of handcuffs?"

"Not as good as you. Nobody was as good as you. Only Jack came close." A look of sadness flashes over her face at the memory of the boy we grew up with. Jack was one of the assassins in our cohort. Small and wiry, an expert lockpicker, and a pretty decent hacker as well. I haven't thought about him in years. "What happened to him, do you know? Does he still work for Bach?" She laughs a little as she realizes what she just said. "You can tell it still hasn't sunk in. I don't know if it ever will. Maybe I'll need to see a body before I truly believe that Henrik Bach is dead."

"I'm sure Valentina can break into the Austrian police records to get you what you need." The water is hot enough, so I unhook the pail and bring it over to Stefi's blanket.

"Hmm," she says noncommittally. She cleans my wound, looking carefully for any signs of infection. There isn't any. It was a clean cut, and Stefi tended to it thoroughly last night. When she's satisfied I'm clear, she opens the first-aid kit and reaches for the numbing spray.

"I don't need it," I tell her with a roll of my eyes. "I don't care if it hurts."

"You might not care that it hurts, but I do." Her voice lowers to a whisper. "I can't bear to cause you pain."

Then why did you run? Why didn't you tell me what you were planning? Why did you let me believe, for eight long, agonizing years, that you were dead?

The words are on the tip of my tongue, but I don't ask.

Asking her why would shatter this fragile interlude, and I don't want to do that.

But she's waiting for me to ask. She's watching me, her eyes wide and wary, her shoulders stiff, every muscle in her body poised to run again.

"I want you to know something, Stef," I tell her, my voice quiet. "The moment that knife hilt slid inside you and you sighed in pleasure, I realized I don't care. Whatever the reason you left, it was eight years ago, and I can't stay angry forever." I exhale in a long breath. "Fuck it. Whatever happened, it was in the past, and I'm a lot more interested in the present."

"You realized you didn't care the second the knife slid into me." She laughs disbelievingly. "That's not real, Joao. That's magic pussy. You have sex brain right now. When it fades, you'll realize that of course it matters. The past influences the present. Like it or not, you can't pretend it didn't happen."

"Sex brain?" I stare at her, dumbfounded. "That's what you think this is about? Don't be ridiculous. This isn't about sex, and we both know it. Last night, I slept so soundly that I didn't even wake up when you left. Me, who wakes up when Mimi pads outside my bedroom. This is about trust, about finding your person. When I saw you at the party, it felt like a giant neon sign popped up over your head. It made me realize I could either wallow in my pain and anger, or I could open my eyes and *see* that you're right in front of me, the second chance I never thought I'd get."

There's a long moment of silence. Stefi's the first to

break it, but she doesn't address what I just said. "Show me your palm," she says instead.

It's tempting to push, but I shove down the urge. My wife needs space, and I'm going to give it to her. Without another word, I hold out my hand. She numbs the flesh and starts to stitch the cut shut with neat, even stitches, her head bent over my hand. "I know you want to ask me why I left," she finally whispers. "But it's because I can't bear to cause you pain that I can't tell you why. The truth won't set you free, Joao. It'll just break your heart. Trust me on this." She looks at me with luminous green eyes. "I never wanted to flee. I just had no other choice."

"I thought you left this morning," I admit. "When I woke up and you weren't there, I thought I lost you all over again."

She shakes her head. "I'm done running. Henrik Bach is dead. Varek Zaworski is dead. If it weren't for my promise. . ." She stops herself abruptly.

"Promise to who?"

Her face closes, and she stays stubbornly silent. I've evidently asked another question she won't answer. I'm casting my mind for a different topic of conversation when she says, "My list is down to two targets. I need to talk to you about one of them."

Her voice is suddenly serious, and my senses go on high alert. I have a feeling I'm finally going to get some answers from my wife. "Tell me."

She swallows hard. "Antonio Moretti," she says. "Your boss is part of Henrik Bach's empire. For the last five years, he's been funding it." Her hand clenches into a fist. "And I've sworn that no matter the cost, I will kill him."

30

STEFI

"You think Antonio Moretti has been funding Bach?" Joao's expression sharpens as he works it out. "Is that why you don't want to go to Venice? You think Antonio's figured out what you're doing, that he knows you're after him, and if you enter his city, he will kill you."

"Yes."

He shakes his head instantly. "That's impossible."

I can tell by the tone in his voice that he doesn't believe me. My stomach sinks. It was always a possibility that this was going to happen, but even though I should have been prepared for his reaction, I'm not. His reaction feels like a knife twisting in my gut.

How do I convince Joao if he's not ready to listen to what I have to say? But I have to try. If the last twenty-four hours have shown me anything, it's that I want Joao in my life again. I'm not willing to let him go without a fight.

"Would you bet your life on it?" I ask him. "Would you bet *mine*?"

He starts to reply and then closes his mouth. I finish stitching his wound, but he doesn't make any effort to take his hand back from mine.

"I have proof of Moretti's financial involvement," I continue. "Every year for the last five years, he's transferred three million euros into Bach's Swiss bank account. He made an effort to hide what he's doing—the transactions are run through dozens of shell companies—but it's him. I know you don't want to listen to me, Joao, but this is real. I have evidence of his guilt."

"How did you find out?" he asks skeptically. "Did you get this information from the same source who told you about Zaworski's party?"

"Yes, it was Q," I retort, stung by his obvious implication that my informant has sold me out. "They're reliable, and their intel is the best there is. I know you don't believe it, but the leak is not on my end. It can't be."

"Would you bet your life on it?" he asks pointedly. "Would you bet *mine?*"

"I hate when you throw my own words back at me," I grumble. "Really hate it." I take a deep breath and think about how else I'm going to convince Joao about Moretti's guilt. "How did you discover I was taking out Bach's network?"

He frowns. "Daniel helped me figure it out. He was the one who saw the pattern, not me."

His voice trails off thoughtfully, and something flickers over his face. Doubt?

"What is it?" I demand. "What did you just remember?"

"Daniel was familiar with one of your targets," he says

slowly. "René Vannier. He said that he recognized Vannier's name from a file on Bach that Valentina, our hacker, had compiled when I first joined the organization. But..."

"But what?"

"But I joined five years ago, and Bach didn't bribe Vannier until—"

"Last year. Why would your hacker bother to keep an eye on Henrik Bach when she must have so many other threats to track?" My heart sinks. As convinced as I was that Moretti was part of Bach's network, I didn't want to do this to Joao. I wanted there to be a loophole, damn it.

"There's more." Joao looks upset. "I asked Daniel why Valentina would have a file on Bach, and he changed the topic almost immediately. I could have sworn he was hiding something." He leans back against the wall, his eyes clenched shut. "I don't know what to believe anymore," he says at last. "If your intel is right, then yes, Antonio looks guilty. But I know the man. I've worked with him for five years, Stef. I've eaten at his house. His housekeeper watches my cat when I travel. I know who he is, and Bach is the last person he'd work with."

He exhales in a long breath. "When Antonio was younger, the Venice Mafia was run by a man named Domenico Cartozzi. This was before my time, but I've heard the stories. Cartozzi was erratic. Violent. He'd be smiling one moment and swinging at someone with a machete the next. When Antonio killed him and took over, he swore to make a better organization. Bach is too much like Cartozzi, don't you see? Antonio would never ally himself with someone like that."

"Maybe you don't know what motivates him as well as you think you do. Or maybe Moretti thought that as long as Bach stayed away from Venice, there was no harm working with him."

"That doesn't track," Joao responds immediately. "I'm the organization's assassin. Do you know how many times I've been asked to kill in the last five years? Less than a dozen."

I open my mouth to argue, but he holds up his hand. "Don't get me wrong. Antonio is ruthless when he needs to be. You don't rise to be the head of the mafia without a willingness to do what needs to be done. But Antonio doesn't relish murder, Stef, not the way Henrik did. He'll only kill if he has no other alternative. I'm so underused that I've started managing his smuggling operations just so that I'm not bored out of my mind."

"You don't believe me."

"That's not what I'm saying. If you tell me you're absolutely sure about the money and the shell companies and the Swiss bank account, I'll accept that. But you're asking me to discredit five years of knowing him, and I can't do that. What if you're missing something? What if your intel is faulty, or what if the person giving it to you has ulterior motives? It's not as if you can trust them after what happened at Zaworski's birthd—"

"We're back to this," I say in frustration. We're talking in circles and getting nowhere, but I have to keep trying. "You think the leak is at my end. You think Q sold me out to the gunmen."

"They knew you were going to be at Varek's party," he says stubbornly.

"And so did your friend Daniel. Maybe he ran to Moretti as soon as he figured out that I was going to go after Zaworski. And then Moretti sent the gunmen."

"It's a good theory, except for two things. First, I didn't tell Daniel about Zaworski's birthday party. I didn't tell anyone."

"You didn't need to. Don't you think your phone has a tracker on it?"

He nods. "Fair enough. But I said there were two things. The second one is this. The gunmen didn't know who they were looking for. They were checking IDs, looking for a fake. Antonio doesn't need to do that. He has a photo of you. Yes, your hair was a different color in that picture, and so were your eyes, but even so. Those guys didn't even know they were looking for a woman."

Okay, he has a point there.

For the first time, a little worm of doubt rears its head in the back of my mind. Could Q have betrayed me, and if so, why? I'm not fooling myself that they have any loyalty to me, but they've been a valuable informant for almost seven years, and they've helped me take down most of Bach's network. Why would they flip on me, and why now?

"So, no," Joao continues. "I don't think that Antonio asked me to bring you back to Venice so that he could kill you. I don't know what's going on with the money trail, but I know this. Antonio gave me his word that he would protect you if you came to Venice, and the man I know *does not break his promises.* He does not stab people in the back."

"You're putting a lot of faith in him," I say softly, my

voice trembling despite my best efforts to keep it steady. "So much loyalty. Is he worth it?"

He stares into my eyes. "This isn't a question of loyalty and what I owe the padrino," he says. "If I believed Antonio was a threat, I would attack because my loyalty to you is far, far greater than anything I owe him. If it comes down to a choice, I will always choose you. But..."

"But what?"

"But you're asking me to ignore my intuition, little fox."

And his intuition has kept him alive more times than I can count. I'm the one who is all about detailed analysis. Joao follows his instincts, and they are superb.

Sudden weariness fills me. "Let's talk about something else. We need to make a plan."

He nods, his eyes troubled. "We're not safe in Poland," he says. "But to get out, you need to be operational, and you're not. We're not going anywhere until your ankle heals."

"That could take a couple of days. We can't risk—"

"It'll take a week, and yes, we can. This is about as secure a base as we can hope for. It's abandoned, and the fields haven't been plowed in at least a couple of years. The nearest neighbor is miles down the road. We'll only light the fire at night so nobody can see the smoke coming from the fireplace." His voice is confident. "We'll be safe here, Stef. It's going to be fine."

His optimism is contagious, and I want to give in. Staying here for a week will mean getting to spend that time with Joao. A week during which the outside world can't intrude. "I only bought us a day's worth of food," I say weakly.

"I'll go into town for supplies this evening once it gets dark. This is Poland's wine region, and even in November, there are tourists in Zielona Góra. I won't stand out."

"You will, dressed like that."

He glances down at his bloodstained tuxedo. "I'll steal a T-shirt off someone's clothesline before I go shopping. Besides, it's not only food we need. I need to call Mathilde and arrange for passports for both of us."

"And then what? We go to Venice? I'm not doing that. Not until I'm positive Q was the leak. And right now, I'm not even close to being convinced."

"I have an idea about that. We could set a trap for them."

"What kind of trap?"

"Dunno yet. But we'll figure it out." He gives me a cocky, confident grin. "As long as we work together, we can do anything. Deal?"

I'm still dubious about Moretti and Joao's faith in him.

But when he smiles at me like that, I can't deny him anything.

"Deal."

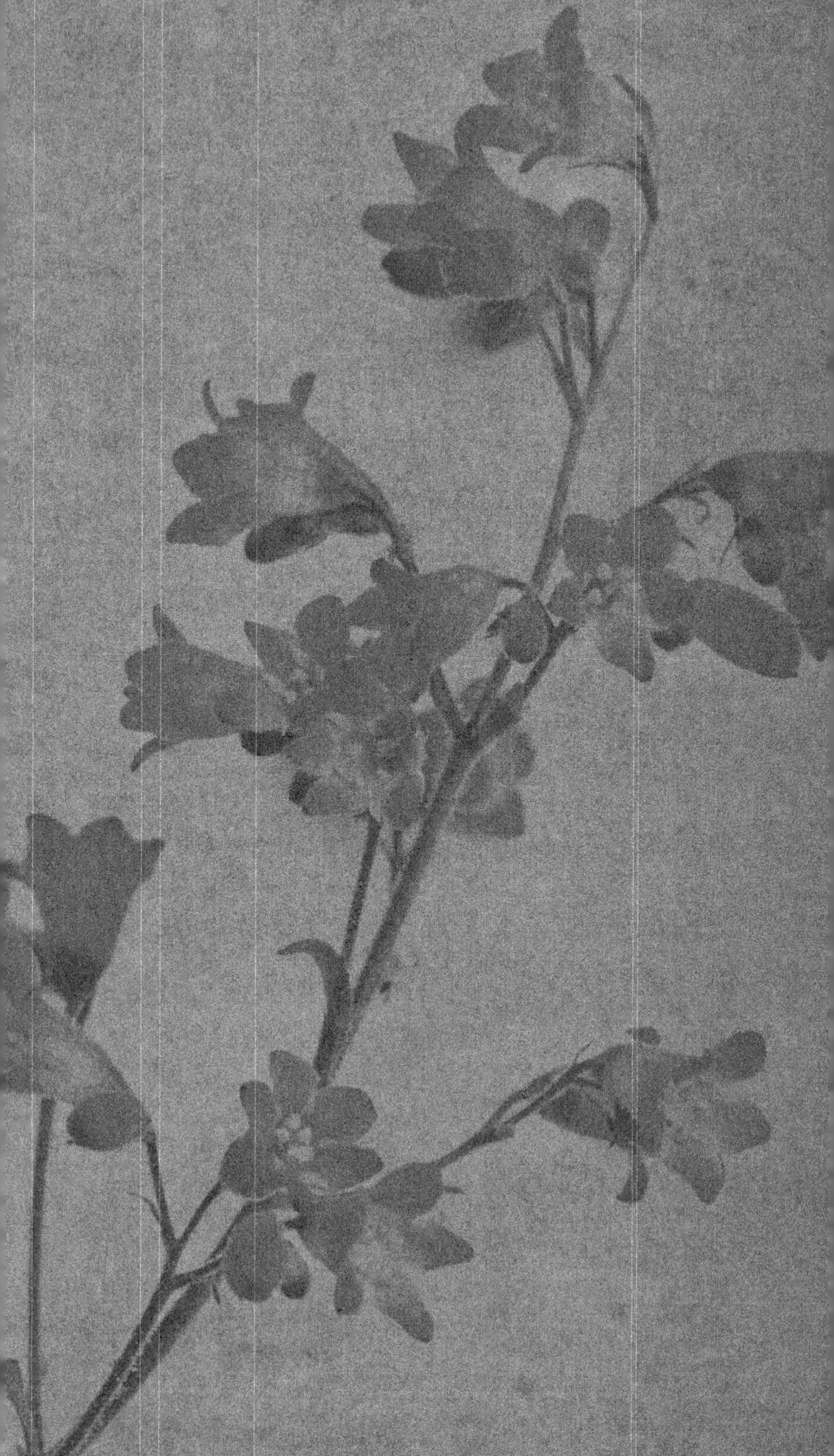

31

STEFI

A week goes by. Joao goes into town once, but when he gets to the only store, he sees my photo, the one Ivana took of me for her escort website, on the TV screen there. Apparently, I'm on the list of Poland's most wanted. It spooks him enough that he leaves without buying much, and when he gets back, we decide it isn't worth the risk of him going into town again.

So we live rough, squatting in the cold and abandoned farmhouse, and sleeping on the ground, one blanket between the two of us. We only light the fire under the cover of the dark. We eat bread and cheese, which sounds pretty good, but after three days of the food becoming increasingly stale, I'd sell my soul for a hot meal.

And despite all of those inconveniences, it's the best week of my life.

Time is a luxury we never had. Our entire relationship was built in the slivers we could steal away from Henrik Bach's paranoid and watchful gaze. We've never had a full week alone, never spent this much time together, and even the danger hanging over our heads can't detract from how magical an interlude this is.

We catch up on each other's lives and fill in the gap of the missing years. We argue about the latest superhero movie and tease each other about the books we're reading. (A fluffy rom-com for me, and something about video games and chickens in a fantasy alt-Chinese world for Joao.)

I've always loved Joao, but in that farmhouse, I fall in love with him all over again.

My ankle gets better, and the swelling subsides. After three days, I can put my foot down without wincing. If I still worked for Bach, he would have pronounced me ready for the next job at that point. Unlike him, Joao gives a shit about me, and he refuses to let me get up.

"It needs more time," he says stubbornly. "Besides, Mathilde isn't ready with our passports."

We have a phone now that Joao bought on his supply run, but it's only for emergencies. We don't use it; we don't even turn it on. The moment we do, the outside world will intrude, and neither of us wants that.

But whether we want it to happen or not, time still flows inexorably forward. Before I know it, it's time to say goodbye to our farmhouse and meet Joao's Berlin contact at a fast-food restaurant in the border town of Szczecin.

I look around the room I've spent all my time in this last week, at the cracked window and the sooty fireplace.

"I never thought I'd say this, but I'm going to miss this place."

"Is it the mice?" he quips. "Or is it the drafty windows and creaky floors?"

It's you. I'm going to miss our togetherness. Because while we've avoided the topic about why I left all week, it's still there, lurking in the shadows. And the moment we leave the farmhouse, everything that keeps us apart is going to rush back to the fore.

"All of the above," I say lightly, hoisting the handbag Joao bought me over my shoulder. "Shall we?"

I've burned my wig and Ivana's red dress so there's nothing tying us to this place. I'm dressed in a pair of cheap jeans, a black T-shirt, and running shoes. I look like I'm already halfway out the door.

I'm not ready to leave.

If I could, I'd stay here with Joao forever and ignore the outside world, but I can't. Mathilde will be waiting with our passports. And once we cross the border into Berlin, we need to put our plan into action, the trap we've hatched to figure out who's leaking my movements.

And I still have two names on my list. Two people I need to kill to keep my promise to Christopher.

Joao laces his fingers in mine. "We're going to sort this out, little fox. And then we're going to live happily ever after. Okay?"

Happily ever after. The words send a poignant longing through me. If only it were as easy as he makes it sound.

When Joao finds out why I ran, his heart is going to break.

I've spent the last week with him under false pretenses, but it's time to tell him the truth.

It's time for me to tell Joao about his dead son.

32

JOAO

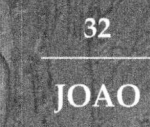

We ditch the car on the outskirts of Szczecin and catch a bus into town. I've arranged to meet Matilde at a low-budget pizzeria located behind the main square.

I met the German woman on my last job for Henrik. I'd been sent to kill Mojiz Qamari, a French-Moroccan gunrunner who lived in Marseilles. Qamari was a piece of crap, and under normal circumstances, I would have had no qualms about taking him out. But it was just six months after Stefi's death, and I was still reeling. I walked into the job, a hollow shell of a man, truly uncaring if I lived or died.

Mathilde was a hacker embedded in Qamari's organization to spy on his dealings. I don't know who she really worked for. I didn't ask her, and she didn't volunteer that information. But she saw I was walking into my death, and she helped me get out.

I have no reason not to trust her. But after the events of the last week, I'm not taking anything or anyone on faith, so we arrive at the pizzeria three hours early and stake out the place, watching for any signs that she's sold us out.

There aren't any. The hacker arrives alone, as promised, a little after two in the afternoon. Once I'm satisfied that she hasn't been followed, we head inside.

My wife stops just inside the first set of double doors. "When we get inside, I'm going to the washroom," she says. "Flush toilets and running water are luxuries I'm never going to take for granted again. You go ahead and meet your friend."

I frown. Stefi's body language is telegraphing that she wants to be anywhere but here. "What's going on?"

"It's nothing," she says, but she doesn't meet my gaze, and I know she's lying. "I just want to clean up."

"Tell me."

She runs her hand through her hair, making it stand up in adorably messy spikes. "It's just. . ." Her voice trails off. "After what I did to you, every single one of your friends has good reason to hate me. I don't know if I'm ready—"

"Listen to me." I take her hands in mine. "I can't promise my friends will love you. But it doesn't matter. You and me, we're a team. We'll be a team always and forever. Nobody—not the padrino and not my friends—will come between us. I promise you that."

"You don't know why I left."

"I know *you*. And that's enough for me." I tug her forward. "Now, come on. Don't tell me you're afraid of meeting Mathilde. The Stefi I knew didn't run from a fight."

Her chin lifts in the air. "I know what you're doing," she says. "You think if you dare me, I'm going to do whatever you want."

I grin as I push open the inner door, and she steps inside with me. "And yet, despite how obvious my actions are, you're coming inside."

Mathilde is sitting at a table in the middle of the room, engrossed in something on her phone. She looks up when we enter and jumps to her feet, a smile breaking out on her face. "Look at you," she marvels. "Still alive after all these years." She turns to Stefi. "And you must be Stefania. Joao was pretty broken up about you. I'm glad you're not actually dead."

Stefi smiles nervously. "Thank you for helping us."

"Of course." She sits back down and pushes a large envelope toward me. "I can't stay long—a friend is picking me up in ten minutes. But this should have everything you need. Car keys are inside as well. I figured you wouldn't want to cross the border in a stolen vehicle."

"Thank you. I really appreciate this."

"It's not a problem. I had to work in a rush, but the passports should stand up to a fair bit of scrutiny. Still, I recommend a land crossing. Take the A6. There's a checkpoint there, but Poland is part of the EU, so security is pretty lax."

"Got it."

"Good luck," she replies, and then, before I have a chance to thank her again, she shakes our hands and is out of there like a whirlwind.

The instant she leaves, a teenage server rushes over. "Where's the woman who was here?" he demands. "She ordered an extra-large pizza with all the toppings. The kitchen is almost done making it. Did she really take off without paying?"

I start to laugh. This isn't the first time that Mathilde has been too distracted to eat. "It's okay," I tell the outraged kid. "She's a friend, and the pizza is for us. But could we get it to go? We're in a hurry."

Stefi waits for the teenager to leave before raising her eyebrow at me. "We are?"

"Yes," I reply. "I'm going to celebrate our new passports by checking into a nice hotel for the night. Someplace with heat, hot water, and flush toilets. What do you think?"

I have good reason to linger in this town. Mathilde would have just crossed the border in the car she left us. If we try to head to Germany immediately, it might set off some kind of security flag. Better to pretend to be tourists coming to Poland from Berlin for an overnight trip. Szczecin sees plenty of those, and we won't stand out at all.

But that's not the only reason for me to delay. I've spent a week alone with Stefi, and I'm not ready for our interlude to end.

"It sounds amazing," my wife replies. "You had me at flush toilets."

The Hunter

We splurge on a really nice room in a fancy hotel. Stefi's eyes light up when she takes in the massive bathtub, easily big enough for two people. "Shower first if you need," she says. "As soon as you're done, I intend to soak in this tub all night long."

I can tell she means it. "Got it," I say with a laugh. "Eat the pizza while it's hot. Don't wait for me."

I shower as quickly as I can, scrubbing off a week's worth of dried blood and grime. My shoulder is healing nicely with no sign of infection, thanks to Stefi, who diligently cleaned the wound each day. When I'm done, I wrap a towel around my waist and head into the room, where the pizza is sitting, still uneaten.

"I told you to eat," I grumble. "Now it's going to be cold."

"I wanted to wait for you," she replies. "Also, I know this is going to come as a shock, but I don't always do everything you tell me." She opens the pizza box, and a look of bliss comes over her face. "Oh God, I never thought I'd be so happy to eat a hot meal in my life."

"It would have been hot if you'd eaten it when I told you to," I say pointedly. "It's lukewarm now."

"Whatever," she says with a grin, leaning forward and putting a slice of pizza in front of me. "Dig in."

True to her word, Stef retires to the bathroom shortly after eating, showering quickly before filling the tub with steaming hot water and sliding in with a sigh of complete happiness.

I go through the envelope Mathilde gave me. She came through like a champion. She supplied not just passports but also credit cards made in each of our new fake names. I take advantage by heading to the boutique across the street for a quick shopping expedition. On the way back, I duck into the hotel bar before returning to our room and knocking on the bathroom door.

"Come on in," Stef invites.

I enter. The bathtub is filled to the brim with bubbles, and Stefi is submerged under them. Her face is luminous, a smile on her soft lips, and she's never looked as beautiful to me as she does in that moment. The only part of her body that I can see is her bare shoulders, but that doesn't matter. My cock knows she's naked under those bubbles and reacts accordingly.

As usual, I'm gaping at her like an idiot. "I thought you'd want a drink." I hold up the bottle of champagne and the two flutes I got from the hotel bartender.

Her eyes light up. "You know I'm never going to say no to champagne. What are we celebrating?"

"Surviving." That was always our toast. After every job we did for Henrik, that was what we drank to: the sheer relief of being alive.

Stefi shakes her head. "I'm done surviving," she says. "No more. I want to thrive." She beckons me with two tempting fingers. "Join me. The tub's big enough."

I don't need any more persuasion. I strip and slide in behind her, yelping as soon as the almost scalding water touches my skin. "I should have remembered you like the water at lobster-boil levels of heat."

"Sorry," she giggles. "I should have warned you."

I pop the cork and pour the bubbly into two glasses. "It's going to warm quickly in this room."

The Hunter

"In that case, I better gulp it down," she replies with a laugh. "Hang on, are you trying to get me drunk?"

"Drunk, sober, it doesn't matter." I kiss the curve of her shoulder. "I like every version of you."

She registers my words, and her muscles tense. "Joao," she says in a whisper. She leans back against my chest, her head resting against my uninjured shoulder. "I need to talk to you."

"I'm not going anywhere."

She doesn't reply immediately. Despite what she said about gulping her champagne down, she barely touches it. The silence stretches until she finally speaks, her voice so soft I have to strain to hear her. "I hadn't been feeling well in the run-up to Puerto Vallarta. I thought I had a stomach bug, figured I ate something that disagreed with me, and eventually, it would go away. But it didn't."

I have a sudden, dreadful feeling about this story.

"On the way to Mexico, they served fish on the plane, and I couldn't stand the smell. I threw up in the bathroom. I was sitting next to a woman in her forties, and when I came back from the bathroom, she gave me a sympathetic look and told me she too had terrible morning sickness in her first trimester."

Shock jolts through me.

She plays with the bubbles absently with her pinkie. "I hadn't even considered that I could be pregnant. Why would I? Bach had all the girls on birth control. But when she said that to me, it struck me that maybe it wasn't a stomach bug after all. Maybe I was pregnant with our baby."

I don't say anything—I can't. I'm reeling. My grip

around her waist tightens, and I hold her against me as if the warmth of her body can shield me from the rest of her story.

"My first reaction was denial. How could I be pregnant? I was on a contraceptive. I took the monthly birth control shots without fail. It's not like Bach gave us a choice about that. And then I remembered I got hurt in Lagos. I got shot in my right arm and was grounded in the compound for six weeks, taking some pretty heavy-duty antibiotics to ward off infection." She exhales in a slow breath. "Antibiotics interfere with birth control."

Does that mean I have a child? A daughter or a son out there somewhere? Likely adopted because as heartbreaking as it would have been to give up the baby, Stefi would have known it was the safest thing to do?

I bite my tongue hard enough to draw blood so I don't ask that question. This is Stefi's story, a burden she's had to bear for eight long years. *All by herself.* The least I can do is to let her tell it at her pace without throwing a barrage of questions at her.

"As soon as the plane touched down in Puerto Vallarta, I went in search of a pregnancy test. I bought one from the pharmacy in the airport and huddled in a bathroom in the terminal to take the test. Two lines. I was pregnant."

There's so much pain in her voice. So much heartbreak. It was eight years ago, but the wound hasn't healed. I can hear it in her voice that it's just as raw as ever.

I hug her close to me in a futile attempt to protect her from her grief, my own emotions churning like a tornado.

The Hunter

I've never felt as helpless as I do in that moment. I want to scream. I want to break things. I want to find Henrik Bach and snap every single bone in his body because of what he put my wife through.

"I was still processing the news when the first cartel assassin tried to kill me," she continues. "She almost succeeded. And I was *terrified*. For the first time in my life, I was afraid, not just for myself but for our baby. The odds of me surviving that mission weren't great. I'd been made, and more cartel assassins were on their way. I was only in my first trimester. If I died, our baby would have died too."

She told me she tried to contact me. On the day she told me how she made her escape, I asked her why she didn't call me, and she said she did.

And I didn't answer.

Bile fills my mouth. It doesn't matter that it wasn't my fault—it doesn't matter that I was on a job of my own and couldn't break radio silence. On the day my wife needed me the most, *I wasn't there*.

"I'm so sorry," I whisper. "Stefi, I'm so, so sorry. I should have been there for you."

"No," she says sharply, shifting to face me. "No. You will not blame yourself for this when it wasn't your fault. Don't you dare. That's not why I'm telling you this story." She traces more patterns in the bubbles. "I had less than an hour to make a plan. I couldn't possibly succeed in taking Peng Wu out; he was too well protected. And if I walked off the job, Bach would have killed me. Sure, all my training didn't come cheap, but—"

"But Bach was a fucking psychopath," I finish for her.

She nods. "It was just a week after he killed Michaela," she whispers. "When I closed my eyes, I could still feel her blood on my face. I was scared, so scared. If I walked off the job, Bach would search for me. If I left you a message telling you what happened, you would have immediately taken off to find me, and he would have killed you. I had to make a choice, and that day, there were no good ones. I couldn't stand the thought of our baby dying, and I couldn't bear it if you died either." She takes a deep, shuddering breath. "So, I chose our baby, and I sacrificed us. Our love, our marriage. Our happiness. I knew it would wreck you if I faked my own death, and I did it anyway."

When Stefi loves, she loves deeply and with every fiber of her being. She loved me, and she loved the baby, so she destroyed herself to protect both of us.

"You should have told me."

"If I told you, you would have tried to find me. You could have been killed, shot the way Michaela was. She begged for her life, but Bach had no pity, no mercy. I couldn't risk it. That first six months, I was a wreck. I cried myself to sleep every single night, but I never once wanted to change my mind *because you were still alive.* The price we paid was heavy, but it was worth it."

"It wasn't just your choice to make." I lace my fingers with hers. "If you asked me what I wanted, I would have told you that I would rather die with you than face a world that didn't have you in it. I would make that choice a thousand times over. I would make that choice every day of my life."

She doesn't respond, not right away. When she finally

resumes her story, her voice is very small. "I know you can never forgive me for letting you believe I was dead for eight years, but—"

"But nothing." I kiss the top of her head. "Yes, I wish you hadn't made the decision you did, but that doesn't mean I don't *understand*." My voice is very, very quiet. "I would have made the same choice you did, Stef. I would have done everything I could to protect you. If faking my own death would have meant you got to live, I would have done it in a heartbeat. Forgive you? There's nothing to forgive."

"I don't deserve your love, Joao," she whispers shakily.

She's rarely wrong, but she's wrong about this. "Let me love you anyway."

"You say that now, but the story's not over. You're not asking me what comes next."

I hold her hand and wait for her to continue. "I eventually ended up in Istanbul," she says. "I needed to hole up somewhere while I gave birth, and that was the one place I knew Bach wouldn't come. For some reason, Turkey's always been off-limits."

"It's because he stole a child from the wrong family."

"Oh." Stefi digests that. "That explains it. Anyway, I went to Istanbul. Got a job at a restaurant and lived with the family that owned it. Then, two weeks before my due date, Pavel Dachev found me."

I grow cold. Dachev used to be a bounty hunter in Henrik Bach's organization, similar to Varek Zaworski, but in the last eight years, he's backstabbed his way into becoming Henrik Bach's second-in-command. Zaworski was an asshole, but Dachev made him look like a choir boy.

"I don't know how he tracked me down." Despite the warmth of the water, she shivers. "But he knocked on the door one afternoon. I was expecting a spice delivery, so I opened it without thinking." Her voice is flat now, flat and drained. "We got into a fight. He knocked me down, and I landed badly. I thought he was going to kill me, but before he could, the restaurant owner and his sons heard the commotion and came to help me. Ozel had a weak knee, but he was still ex-military. Special Forces Command. Dachev was forced to run for it. But the fall. . ." She swallows. "I went into labor, but our baby. . ." She shakes her head. "Christopher didn't make it."

I hear the name and pain tips through my heart. Stefi didn't just fantasize about where we'd live and what we'd call our cat. She also had the name of our firstborn picked out. Christopher if it was a boy, and Magali if it was a girl.

"Oh, Stefi," I say, trying to keep the grief out of my voice and failing miserably. All I can do is hold her close. "I'm so sorry, little fox. I should have been there. I should have never stopped looking for you." My heart stops as I realize something even more heartbreaking. "Wait a second. If I'm calculating the timing correctly—"

She nods tightly. "As much as I hated leaving you, at least I was comforted because I knew it was for the baby's sake. That this was the best thing I could do for him. But then, when I lost Christopher..."

"By the time you lost Christopher, I had already faked my own death," I finish. What horrible, star-crossed

The Hunter

timing. This is the part that I don't want to face. The brutally ironic part. If I hadn't pretended to drown in Marseilles, we could have been *together*. I could have been with her all these years.

"I contacted Tommy Power," she says tonelessly. "I pretended to be a potential client, and he told me that you'd drowned. Just like that, I had nothing. My choice was supposed to keep our baby alive and you as well, but it all went painfully wrong because both of you were dead."

There's more. I know there is. "What happened next?"

"I. . . I tried to kill myself," she whispers. "After that, they locked me up in a psych ward."

Tears prick my eyes. Stefi carried all of that alone. I should have been there to comfort her after the loss of our child, and instead, I wasn't around. I hadn't been around in Mexico when she was terrified out of her mind, and I hadn't been there in Turkey when she mourned her baby.

At the same time as my wife was suicidal, when she needed me to love her and support her and be a shoulder for her to cry on, I'd been traveling around the world, trying to *find myself*.

"You're blaming yourself."

"I'm plotting Pavel Dachev's death." It's only half a lie. Dachev doesn't know it, but the moment he touched my wife, he signed his death warrant. I don't care how powerful the Bulgarian is and how untouchable he's supposed to be. I intend to kill him.

"I know you, remember? You might be swearing vengeance, but you're also blaming yourself. I did the same thing—that's why I tried to kill myself. But this isn't your fault, and it isn't mine. When I was recovering in the hospital, I realized something. I found myself in an impossible situation because of Bach and all the people who covered for him, people who enabled him to do what he did. When I got out, I went to the cemetery, and I swore an oath at Christopher's grave. I wouldn't rest until I took out all of Bach's network. And now I have two people left. Antonio Moretti and Pavel Dachev."

I don't have a response to that. For the first time, I have no desire to argue for Antonio's innocence. By this time tomorrow, our trap will be set, and we'll know where the leak is coming from.

And then what?

Stefi's determined not to go to Venice, and I'm just as determined to keep her safe.

We're at an impasse.

Sooner or later, *something's gotta give.*

33

STEFI

There's a dress spread out on the bed when I get out of the bathtub. It's a simple sheath, emerald-green in color, with just enough ruching at the waist to be flattering.

I swirl around to stare at Joao. "You bought me a dress? When? Why?"

He shrugs his shoulders, as if it's no big deal. "I made us dinner reservations," he says. "I figured you'd want something to wear that isn't the same pair of jeans you've been wearing for a week in a row. There's a boutique across the street, and the dress was in their window. I took a guess on the size."

"You made a dinner reservation?" I repeat like an idiot. Beautiful dress, nice restaurant—this feels a lot like a date. Anticipation winds through me. I haven't been on a date with Joao in a very long time.

"You've heard of the concept?" he teases. "A couple of glasses of wine, food that isn't stale or out of a can, dessert to finish. What do you think?"

"I love it."

I catch a glimpse of my hair in the mirror and grimace. It's thin and stringy, an indeterminate shade of brown, and it looks like someone was wearing a blindfold when they cut it. It could use some attention from a stylist who knows what they're doing. Who am I kidding? They would have to work overtime to restore this to some semblance of style.

"What time are we eating?"

"Eight. Why?"

I glance at the time and see that it's a little after five. Wow, I was in that bathtub for ages. "I saw a salon downstairs. I thought I might do something about this." I wave a hand in the direction of my hair.

"What's wrong with it?"

Men. "It's a disaster; that's what's wrong with it."

"It looks fine to me." I start to ask him if he's being willfully blind or just insane, but before I can get that thought out, he holds up his hands. "I'm never going to think you look anything but beautiful, but if you want to go to the salon, knock yourself out." He hands me an envelope. "There's ten thousand euros in there."

"How expensive do you think a woman's haircut is?"

He doesn't answer; he's too busy handing me more things. A passport, a phone, a pair of credit cards. "Wow," I say cattily. "Mathilde must really like you."

He grins. "Jealous?"

Absolutely. "Not at all. I'm just wondering if it's safe to trust her."

"You have to trust someone, sometime." He levels a look at me. "For example, you have a bad habit of trying to run away from me. First in Zurich, then in Paris. But instead of putting a pair of handcuffs on you, I'm giving you a passport and the means to escape because I trust you won't disappear on me."

If I think too hard about the way he's trusting me, I'm going to start crying, so I make a joke to tide me over the moment. "A blow to the heart," I say, clutching my chest in mock agony. "This coming from the man who pointed a gun at me less than a month ago and ordered me to strip." I grin and tilt my head to the side. "We keep circling back to handcuffs. I mean, you could try it, but you know I can get out of them."

He laughs out loud. "As you admitted in the farmhouse, not as quickly as me. And now that you mention it, I'm getting some very interesting ideas." He glances meaningfully at the bed. "What do you say, little fox? We do have a few hours before dinner."

I'm about to take him up on his offer when I catch another glimpse of my reflection in the bathroom mirror, and it's horrifying enough that I push down my desire and shake my head. "It's a tempting offer, but I need to fix this disaster." I stand up on tiptoe to kiss him. "What are you going to do while I'm gone?"

"I'll amuse myself," he says. "And before you ask, no, I'm not going to contact anyone in Venice. Not yet. Not until we get to Berlin. I figured I'd finalize the plan details now that I have a laptop."

A spike of anxiety goes through me at his mention of Venice, but I push it aside. I have a date tonight, a date with Joao. I've been promised good food and drink and possibly some fun with handcuffs. It's going to be a perfect evening, and I'm not going to let anything ruin it.

I head to the salon downstairs. The stylist takes a despairing look at my hair and throws his hands up in exaggerated horror. "Who did this to you?" he demands. "This is a crime scene, an offense against humanity, a stain—"

"Can you fix it?" I ask, interrupting him. For all I know, if I let him rant, his diatribe could go on for another five minutes.

"I'm the only person in a three-hundred-kilometer radius who can," he replies arrogantly. "People come to me all the way from Berlin so I can cut their hair." He nudges me toward the shampoo station. "The sooner we get started, the better."

Henri might be dramatic, but he clearly knows what he's doing. An hour and a half later, the dull brown is gone, replaced by a flattering shade of red that's close to my natural color.

"So, what's the occasion?" he asks as he dances around me with a pair of scissors. "What brought you in today?"

"I have a date."

"A first date?"

"No. But it feels like one." For the first time in eight years, I'm free of the guilt, and it's not until I confessed the truth to Joao that I realized how crushing a weight it had been.

Back in Paris, Charlie asked me if I'd dated anyone else in the last eight years, and I said something vaguely

The Hunter

discouraging to stop her from probing further. The truth is, I've never wanted anyone else but Joao.

It makes me nervous to hope for a future with him, but though I try to tell myself I'm being unwise, I hope anyway. There are no more secrets between us. Maybe—just maybe—we can get a fresh start.

Once my hair is done to Henri's satisfaction, he hands me off to Lina, who does my makeup and insists I get a manicure and a pedicure. I've never been this thoroughly pampered in my life. The warmth of the water Lina soaks my feet in, the soothing scents of the creams—it feels indulgent, almost frivolous, and yet I can't deny how much I enjoy it.

If you give up on your mission and go to Venice with Joao, your life could look like this.

It's a quarter to eight by the time I get back to the room. Joao is already dressed and sitting on the couch, reading something on his computer.

He looks up when I get in.

"Sorry that took longer than I anticipated," I say apologetically. "Give me a minute to change, and we can leave."

"No rush." I'm still in the clothes I wore this morning—jeans, T-shirt, running shoes—but he still gives me a slow once-over, and his eyes turn hungry. "You look good, little fox. Really good. Come here a second, will you?"

There's a very obvious invitation in his eyes. "I know how this works," I reply, resisting it with all of my willpower. "I come over there, we get naked, and we never make it to dinner. And I was promised wine."

Amusement touches the corners of his eyes. He

crooks his fingers, and I start making my way toward him before I realize what I'm doing.

"I have something for you," he says. "Something I've wanted to give you for almost a month now."

He gets to his feet, closes the distance between us, and unhooks the chain around his neck. My eyes widen when I see what hangs from it.

"Show me your hand," he says quietly.

I hold it out. It's shaking. I'm shaking. The expression on Joao's face. . . He looked like this in Copenhagen, when he said 'I do.' "You kept it," I say in a whisper, staring at the ring he's holding, the same thin band of gold he slipped over my ring finger nine years ago when he promised to love me forever. He must have taken it off the assassin's body in Mexico. "You kept it all these years."

"Of course I did." He takes my hand in his, his touch warm, his thumb caressing my palm. "It's been close to my heart, but now it needs to go back where it belongs." His voice is openly possessive. "My ring, on your finger." He stares into my eyes. "Yes?"

My heart is racing, and there's a tightness in my chest. But my answer is very, *very* certain. There's never been anyone I've wanted the way I've wanted Joao. "Yes."

He looks like a warlord claiming his bride when he slides the golden band into place, but his touch is soft, almost reverent. My breath hitches as the cool metal settles against my skin, a stark contrast to the flushed heat running through my body. My chest feels like it might burst from the mix of emotions running through me—love mixed with relief, joy mixed with a very dangerous hope.

The Hunter

"My wife," he growls, his voice rough and possessive. "Mine."

He pulls me into his body and kisses me hungrily, and I respond, standing on tiptoe, clutching his shirt, and kissing him back. We stay that way for a long time, bodies pressed up against each other, and then he pulls back with visible effort. "As much as I want to tear your clothes off you, I promised you a nice meal. Go get dressed." He brushes his thumb over my lower lip. "The sooner we eat, the sooner we can get back to this."

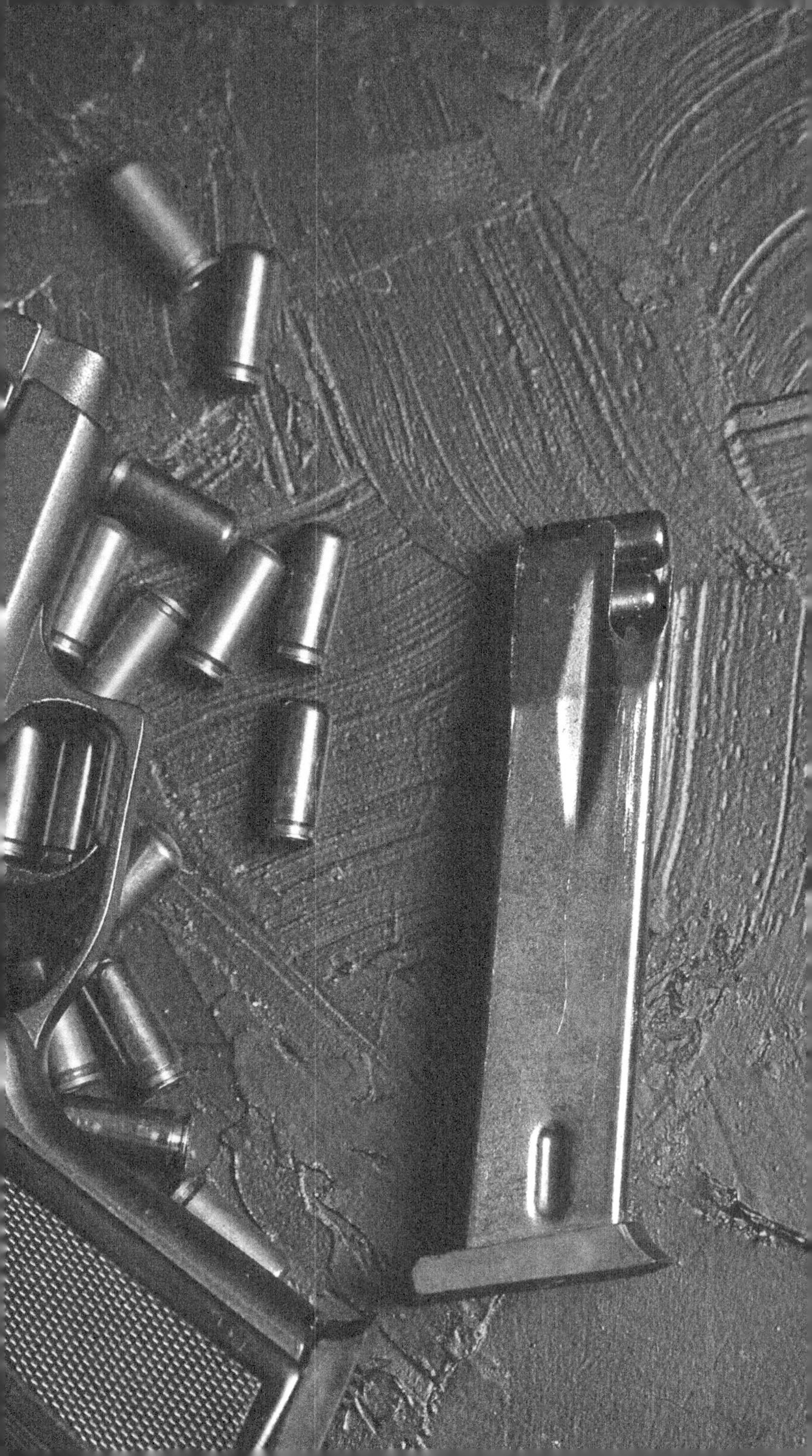

34

JOAO

The restaurant I picked is old-school romantic. Spotless white tablecloths, soft golden lighting dripping from the crystal chandeliers, and pink candles on the tables.

The hostess leads us to a corner table. I pull Stefi's chair out for her, then take my own seat across from her. Stefi waits for the hostess to leave, then raises her eyebrow. "You're sitting with your back to the room," she says. "Not worried about danger? What if someone sneaks up on you?"

I flash her a grin. "There's no danger. My wife's watching the room, and I pity the fool who tries to take her by surprise."

I can't stop looking at her. Her hair has been styled into bouncy curls, she's done something with her eyes that makes them look larger and more luminous, and her lips are painted a soft pink, the precise color of her nipples.

A smile touches her lips. "You're flattering me."

"I'm not. You've always been better at threat assessment."

"I had to be," she replies. "I wasn't as naturally talented as you, so I had to work ten times harder. It was the only way to survive."

For a moment, I'm speechless. I don't often think about the way we were brought up, but her words are a reminder that we've both fought hard to be alive. And now, against all odds, we're together again. Seeing my ring on her finger sends a rush of warmth through me. I almost can't believe she said yes. After everything she's been through, she still said yes.

My wife. *Mine.*

I look at her face, at those luminous green eyes, and I make myself a promise. This is the second chance I never thought I'd get, and I'm going to do everything in my power to ensure that nothing can come between us. This last week has made me fall in love with my wife all over again. I can't—*won't*—lose her as soon as I've found her.

The waiter arrives with menus, pulling me out of my thoughts. "Do you want some wine?" I ask Stefi. "I looked up their wine list when I made the reservation. It's a pretty decent selection."

"You choose. I'm not picky."

"White or red?"

"White, please."

I order a Reisling from a local winery whose name I recognize. The waiter nods and disappears. "Are you a wine expert now?" Stefi asks curiously.

"Not an expert, no. But Antonio owns multiple wineries, and we also smuggle wine. I've learned enough to be able to detect the obvious fakes."

Her lips tighten at the mention of Antonio. The waiter arrives before she can say anything, pours the wine into our glasses, and takes our food order. Once he's gone, I lift my glass to Stef. "A toast. Not to surviving but to thriving."

"You remembered what I said."

"How could I not?" I look around the room. "In all the time we've been together, we've never once done this. Gone on a proper date, sat in a nice restaurant, spent hours together without looking over our shoulders."

"You have, though," she says, not meeting my eyes. "Before you found out I was still alive, you had a stable life in Venice. You had all this, right?"

"Define 'all this.'"

"You know," she says. "Nice restaurants, fancy meals, dinner dates."

"You think I dated?" I shoot her an incredulous look. "There were no other women. You're the only one for me, Stef. It's always been you."

Her head snaps up. "No," she says, sounding almost angry. "No. I was *dead,* Joao. You didn't promise me monogamy from beyond the grave. I didn't want that; I never wanted that. You were supposed to move on. You were supposed to forget me and find love with someone else. That was the deal. That was the only reason I was able to walk away from you."

My brows furrow. "It wasn't a deal I agreed to," I

respond. "It's not as if you consulted me on what I thought about the matter."

Am I angry with her choices? A little bit, yes. She was making the best decision she could, and in her shoes, I would have done the same thing, but that doesn't stop me from wanting to rage at the life that was stolen from us. I'm angry we never got to linger over romantic meals. I'm angry we never had the wedding she wanted, and I'm angry I never got to hold my son in my arms.

I take a deep breath, unclench my fists, and force myself to take a sip of wine. "I knew you'd want me to find happiness with someone else," I say quietly. "And I would have, *as soon as I stopped mourning you.* The instant I could think of you without feeling like I was going to drown from the pain of your loss, I was going to date again." The wine is cold and tart in my mouth. "It just never happened. Every time I thought about you, every time I was forced to face the fact that I'd never see you again, it felt like I was being flayed alive."

I stare into her green eyes, as familiar to me as my own. "It didn't matter that you were dead, Stef. How could I be with another woman when all I could think about was you? You're the only woman I've ever wanted."

"*Eight years,* Joao," she whispers. "You waited eight years."

I reach across the table and link my fingers in hers. "I would have waited eighty."

She looks like she's about to cry, so I change the subject to distract her. My wife hates being vulnerable in public. "What about you?" I ask. "Did you date anyone?"

The Hunter

She shakes her head. "You know I didn't. *I couldn't.* You were always there. And maybe I could have tried to forget you by deadening my senses with alcohol and picking someone up at a bar, but why would I do that? You've always been the best thing in my life. As much as it hurt to remember you, you were the one person I never wanted to forget."

I swallow hard. "We're a pair of fools, aren't we?" I reach across the table and link my fingers with hers. "You pushed me away to protect me, and I would do the same thing. But maybe we don't have to. Maybe we should try making these decisions together."

"Would you?" she asks me quietly. "Could you? If we find out that the leak is on my end, you're going to do everything in your power to get me to Venice, aren't you? It doesn't matter that Antonio Moretti funded Bach's sick, twisted business for five years. As long as he promises to protect me, it doesn't matter to you what else he did." She stares at me with challenging eyes. "Tell me I'm wrong. Promise me you won't force me to come with you to Venice."

I've been thinking about this all week, and I know what my answer is going to be. "That's not a promise I can make."

Her face falls, and I feel like a complete asshole for disappointing her. But it's better to tell her a truth she hates than a convenient lie.

Someone is after my wife. Someone sent a team to Zurich to take her out, and that same person sent armed men into Zaworski's party to find her, willing to risk the wrath of some very dangerous and powerful people.

And when it comes down to it, I'd ally myself with the devil himself to keep her safe.

Even if Stefi will never forgive me for it.

Even if it crushes our marriage into the ground.

Even if it destroys the second chance I never expected to have.

35

STEFI

For the rest of the meal, we talk about lighter things. I ask Joao about his life in Venice, and he delights me by telling me he has a cat. "I found her cowering outside my door a couple of years ago, and I started feeding her." He grins. "She moved in a couple of months later. Her name is Mimi."

"Mimi?" A smile breaks out on my face. "That's what we were going to call our cat."

"I remember, little fox. I remember all our plans. Why do you think I ended up in Venice?"

My heart constricts painfully. "Because of me?"

He nods. "You always wanted to live there. I even bought a house near the water because that was your dream."

A lump rises in my throat. Even when Joao thought I was gone, he still found a way to hold on to me, to stay connected to the life we dreamed of building together. I've always been there with him, and that realization is both beautiful and incredibly painful.

Because the universe has a sick and twisted sense of humor. Venice might be the city I've always dreamed of living in, but Antonio Moretti runs it.

I don't tell Joao what I'm thinking because I don't want to ruin our nice dinner by having the same discussion over and over again. Joao trusts Moretti, and I don't, and neither of us is going to change our minds without overwhelming proof.

"You bought a house?" I ask, hungry for every detail about his life. "Tell me about it."

"I bought it three years ago," he replies. "It's in Giudecca. An old palazzo came up for sale, and a bunch of us got together, bought it, and converted it to row homes."

"When you say a bunch of us..."

"Tomas, Daniel, Goran, Matteo, and Paulina," he says. "We all work for Antonio." Amusement touches his eyes. "It's a good thing I like my coworkers because they're also my neighbors."

I suppress the urge to ask him who Paulina is; my attention is caught by a more familiar name. "Tomas is Alina's boyfriend, isn't he?"

"Fiancé now."

A shadow passes over his face when he mentions Tomas. I can guess what caused it. Me. After my attempt at abducting Alina, I can't be popular among his friends. "Does he know you've been looking for me?"

He nods. "He knows."

"And?"

"And what?"

He's being evasive. "And what does he think?"

"It doesn't matter."

"He hates me, doesn't he?"

"It doesn't matter," he repeats stubbornly. "I don't need Tomas's approval, or that of any of my other friends. They will be polite to you, or else."

I stare at him unhappily before turning my attention to my food. I hate this. As much as he'll deny it, I'm a bomb tossed in the middle of Joao's peaceful life. I'm already making him choose between his boss and me, and now I'm going to be the person who comes between him and his friends.

The food is delicious, and it's warm in the restaurant. Tonight, when I fall asleep, it'll be on a comfortable mattress. If I'm cold, I can turn up the heat. If I need to clean myself, I can hop into the shower stall, open a tap, and get hot water on demand.

Despite all of that, I want, more than anything, to be transported back to our farmhouse. Where it was just Joao and me, and the outside world couldn't intrude.

We're going to set our trap tomorrow. In less than forty-eight hours, we'll know where the leak is coming from. And I can't shake the premonition that our time together will soon be coming to an end.

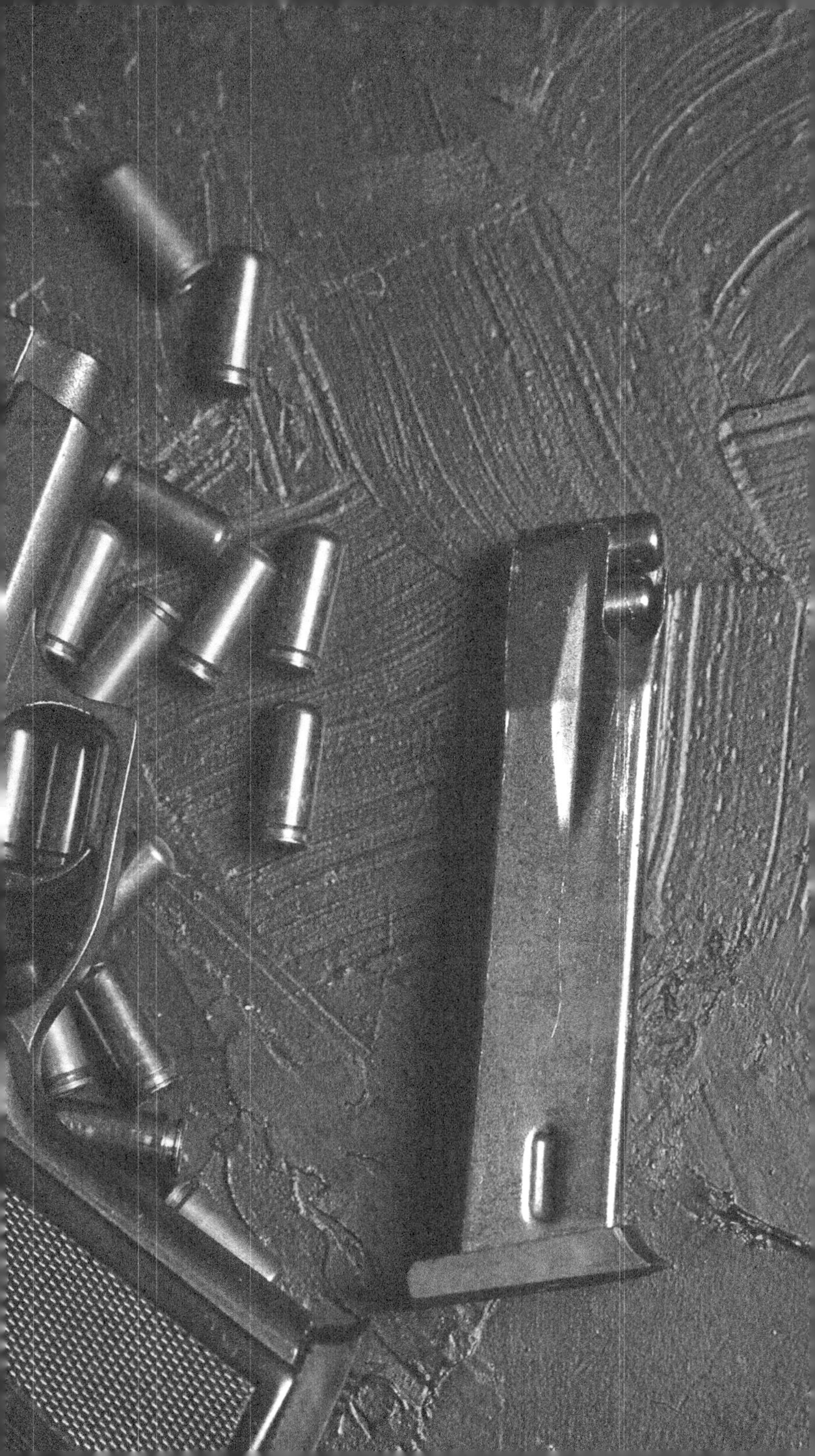

36

JOAO

Stefi wants to visit a nightclub after dinner. "Let's go dancing," she says when we finish our meal, her eyes too bright and her voice filled with false cheer. "I want to do all the things we never got to do."

The conversation about my friends upset her, but I don't understand why it matters so much. Doesn't she know that I don't care? She's my everything—I will *always* choose her.

But if my wife wants to dance to Polish pop, then that's what we're going to do, because I would happily give her everything she desires and more.

The nightclub options in Szczecin are not extensive. There are two choices, and we take a cab to the noisier and more crowded one. Once we arrive, we pay our cover and head inside.

Not going to lie; I'm a little grumpy about the crowded venue. I'm reasonably certain nobody knows we're here, but even so, masses of people are always risky.

Someone could walk right up to us and shoot, and we wouldn't even realize it until it was too late.

But one look at Stefi's face, and I know she's done with threat assessment. If I'm being honest, so am I. It's hard to be on high alert all the time. It's no way to live.

I brave the crowds and get both of us beers from the bar, then let her drag me onto the dance floor, doing my best to look cheerful about it.

Stefi puts her arms around my neck, her body pressed tight against mine. "Guess what?" she whispers. "I'm not wearing any panties."

Looks like the music is putting her in a better mood. That's good—I hate seeing Stefi upset. I know from experience that she'll talk only when she's ready to, so rather than push the conversation back to Venice, I follow her lead. "Tsk, tsk," I say sternly into her ear, fighting back a smile. "Is that any way to behave, Signora Carvalho?"

She gives me a startled look. "Signora Carvalho," she says, testing the name out on her lips. "I like it." Her smile widens, and she winks at me. "I'm a bad girl. What are you going to do about it?"

A young guy who's had too much to drink starts grinding into my wife from behind. I stare at him, murder in my eyes. "Try that again, and I'll kill you," I tell him flatly.

No matter how drunk you are, there's a lizard part of your brain that tells you you're in mortal danger. The guy looks at me, knows I mean every word, and hastily beats a retreat.

Stefi just chuckles. "Jealous?" she teases.

"I'm trying to decide if breaking his arms and legs is worth the hassle."

She laughs again. "Forget him," she breathes into my ear. "I don't want to spend the night in a Polish prison. We have better things to do."

We do indeed.

I look around and realize that nobody's watching us. A group of young women wearing identical tight pink T-shirts and short skirts have just entered the club, hooting and hollering and laughing loudly, and all eyes are immediately on them. It's a bridal shower, from the looks of it, and judging by how unsteady some of the women are on their feet, this isn't their first stop.

I take advantage of the crowd's distraction to glide my hand under Stefi's dress and feel her bare cunt against my fingers.

Her eyes go wide, and she sucks in a breath from the sudden touch.

But she doesn't pull away.

"So wet." My voice comes out in a low growl. "Such a bad girl, going out without panties." I pet her clit, and she clamps down on my finger, and fuck me, that's hot. I steer her to one side so she's up against a wall and shield her from view with my body. Then I hold up my bottle of beer. "I'm not a fan of the lager."

"Umm, okay?" She has no idea where I'm going with this, but from the sparkle in her eyes, she's okay with being surprised.

"It doesn't have any taste." I take her wrists firmly in my hand and pin them above her head, then slide the bottle up her skirt and slowly ease the neck inside her slick cunt. I pull it out and take a long drink, the heady taste of her mingling with the cheap beer. "Much better."

"Joao," she exhales, half-shocked, half-turned on.

"Yes, Stefi?" I slide the bottle in again, pull it out, and have another drink. "Is something the matter?"

Her eyes start to glaze over, and then she shakes her head. "No," she protests. "This isn't fair." She looks around the room. The bride-to-be is doing shots off some guy's abs, and everyone is riveted by the spectacle. Something tells me this isn't a daily occurrence in Szczecin. "You already made me come in a crowded room in Warsaw. It's my turn to return the favor."

I'm about to ask her what she has in mind when she unzips my trousers and reaches for my cock. Predictably, it's hard and ready for her. She strokes up and down my length once or twice, then, before I even have a chance to process what she's doing, she drops to her knees right there, wraps her pretty pink lips around my cock, and takes me into her mouth.

Fuck.

I think I've died and gone to heaven. I can't see the club entrance, and I don't care. Neither of us is watching the crowd for threats, and it doesn't matter.

She takes me deep, her cheeks hollowing out, and her tongue sliding around my length, and my knees almost buckle it's so good. Pleasure jolts up my spine. "Stef," I groan, sliding my fingers through her curls. "You're killing me here."

She looks up at me with a smile in her eyes, then takes me in deeper, licking the underside of my cock from the base to the head. I think I'm going to lose my mind.

The Hunter

She sucks me deep, completely focused on my pleasure, her head bobbing on my length, her curls dancing.

The squeeze of her mouth is perfection.

My grip on her hair tightens, my vision starts to blur. My head falls back, and my hips thrust forward. It doesn't take long for my balls to tighten. "I'm going to come," I growl, gripping her shoulders to warn her. Her vivid green eyes sparkle even more, and she takes me deeper down her throat, and that's all it takes. I erupt into her mouth.

She swallows every drop, then gracefully rises to her feet and holds her hand out for my beer.

My head still swimming from my climax, I hand the bottle to her, tuck my cock away, and zip up. She drains the rest of the contents, then she winks. "You're right about the beer. It *is* pretty tasteless." She gives me a cheeky grin. "Want to get out of here?"

"I thought you'd never ask."

ON THE WAY back to our hotel, we pass a sex store.

I don't know why I'm surprised. Even in the age of the Internet, every tourist town probably has a sex store tucked away in a side street. This one looks nicer than most. The window is brightly lit and decorated for the holidays. Dildos in shades of red and green are strewn around a male mannequin, who's dressed in a Santa hat, a leopard print thong, and nothing else.

Stefi starts to giggle. "You should buy it," she says through her laughter. "I would pay serious money to see you in a thong."

I change directions and walk toward the shop door.

Stefi's eyes go wide. "Seriously?" she asks in delight. "You're going to buy it?"

I open the door and beckon for her to enter. "Sorry, little fox. I would do anything for you, but I draw the line at a thong that looks as thin as dental floss. We're here for handcuffs." We head inside, and I direct her to the rear of the store, past the neon pink fur cuffs and the leather restraints to the basic steel variety. "I thought we'd play a game. Wanna see who can get out of them first?"

Stef could never say no to a challenge. "What do I get if I win?"

"I'll go down on you. But if you lose—"

"I'll have to go down on you? So basically, win-win?" Her teeth flash in a grin. "You're on."

We pay for our handcuffs, then head back to the hotel. She wriggles out of her dress, and I suck in a breath and reach for her, blindsided as always by how beautiful she is. I kiss her deeply, my pulse racing, then push her back on the bed and feast on her.

It takes us a while to get to the handcuffs, but we eventually take them out of the shopping bag. I pull her hands behind her back and put the cuffs on, kissing her neck and her shoulders as I do. Then I get mine on. "Ready?"

Stefi's eyes are bright with anticipation. "Ready," she responds. "Let's do this."

Eight years ago, I was faster than her at getting free.

The Hunter

Tonight, she wins easily, getting out of her handcuffs a full minute before I do. I'd like to blame the fact that she's naked, but that's just an excuse. She's just better than me. She's spent the last eight years on the run, and it's honed her skills into a blade. While I'm struggling to get out of the restraints, she slides her hand down her stomach to her cunt and slips a finger inside.

"Don't mind me," she says innocently. "I'll just entertain myself while I wait for you to break free."

Watching her touch herself does not help. She strokes two fingers down her slit and then places them on my lips. I forget all about getting free and suck them into my mouth, my cock jerking at her taste, my brain turning into mush.

"No, no," she chides, laughter in her eyes. "This won't do. What if you're in danger and need to get out of your restraints?"

"I'll sit back and wait for you to rescue me." I twist my wrists, and the cuffs release with a click, and then I pounce on her, sweeping her into my arms and tossing her onto the mattress. "Now, I believe I have a forfeit to pay." I spread her legs hungrily. "And Stef, I always pay my debts."

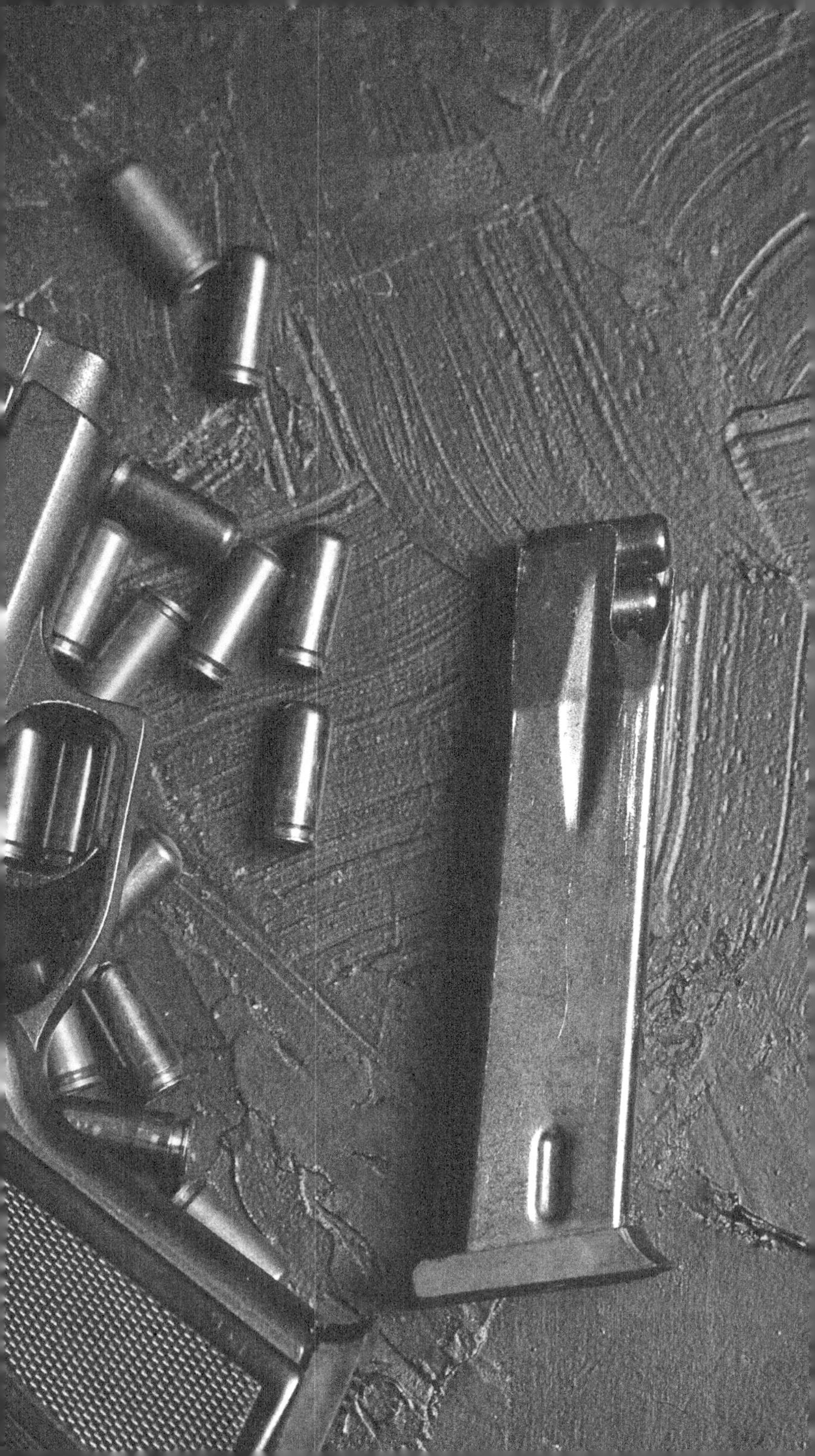

37

JOAO

The next morning, we check out of our hotel and cross the border into Germany. There's a checkpoint on the A6, as Mathilde predicted, but the officer barely gives our fake passports a glance before waving us through.

We arrive in Berlin by noon. The first thing we do is find a computer store and buy a couple of laptops and a half dozen burner phones. Then we check into a hotel, even though we have no intention of spending the night, and put our plan into action.

I go first. Using one of my burner phones, I dial Daniel's number. It doesn't even ring once before it's picked up, but it's not Daniel's voice that comes through the receiver. It's the padrino himself.

"Joao," he says, sounding relieved beyond measure. "Thank fuck you're alive. We've been frantic with worry."

Why is Antonio picking up Daniel's phone? "You have?"

"Of course we have," he responds. "For fuck's sake, I

thought you were dead. Your phone was out of commission, and your car hasn't been moved all week. Then there are the rumors of gunmen breaking into Zaworski's party, plus all of Poland is on high alert—"

Guilt surges in me at the obvious worry in his voice. I'm not used to anyone except Stefi giving a shit about me. "I'm fine. I needed to lie low for a while."

"So much so you couldn't check in?" he demands. "And where's Stefania? Are you with her? Where are you now?"

Stefi's listening to this conversation with an intent look on her face. When Antonio mentions her name, she stiffens, and I can already predict what she's thinking. She's convinced the padrino wants my location so he can send troops to kill her. I don't agree. To my ears, Antonio sounds genuinely concerned for our safety.

"Yes. We had a little bit of trouble, but we're in Berlin now. I'm bringing her in, but—"

"I can send a plane to pick you up in three hours. Dante and Goran are ready to pull you out."

We predicted he might say that. "Not in Berlin," I reply. I hate the idea of lying to the padrino, but if we're to find out where the leak is coming from, I *need* to stick to our plan. "I might have picked up a tail, and I need to lose them first. Can Dante and Goran meet us in Nuremberg?"

"Sure. What address?"

Stefi and I thought long and hard about our plan. The obvious trap was to give each side a different location as bait, stake out those spots, and see who bit. But there was one crucial flaw with that approach; we would have to be separated, each one of us monitoring a different spot, and I flat-out refused to let her out of my sight.

So instead, we picked two locations in the same suburban shopping center on the outskirts of Nuremberg. One is a coffee shop, and the other is a Thai restaurant. There's a parking lot across the street where we can stake out both establishments. It's not ideal—we chose the shopping center by looking at a map online instead of doing an in-person recon—but it'll have to do.

I reel off the address of the coffee shop. "Got it," Antonio replies. "When?"

"Tomorrow. Eleven in the morning."

"Dante and Goran will be there." He exhales in a long breath. "See you tomorrow, Joao. Until then, do me a favor and stay safe. I would hate to lose you."

He hangs up, and I stare at Stefi, who's biting her lip and looking as conflicted as I feel. "One down, one to go."

The padrino sounded almost frantic with worry. He must be to send his second-in-command, Dante, to pull me out. I've been in Venice for five years, and I'm still not used to the idea of someone caring about me. To Henrik, we were tools to be used until we broke and carelessly discarded when we were no longer functional.

But Antonio's never been that way. He values each and every member of his organization. I'm pretty sure his concern was real.

And if it's not...

I guess we'll find out in Nuremberg.

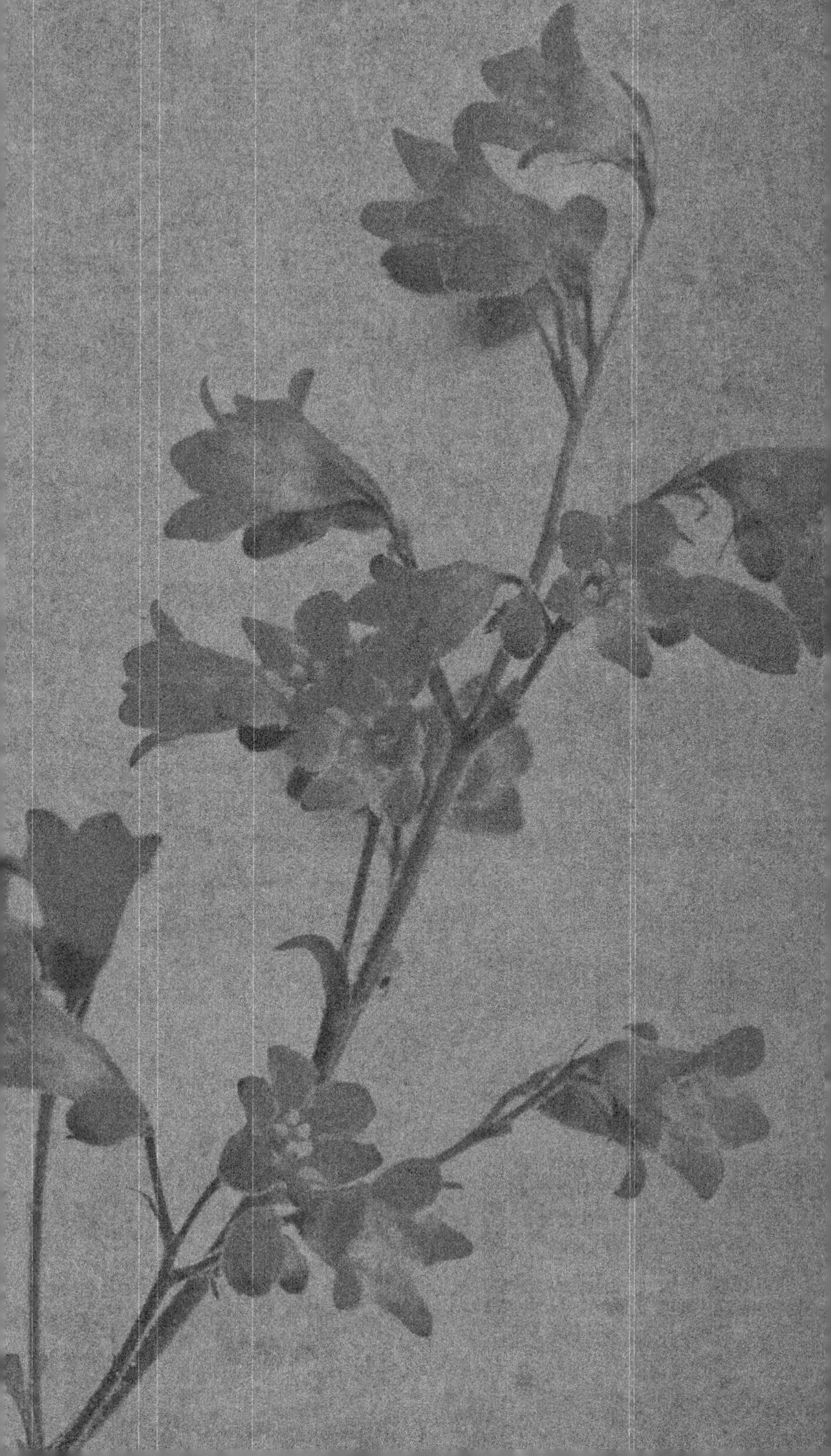

38

STEFI

Once Joao is done talking to Moretti, I message Q. "He might not reply right away," I warn Joao. "It often takes him a day or two to get back to me."

"Oh, I have a hunch you'll hear from him much sooner than that."

I glare at Joao. He's absolutely convinced that Q has sold me out, and increasingly, I'm starting to suspect the same thing. Joao has really good instincts, and it would be foolish to ignore him.

"It doesn't make sense," I say, repeating an argument we've had many, many times in the last week. "Without Q's intel, I wouldn't have been able to take out half the people I did."

"You don't know who Q is," he says. "You don't know their motivations."

"I have my theories."

"Yes, that Q is one of Bach's assassins. Even if that were true, that doesn't mean they wouldn't sell you out."

The laptop beeps, cutting off our discussion. My heart sinks. As Joao predicted, I have a reply from Q.

> Q
>
> Congratulations on taking out Zaworski.
> Did you manage to get out of Warsaw?

> I did. I've been laying low in Nuremberg.

> Germany? No problems crossing the border then?

Q's never been the type to offer congratulations, and they've never once wanted to know where I was. I silently curse Joao. He's made me ultra-suspicious, ultra-vigilant. For all I know, Q's just making conversation, and I'm being paranoid about nothing.

> None I couldn't handle.

> Who's next on the list?

> Pavel Dachev.

> The Butcher of Bulgaria? I can help you with that. He spends most of his time in Sofia. His estate is supposed to be impregnable, but there's always a way in.

> How much will it cost me?

> Fifty.

I miss the days when Q's usual rate was ten or twenty thousand.

The Hunter

I glance at Joao. "If he really knows how to get to Dachev—"

"Set the trap," he says implacably.

I make a face, but he's right.

> Fifty is fine. But my computer was hacked, and I don't know who did it. Could you put the info on a USB key and mail it to me?

Q seems confused.

> Mail? Physical mail?

> Yes. Can you send it to this location in Nuremberg? It's a Thai restaurant. I'll be there at eleven tomorrow to pick it up.

> Yeah, okay. I can do that.

I log off and stare at Joao. The trap's set. Now, we just have to wait and watch to see who takes the bait.

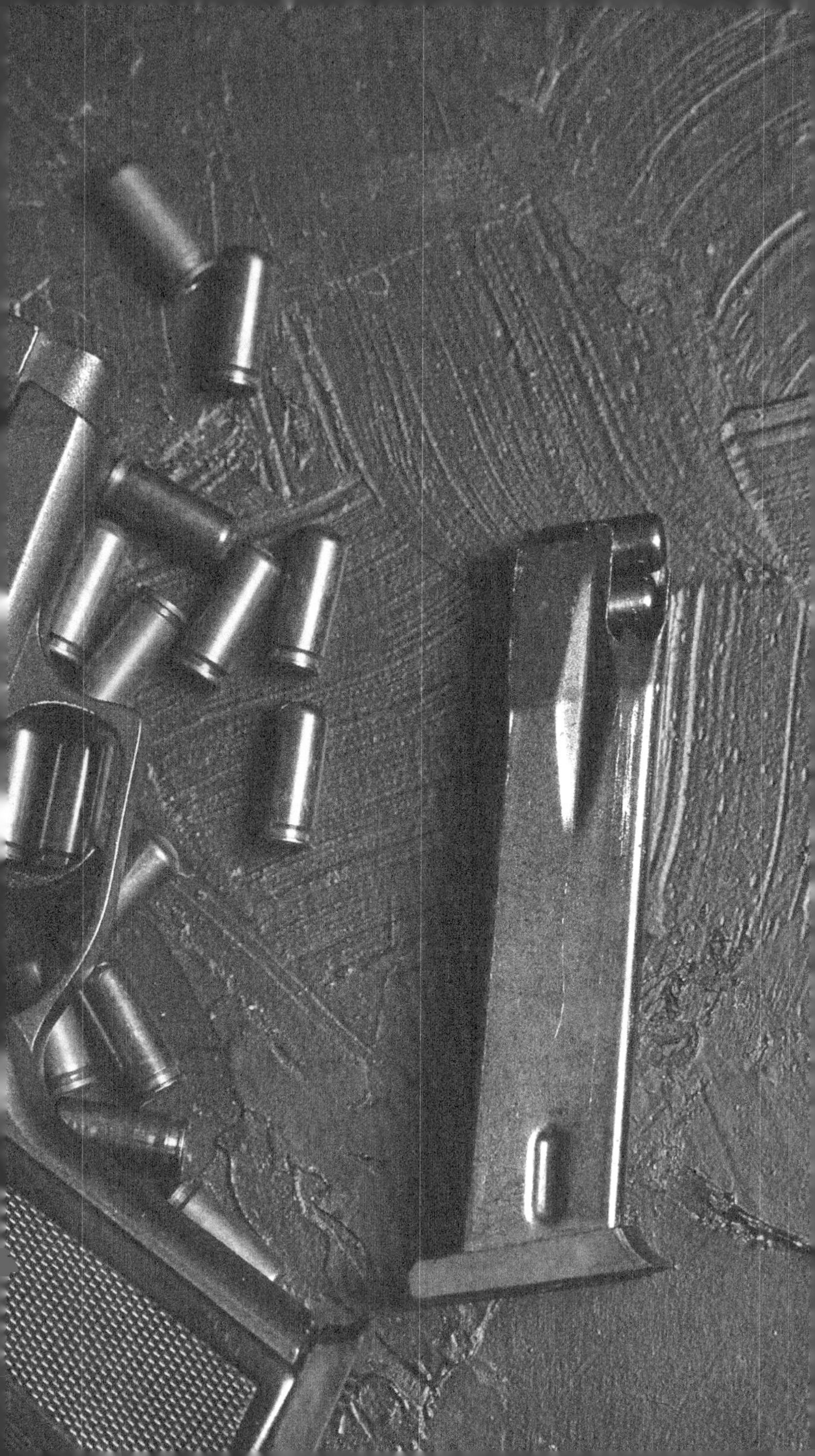

39

JOAO

After we set our trap, we make the five-hour drive to Nuremberg and stay busy with logistics for the rest of the evening. We rent a windowless van and replace the rental company logo with that of a local construction company. The same company is repaving the sidewalks in the neighborhood, so nobody will give our parked vehicle a second glance. I wear a reflector vest and a hard hat and plant our surveillance cameras in the parking lot across the street during the day, and such is the magic of my makeshift uniform that nobody pays us any attention. While I'm doing that, Stefi buys half a dozen monitors so we can watch the camera feeds.

As we set everything up, I have a newfound appreciation for my wife. I've never had to do this kind of boring operational setup on my own. I went from Bach's organization to Antonio's, so someone always gave me the intel I needed for a job. I always had easy access to cars, passports, money and weapons—everything I needed to complete my mission.

Not Stefi. She had to do it all on her own. And despite having none of the support I take for granted, in seven years, she's managed to wipe out almost all of Bach's network. My wife is a force of nature, and anyone who underestimates her does so at their own peril.

"I'm starting to realize why you don't want to hear about Q's betrayal," I say out loud that night when the two of us are finally in bed. Our hotel in Nuremberg isn't nearly as nice as the one in Szczecin, but the bed is comfortable enough, and let's be honest, I'll take up permanent residence in a pest-infested farmhouse if it means that Stefi's there with me. "For seven years, they were the only team member you had, the only person in your corner. It's got to hurt to realize they sold you out."

"Don't get ahead of yourself," she replies, propping herself up on one elbow. My cock hardens instantly. Stefi sleeps naked, and though we've slept together for the last nine days, my cock still hasn't adjusted. "We have no proof it's Q."

"We will."

"So cocky." Her gaze falls to my rapidly hardening erection. "In more ways than one."

"That is an awful pun," I tell her sternly. "It's so bad that you should be punished."

She bats her eyelashes at me. "Are you going to put me over your knees and spank me?"

My throat goes dry at the thought of Stefi naked and wriggling on my lap. "If you'd like."

"You can spank me," she replies, "if you can pin me down. Deal?"

I lunge toward her, but she's already slipped away. Fuck, she's fast. I get to my feet, and she watches me from across the bed, her eyes laughing.

"You didn't say deal," she accuses through her giggles. "You have to say it before we start."

"I cheated. What are you going to do about it?" I crook a finger at her. "Come here."

"If you want me, you're going to have to catch me."

"Deal," I say, lunging forward again. I catch her, of course. It's not a fair fight—she's laughing too hard to be able to dodge out of the way. I spank her and lick her pussy until she's breathless, then the two of us collapse on the bed, still laughing.

This could be my life, I think. Me and Stefi, together forever.

But even as I say it, I cross my fingers. Imagining a future filled with love and laughter feels like I'm tempting fate.

And that feels like a very foolish thing to do.

We didn't want to park the van directly across the street from the plaza—it was too risky. Thankfully, there's another parking lot on a parallel street, so we're using that one for the stakeout.

The next morning, we arrive at dawn, park the van

near the exit so we have a fast way out, and turn on the monitors. Six camera feeds fill the screens, four from the front of both the Thai restaurant and the coffee shop and two from the parking lot we're in.

And then we wait.

An hour goes by, and then another. The coffee shop does a steady stream of business in the morning, serving impatient people who need caffeine to face their workday. At the Thai restaurant, a van arrives, and a woman in a white apron unloads trays of produce before signing for the delivery.

Stefi and I drink hot coffee out of a thermos and ignore our grumbling stomachs. We've both done this kind of boring surveillance, but never together. It's nice to share this experience with her. "Is it weird that I'm enjoying this?"

"I'm enjoying it too," she admits. "Normal people enjoy wine tastings and picnics in the park, while you and I get our kicks from watching a bunch of monitors for hours on end."

"Normal is overrated." Her words make me realize something. Stefi fantasized about our house, our cat, and even the names of our children, but I don't remember her ever talking about doing a different job. "Have you ever thought about what you would do if it wasn't for this?"

"All the time."

"And?"

"Is it weird to say I don't care? I just want a job where I earn enough money to live. I want to go for morning runs, spend most of my weekend at a beach, and curl up in a corner and read a good book while drinking a cup of apple tea." She gives me a wry smile. "After everything that's happened, I want the most boring life imaginable."

The Stefi I knew drank coffee, not apple tea. She must have acquired a taste for it in Istanbul.

"I can relate," I reply. "My life is a little bit like that. It's boring, but in a good way."

"You said you didn't do much killing."

"Hardly at all, and I'm happy about it. I'm good at killing people, but I don't like it. In fact, when Antonio offered me this job, I only took it on one condition. If he wanted me to kill someone, he needed to explain why, and I had the right to turn it down. In five years, he's never once broken his end of the deal."

Every time I mention the padrino, she usually has something cutting to say. This time, though, she just looks thoughtful, which gives me hope. Maybe the idea of Venice isn't as poisonous to her as it's been in the past. Maybe she's starting to entertain the idea of hearing Antonio out.

Last night, I thought I was tempting fate by imagining a future with Stefi. Today, in broad daylight, my worries feel very far away, and I'm filled with happy anticipation for our future. Yes, we have some issues to work out—well, one issue—but I'm feeling good about it. We love each other, we want to be together, and we're going to make it happen.

Everything is going to be okay.

She takes another sip of coffee and squirms in her seat. "I need to go to the bathroom."

"Pee into a bottle," I tell her. "Someone could see you if you get out. They have your picture now, remember?"

She gives me an incredulous glance. "Pee into a bottle? Are you nuts? Newsflash: I don't have a penis, so aiming isn't as easy as you're making it sound. Also, I'm not going to pee in front of you. I'd like to retain some sense of mystery."

"Oh, for fuck's sake—"

"There's a fast-food restaurant a block south of here," she continues. "I'll go there."

"Stef..."

"Joao, don't be paranoid. This parking lot is deserted. The only person here is that kid on his skateboard."

I look at the screens and realize she's right. There's no one around except for the lone preteen practicing tricks in the far section of the lot. It's nine forty-five. The breakfast rush is over at the coffee shop, and it's too early for the lunch crowd at the Thai restaurant. Everything is as quiet as it's going to be. "I'll come with you."

"Who'll do the surveillance if you do?" she asks pointedly. "I'll be fine."

She's right; I am being paranoid. "Okay," I say grudgingly. "Go pee."

She gets out, and I monitor her progress on the screen. The kid is wearing headphones and doesn't notice her until she's almost in front of him, and then he promptly wipes out. Stefi helps him out and says something with a smile. I keep my eyes glued to the screen, feeling uneasy and not able to explain why, and it's not until she returns that I'm able to breathe again.

"Here you go." She holds out a sandwich to me. "I thought you could use something to eat. It's ham and cheese."

"Thank you, little fox."

At half past ten, a black SUV pulls up in front of the coffee shop. The driver parks at the side of the road, in flagrant disregard for the No Parking sign, and Dante Colonna, the Venice Mafia second-in-command, and Goran Karaman, one of the enforcers, get out from the back.

I zoom in until I can see the driver, and when I recognize him, a wave of relief goes through me.

"What is it?"

"They're not expecting any trouble," I reply. "If they were, they never would have brought along Ignazio."

"How can you be so sure?"

"Ignazio is nineteen," I reply. "And easily distracted. If you flutter your eyelashes at him, he'll forget the mission. If he sees a stray dog or cat, he'll befriend it and bring it home. Antonio wouldn't put him in a dangerous situation." I exhale in a slow breath and feel a smile break out on my face. "The leak isn't in Venice. I'm sure of it."

Ignazio turns on the four-way flashers and stays in the car. Goran stands outside the coffee shop with a cigarette in his hand, pretending to talk on the phone, while Dante goes inside.

Stefi watches them on the screen. "You think they're armed?"

"Yes. They might not be expecting danger, but that doesn't mean they won't be prepared for it. They'll all be armed, even Ignazio, as unwise as that is."

"Why is that unwise? Is Ignazio not competent?"

"He's *nineteen*."

She smiles. "Not all nineteen-year-olds are clueless,"

she says. "After all, we got married when we were younger than that, and we certainly thought we knew what we were doing."

"Thought being the operative word. What were we thinking? Bach would have killed us if he found out." I give her a wry smile. "Just goes to tell you what a fool I am when it comes to you."

"Do you regret it?"

We should be looking at the screens in front of us, not having this conversation. "Regret it? I'm congratulating the eighteen-year-old version of me for having excellent taste." The memory of who we were at eighteen wraps around me. Maybe we hadn't been reckless, but defiant, choosing each other in a desperate bid to hold onto something good in a life that offered so little of it.

Our baby had been part of that hope. When I think about him, a hollow ache fills my chest. We lost him before he could draw a breath, but he's still part of our story. I glance at her, serious now. "Will you take me to visit Christopher's grave in Istanbul?"

"Of course," she says. "He was your son, too." She lapses into silence and then asks, "You were nineteen, same age as Ignazio. If you found out I was pregnant, how would you have reacted? Would you have wanted to be a father?"

"You were nineteen as well," I reply. "Just as young as I was, and you had to deal with everything on your own." Even thinking about what she must have endured makes me rage. It's a pity Bach's dead because I've thought of at least a dozen ways of making him pay for what he did to her. To us.

"It was our baby, Stef," I continue. "A little piece of you and a little piece of me. Of course I would have wanted him. I probably wasn't ready to be a parent, but it wouldn't have made a difference. I would have loved our baby with all my heart."

I want to ask her if she still wants children, but I don't want to upset her if it's a sore subject, so I hold my tongue and keep my attention on the screens.

Nothing is happening. Dante is still inside the coffee shop, Goran is still pretending to smoke his cigarette, and Ignazio is still ready to get them out of there at a moment's notice. I glance at my phone. It's almost eleven, almost time for Q to make their move.

"What about now?" Stefi asks, after a few minutes of silence. "Do you want children now?"

"I want you. Anything else is a bonus."

"You're avoiding the question."

"No, I'm not. I would love children if you want them. If you don't, then we won't have them."

"Is it really that simple?"

"Yes," I reply, lacing my fingers in hers and brushing my lips over the back of her hand. "It really is. I love you, Stefi. I've tried living without you, and it was garbage. Zero out of ten, do not recommend. I spent eight years feeling like an essential piece of my soul was missing. You were the first person on my side, the only person I could always trust. I found my soulmate when I was ten, Stef. I know how lucky I am, and I never want to let you go."

Before she can react, a car pulls up outside the Thai restaurant. Four men jump out. They're dressed in jeans and thick sweaters, but even though they're trying to blend in, they can't. The way they move gives them away immediately. They're all ex-military.

This is a mercenary unit sent to capture or kill my wife. I push the rage deep down inside. My fury can wait. One day, I will make Q pay, but today, my priority is to get Stefi to safety.

She stares at the screen in shock. "It really was Q," she says in a whisper. "I wish I understood why." She slumps in her seat. "What do we do now?"

Before I can answer, there's a sharp staccato of machine gun fire from the parking lot. A deafening cacophony shatters the quiet, and the van rocks as bullets pound the metal sides.

I dive over her on instinct.

But I'm a second too late.

I watch in horror as a bullet tears into my wife. She stares at me, uncomprehending, as blood spreads from a wound on her left side, then her knees buckle, and she slowly slides to the floor.

The world goes still. Time slows to a viscous crawl. Images flash in front of me like stills from a movie: the monitor that shows the skateboarding kid holding a machine gun in his hands and shooting at us, the vivid red of Stefi's blood, and the strained gasps of her breathing.

Put pressure on the wound, a voice in the back of my head screams. *Stop the bleeding before she dies from the blood loss. Keep oxygen flowing to her brain.*

I take off my shirt and put pressure to her side, desperate to stop the pulsing flow from the vicious wound. I lock my mouth on hers, giving her the air from my lungs, the air that's coming in choking gasps as she struggles to live. My eyes fall on the phone, and I grab it with the ferocity of a drowning man, dialing Dante's phone number. "Help," I shout. "We need help."

"Stefi," I rasp between breaths. Her eyes flutter as she struggles to focus on me, and her lips part, as if she's trying to say something, but no words leave her mouth. "Stay with me, little fox. Please, I beg you." Tears stream down my eyes and blur my vision. "Hold on for me. Just for a little bit. Because I can't make it without you."

I whisper her name over and over. Her anguished face is the only thing I see. Her strained breathing and her weakening heartbeat are the only things I hear. I don't register the machine gun fire dying away, and I don't notice the van door being wrenched open.

And then Dante and Goran are at my side. Dante screams an order, and the next thing I know, the van is moving, being driven at full speed down the road.

But I barely notice what's happening around me.

I can only look at her. My soul mate, *my wife*. Lying in my arms, a pool of blood spreading from the wound on her side.

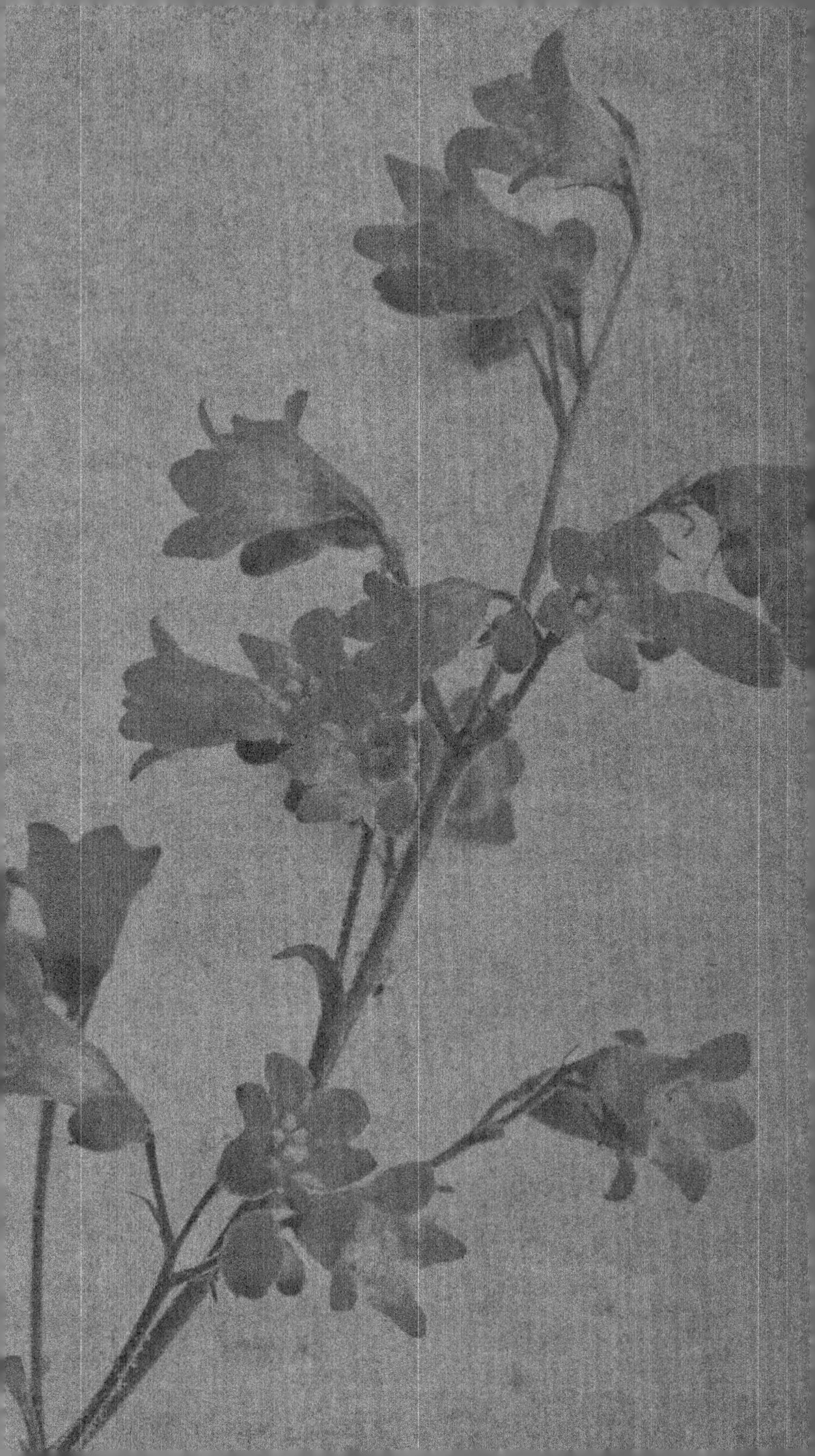

40

STEFI

I wake up, disoriented and groggy, in a room with yellow walls.

My eyes roam around the space. Above my head is a glass chandelier that illuminates the space with soft golden light. Directly across me is a large window, but the white gauze curtains are closed, and I can't see enough of the outside to know where I am.

I try to sit up, and a wave of pain washes over me, and a thin, urgent beeping fills the air. I look down and realize I'm in a hospital bed, surrounded by medical equipment. An IV is stuck in my right arm, and a large gauze bandage covers my midriff.

Bile fills my mouth. The last time I woke up in a hospital, I'd been strapped to the bed. I cried out, and a hard-faced doctor entered the room. "You tried to kill yourself," he told me. "For your own safety, I'm placing you in a psychiatric hold."

But am I in a hospital now? Bed aside, this doesn't

look like any medical facility I've been in. It's too quiet, too peaceful. And it doesn't smell like one.

What happened? I search my memory, trying to remember the chain of events that led me to this unknown place. Joao and I were in the van, watching four mercenaries walk into the Thai restaurant. I think I said something about Q, something about how shocked I was that they sold me out.

And then what? As hard as I try to retrace my steps, I draw a blank.

A tall man dressed in scrubs enters the room. "Oh good, you're awake," he says. "Don't try to get up. You lost a lot of blood, and you've been sedated for the last two days. How are you feeling?"

I might not remember the chain of events that led me here, but I do remember what it feels like to be shot. "Like a bullet ripped through me."

"You have that right," he says. "You were extremely lucky. If you'd reached the emergency clinic ten minutes later, you'd be dead."

I wriggle my toes experimentally, and the doctor notices. "No, you're not paralyzed. Like I said, you were extremely lucky. I've already yelled at Joao, and now it's your turn. The next time you're going to do something dangerous, wear a vest. It won't completely prevent you from dying, but it'll increase the odds that you'll stay alive." He smiles at me to rob the sting from his words. "My name is Matteo Ferrini, by the way. I'm Antonio Moretti's physician."

"Moretti?" Ice drenches my spine, and I try to sit up again. "You're saying I'm in—"

"Venice," Joao says from the door. His gaze locks onto me, and what he sees there must reassure him because he takes a deep, shuddering breath of relief. "You're in my house in Venice."

On some level, I've known ever since I woke up that I'm in Venice. Where else could I be? But my stomach still sinks. Joao knew how I felt about Moretti. How could he bring me here? I want to scream, but even my aborted attempt to get up has left me exhausted. "What happened?"

He comes up to my bed and brushes a strand of hair away from my face, his touch infinitely tender. "What's the last thing you remember?"

"Q betrayed us. I saw the car with the four mercenaries, and then, nothing."

"The kid on the skateboard had a gun in his backpack. He opened fire on us."

"But he was just a ki—" I fall silent. I know better than most that in the hands of the right person, even children can be molded into deadly, lethal weapons.

He nods grimly. "One of Henrik's. Looks like Pavel Dachev's taken over the empire, and he's lost no time putting the kids to work." His expression promises murder. "Dachev made a mistake—he showed his hand too soon. He's going to live just long enough to regret it."

The doctor, Matteo Ferrini, is still in the room, pretending he's not eavesdropping on our conversation. When he introduced himself, I didn't put it together, but I remember now where I've heard his name before. He's one of Joao's neighbors, and like the rest of Joao's friends, he probably hates me.

"When you got hit, I called Dante for help," Joao continues. "They rushed over, and the kid got away. Chasing him wasn't a priority—getting you to a hospital was." He gives me a reassuring smile. "Don't worry; your DNA isn't in the system. Valentina was able to hack into the hospital's network and erase all signs of your presence."

And then, when I was stable enough to travel, they must have loaded me onto a private plane and flown me to Venice.

Venice, the city run by a man who funded Henrik Bach's operation for the last five years. If a young child shot me, it's because Antonio Moretti's money paid for his training.

I feel like crying. Yes, I'm still alive, but at what cost? Everyone is ignoring Moretti's complicity, especially Joao. Although I knew it was going to happen, it still feels like a gut punch.

Like me, Joao grew up in Bach's academy. Is my safety so important that he can ignore the fact that Moretti's millions have probably paid for the abduction of God knows how many children? It's a question I want to throw at him, but there's no point. I already know the answer.

Joao would do anything to keep me safe.

But today, his protectiveness doesn't feel like a warm blanket around my shoulders. It feels suffocating, like the padded walls of the psychiatric facility I was held in.

I avoid looking at my husband. "When can I get up?"

The doctor answers. "I like my patients up and moving as quickly as possible," he says. "But you'll have to take it very easy. For the next week, only three or four ten-minute stretches a day. After that, we'll discuss a rehab program." He gives me a stern look. "The bullet might have missed your major organs, but there was still a lot of tissue damage, and you lost a lot of blood. I'm familiar with your history and the way you were brought up, and it sounds like the doctors who worked on you in the past would have certified that you had recovered after only a week or two. But that's not how I work. This injury will take six weeks of recovery at a minimum."

"I can't—"

Dr. Ferrini continues over my protest. "If it were up to me, I'd keep you in the hospital, but Joao insisted you recover in his house." He turns to my husband. "Infection is a real risk for the next couple of weeks, so keep that cat of yours away from her until the wound heals. And no sex, Joao. Everything that counts as sexual activity is completely off the table until I authorize it. Are we clear?"

Joao stares at the doctor as if he's grown a second head. "She almost died, Matteo," he snaps. "Do you think I'm going to fall on her like an animal in heat? Her recovery comes first. Of course I can control myself." A cat's plaintive meow sounds from the other side of the door, and a brief smile flashes across his face. "Mimi might have a harder time adhering to your rules."

"Make it happen," Matteo says unsympathetically before turning back to me. "Whenever you feel up to it, the padrino would like to see you."

"Not until she's ready," Joao says, his voice hard. "Stefi's recovery comes first."

"I'm ready now." My words are a lie. As furious as I am, I can barely keep my eyes open. The pain is the only thing keeping me awake. "You might all tiptoe around him, but I refuse to walk around in awe of your precious padrino. I know what he did. I'm going to confront him with the evidence, and I don't care if he kills me. The rest of you might be able to ignore what Antonio Moretti did, but I can't. I won't."

"Stef. . ." Joao sounds strained and desperately worried. "Please don't stress yourself. You need to stay calm to recover—"

I cut off the rest of his sentence. "I don't want to talk to you." I don't want to see the dark circles under Joao's eyes, evidence he's barely slept a wink ever since I got shot. I don't want to see the corresponding sleeplessness in the doctor either, proof that he's been working around the clock to save my life. Maybe it's stupid and self-destructive of me, but I can't pretend Antonio Moretti wasn't funding Bach's network. I can't lie to myself to stay safe.

My heart feels like it's going to explode. "Stef, please," Joao begins, but before I swallow the lump in my throat and respond to him, one of my devices connected to me starts to beep.

The doctor jumps to attention immediately. "Continue this discussion later," he snaps. "She needs to rest, and this argument isn't good for her." He takes a vial from a tray. "This is a sedative," he says to me. "It'll also help with the pain. May I add it to your IV?"

"Do what you have to do," I respond bitterly. "But stop pretending I have a choice in the matter. The bed is softer, and the amenities are nicer, but I'm still a prisoner here."

The Hunter

Joao looks stricken. His face is the last thing I see before exhaustion tugs me under.

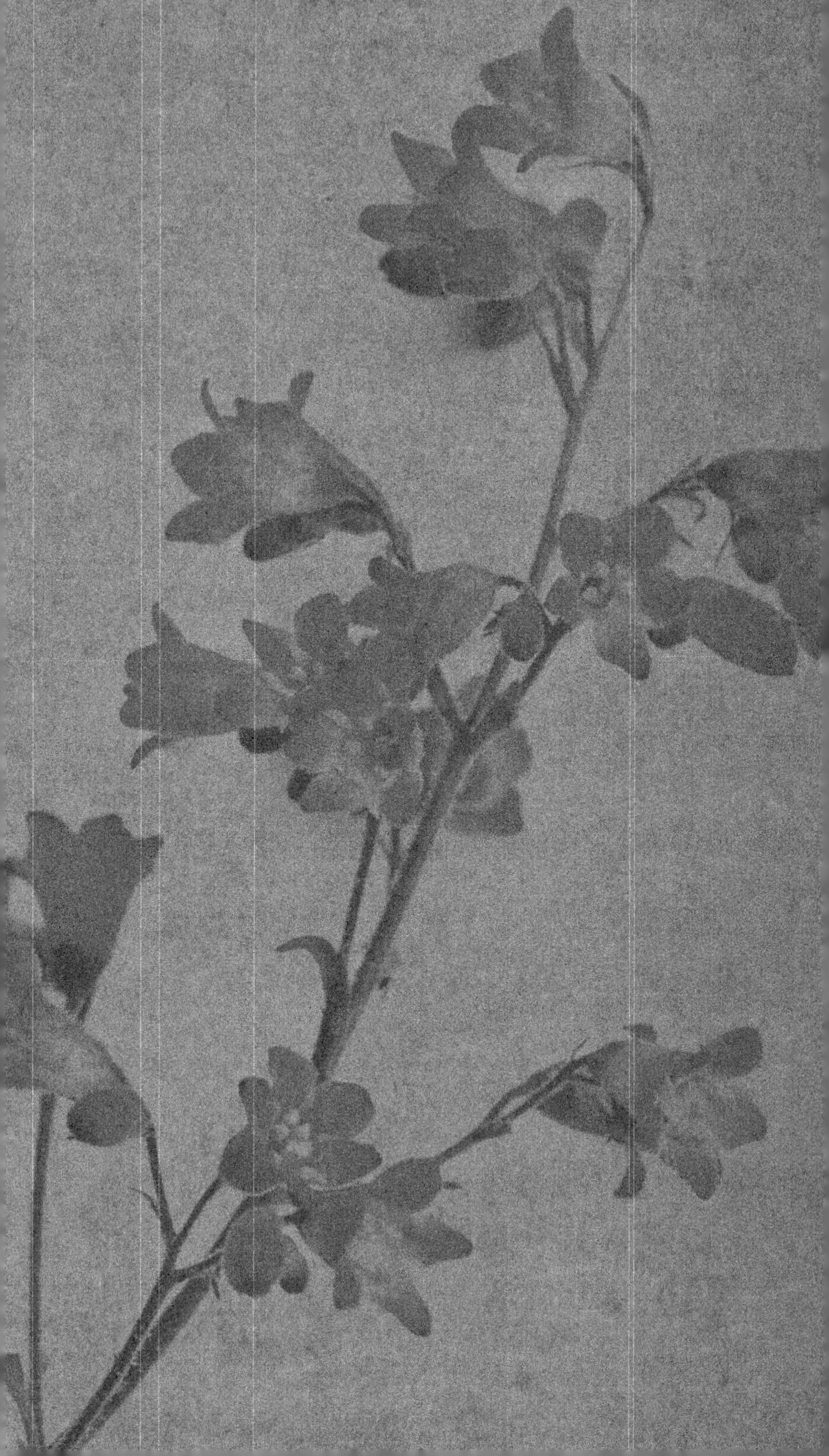

41

STEFI

Joao is sitting in an armchair in my room when I wake up, reading something on his phone. He must be absorbed in what he's doing because he hasn't noticed that I'm conscious again. I take advantage and study him covertly through my eyelashes.

He looks exhausted. He hasn't found time to shave, and it's not as much stubble that lines his jaw as it's the start of a beard. As mad as I am, and as awful as I feel, I still think it looks hot.

He looks up. "Hello, little fox," he says with a smile. "You gave us all quite a scare there. How are you feeling?"

His concern reminds me that I'm still mad he brought me to Venice. "I'm not happy with you."

"Fair enough," he says mildly, refusing to get drawn into an argument. "I'm just going to continue to sit here." A plaintive meow sounds from the other side of the closed door, and a small body thumps against it. "Meet Mimi," he says with an affectionate laugh. "This is the first time her wishes have been thwarted, and she does not like it."

I smile before I can help myself. "You shouldn't have brought me to Venice," I say sulkily. I'm aware I'm acting like an ungrateful child, but I'm in the city run by a man I've sworn to kill, and everybody around me is pretending like there's no problem here whatsoever.

"In normal times, the two of us would sort this out by having a screaming match followed by passionate sex," Joao replies. "But unfortunately, Matteo has ruled out both things and told me that my job is to keep you calm and happy. So, I'm just going to agree with everything you say."

"And now you're patronizing me," I snap.

"What do you want me to say, Stef?" he asks, suddenly sounding weary. "You spent twenty-four hours in a hospital in Nuremberg. The kid who shot at us got away when Dante and Goran showed up, and I fully anticipated him running back to Dachev. All the time you were in surgery, I kept expecting a mercenary team to burst through the hospital doors, guns blazing. And if they did, who was going to fend them off?"

He gets to his feet restlessly and draws the curtains open. Brilliant sunlight floods the room. "There were only three of us," he continues. "Four, if you count Ignazio. Dante and Goran are crack shots, but we were severely undermanned. There weren't even enough of us to guard each entrance and exit of the hospital, damn it. We were sitting ducks there."

A shudder runs through him. "It was the worst twenty-four hours of my life, even worse than Puerto

The Hunter

Vallarta. I kept picturing you getting shot to shreds, dying in front of my eyes. The padrino got a team there in record time. Three hours after you went into surgery, he sent six people as reinforcements. But when the king of Venice masses his troops outside his home territory, people take note. It's the sort of thing that gets viewed as an act of war. He couldn't send any more, and we had no idea how many people Dachev could mobilize in Germany. Yes, we were safer there than in Poland, but home is where we needed to be." He stares at me, his eyes bleak. "Be angry if you want. But you're alive."

The way he's telling it, he didn't have any other choice other than to bring me to Venice. And I, more than most, should understand impossible choices. After all, I had to make my own impossible choice eight years ago.

And Joao forgave you for it, my conscience reminds me. *Instantly, readily. Without a word of reproach.*

Damn it. I'm feeling things I don't want to feel right now. I look outside the window to avoid looking at Joao, and the sheer beauty of the view outside hits me like a punch.

It's spectacular.

Immediately in front of me, the water, an impossible turquoise, sparkles where the sun's rays fall on it. Across the lagoon, the houses are painted in vivid shades of ochre, yellow, and rust. To the right, the twin domes of the Basilica Santa Maria della Salute reach for the sky. Boats of all sizes zip around on the water. The large tour boats are crowded with tourists, even in November, while the smaller water taxis hold one or two people.

It's a scene out of a postcard, and it's my childhood fantasy brought to life.

"Nice view," I admit grudgingly. "I can't complain about that. And this bed is nice too. It's the most comfortable hospital bed I've ever had."

I should stop there, but I can't—the same words from yesterday tumble from my mouth before I can force myself to hold back. "I'm still a prisoner, though. Under the guise of protecting me, you're going to force me to stay in Venice."

"Oh, for fuck's sake." Joao has the patience of a saint, but it's hanging on by a thread. "You are not a prisoner. As soon as you're fully recovered, you can leave."

"Really? Just like that. And you're not going to stop me? What's the catch?"

"Not a catch. Just a promise. Wherever you go, I'm coming with you."

I stare at him in shock. "What about your life here? Your cat, your friends? You're going to give all of that up to live out of a suitcase with me?"

He sets his jaw in a stubborn line. "I don't know why you're surprised. I've already told you, Stef. I love you. I've tried living without you, and I'm not going to do that again. It doesn't matter that you hate me right now—I love you anyway. I'm just going to keep loving you until the day I die."

There's a lump in my throat. "Does my choice not matter?"

"Your choice is the only one that does," he responds, his expression serious. "Tell me you never want to see me again, and I'll stay away. But that is the only thing that's allowed to come between us. Nothing else. Not this stupid shit with the padrino, not some child with a gun, not Pavel Dachev, nothing else."

I blink furiously to keep the tears from falling. Why does Joao have to be so damned perfect? Why can't he be more like me, held together by revenge and not much else?

I try to stay angry with him but can already feel it drain away. I look around the room and my gaze rests on the orchids overflowing from the two tall vases on either side of the window. "Nice flowers. Where did you find cattleyas?"

"Is that what they're called? I called a florist Signora Moretti recommended and told her that orchids are your favorite flower."

His thoughtfulness makes me weepy. I blink the tears from my eyes. "They're breathtaking. Thank you."

His expression turns tender. "You're welcome."

Mimi throws herself against the door and yowls indignantly, interrupting the moment. I laugh at her angry tirade and regret it immediately when a hot knife of pain slices through me. I exhale slowly, counting to ten to keep from screaming aloud. Joao holds my hand, his expression distressed.

"I'm fine," I tell him to stop his worrying.

"Sure you are."

"Stop hovering over me."

"Are you trying to distract yourself from the pain by starting another fight with me?" he asks. I don't have to answer; my expression gives me away. "Here." He holds out a phone. "This might help. I thought you could call Charlie."

Charlie. "Oh God, I can't believe I forgot to call her. She's probably going out of her mind with worry." The last time I talked to her, I told her I'd call back in a day or two, and it's been at least twelve. She probably thinks I'm dead.

"I checked up on her when we got back to Venice," he replies. "I knew you'd want to make sure she's okay. She knows you got hurt, but that you're recovering nicely."

"You called her?" My heart swells with emotion. "Why are you making it so difficult for me to be mad at you?"

He chuckles. "It's part of my master plan to make you fall in love with me. What do you think of the color of the walls?"

"Make me fall in love with you?" I gape at him in shock. Is he out of his mind? "I'm *already* in love with you, you idiot."

His head snaps up. "You are?"

"For a supposedly smart guy, you can be pretty dumb sometimes. How do you not know that? Of course I'm in love with you."

"But you're angry with me," he says. "You're pissed off that I brought you to Venice."

"A little. Both things can exist in the same space at the same time." He looks confused, and I don't blame him. Right now, even I don't understand my own emotions. "I love the color of the walls. I didn't think you liked yellow as much as I did, though."

His expression makes it clear he realizes I'm changing

the topic. "I don't," he replies. "I painted them yellow because that's the color you were going to paint our bedroom walls. I thought if I lived in the house of your dreams, in the city of your dreams, it would feel like you were here with me. Spoiler: it didn't." He smiles cheerfully. "But that's the past. What matters is that you're here now."

My heart clenches painfully. "You're not listening to me. Stop pretending we don't have any problems."

"No, Stef," he says, determination etched into every syllable. "You're the one who isn't listening. I'm not going to let anything get in the way of us. Don't like Venice? Great, we'll move. Hate all my friends? I'll get new ones. Mimi annoying you?"

"I'm going to interrupt you before you offer to give up your cat for me," I tell him. "And no, I'm not going to make you get new friends; that's super controlling. They have every right to be pissed off with me. And when I get up, I need to find Alina and apologize."

"Funny you should mention Ali," he says, a little too innocently. "She wants to meet you too. Her phone number is programmed into your phone."

His sunny optimism is giving me hope, and I can't have any. As a teenager, I dreamed about a happily ever after in Venice with Joao, and then I was forced to leave him. I hoped for a stable life in Istanbul, but Pavel Dachev found me, and I lost Christopher.

I've learned the hard way that hope is the most dangerous of emotions.

I have to stop this conversation before I start wanting things I can't have. "I'm going to call Charlie," I murmur.

"But first, I need a nap." I give him a pointed look. He looks like he hasn't slept in *days,* and I don't like it. His shoulder is still healing, and he needs to rest. "You should try one too. You looked wiped."

He grins. "Whatever you say, sweetheart."

My one-hour nap turns into three. It's late in the afternoon when I finally call Charlie.

"Stefi," she exclaims. "I've been so worried. Joao told me you'd been shot, and I *freaked out*. I've been so stressed that yesterday, I looked in the mirror, and I saw a gray hair. Gray!"

I bite back my grin. "I thought Joao told you I was fine. Is it at all possible that you're imagining the gray hair?"

"Absolutely not," she says indignantly. "And yes, your extremely hot husband did tell me you were fine, but that didn't stop me from imagining the worst. Where are you?"

"Venice." It feels really good to hear her voice. It's a little slice of normalcy in an increasingly chaotic world. "Tell me what you've been up to."

"Nothing."

She sounds disconsolate, which isn't like her at all. Worry trickles down my spine. "What do you mean, nothing? Did you get that job at the grocery store?"

"No, I didn't apply."

The Hunter

"Why not?" I feel like a nagging parent. "I thought you liked Madame Allard."

"I just haven't gotten around to it," she mutters. "I talked to my mother. She's found a new guy. *Already.*"

Oh dear. "Anyone you know?" I ask casually. Who do I need to kill now?

"Yeah, I know Saul," she says bitterly. "He's a friend of Brando's. The way he used to look at me made my skin crawl."

I feel like strangling Severine Bellegarde. She should be protecting her daughter, not subjecting her to one creepy guy after another. "Have you been going to the youth center?"

"I went a couple of times."

It sounds like she's been sitting at home, all alone, brooding. And there's enough darkness in Charlie's past to overwhelm her. When I was there, she kept herself busy by cooking for me and bossing me around, but without me, she seems to be a little unmoored.

"Why don't you come to Venice for a bit?" I ask. "You could stay with us while I recuperate. Joao has a three-bedroom house, so there's plenty of room for you."

"I don't want to be a burden. You've already done so much for me, and—"

"Charlie, if you don't show up, I'll have to cook my own meals. Or worse, have Joao do it." I have no idea if my husband can cook, and of course I don't want Charlie to be some kind of live-in help. But she's more likely to come to Venice if she feels like she's helping me out.

"You mean it?" she asks cautiously.

"If I didn't, would I make the offer?"

"Joao suggested I visit too, but I told him no. I figured you'd want alone time with your husband. Or maybe you'd think that I was hitting on him. Which I'm not, don't worry. I've decided I don't like guys any longer."

"You're into girls?"

"No, I don't like anybody."

"That's fair." If I were in her shoes, I'd feel the same way. "I would *love* to have you here. And if Joao suggested it, you know he's on board as well. Can you get on a train by yourself?"

"Your husband told me I needed an escort and that he'd send someone. Some kid called Ignazio." She sounds disdainful. "I told him I don't need an escort and can take care of myself, but he insisted. I can be in Venice next week if you're sure."

"I'm absolutely sure," I tell her firmly. The truth is, I need Charlie as much as she needs me. The couple of months I lived with her were the most normal my life has ever felt.

The next few weeks are going to be... rocky. I'm going to need all the normalcy I can get to survive it.

42

STEFI

In a week, Matteo—I tried calling him Dr. Ferrini but he wasn't having it—is happy enough with my progress that he gives me permission to go downstairs. "It's probably safe enough for you to meet Mimi as well," he says in response to a long, plaintive yowl. "As long as Joao is supervising and stopping her from jumping on you." He fixes me with a stern look. "Don't pick her up, no lifting anything heavier than a kilo just yet."

Leaving my makeshift hospital room cheers me up immensely, as does the shower that Matteo allows me to have. Joao insists on helping me with the latter task, and for a change, I don't pretend I can manage on my own.

He makes me sit down on a chair in his shower stall while he washes me gently with a handheld shower, taking care to keep my wound dry. He massages shampoo and conditioner into my hair and rinses them out with warm water. The whole experience leaves me feeling unbelievably pampered.

And turned on. It doesn't help that Joao is naked. It makes perfect sense as he's in the shower with me, and it's only practical for him to take off his clothes, but when I see his massive erection, my lizard brain immediately starts screaming for sex. Which Matteo refuses to let me have because it'll interfere with my healing.

"You want me to take care of that?" I ask him hopefully as he smooths lotion into my skin. I keep forgetting that I'm annoyed with Joao for bringing me to Venice. "Matteo didn't forbid me from going down on you."

"That's a tempting offer, but no, thank you. You need to heal, not get me off."

"Why not both?"

"Not going to happen."

"Since when did you get so rule-abiding?" I grumble. "I don't like it."

He laughs and kisses my forehead. "I have it on good authority that you love me."

"Once again, throwing my own words back at me. Can I borrow one of your T-shirts? I don't have anything to wear."

"Right. About that." He opens his dresser and pulls out what looks like three neatly folded blankets. "I bought you some warm and comfortable lounge sets." He holds them up. "Pink, charcoal, or red?"

I'm incredibly touched. "Pink, please." It's a soft pastel pink that feels unbelievably cozy. "It's perfect. Thank you, Joao."

"You're welcome, little fox."

Once I'm dressed, Joao helps me down the stairs and

into a plush leather recliner. Mimi promptly comes over to investigate. She sniffs my outstretched hand, then rubs her cheek against me, plops herself on my feet, and promptly takes a nap.

"Typical," Joao murmurs in mock disgust. "I feed her and clean her litter, yet one look at you, and she's glued to your side."

"I didn't take you to be a sore loser," I tell him with a grin, and then my smile fades. As much as I want to stay here all afternoon, I've already been in Venice for a week, and I can't avoid reality forever. If I'm well enough to get up and go downstairs, I'm well enough to confront the king of Venice. "I need to meet Antonio Moretti."

"I figured you'd say that," Joao replies. "He lives around the corner. Let me call him."

He steps out of the room to make the phone call. "He's coming over," he says when he returns. "He said he'll be here in fifteen minutes, give or take."

"He's coming here? I'm a little surprised. This guy runs the city but is willing to visit one of his underlings instead of having us visit his palazzo and kiss the ring?"

"Well, it's not like you can walk to his house in your condition." He fixes me with a serious look. "Can I trust that you won't kill the padrino?"

I can't tell if he's joking or not. "Are you planning on stopping me?"

"Yes," he replies. "If you kill Antonio, you won't make it out of Venice in one piece. And I don't know if you've noticed, but I've been trying *very hard* to keep you alive."

Something tells me that if I attack Moretti, it won't

just be my life I'm risking. It'll also be Joao's, and that, I'm not going to do. "I won't touch him. Am I allowed to yell at him, or do I have to treat him like he walks on water?"

He gives me a wry smile. "Yell all you want."

"What, you're not worried he'll have me killed if I look at him the wrong way?" I ask snidely.

"No," Joao replies calmly, refusing to be provoked. "I already told you—he's guaranteed your safety."

Lo and behold, fifteen minutes later, there's a knock on the front door. Joao opens it, and Antonio Moretti enters the room.

He looks like his pictures. Dark hair, dark eyes, broad shoulders. Although, the photos don't do a good job conveying the relaxed calm with which he holds himself. This is a man who's comfortable with his place in the world and has no need to impress anyone.

"Thanks for getting me out of there," he says. "Lucia's hosting a movie night. It's one rom-com after another." He turns to me and holds out his hand. "It's good to meet you," he says. "Matteo tells me you're recovering well. I'm glad."

"Are you?" I ask, my voice harsh. Joao winces at my tone, but I don't care. I'm not physically attacking Moretti —that has to be good enough.

"Yes," he says. He sits down across from me, and Mimi, the traitor, gets up from my feet and jumps onto his lap. "But I get the sense I'm missing something."

"Fifteen million somethings," I bite out. "Did you really think you could hide your yearly payments to Henrik Bach?"

The Hunter

A look of shock flashes over Moretti's face. "Fuck," he swears, running his hands through his hair and looking deeply discomfited. "You weren't supposed to find out about those."

Joao's head snaps toward his boss. "You really paid Bach?" he asks, sounding betrayed. "After everything I told you about that psychopath, after the dossier Valentina compiled on him, you still funded his operation? Why?"

The mafia head looks at me and then Joao. "I would have preferred you never find out. But what's done is done." He exhales in a long sigh. "Six months after Joao came to Venice, the first bounty hunter showed up. Bach really didn't like when his assassins tried to escape, and he was determined to get Joao back."

He leans back in the chair and absently pats Mimi's head. "Leo, my enforcer, foiled the attempt, of course, but it didn't stop there. Four more bounty hunters came to Venice that year."

I have a very bad feeling about this story.

"They weren't very good," Moretti continues. "Bach was willing to pay a million euros for your recovery, and that kind of money brings a lot of people out of the woodwork. But the truly competent bounty hunters—people like Varek Zaworski and Pavel Dachev—stayed away. They knew better than to abduct someone from Venice." He gives me a very dry look. "It's generally considered a bad idea to make an enemy out of me."

"Touché."

"We sent the first dozen bounty hunters back in body

bags before Bach upped his offer by half a million. We killed another six, and it became two million. In the meantime, I had to keep Joao in Venice. Inside my city, I could protect him. Outside? There were no guarantees."

"I can protect myself," Joao says, his voice hard.

"It was too risky," Antonio counters. "If one of them got lucky. . . No. I wasn't going to gamble with your life. But at the same time, I couldn't keep you in Venice forever. It would have been like trading one prison for another. The situation wasn't tenable. I knew it, and Bach knew it too, which is why he called me. He said he could keep sending his bounty hunters, and one of them would eventually get through because we couldn't kill them all. I told him to go to hell. Then he warned me that he wasn't going to stop trying, and when he ran out of bounty hunters, he was going to order his trainees to step in."

My throat goes dry. If Joao knew who Bach sent to bring him in, he wouldn't shoot back. We all went through hell. I don't know if any one of us could kill our own.

"You were a valuable employee, Joao," Moretti continues. "But it was more than that. My childhood was nowhere as difficult as yours, but we both grew up in difficult circumstances, and I've always felt a sense of kinship with you. Bach was setting you up for a choice that would tear you apart. I didn't want that to happen."

"So, instead, you gave in to Henrik's blackmail," Joao says tonelessly. "You paid him off."

I can't say anything. All my anger, all my recrimination, suddenly drains away to nothing. Antonio Moretti's money kept Joao alive. How can I hate him for it?

I'm a hypocrite, the worst sort of hypocrite in the world. For all that I accused Joao of looking the other way and tolerating the lesser evil for my safety, I'm doing the same thing. I don't want to rail against Moretti for what he did—I want to thank him.

"Not happily," Antonio replies. "It was a stopgap measure, one that bought me time. As soon as I paid Bach off, I put a plan into action. For the last five years, I've been working on ruining him financially. I've had to proceed slowly and carefully, not letting anything be traced back to me for fear that it might endanger Joao, but I wasn't going to rest until Bach's empire was destroyed."

He glances at me. "I have many projects on the go," he says. "I didn't know about your existence until Cici sent me her intel, and it wasn't until much later that I realized what you were doing. But you and I have the same goal."

"It appears we do," I mutter. I know I sound ungracious, but in my defense, Antonio Moretti has been on my list for five years. I'm having difficulty thinking of him as anything other than an enemy.

But it turns out I owe him a huge debt of gratitude. Moretti set out to ruin Bach; that's why he's been weaker these last few years. And I know I couldn't have taken out as much of Bach's network as I did if it had been operating at full strength.

Antonio gives me a half-smile. "I've also heard I'm on your hitlist."

My gaze flies to Joao, and Antonio shakes his head. "No, Joao didn't tell me. He said that you freaked out when you found out he worked for me. There was really only one reason you'd have that reaction, and that's if you found out I was paying off Bach."

I clear my throat. "You're no longer on the list; you should have never been on it in the first place. I didn't understand what you were doing." I take a deep breath. "I'm sorry about that."

He shakes his head. "No apologies needed," he says. "And about Alina. . . I wasn't thrilled about your attempt to kidnap her, but given the extenuating circumstances there, I'm willing to let bygones be bygones."

Joao looks discomfited, though not for the reason I think. "Padrino, about the money. I—"

The mafia boss holds up his hand. "And this is why I didn't want you to find out. If it makes you feel better, Joao, I've made more money destroying Bach's business than what I paid him. Please let's not discuss it again." He phrases it as a request, but it's definitely an order. He turns back to me. "Let's get back to business. Who's left on your list?"

"Just one person. Pavel Dachev."

He grimaces. "A hard target. Your gunshot wound hasn't dissuaded you from trying to take him out?"

Antonio Moretti doesn't know about the promise I made at Christopher's grave. "No. I won't stop until I'm done."

"I was afraid you'd say that. Dachev is scum, but for all kinds of complicated reasons, I can't be seen taking him out." His smile is vicious. "What the two of you do, on the other hand, is up to you. He tends to be a hard person to find. I'll ask Valentina to help you." He gets up to leave. "If anyone can track him down, it's her."

The Hunter

"Thank you."

All this time, I've thought of Moretti as the enemy, a man standing in the way of Joao and my happiness. But he's not. Moretti might be ruthless, but he's also deeply protective of his people, a man who not only values loyalty, but also offers it to his people.

And I'm glad, so glad. All this time, I've hated the idea that I'd be tearing Joao's life apart when I killed Moretti. I've hated the idea that I'm making him choose between me and the life he's built here.

And now he doesn't have to.

Joao walks Antonio out and then comes back inside with a grin on his face. "What?" I ask, my cheeks flaming at the knowing look on his face. "If you're going to say, 'I told you so,' then let me warn you that being cocky isn't attractive."

He laughs. "Oh, I think you love when I'm cocky. But I wasn't going to rub your nose in it. I'm just thinking that we're in the city of your dreams, and there's still a few hours of daylight left. Matteo grudgingly agreed that as long as you stayed off your feet and didn't go anywhere too crowded, it was safe enough to go out. If you're very nice to me, we could go out in my boat for an hour. Cruise the Grand Canal, see the Ponte di Rialto—"

"You have a boat?" I blurt out.

"Of course."

"How nice do I have to be?" I flutter my eyelashes at him and make my best come-hither face.

Joao gives me a stern look. "Not that nice," he says. "Get your mind out of the gutter. You just got shot. Matteo hasn't cleared you for sex."

"You don't want me?" I pout.

"Stefi, there's never a moment that goes by when I don't want you. But I care far more about your health than the state of my cock." He sweeps me into his arms, and I bite back a squeal of surprise. "Now, shall we go? Venice awaits, my lady."

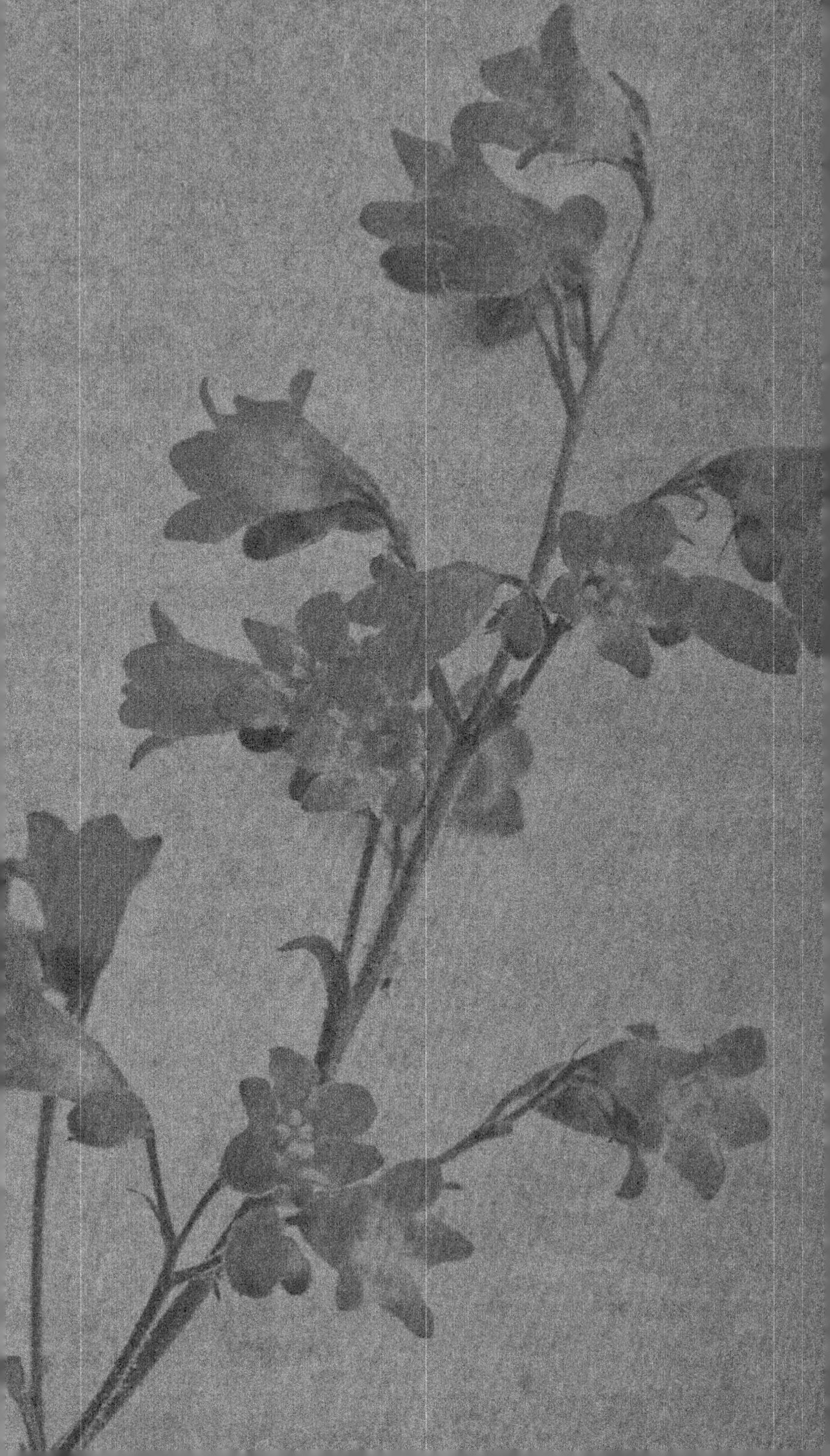

43

STEFI

Since I found out that Joao was alive, anytime I let myself dream about living in Venice with him, Antonio Moretti's financial support of Henrik Bach was always the thing that stopped me cold. It was always the biggest impediment to our happiness.

Turns out Venice's fearsome padrino isn't the biggest hurdle. It's Joao's friends. They do not like me, a thing that becomes rapidly clear over the next few days.

Dinner invitations arrive addressed to Joao, not to me. He turns every single one down. He also skips his weekly poker games, insisting he can't possibly leave me, but I know the real reason. It's because I'm not welcome.

Charlie arrives in Venice a week after our conversation and gets immediately integrated into the social circle. There are a handful of young girls her own age—Francesca, Dina, and Lavinia—and she's immediately and warmly invited into their ranks. She doesn't speak any Italian, but they seem to get along just fine anyway, with makeup tutorials on TikTok serving as their shared language.

Me though? I'm being frozen out.

For two weeks, I try to pretend it isn't happening, but when Matteo gives me the okay to go outside in carefully controlled doses, I can't put it off any longer. I've been letting my recovery serve as an excuse, but the truth is, I need to talk to Alina. It doesn't matter if she gives me the cold shoulder. The apology I owe her is long, long overdue.

Joao's been working from home during my convalescence, but he finally returns to work one overcast Monday morning, three weeks after I arrived in Venice.

"Are you sure you can manage?" he asks me as he gets dressed. "Our headquarters is less than a ten-minute walk from here. I'll be back for lunch, but if you need me before that—"

"I'll be fine."

I perch on the edge of his bed, sip my coffee, and watch him through lowered lashes. For the last three weeks, Joao's been casually dressed in jeans and T-shirts, but today, he's wearing a suit, and he looks good. Really good. So good that my libido is screaming at me to ignore Matteo's strictures.

"What will you do all day?"

"I don't know. Read a book, take a nap. Charlie said she'd teach me how to make beef bourguignon, so maybe I'll do that today." I don't tell him I'm planning to visit Alina because I'm afraid he'd offer to come with me, and I'm even more afraid I'd take him up on it. But I can't do

The Hunter

that. *I* tried to kidnap Alina, not Joao, and this is my mess to clean up.

"Isn't that a really complicated dish to make? Don't overdo it."

"Stop worrying, I'll be fine."

He gives me a deeply skeptical look but finally heads out the door. Once he's gone, I get dressed and head out.

Ignazio is hovering outside the front door. "Are you looking for Charlie?" I ask him.

I don't know exactly what happened on the train ride from Paris to Venice, but Charlie claims to hate Ignazio while constantly sneaking glances at him. Ignazio has dropped by at least a dozen times with questions for Joao, questions that are easily asked by text and don't need an in-person visit.

"No," he replies, the tips of his ears going red at the mention of Charlie. "Signor Carvalho asked me to keep an eye on you."

"Did he now? Good. Then you can give me a ride across the harbor to Alina's gym."

"Umm—"

"Or I can catch a water taxi."

The poor kid decides it's easier to keep an eye on me if he gives me a ride. "I'll take you there," he says reluctantly.

I feel bad about manipulating him, but I can't let anything stop me from my task.

Ignazio helps me into a nearby boat, and we speed across the lagoon. In no time at all, we arrive at the pier. Ignazio docks the boat and escorts me to Alina's gym. It's only a short walk, but my footsteps drag as I near it. A pit of guilt opens in my stomach every time I think about what I did to Alina and how bad things could have turned out for her if I'd succeeded. If Tomas hadn't been in time to rescue her, she'd be in Russia right now, the unwilling bride of a vicious Russian crime lord.

Alina is at the front desk of her gym when I walk in. She catches sight of me and stiffens instinctively, then forces a smile on her face. "Stefania, right?"

Stefania was what Bach used to call me. Every time I hear someone call me that, I feel a little lurch in my gut. "Call me Stefi."

"Okay." She looks at me, and her forehead creases in worry. "You don't look too good. You shouldn't be up. Does Joao know you're here?"

My stomach is roiling, and I'm sucking in breaths to keep from throwing up. Guilt is one hell of a drug. "Are you going to tell on me?"

"No, but I am going to insist we grab a coffee next door so you can sit down."

We head to a coffee shop, and Alina gets us both espressos. "How's your recovery going?"

"Slow. I'm driving Joao crazy, I'm sure." I take a sip of my espresso before letting out a deep breath. There's no point beating around the bush. "I'm sorry I tried to abduct you. At the time, I thought I didn't have any options, but—"

"Joao told us you did it to protect Charlie."

I nod. "I wish I'd tried harder to find a different way to save her." I stare down at the tablecloth. "She needed my help, but that didn't give me the right to involve you, and I'm truly sorry I did."

"I met Charlie yesterday."

That's not what I expected her to say. "Did you?"

"She came into the gym. Wanted to learn self-defense." A smile flickers over her face. "She thinks very highly of you. She said she wouldn't have survived without you."

I shake my head. "I had nothing to do with it. She's the one who had to survive, not me."

"Why do you say that?" she asks quizzically. "Joao told us a little bit about your childhoods. Surely, it wasn't easy to survive Bach."

"It's. . ." I hesitate, trying to find the best way to word my thoughts. "Whatever else Bach was, he wasn't interested in us. Sexually, I mean. He didn't whore us out. What Charlie had to go through. . . Nothing that happened to me was as bad."

"Sexual violence is deeply terrible," she says. "I would never trivialize it. But it isn't the only form of violence. Abuse is abuse, whatever form it takes, and what you went through was absolutely abusive. And, at the risk of being an armchair therapist, I think that when you saw a young girl in trouble, it reminded you very much of yourself, so you instinctively did what you could to help her." She takes a sip of her espresso. "Do you know my mother's story?"

I blink at the sudden topic change. "No."

"My mother met my father when she was Charlie's age. He was thirty-one."

"Ah." I didn't like Vidone Laurenti when I met him, and now I like him even less. There's a special place in hell reserved for a grown man who would prey on a teenager.

"He decided she would be his, and he didn't take no for an answer. She never talked about him. I used to harass her for details about him as a child, never realizing their relationship wasn't consensual." Her expression is sad. "It wasn't until she discovered she was pregnant that she got the courage to flee."

"I can relate to that." The safety of my child was the only thing that could overcome my fear of Bach.

She looks up. "You can?"

Oh, right. Nobody in Venice would know about my pregnancy. Joao would never discuss Christopher without my consent. But maybe because Alina's always been warm and welcoming toward me, I feel comfortable telling her the whole story. "On my last mission, I found out I was pregnant. That's why I disappeared." A shadow passes over my heart. "I couldn't contact Joao for his own safety, and then I lost my child."

"I'm so sorry," Alina says, her expression stricken.

"Please don't feel sorry for me. It doesn't change anything I did to you."

"No, it doesn't," she agrees. "But there's a reason I brought up my mother. Nobody helped her. Everyone could see what was happening, and not a single person intervened. You were different. You saw what was happening to Charlie, and you helped her." She takes another sip of espresso. "Besides, as Joao pointed out, if you were really trying to abduct me, it was a very sloppy attempt. I mean, come on. You left me with my phone. A phone that was transmitting my location information to anyone determined enough to track it down."

I don't know what to say. She's offering to forgive me, just like that, but I don't deserve it.

"Look, can we both agree to move past it? If it makes you feel better, we can get into the ring and beat the crap out of each other. Once you heal, of course."

"Thank you," I say softly. "But just so you know, I wouldn't last a single round. I'm terrible at hand-to-hand combat."

"Why do I have a feeling that you're not as bad as you're pretending to be?" she says. "No, don't deny it. I've seen Joao fight."

"I'm nowhere as good as him, unfortunately."

"If you say so," she replies skeptically. "Tell me, has Matteo cleared you to go out yet?"

"Conditionally. I'm supposed to take it easy for the next two weeks. Hopefully I'll get the all-clear after that to start working out again. My muscles are going to atrophy if I sit around much longer."

"Once Matteo pronounces you healed, you need to join us for drinks. We have a girls' night out every Thursday. What do you think?"

"I don't think anyone wants me there."

"Nonsense," she replies. "Tell me if anyone's giving you grief, and I'll threaten to beat them up." She grins. "We're a family here, which means we sometimes drive each other crazy. If anyone should be annoyed with you, it's me, and I'm inviting you. Say you'll come."

"I'd love to." I try to take a sip of the espresso, but my stomach roils again.

Alina notices. "You've barely touched your coffee," she says, looking concerned. "Are you feeling okay?"

I feel awful. "This is more activity than I've had in two weeks, and the espresso isn't sitting well," I say with a wan smile. "I should probably get back home and lie down."

She starts to say something and then stops herself. "Of course," she says. "I see Ignazio hovering outside. Let me get him, and then we'll get you home."

ANOTHER COUPLE of weeks go by. Valentina Colonna, the mafia hacker, is doing her best to find Pavel Dachev, but he's proving to be elusive.

And there's nothing I can do except heal and wait.

A part of me is chomping at the bit to find the asshole who ordered a young child to open fire on me. It's the same part that burns to scratch the last name off my list and finally avenge my son.

But despite my impatience, I'm also happy.

Joao and I are living together in my dream city. When the weather is nice, he shows me all his favorite places in Venice. We take a trip to Murano to see the glass blowers and another to Lido to walk along the beach. I pretend I'm a tourist and take a scenic tour of the city on a gondola. We stop in local bars for an ombra and cicchetti, though my stomach is still rebellious, and even a sip of wine makes me queasy.

On cold and blustery days, I sometimes head to one of the many museums dotting the city, or, more often than not, I curl up in my pajamas and read, Mimi napping next to me. Every night, I fall asleep with Joao at my side, safe and secure, with nobody wanting to kill us, and that, more than anything else, is a dream come true.

Charlie lives with us, and that's pretty great as well. Her friend Francesca is a runner, too, and no matter how cold it is, the two of them wake up at dawn to go for runs. She's found a job as a tourist guide for French tourists, and she's taking Italian lessons every evening. Being in a safe and supportive environment agrees with her.

Joao's happy about the delay in finding Dachev. "I almost lost you," he says. "I want you to be fully healed before we go in search of Dachev again. To be honest, I'd prefer you to stay behind, but—"

"But it's not going to happen."

"I know," he says unhappily. "I've resigned myself to it."

Before I know it, five weeks have gone by since I got shot, and it's time for my last check-up.

We're about to leave for Matteo's clinic when Joao gets a phone call. I can only hear his end of the conversation, but it sounds like a crisis. Sure enough, when he hangs up, he looks harried. "One of our ships got boarded by customs agents in Greece," he says. "It's a mess."

"Go handle it. I can go to this appointment on my own."

"Are you sure?"

"Absolutely. It's a routine check-up, and Matteo's clinic is just around the corner." I'm hoping the doctor will tell me I can start having sex again. For the first couple of weeks, I was in too much pain to be horny, but lately, it's been *torture* to sleep next to Joao and not fool around. I push his shoulder. "Go. I'll be fine on my own."

Once he heads out, I walk the five minutes to Matteo's Giudecca clinic. I tell the receptionist my name and barely have time to take a seat before Matteo shows up to usher me inside. "How are you feeling?" he asks once he's taken a blood sample.

"I'm great."

"No pain?"

"A twinge or two, nothing serious. The queasiness is the only thing that's still bothering me."

His expression sharpens. "What queasiness?"

"I'm nauseous a lot. I figured it was because of the stomach wound."

"You shouldn't be nauseous," he replies. He opens a drawer and pulls out a specimen cup. "I'm going to need a urine sample."

"Awkward."

He rolls his eyes. "I am a doctor, Stefi." He opens the door for me. "There's a bathroom down the hall."

I pee into the cup and return to Matteo's office, my face flaming. "Here you go."

"Wait here," he says, taking it from me. "I need to run a couple of quick tests."

He's gone for ten minutes. "It's probably nothing," I tell him when he returns. "I'm sure I'll be fine in a week or two. I've always been a slow healer."

He clears his throat. "Stefi," he says. "This isn't a side-effect from your wound."

"It isn't?"

He shakes his head. "No. You're feeling nauseous because you're pregnant."

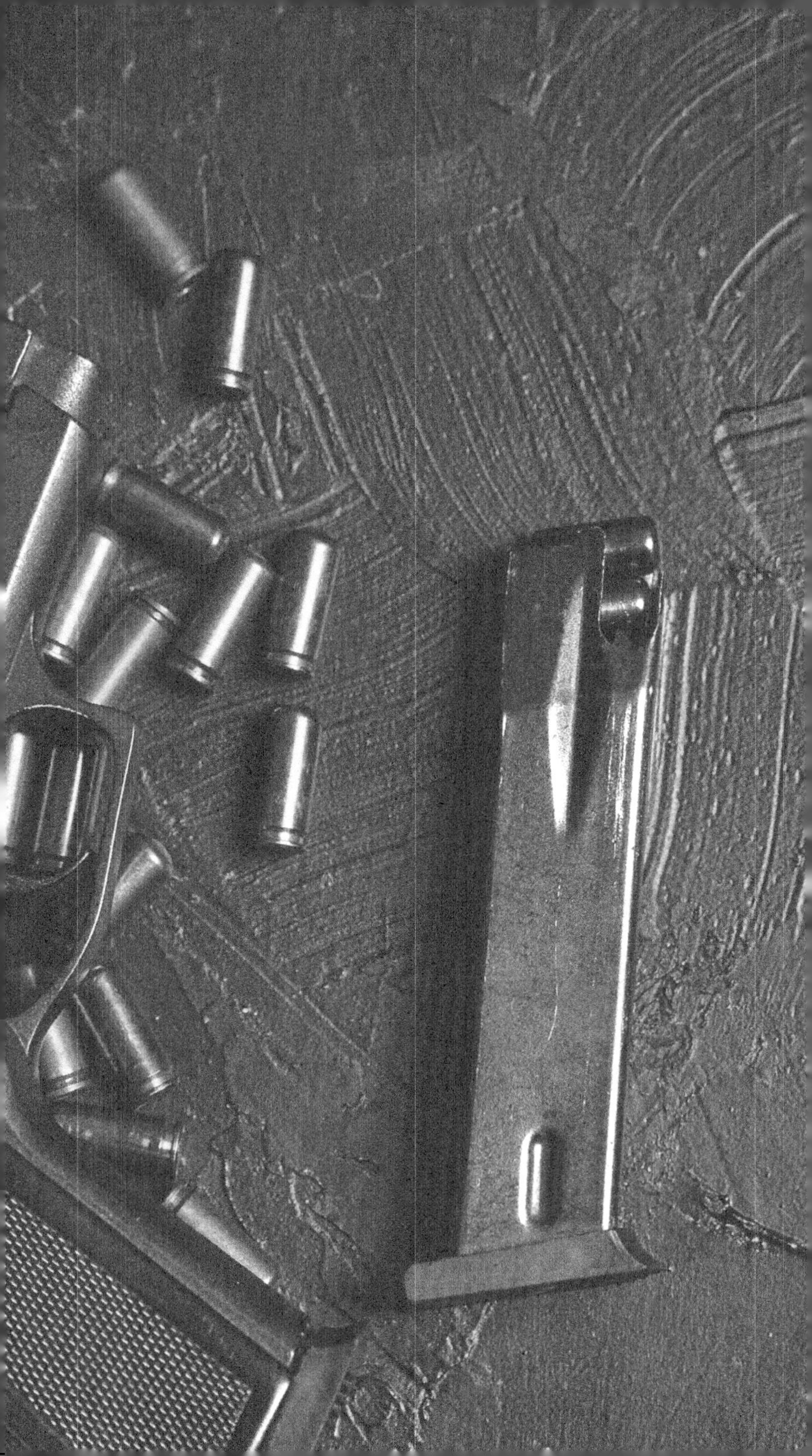

44

JOAO

I've just about smoothed over the customs situation in Greece when Valentina stops by my office. "I have good news and bad news," she announces. "Good news: I have a lock on Dachev's location. He's completed his takeover of Bach's empire and is throwing himself a victory party in Sofia."

"You think we should attack him there?"

"God, no. Sofia's a deathtrap. The party is Dachev's way of celebrating in public. But he also likes to celebrate by fucking the mistress he has ensconced in a beachside villa in Varna."

"He has a mistress?"

"It's very hush-hush. And because it's such a secret, he travels to Varna with only one bodyguard. That's your way in."

"What's the bad news?"

"The party is tonight. Which means Dachev will be in Varna tomorrow." She gives me a sympathetic look. "I know it's soon, but this is as good as it's going to get, Joao.

Dachev isn't easy to locate, and before you ask, finding him in the future won't be as simple as staking out his mistress's house. She's been with him for a year, and he never sticks around for longer than that."

Fuck.

I hate this. Stefi is going to insist we take off immediately for Bulgaria, and I don't want her to go. She got shot just five weeks ago, for fuck's sake, and isn't fully recovered. The smell of food makes her sick, she barely eats, and she's even having trouble tolerating coffee.

Valentina might be right, and Dachev might truly be unprotected. This mission might be straightforward, and Stefi might not be in any danger. But I don't know that for sure, and I've learned from bitter experience to never expect things to go according to plan.

I *hate* the thought of Stef going on this mission with me.

You could just go by yourself, a little voice inside me whispers. *You could tell her you have to fly to Athens to straighten out this situation and head to Bulgaria instead. She doesn't need to kill Dachev—you could kill him for her.*

She'd never forgive me if she found out. But would she find out? Valentina might disapprove of what I'm thinking of doing, but she would keep my confidence.

Stefi's safe in Venice, safe and happy. After so many years apart, we're finally living together as a married couple. I'm finally able to give her the life she's always wanted.

One little lie, and she'll be safe.

One little lie, and we'll live happily ever after.

Would that really be the worst thing in the world?

45

STEFI

The moment Joao comes back home, I can tell that something is up. His shoulders are tense, and there's a hard look in his eyes. "How was your doctor's appointment?" he asks.

"All good. I'm clear to resume normal activity."

"Excellent," he replies, though he doesn't sound thrilled. "That's great. I have some news for you. Is Charlie home?"

I shake my head. "She went to see a movie with her girlfriends. I asked her if Ignazio was going to be there, and she told me she hasn't changed her mind and still hates guys. I told her that if Ignazio was bothering her, she should tell me and I'd take care of it, but she blushed furiously and told me he wasn't that bad." I take a deep breath. I'm babbling about Charlie because I'm nervous about what my pregnancy will mean for us. "I have some news, too."

All afternoon, I've been struggling to process the news of this baby. After Christopher, I threw hope for another child out the window. I don't really think I ever expected to survive my quest, let alone be pregnant again. I'd lost the love of my life and then my baby boy and was reconciled to being alone forever.

But I'm pregnant again. I must have conceived that first night at the farmhouse—that was the only time we didn't use protection. This baby—our baby—is a miracle, the second chance I never thought I'd have. The second chance I never deserved.

My emotions have been like a wild pendulum since I heard the news. I go from giggling in sheer delight to expecting the worst. Matteo gave me a thorough exam and told me everything looked fine, but that doesn't completely reassure me.

My palms are sweaty, and I can't stop smiling. Joao and I are going to have a baby.

"Flip to see who goes first?"

"Sounds good."

He fishes a coin out of his pocket and tosses it in the air. "Tails," he says when it lands. "I win." He exhales in a long breath. "Valentina has a location for Dachev. He's going to be in Varna with his mistress tomorrow night. His secret mistress, so he'll only be traveling with one bodyguard."

My heart leaps in my chest, and then I register the timeframe. "Tomorrow? That soon?"

He nods grimly. "Valentina warned me that if we missed this opportunity, there was no guarantee she'd be able to find Dachev again. I wish the timing were better. I wish you had longer to heal and recover, but if Matteo said you could resume regular activity. . ." His voice trails

The Hunter

off. "We could travel to Bulgaria together and take him out."

He didn't want to tell me. I can see it in his face, in every line of his body. More than anything in the world, Joao wants to protect me from harm.

And it would have been so easy for him to keep Dachev's location a secret. After all, how would I ever find out he had a lead on the man who killed my baby? Valentina doesn't like me enough to break Joao's confidence.

But as much as he'd prefer to wrap me in cotton wool, *he didn't*. He told me the truth.

"You wanted to hide this from me, didn't you?"

A flicker of guilt crosses his face, but he doesn't lie to me. He nods, his jaw tightening, as if bracing for a blow. "I did. Are you mad at me?"

"No." Matteo warned me about hormonal changes and told me I might be more emotional than normal. He's certainly right about that because I'm fighting the urge to burst into tears. "Your first instinct was to want to protect me. How can I be mad about that? It makes me feel cherished." I give him a tremulous smile. "You could have hidden Dachev's location from me, but you didn't. What you wanted to do doesn't matter as much as what you did."

And now I'm faced with a dilemma of my own.

I desperately want to kill Dachev. I want to see him suffer and die more than anything in the world. I want him to beg for his life while I line up the gun. He's the only target left on my list, the list that has consumed my life since the moment I walked out of that psych ward in Istanbul.

He killed my baby, and I've waited so long to avenge his death. I owe it to Christopher to kill Pavel Dachev.

But if I tell Joao I'm pregnant, he's not going to want me to go to Varna.

If I don't tell Joao... if I just wait two more days to break the news...

I take a deep breath. "I'm pregnant." My hands tremble as I wait for his reaction. This is such a big deal, such a life changing thing, and even though I think he's going to be happy, I can't be sure.

Shock flits across his face for a second, and then he breaks out into a wide smile. "We're going to have a baby? Stef, that's amazing news." There is a sheen of tears in his eyes. "Do you want this?"

I nod, a lump in my throat. "I really do."

He envelops me in a hug. "Me too," he says, his voice thick. "I want this so much. I'm so happy."

He holds me in his arms for a long moment before pulling back and studying me intently. "You still want to go to Varna, don't you?"

"Dachev made me lose Christopher," I whisper. "I made our baby a promise. More than anything, I want to keep it."

He nods. I'm waiting for him to tell me it's a bad idea, waiting for him to forbid me to go.

But he doesn't say it. He knows how important this is to me, so as much as he wants to, he doesn't tell me I can't come.

He leaves the decision to me.

The Hunter

And because he doesn't do anything to stop me, I stop myself.

I just found out I'm pregnant. There are now things more important than my revenge. And if Christopher was alive, I know he'd agree. He'd tell me to protect his baby brother or sister.

"I don't want to take any chances with this pregnancy. I don't think. . ." I start to choke up. It takes me a minute to steady my voice. "Will you kill Dachev for me, Joao?"

"Happily." His eyes search mine. "You're sure?"

I nod. "I'm sure. Sometimes, you have to lose the battle to win the war. I'm making the right choice." I drop my gaze from his. "It still sucks."

He squeezes my hand. "It does," he says. "You don't have to stay here, though."

"What do you mean?"

"You don't have to remain in Venice while I go to Bulgaria. You could travel with me and provide operational support. That way, you'd still be involved."

There's not much support to be provided, but Joao can tell I hate the idea of him going into danger all by himself, and he's offering me a solution that works for both of us. I smile at him, my heart lifting. "I'd like that very much."

He grins. "Do you realize we just had a moment of personal growth? We both curbed our natural instincts to protect the other person and decided to trust each other."

Joao's right. We had a problem, and we solved it *together*. We didn't unilaterally make decisions to protect the other person. We had a discussion and came to an agreement. "Huh. Does this mean we're growing up?"

He laughs. "Probably good timing, given that we're going to have a baby."

I beam at him. The future is bright and filled with promise and close enough to reach.

Just one more death to go...

And then we're going to live happily ever after.

46

JOAO

The padrino doesn't officially support our attempt to take Dachev out, but he still lends us his private plane. We land in a small airfield the next day, half an hour inland, and drive to our destination.

Varna is a coastal town on the Black Sea, and during warmer months, it's probably filled with tourists. Not so in December. It's not empty by any means—it's still Bulgaria's third largest city—but the beach is deserted, and all the restaurants along the boardwalk are closed for the season.

Dachev set his mistress up in a seaside villa about a mile north of the main boardwalk. We drive by to scout the location, and the security is as lax as Valentina promised. No armed men patrolling the streets, no guard dogs, just one bored-looking security guard who appears to be half-asleep.

No one is patrolling the perimeter, and there are no

cameras mounted on the streetlight posts to monitor who's coming and going.

"Could it really be this easy?" Stefi marvels.

"Maybe," I say, though I'm as skeptical as Stefi. "From everything I've heard about him, Dachev is a deeply private man who stays hidden by keeping a very low profile. Armed guards would be out of character for him."

She chews on her lower lip. "I don't know. . . Eight years of searching, and it's down to this? All you have to do is break in and shoot Dachev? Something doesn't feel quite right."

I don't have a good feeling about this either. I'm never anxious about a job, but I'm anxious today, nervous and twitchy. Then again, that could just be because my wife is here. I know that she's more than capable of taking care of herself, but that has never stopped me from worrying about her.

"Most of my jobs for the padrino have been easy," I say to reassure her. "Unlike Henrik, he doesn't cheap out on intel and operational support." It's almost dusk, almost time to take out Dachev. "You've got the spare license plates?" I'm asking the question more from nerves than anything else. Stefi's not going to miss any of the details.

"Yes." She opens a map on her phone and zooms in on the street parallel to the villa. "This is where I'll be parked," she says. "It's a straight shot to the highway from here and then to the airport."

"Got it." The spot she's picked is the logical place to park. We discussed it on the flight over and drove by earlier to make sure Google Maps wasn't putting us in the middle of a swamp. She's repeating herself because she's nervous, too.

"This is going to be straightforward," I tell her. But I'm not sure who I'm trying to convince.

Her, or myself.

SHOCKINGLY, it really does appear to be easy. I disarm Elena Alexandra's security guard, break into the house, and find a very naked Pavel Dachev in bed with Elena. They're engaged in some very vigorous lovemaking using the fruit bowl next to them as props. (Don't ask: it involves multiple bananas.)

I point my gun at them, and Elena screams. She's not a part of this, so I throw a plastic zip tie in her direction. "Put those on," I order. "Arms in front of you. Tighten them with your mouth. And not a word. I don't want to kill you, but if you scream, I will."

Pavel tries to fumble under his pillow for a weapon, and I shoot him in the hand. "The next shot will be to your head," I tell him calmly.

"Who are you?" he demands shakily, staring down at the shattered bloody mass that was his hand. "What do you want? You don't have to hurt us. If it's money, I can—"

"It's not money," I reply. Stefi has both audio and visual access to this conversation through the camera I've pinned to my shirt. "Before you die, I want you to know why. Eight years ago, you tracked my wife down in Istanbul. She was visibly pregnant, but you didn't give a fuck. You fought with her and pushed her to the ground, and because of what you did, she lost our baby." I raise my gun to his head. "This is for Stefania and for Christopher."

"Stefania, Henrik's little runaway in Istanbul?" Something flickers in his eyes—fear? —and a muscle ticks in his jaw. "Why would you kill me? I let her live."

In my ear, I hear Stefi's harsh intake of breath. "Explain," I snap. "Quickly."

"I could have told Bach she was still alive, but I didn't. Instead, I told him I killed her. That's the only reason she's still alive."

I roll my eyes. "You told him she was dead and then collected the bounty on her, and you're trying to frame that as an act of altruism? I don't think so."

My finger starts to squeeze the trigger.

"Not just that," Dachev yelps. "Who do you think fed Rachid the information he gave her? That was me. Every piece of intel that she got came from me. Vannier, Benita, Warren, Medina, Bates, Rodriguez. She wouldn't have been able to kill any of them without my help."

"You're talking about Q?"

"Was that what he was calling himself?" he asks with contempt, forgetting for a moment that my gun is pointed at his head. "If that idiot hadn't died in September..."

I go still. "Q is dead? When? How?"

"Rachid Nenne died from a heart attack at the tail end of September. Why do you care?"

Because Stefi was talking to Q in October.

All along, I've been wondering who Q was working

The Hunter

for and who he betrayed Stefi to. But it looks like I've been asking the wrong question.

I should have been asking who Q was.

Because the person who gave Zaworski's location to Stefi wasn't Rachid Nenne.

No.

Someone figured out that Nenne was Stefi's source for intel.

They killed him, and they took his place.

They led my wife into a trap.

Who?

Who is behind all of this?

"Did anyone know about Nenne?" I demand. "Did anyone know you were feeding him information?"

"Nobody. A boy walked in on me once when I was talking to Rachid, but he was just a kid."

Ice drenches my spine. "What boy?"

His eyes slide away from me, and a prickle of unease creeps up my neck. "Ewan Wagner," he replies. "One of Henrik's trainees. The last one left."

Everything falls into place with a click. "You idiot," I say, forcing the words past the lump in my throat. "People in Bach's network mysteriously start to die. Henrik's trainee walks in on you feeding information about your rivals to Nenne, and a few months later, Bach conveniently dies in a car accident, and *you didn't think anything of it?*"

Realization hits his eyes. "No," he says. "It can't be. Bach is still alive?"

"Of course he is." Stefi doesn't say a word. She's got to be as shocked as I am. "He knew you were betraying him, but he didn't know who was taking out his network."

Not until Poland. As soon as we were made at Zaworski's party, he knew who we were. He must have lost track of us in the farmhouse, but he picked up the trail again in Nuremberg. He wouldn't have been able to touch us in Venice, but he didn't have to.

All he had to do was sit back and wait for us to take Dachev out.

My mouth goes dry with fear. I tap my earpiece furiously, my voice urgent. "Stef, get out of there. It's a trap. Can you hear me? Bach's still alive."

I look down at the scum on the bed, and my finger tightens on the trigger. Dachev lets out a terrified whimper. It's finally sinking in that death is staring him in the face. He cradles his shattered hand and looks up at me, desperation written all over him. "I have information," he forces out through stiff lips. "Information I want to trade for my life."

He's already told me about Q, already revealed enough for me to work out that Henrik is still alive. "After what you did, what do you think you can tell me will pay for your life?"

"The boy," he replies, his eyes glued to my trigger finger. "Do you know who he is?"

"Get to the point before I lose what little patience I have," I snap.

"He's seven and a half years old." He wets his lip with his tongue. "Seven and a half years ago, I went back to kill Stefania, but I found her in a hospital in the middle of giving birth."

The Hunter

Ice drenches my spine. I'm on the verge of figuring it all out, and it's all pointing to one inescapable, terrifying conclusion. "What did you do, Dachev?" I ask, my voice trembling.

"I bribed a nurse to swap her baby with a dead one," he says.

No. It can't be. He has to be lying. The air feels too thin, like all the oxygen has been sucked out of the room. My hand trembles, and for a second, I can't breathe. No. This can't be true. It can't. The timeline rushes through my mind—a frantic, disjointed calculation. Seven and a half years. It matches up. And why would Dachev lie about this? He's hoping this information will buy him his life.

Stefi mourned her son for years. She was so fragile after his death that she tried to kill herself. All so this man could do what? Make a few thousand euros selling a child to Bach? I think about her grief, the grief she's been carrying inside her chest for almost the last decade, and fury fills me, threatening to burn me from the inside out.

Dachev looks up at me. "I put him in an orphanage until he was old enough, and on his fifth birthday, I gave him to Bach. He's still with him. Stefania's son isn't dead. He's very much alive."

My mind explodes with rage. Ewan, that child with the too-thin frame, the little boy who held a machine gun in his hands and rained destruction down on us, is our son. I feel like I'm drowning, and I can't even imagine what Stefi's feeling right now. Everything we've known and believed is being reshaped by this revelation, and it's too much. My anger builds to a crescendo and shatters outward. I shoot Dachev between the eyes, a quick death he does not deserve.

His mistress lets out a terrified whimper, but I don't care; I barely register it. I have more urgent matters on my mind. I'm tapping my earpiece urgently. "Stef, did you hear all that? The child with Bach, that's our son. That's Christopher."

A chuckle fills my ear. "Your wife is otherwise occupied, Signor Carvalho," Henrik Bach says. "If you ever want to see her alive again, come to the dock. Alone. Look for a boat called *The Good Fortune.*"

Then the line goes dead.

47

STEFI

I sit behind the steering wheel of our getaway car, straining to listen to Joao's conversation with Pavel Dachev. "This is for Stefania," he says, "and for Christopher."

My eyes fill with tears. Stupid pregnancy hormones. But when I hear Joao remember our dead child and tell Dachev he's killing him for Christopher, it begins to heal a wound inside me that I thought would stay raw forever.

I will always grieve the baby I wanted so much that I risked everything to protect him, but I now realize there's room in my heart for happiness. Joy will never totally replace sadness, but the two emotions can coexist.

I'm so lost in my thoughts that I miss the next part of the conversation. I hear Dachev telling Joao that he's been feeding Q the information I bought from him, and then he says something that makes the hairs on the back of my neck stand up. "If that idiot hadn't died in September…"

I freeze. Q died in September? But that can't be. He

tipped me off about Zaworski's party six weeks ago, and I told him I'd be in Nuremberg a week after that.

If I wasn't talking to Q, who was I talking to?

My brain is just beginning to put two and two together when I hear Dachev's next words. "Seven and a half years ago, I went back to kill Stefania, but I found her in a hospital, in the middle of giving birth."

My palms turn sweaty, and my heart starts to race. What's Dachev hinting at? What's he saying? Did he... Could he...

"What did you do, Dachev?" I hear Joao ask.

Then I hear the words that change everything. "I bribed a nurse to swap her baby with a dead one. Stefania's son isn't dead. He's very much alive."

The boy that shot me in Nuremberg...

That's Christopher.

That's our son.

It can't be, but it really is. For a moment, I can't breathe. The world tilts, and my vision blurs as Dachev's words play in an endless loop in my mind. Christopher is alive. The baby I wept over, the baby I buried in Istanbul and whose grave I visit every year and whose death I've never stopped mourning...

Is alive.

Impossible relief surges through me, a flicker of hope so bright it's almost blinding. My son lives. The last two months have been filled with miracles, and this is the most unlikely one, the most joyous...

But my happiness quickly turns sour as the next horrifying realization dawns on me. Christopher is alive, but Dachev *gave him to Bach.* A tidal wave of rage washes

The Hunter

over me. The same monster who stole our childhoods, who turned us into deadly weapons, has my son.

And suddenly, there's no room for confusion or hesitation. An icy determination settles over me. I will do whatever it takes to find Christopher and get him out, and I'll kill anyone who stands in my way. *This ends now.*

My thoughts are still racing, colliding with one another, when the passenger side door opens, and a man slides in, his gun pointed directly at my temple. "I'm not at all happy with you, Stefania," Henrik Bach says, his voice as cold as ice. "You've been a thorn in my side for far too long, and now you're going to pay the price. Both you and your precious husband."

I scramble to open the car door, but a movement in the corner of my eye stops me. Ewan—Christopher—appears outside the driver's side door, pointing a blunt-nosed Glock 19 right at me. "Don't even think about running, or Ewan will shoot you dead. Won't you, Ewan?"

For a moment, I can't think. It's not fear that holds me captive; it's sheer, blinding fury. I haven't set eyes on Bach in eight years, but seeing him now, with his pretentious gold-rimmed glasses, his moth-eaten cardigan, and his slicked-back hair, hot anger bubbles to the fore. This is my child that he's using to threaten me. My baby, taken from me all those years ago.

And I'm going to make him pay.

"You know something, Henrik? I'm delighted to find you here, alive. Both Joao and I felt terrible that we weren't able to give you the death you so richly deserve. Looks like we're going to get another chance, after all."

His face twists with rage. He's not used to being talked

to this way by one of his trainees. We're supposed to know our place, which is always under his boot.

"You fucking cunt," he snarls, his face twisted in an ugly scowl.

Then he swings the barrel viciously across my face and temple.

And the world goes dark.

48

STEFI

I wake up on a boat, my jaw aching and my head throbbing. The pain is making me nauseous like it always does, but I push it down and do my best to ignore it.

This isn't good. This isn't good *at all*.

I take stock of my situation. I'm tied to a wooden chair in the middle of a cabin. My hands are behind my back, my wrists secured by metal handcuffs. My ankles have been bound to the legs of the chair with nylon rope. It's thin—only the diameter of my pinkie—but from experience, I know it's near unbreakable. The only thing that'll work against it is a sharp knife, and my blade, the one Joao gave me, is gone.

I feel a set of eyes on me. I turn my head as best as I can and see Christopher staring at me. My breath hitches as I look at him, taking in every detail. His sharp cheekbones and ocean-blue eyes are from his father, but the stubborn set of his jaw is all me.

This is my son. Alive, close enough to touch, *and he has no idea who I am.*

Tears prickle in my eyes, but I blink them away. I have to stay strong for him. But I don't know what to do. Should I tell him who I am, or should I hold my tongue? I want to; God knows I want to gather him into my arms and hug him tight. I want to kiss his face and rock his too-thin body, and I want to tell him that he's my world, he's my everything, and his father and I are going to rain fury down at the people that did this to him. We're going to make this right.

Except I can't promise him that. All I can offer him is hope. Hope that we're going to escape. Hope that we're going to be reunited, hope that we can become the family we never got a chance to be.

I can't tell him the truth. Right now, he sees me as the enemy because of Bach's lies. But if he finds out that the woman he shot is his mother, how will he react?

It could shatter him.

And I can't risk that. *I won't.*

My emotions don't matter; I need to do what's best for my son. "Hey," I say softly, careful to keep my voice calm and unthreatening. "Ewan, right?"

He nods but doesn't say a word.

"How old are you?"

"Almost eight," he mutters.

Seven and a half, actually. I remember myself at his age. How alone I was, how powerless I felt. How much I hoped that my parents would improbably find me and rescue me from the horror I found myself in.

His eyes are haunted and he's too thin, too skinny.

The Hunter

Fucking Bach is probably withholding food. Starving us was one of his favorite training methods. My stomach churns as I think about what he must have gone through, and a wave of self-loathing washes over me. While I was busy tearing down the spider web that is Bach's vast and evil network, my son was at the mercy of this monster. I couldn't save him from it. I couldn't protect him.

"I'm so sorry," I whisper.

"About what?" His voice challenges me to pity him. "You're the one who's gonna die."

I search desperately for the right words. "I used to be you. I was taken from my parents and brought to Bach when I was five." I exhale in a shaky breath. "Do you remember your mother?"

He shakes his head. It's what I expected—what else could it be? I never even got a chance to hold him in my arms. I blink back the tears that fill my eyes and threaten to spill down my cheeks.

"Me neither. All I can remember is the way my mother smelled, like jasmine mixed with incense. Every time I get a whiff, it brings me comfort."

His expression softens for an instant before he abruptly turns away. Crap. I shouldn't have tried so hard. I don't want to push him away. To Christopher, I'm a perfect stranger, and he has no reason to trust me. He's learned through bitter experience not to trust the adults in his life.

I cast about for a neutral topic of conversation, something that would keep him here, talking to me. "Where am I?"

"On a boat," he says, stating the obvious. "We're

docked." He jerks his head toward the deck. "He's waiting for your husband."

Joao. Of course Bach would have called him. He doesn't just want to kill me; he wants to kill both of us. My heart clenches. As much as I want to entertain the fantasy that Joao will go back to Venice for reinforcements, I know better. Joao knows Christopher is still alive and being held prisoner by Bach. My husband is on his way here, murder in his heart.

Footsteps sound above my head, and Christopher—Ewan—flinches like a puppy that's been kicked over and over again. Rage fills me. "Where's the rest of your cohort?"

He looks confused. "Co-hort?"

"The other children, where are they?"

"There was one other. . ." His voice drops to a whisper. "It's just me now."

My poor, poor baby. All of Bach's insanity—his insane mutterings and his wild mood swings—have been directed squarely at him. "I'm so sorry," I say again, though the words don't feel adequate to this situation. "I'm so, so sorry, Ewan. I can't do a damn thing about the past, but we're going to get out of this. Things are going to change."

"No, they won't," he says tonelessly. "You tried to run, but he found you, and you're his prisoner again. Nothing will ever change."

"I know it seems that way, but Bach isn't going to get away with it this time." If Henrik kills Joao, he'll be declaring war on the Venice Mafia, and Antonio Moretti will not let him get away with it. One way or the other, it's

The Hunter

the end of the line for Bach. Joao and I might die here today, but Christopher will survive, and I cling to that silver lining.

"My husband will find me," I continue, my voice confident. "And he will kill Bach. We're going to help you, Ewan. Things are going to get better."

"You shouldn't lie to him," a cold voice says from the doorway. Bach enters the cabin. "I see you're up, Stefania. You missed the call I had with your husband, but rest assured, he's on his way. And then I'm going to take the greatest of pleasure in killing you both."

Just then, there's a clattering on the deck. Christopher disappears from the room and returns a moment later with Joao. My heart sinks, and I shoot him an apologetic look. "Sorry about this. I shouldn't have got caught."

"Hello, Joao," Bach says, retreating a very safe distance away from my husband and keeping his gun trained on me. There's an unspoken message there. *Try anything, and I'll kill your wife.* "It's been a while."

Joao ignores Henrik. "No worries, Stefi," he responds to me, as if Bach hadn't spoken, staring at our son with open yearning in his eyes. "I'm right where I want to be." His mouth twists into a smile that does not reach his eyes. "Look on the bright side. Henrik didn't die in a car accident. Now we get to kill him."

Like me, Joao is not going to give Bach the satisfaction of watching us fall to pieces. Bach can kill us, sure, but we won't cower. Enough is enough—neither of us will do anything to traumatize our child further.

Moretti will find Bach, and my son will be rescued. As

for Joao and I... if we're going to die, then this is the way I want it to happen. *Together.*

"That's exactly what I was thinking," I reply. "And I don't know about you, but I want to take my time. Savor the moment."

Christopher watches us in confusion while Bach's face turns an extremely satisfying shade of purple. This isn't the scene he had in mind. We should be begging for our lives, and instead, we're grimly plotting the best way to kill him.

"I don't think you understand the situation," he spits out. "So let me spell it out. I have a gun, and the two of you do not." He gestures with his gun. "Search him," he orders our son. "Make sure he's unarmed."

Christopher pats Joao down as thoroughly as he can but finds nothing. "I could have told you that," Joao says when he's done. "Stef and I don't need weapons to kill you, Henrik, and if you don't remember that, you're an even bigger fool than I took you for."

"Tie him up," Bach snaps. "Tie them separately, not back-to-back. I don't want them freeing each other." His mouth twists into a malicious smile as he watches my child work. "I've spent a lot of time finding the perfect death for the two of you. I think you're going to love what I've come up with."

"He's waiting for us to ask," Joao says, a bored note in his voice. "He hasn't realized that we don't give a fuck."

Winding Henrik up is its own reward, but that's not the only reason Joao's doing it. The angrier Bach gets, the less attention he'll be paying to what Joao is actually doing, which is testing his bonds and flexing his wrists against the handcuffs to see if he can get them to release.

I need to keep Bach angry and distracted. "What a fucking coward you are," I tell him. "A grown man hiding behind an eight-year-old child? You couldn't even shoot me on your own in Germany; you sent Ewan to do it. Pathetic."

A vein throbs in Bach's forehead. He wants to hit me so badly, but for some reason, he's holding himself back. "He should have killed you," he grinds out. "I was quite unhappy about his failure."

My heart leaps in my mouth. "Did he hurt you?" I ask Christopher urgently. *"What did he do?"*

My son doesn't respond, not at first. But Bach loves to show off his handiwork. "Show them, Ewan," he says.

Christopher silently lifts up his shirt. Down his right side is a line of relatively fresh and angry-looking burns. I stare at them for a second, unable to comprehend what I'm looking at, and then Joao growls deep in his throat. "You burned a child?" he spits out, fury infused in every syllable.

Oh God. I nearly lose the contents of my stomach. The round marks are cigarette burns. He held his cigarette against my son's skin to punish him, not once, but three times.

"You fucking psychopath," I snarl, so angry I can't see straight. "You burned a child. You're going to pay for this." I look at the young boy in front of me, and tears fill my eyes. "What he did was wrong," I whisper. "I know it feels like nobody cares, but I do. We're going to get you out,

Ewan. Hold on for just a little bit longer. The end is almost in sight."

"You really shouldn't give him false hope. After all, in a couple of hours, you'll both be dead. I have something truly special in store for you. In fact, it was Ewan here who gave me the idea. He was watching a documentary about sharks. Did you know that a colony of great white sharks has recently migrated to the Black Sea? No? Me, neither. It caused quite a consternation as the sharks swam from the Mediterranean, through the Turkish Straits, and into the Black Sea. The marine biologists at Istanbul University tagged them, and there's even a website that broadcasts their location."

He rubs his palms together in glee. "I've killed a lot of people in a lot of ways, but I've never tossed anyone into shark-infested waters. I'm so looking forward to it. And on that happy note, I need to leave you. Someone needs to get this boat underway, after all. Ewan, come with me."

I turn toward Joao as soon as Henrik leaves. I can't talk about Christopher without breaking down, so I ask about the handcuffs instead. "Any luck?"

He shakes his head grimly. "No. I'm sorry, Stefi. I can't get free."

"Me neither. We're not going to get out of this, are we?" I take a deep breath. "Can I tell you something terrible? As much as I wish you were safe in Venice, there's a small, shameful part of me that's glad you're here with me."

"I'm glad I'm here too," he replies. "Together 'til the end."

The Hunter

I'm about to reply when I feel something sharp on the seat of my chair.

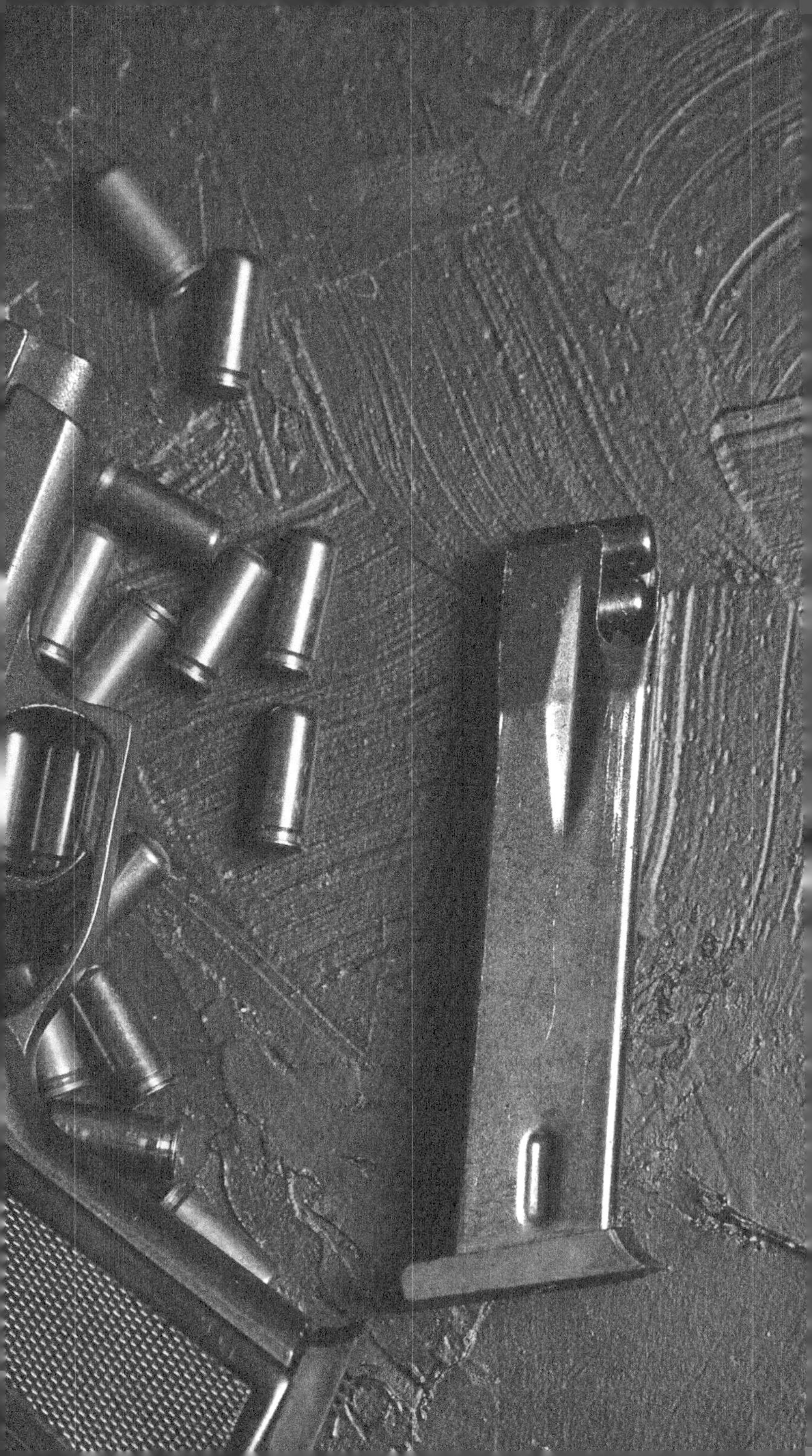

49

JOAO

Stefi and I, we're pretty good at surviving. We had to be. This time, though? I think our luck might have run out.

If this is the end, I'm glad we're going to meet it together. I say as much to Stef, but she's not listening. All of a sudden, her back straightens, and her head lifts up in hope. "I think I'm sitting on a paper clip," she says, life returning to her voice. "Christopher must have left it for me."

That's my boy. My heart fills with warmth, and I smile widely at my wife. "Good thing you've been practicing how to get out of handcuffs."

Her cheeks turn pink. "Is now the time to reminisce?"

"When better?" I can hear footsteps. "I'll keep Bach distracted while you get out of them."

She nods tightly and then gets to work. Her hands are locked behind her back, and the clip is out of reach. She rocks the chair back and forth, a little at a time, and it slides back. I watch, my heart in my mouth. If she leans back too much... If it falls out of reach...

Her fingers close around the thin steel just in time because Henrik comes marching back into the cabin, a gun in his hand, and my son slinking behind him, looking like a beaten puppy.

"Ewan's going to untie your feet, and you're going to walk up to the deck," he says. "Please don't try to do anything heroic; if you do, I'll shoot you in the kneecaps and then toss you to the sharks. And if you're under any illusion that you can get to me by using Ewan as a hostage, let me assure you that I will have no problem shooting him either."

Cold resolve hardens in my heart. Stefi's going to get out of her cuffs, and then we're going to make Bach pay. He doesn't know it yet, but he will not live past the end of the day, even if I have to die to ensure it happens.

"Nothing's changed, then," I sneer. "Loyalty's never been a two-way street for you, has it?" I glance at Stef. The paper clip is out of sight, but she's going to need time to work on the cuffs, and I have to prevent Henrik from noticing. That's easily done. It was never hard to get Bach angry. "I suppose that's why you find yourself all alone, reduced to using a child to do your bidding. My wife's taken quite the wrecking ball to your empire, hasn't she? How far you've fallen from the glory days."

His lips tighten, and he hits me so hard across the jaw with the butt of his gun that my chair falls backward. "Get upstairs," he snaps. "One more word out of either of you, and I will slice your tongue out before I throw you overboard."

The Hunter

I give Christopher my best reassuring smile as he kneels beside us, his small hands fumbling slightly with the rope. Henrik supervises, his eyes sharp and alert for trouble, but neither Stefi nor I fight back.

Not yet.

We proceed up the stairs without incident. The waves are choppier now, and the small boat is being tossed relentlessly over the water. The sky is darkening rapidly, and a storm is coming. It's the right time of the year for the cyclones that form in the Black Sea. In normal times, I wouldn't be thrilled about being caught in the middle of one of them, but Bach's a notoriously poor sailor, so this could work to our advantage.

He looks a little green as the deck rises and falls under his feet. Unfortunately, his grip on his gun is just as firm as ever. "Bind them to the rail," he orders, his weapon trained on us.

Christopher complies without a word. He drags a short length of chain across the deck, loops the chain through the handcuffs on our wrists, and threads it around the rail. If he notices the paper clip clenched in Stefi's fists, he doesn't let on. When he's done, we're standing side by side with our backs to the rail, positioned in such a way that Henrik can't see Stefi working to get out of her cuffs.

Bach doesn't seem to realize how we've been bound until our son is done. It's only when the boy steps away that he expresses his disapproval. "No, no!" he spits out, the gun going in all directions as he gesticulates. "I want them to be able to see the water."

"You want me to retie them?" Christopher asks.

No, I can't let that happen. Our hands are tied behind our backs. If we're facing the water, then Bach will be able to see Stefi getting loose. He's on the verge of answering, and I've got to provoke him before he gives the boy the order.

"Can't bear to see our faces?" I taunt. "Could it be that after a lifetime of being an utterly terrible human being, you're finally having a tiny attack of conscience? No, that can't be it."

"That's it," he yells, aiming his gun at my leg, pointing directly at my kneecap. "I warned you, Joao. I told you to shut your fucking mouth, but you can't follow even the simplest of instructions." His finger starts to pull the trigger...

I tense instinctively, waiting for pain to tear through me.

"They're here," Christopher shouts, a pair of binoculars glued to his eyes. "We found 'em."

The bullet misses my knee and hits my thigh. Pain sears through me, and I grit my teeth against it. Stef gasps out loud and takes a step toward me, but I shake my head. "I'm fine." My leg feels like it's on fire. It takes all my willpower not to show the excruciating agony on my face, but I won't grant Henrik the satisfaction of hearing me scream.

I won't frighten Christopher. And more importantly, I will do *nothing* to worry Stefi. Especially not now, when she's pregnant. I cannot stress her out, so if it means gritting my teeth and pretending like it's just a nick, then that's what I'm going to do.

But in the back of my mind, a countdown starts. My

hands are tied behind my back, and I can't apply any pressure on the wound, let alone a tourniquet. I don't think the bullet hit the femoral artery, but even so, it's not looking good for me.

I got to meet my son before I died, but I would have really liked to meet our baby.

I paste a reassuring smile on my face, but Stefi's not buying it. She's panicking. She knows what I've worked out. That even if I somehow manage to staunch the flow of the blood, I'll still have lost too much of it. If I'm not rushed to a hospital, there's a very real chance I'm going to die.

And we're in the middle of the Black Sea, hours away from medical care, with the storm only getting worse.

"Joao," she whispers through bloodless lips. "Hold on, okay? It's going to be okay. Everything's going to be okay."

It's not, and we both know it. But I nod as if I buy it because if she cries, I don't think I'll be able to bear it. And selfishly, I don't want her tears to be the last thing I see before I go. I want to see my wife smile as brilliantly as a summer sun. I want to see her green eyes sparkle with laughter.

I want—*need*—to see her *happy*.

Henrik's not paying any attention to us. He's not even gloating about the blood gushing from my leg in hot red spurts; he's too busy leaning over the rail of the deck, staring into the distance with Christopher's binoculars, distracted by the appearance of the sharks.

Stefi takes advantage. Her face pale, her eyes fixed on my bleeding thigh, she works on the handcuffs, and I see her shoulders slacken as they fall free. It takes her another quick moment to undo my handcuffs and free me, and—

"Cut the engines," Bach tells Christopher. "Then come here."

My son doesn't react as he turns the key for the engine. But I'm looking at him, and I see the way his shoulders tighten ever so slightly, as if he's bracing for pain. His eyes dart to the small folding knife that Bach's taken out of his pocket and then to his face, and he shuffles over, his face bloodless.

Bach opens the blade. "Hold out your arm," he orders.

It happens so quickly that I don't even realize what he's doing until it's too late. My son doesn't even try to protest. He bites his lower lip hard when Bach slices his forearm and holds it out so his blood can drip into the water.

Stefi makes a choked noise in her throat. Fury engulfs me. I am going to tear him apart with my bare hands. I clench my fists, my nails biting into my palms before I make eye contact with my wife—

And after that, everything seems to happen almost at once.

Moments after Christopher's blood drops into the sea, the dorsal fin of a shark carves through the water, heading straight for us. Stefi moves like a blur, her hand flicking up and swinging the loose handcuffs like a weapon. They catch Bach across his face, snapping his head to the side, and in that moment of inattention, she kicks his gun free.

He rushes for her, murder on his face, and I step in

The Hunter

front of him. Just a small step, but the moment my injured foot touches the deck, I start to buckle. Hot, agonizing pain tears through me, and my vision goes blurry. I'm not going to last very long. I'm not going to last, and then I'm going to leave Stefi and Christopher alone with this madman.

Stefi, who's pregnant with our baby.

Christopher, who's already been the target of Bach's rage more often than any child should.

And it's that thought that provides me superhuman strength. Clutching the deck rail for support, keeping as much of my weight off my leg as possible, I position myself so that my body is between Henrik and my wife.

He charges again, fury etched all over his face. I make a grab for him, my fist connecting with his jaw...

Just then, the deck tilts sharply as the boat dips into a deep swell...

Henrik, already a bad sailor, loses his footing...

And I push him over the edge.

He goes overboard, falling into the water below with a thin scream.

The shark swims closer.

"Help!" The man who kidnapped Stefi and me when we were children, who beat, tortured, and starved us, screams. He gets one arm out of the water and lurches desperately for the ladder on the hull of the boat, but the skies open up just then, and he can't quite reach it in the deluge.

I watch with cold satisfaction as Bach struggles to reach safety. "Help!" he screams again. "Ewan, get me out of here."

My son doesn't move a muscle.

A shark fin slices closer through the water, the smell of blood already attracting it. Henrik Bach screams once more, thin and shrill and loud...

The water turns red and bloody as the creature bites down, and then...

It's over.

I turn away, darkness pressing in from all sides. Christopher doesn't take his eyes off the carnage, but Stefi hurries to my side. "Hold on," she begs, tearing off her shirt and fashioning the sleeve into a tourniquet. "Help is on the way."

"You don't have to lie to me," I whisper. The timer is still running in my head, and I know what it means. "I'm good. Bach is dead, and you're okay, Christopher's okay, and our baby is going to be okay, too. That's enough for me."

She bends down and kisses me, tears coating her eyes. "Joao," she says, and then I hear it, a low thrum that's rapidly getting louder, even louder than the storm that's building around us. A black helicopter appears in the sky and drops like a bird swooping over the water. A man emerges from it, winches down in a harness, and lands on the deck.

It's Daniel.

"How?" I ask Stef in complete incomprehension. I'd been searched for recording devices when I came on board, and she would have been searched, too. How on Earth did Daniel know where to find us?

She tries to sound cocky, but the best she can manage

is a tremulous smile. "You should know by now," she says, "that I always have an exit plan."

50

STEFI

Valentina and I set up the exit plan back in Venice the day before Joao and I flew out to Varna. As soon as we decided I would go along to provide operational support, I called the hacker. "I need your help," I told her. "This hit looks easy, but something is making me uneasy, and I've learned to listen to my instincts."

"I'll be able to track you," she responded. "And I know Antonio wants to stay out of this, but we both know that he's going to have people ready to respond if you run into trouble."

"How will you track us? Through our phones?"

"Yes."

I frowned. "But that's not foolproof, not at all. After all, in Poland, both Joao and I were able to evade detection just by throwing away our phones. Do you have anything better?"

She gave me a long, thoughtful look. Valentina might

not like me, but she wanted to keep Joao safe as much as I did. "I've been working on something," she said, handing me a pair of gold earrings. "There's a tracker embedded in the metal."

"Won't it show up in a scan?"

"No, that's the clever part. The tracker doesn't broadcast until an hour after you activate it." She gave me a very serious look. "Even though I've been waiting for an opportunity to test them in the field, I hope you don't have to activate it."

But I had needed it. And because I swallowed my pride and asked her for help, Joao's going to make it.

Daniel winches Joao to safety. While he does that, I push aside my panic about his wound and move next to Christopher. He's still standing by the railing, staring at the spot where Bach went down, as if making sure there's no hint of him resurfacing.

My heart hurts for him, and I ache to take him into my arms. He thinks he's alone and he's scared, and I can remember feeling the exact same way.

But I always had Joao.

"Thank you for the paper clip," I tell him quietly. "Without you, we would have died out here."

He nods and gives the chopper an uneasy look. "I should get out of here."

"Where will you go?"

He shrugs, his expression stoic. But I've been him, and I know how he feels. I know the fear and the loneliness, the sinking realization that nobody cares whether you live or die.

I want to tell him he's not alone. That we're his

The Hunter

parents, that we're sorry—so sorry—that we let him suffer all these years, but things are going to change. That we're going to love him for the rest of our lives.

But Joao needs to be part of that conversation, too. This time around, I'm not going to act without talking to him first.

I settle for squeezing Christopher's shoulder, trying not to cry when he flinches away from my touch. "The authorities will want to put you in the system," I say quietly. "But the system doesn't understand people like us. If you'd like, you could live with Joao and me."

He stares at me with a strange look on his face. "Why?" he blurts out. "I tried to kill you."

I don't know how to answer this. Even if he wasn't our son, I'd make him this offer. He's just a child. He needs love, not anger and recrimination. "You did what he made you do, and if you hadn't obeyed, you would have been punished even more harshly." I'm never going to forget the cigarette burns on his skin. "I worked for Bach for six years, and in that time, I killed a lot of people. Who am I to judge you for what you did? My hands aren't clean." I smile tentatively. "Think about it, okay?"

He nods shortly. I want to say more, but there's no more time to discuss anything else. Daniel is back down, this time with a basket that will fit all three of us. When we reach the chopper, I see a familiar face. Matteo is bent over Joao's injured leg, and he's already got him hooked up to an IV.

My husband is pale but conscious. His gaze darts over at Christopher, and what he sees there must reassure him because he reaches out and squeezes my hand. "Hello, little fox," he murmurs. "Nice exit plan."

I squeeze him back and lean on his shoulder. My quest is over. I didn't think I'd survive it, but here we are. *Together.*

And then we're flying out of there, back to safety.

51

STEFI

Three days after Joao is discharged from the hospital, we sit down with Christopher in our living room to tell him the truth.

We're not alone. Dr. Alvarez, a therapist that Valentina recommended, is there with us, but even her warmly reassuring smile doesn't help calm my nerves. A thousand butterflies flutter in my stomach, and I feel even more queasy than usual.

I grip Joao's hand hard enough to cut off circulation. Dr. Alvarez leans forward. "Ewan," she says gently. "Stefi and Joao have something very important to share with you."

Our son has been living with us for the last week, but he's cautious, wary, and mistrustful. He looks suspicious now. "What is it?" he asks, a belligerent note in his voice. "Is it time for me to leave?"

My heart squeezes painfully. *Not that, never that.*

"No," Joao responds quietly. "Ewan, Stefi and I recently learned something about you." He draws a breath. "And something about us. Almost eight years ago, Stefi had a baby, but she thought she lost him during childbirth." He draws a breath. "Turns out that was a lie. Because our child was actually alive."

Our son goes still, his arms crossed over his chest in a defensive gesture. "And?"

My throat is tight, but I force the words out. "That child is you. You're our son."

His eyes widen, and he leans back in his chair as if trying to put space between us. "No," he says flatly. "Henrik told me that my parents were dead." His voice rises. "Why are you lying to me?"

I give the therapist a helpless look and she intervenes. "I know it's a lot to process, Ewan," she says calmly. "It's okay to feel confused or upset."

His hands shake, and he digs his fingers into the chair cushion. "I'm not confused," he says. "They are. They aren't my parents. That's a lie."

I don't know how to get through to him. "I named you in the hospital," I whisper. "Christopher. I held a dead baby in my arms and wept, and I buried you in a grave I visit every year." My eyes are wet with tears. "Ewan Wagner might have been the name Bach used, but it's not your name. You're... you're our son Christopher."

Joao slides off the couch and onto the floor. "I've missed—we've missed—almost eight years of your life," he says, his voice thick. "We weren't there when you needed us. We didn't protect you or keep you safe. And I'm sorry, Christopher. I'm so sorry. I would do anything to turn back time and fix the past, but I can't." He holds his hand out to the boy.

"All I can do is promise you that we're here now, and from this moment on, we will *always* be here for you."

I hold my breath as Joao waits, his hand outstretched, for our son to respond.

Christopher's breathing quickens. He stares down at his hands. "You can't be my parents," he says again, but there's a new note in his voice. It's not just anger and fear now. There's a faint undertone of hope. "If you were, why didn't you find me?"

"We didn't know you were alive," I choke out, my voice breaking. "If we'd known. . ." I follow Joao's lead and stretch my hand out. "I would burn the world down to keep you safe."

He doesn't respond for a long time.

Dr. Alvarez puts an encouraging hand on our son's shoulder, and I blink my tears back at how bleak he looks. "You don't have to say anything," I promise him. "Not today, not ever. We're always going to be here."

"I don't have to leave?"

"Never," Joao vows. "This is your home now."

"Okay." He still doesn't look up at us, but he stretches his hand out, too. For a moment, for one brief *shining* second, he lets his hand brush over ours. And then, scrambling to his feet, he runs out of the room.

Dr. Alvarez looks pleased. "It probably doesn't seem like it, but that went really well."

The tears spill down my cheeks, and Joao envelops me in his arms. "It did?" I ask hopefully.

"It really did," she reassures me. "I'll be back tomorrow, and we can pick up where we left off. Okay?"

Hope. There was a time when I wouldn't let myself feel that emotion, but I cling to it now. "Okay."

Charlie returns home just as Dr. Alvarez is leaving, her arms laden with shopping bags. She takes a look at our faces and immediately guesses what happened. "You told him? How did it go?"

"He hasn't run away yet," I reply, my voice shaky. "So, so far, so good, I guess."

She rolls her eyes. "You two," she says. "He's not going to run away. Why would he?" She pats my shoulder. "Stefi, you know why you can't get rid of me? You didn't just tell me I'd be safe—you made me *feel* it. Ewan knows the difference between the people that make promises and the people that actually *keep* them. He's going to be okay, I promise." She raises her voice. "Ewan, come help me with the shopping."

From the next room, there's a beat of silence before my son appears in the doorway. His eyes flit between Charlie and us before he takes a step toward her. "You bought a lot of food."

"I did." She hands him a couple of shopping bags. "Help me carry this into the kitchen, will you?"

"Okay." He starts to take a step toward the door, and then he adds, "And my name isn't Ewan. It's Christopher."

I freeze. For a moment, I'm too stunned to speak. I exchange a disbelieving look with Joao, and he squeezes my hand tight. My heart feels like it's about to overflow with happiness. Our son claimed his name. His real name, the one we chose for him.

Charlie blinks, her usual breezy confidence faltering for an instant before she recovers. "Okay," she says, her

The Hunter

tone light. "Christopher, please help me carry the bags into the kitchen." She tousles his hair. "And don't slam them down on the counter, please. You don't want to crush the tomatoes."

My son rolls his eyes. "If you didn't want the tomatoes crushed, why'd you put them in the bottom of the bag?"

Joao and I watch the two of them squabble good-naturedly as they leave the room. When they're out of earshot, he smiles down at me. "You know something?" he says. "I really think it's going to be okay."

"I do, too," I whisper. "I really do."

He kisses my forehead and brushes a finger over my wedding band. "There's nobody left on your list," he says, a look of contentment settling on his face. "So what happens now?"

"I've always wanted to live with my family in a house with yellow walls and windows that overlook the water," I tell him, my heart beating in my chest. The last week has been so busy, and we've both been so worried about Christopher that we haven't had a chance to talk about us —about our future.

"I've dreamed about waking up every morning next to the man I love, and I want a chance to do that." My voice drops to a whisper. "I promised you I'd love and cherish you for the rest of my life, and I'd like to keep that promise. If you want me to, of course."

He gives me a disbelieving look. "Stef," he says. "Have you not been paying attention for the last eight weeks? Of course, I want you." He pulls me close and kisses me on the lips, long and hard. "If we weren't already married, I'd ask you to marry me right now, all over again. You are the first person I think about when I wake up and the last thought in my mind before I sleep. You are my home and my family, my past, present, and future."

He rests his hand lightly on my stomach. "There's only one problem."

"What is it?"

"Charlie's got one of our two spare bedrooms," he says. "Christopher has the other." He gives me a cheerful grin, and I feel myself smile back in reply. "We're going to need a bigger house."

EPILOGUE
STEFI

Three years later

I never thought I'd be an overprotective, hovering mother, but it turns out I am. Considering the circumstances, can you blame me? But as protective as I am of my two babies, when Joao suggests a weekend away for our twelfth wedding anniversary, just the two of us, I'm tempted.

So tempted.

Does it have something to do with the fact that Magali is going through her terrible twos phase? Yes, it does. I love my daughter with all my heart, but the last couple of months have been *a lot*. Almost overnight, my sweet toddler has turned into a yelling, kicking, and screaming monster. She doesn't want to get dressed—she'd rather run around naked. She doesn't want to eat the food I make her—if it's not either pancakes or French fries, she's not interested.

And worst of all, she's stopped sleeping through the night.

I shouldn't complain. I'm fortunate enough to have a ton of help. Christopher is more responsible than any ten-year-old has a right to be, and he's happy to play with his baby sister for hours on end. If Joao and I want to go out for dinner, Charlie is always ready to watch her, and Lucia Moretti has Magali over for a playdate with her daughter Anna-Teresa at least once a week.

And despite all that, *I'm exhausted.*

Probably has something to do with turning thirty. Joao and I both reached that improbable milestone this year, something that we thought would never happen.

"We can't go away," I say regretfully. "Who'll watch Magali?"

Charlie looks up from the book she's reading. "I will," she says. "And Christopher will help too. Right, Chris?"

He nods.

"You're volunteering to watch Magali for the whole weekend?" I ask Charlie disbelievingly. "You do know what you're getting yourself into, don't you? You have heard her scream all night long?"

"Don't worry," she replies airily. "We'll handle it. If she's bad, we'll just tie her to her crib."

"Sure, but—" I start to say, and then her words sink in. "Wait, what? What are you planning to do to my daughter?"

Joao snorts a laugh. Christopher shakes his head, a small smile playing about his lips. "That was so awesome," Charlie says through a flood of giggles. "You should have seen your face. Don't worry, Stefi, we can

The Hunter

handle Magali. Besides, she always behaves for her big brother."

I look at my son. "What do you think?"

He nods again. "I think you should go. You deserve a nice trip away."

My heart melts. For all of Christopher's quietness, he's grown into such a thoughtful, steady boy. It's moments like this that remind me of how far he's come in the last three years.

"So?" Joao says expectantly. "What do you think?"

I don't know. . . Oh, what the hell. "Let's do it."

Joao smiles widely. "Perfect," he says. "I'll make the arrangements." He looks at Christopher. "Whatever you do, do *not* let Charlie tie Magali to the bed."

A rare smile crosses our son's face, and I get a sudden sense of the man he's going to be when he grows up. Under his stoic facade, he's deeply protective of the people he loves. "I won't."

Joao won't tell me where we're going. I ask him several times in the days leading up to our wedding anniversary, and he always shakes his head. "It's a surprise, little fox."

"I don't like surprises," I grumble.

"No," he says sunnily. "You love them."

He's not wrong about that. "If I don't know where we're going, how will I know what clothes to pack?"

He gives me a slow smile that warms me up from the

inside out. "Stefi, we're going to be alone for the first time in three years. Trust me, you won't need clothes."

My pulse speeds up at his tone. As any parent to a young toddler probably knows, sex can sometimes take a back seat to everything else. And while I love being a mom, I do miss the version of me that did crazy things like give Joao a blowjob in a busy Polish nightclub.

"We're going to spend the entire weekend naked?" I ask, my voice coming out breathless. "We can't do that. We'll have to eat sometime, right?"

"Wrong," he says, winking at me. "What a sad lack of imagination, Stefi. If we need food, we'll just order room service."

It's not until we get to the airport Saturday morning and check in for our flight that I discover where we're going. *Berlin.*

"Berlin?" I ask curiously. I haven't been to Germany for ages, not since I got shot in Nuremberg. "Why Berlin?"

"We're not staying there," Joao replies. "We're going to rent a car and cross the border into Pol—"

"Wait, are we going to Szczecin?" I ask, my face breaking out into a delighted smile. "I was just thinking about that dance club we visited. Remember it? That was a fun night." The blowjob at the nightclub was followed by a visit to a sex store, and then we had a 'who's going to get out of a set of handcuffs first' contest, which ended in more sex. Even now, if I think about the things Joao did to me that night, I start to blush.

"No comment." Joao gives me an amused glance. "I

The Hunter

already gave too much away. I'm not saying anything else that's going to ruin the surprise."

It's a short flight to Berlin. I settle in my seat and close my eyes for a second, and before I know it, we're landing. "Sorry about falling asleep on you," I say ruefully. "I'll be better company from now on, I promise."

"You're fine." He takes my backpack from me and leads the way toward the rental car counters. "You couldn't have had any sleep last night."

I didn't. Joao woke up to deal with Magali most of the week, so last night, I was determined to let him get a full night's rest. "I'm fine," I lie through my teeth.

"Sure you are."

At the rental car terminal, he takes care of the paperwork and collects the keys, then he leads the way to our car and gets behind the wheel. "Tell you what. I'll drive, and you can take a nap. I'll wake you up when we get there."

Szczecin is a couple of hours away from Berlin. A two-hour nap sounds amazing. "You're sure?"

He kisses the top of my head. "I'm absolutely sure."

Despite Joao's offer, I fully intend to stay awake on the drive. But my husband knows me better than I know myself, because the moment we hit the highway, my eyes tug shut.

When I wake up, we're not in Szczecin.

We're in front of the farmhouse, the one we squatted in for a week while we were on the run.

My mouth falls open with shock and I stare at my husband in disbelief. "Is this..."

Joao grins proudly. "Yes, it is." He gets out and comes around to open the passenger side door. "Your palace awaits, milady."

I step out and take in the building in front of me. The farmhouse has always occupied a special place in my heart. This is where Joao and I came together, this is where I fell in love with him all over again, this is where Magali was conceived...

I never thought I'd see this place again. I can't believe we're here.

Time has been kind to the farmhouse. The chimney isn't a crumbling wreck any longer, and the glass in the windowpanes looks new. The wood on the front door has been polished until it gleams. I stare at it, taking in the changes, and then I clue in. "Crap, it isn't abandoned—it looks like someone's put in a lot of work into fixing it up. We better leave before the new owners..."

Then I register the grin on Joao's face and my words trail away. "Who are the new owners, Joao?"

My husband hands me a thick brass key. "We are," he says. "And it better look amazing. You won't believe the number of times I've had to call the contractor." He pushes me gently toward the front door. "Come on. You're going to want to see the inside."

The inside has been transformed. Gone are the mouse droppings, the spider webs, and the gloom. Instead, there are soaring ceilings, exposed wooden beams, and twin skylights flooding the room with natural light. The fireplace that gave us warmth is still there, but it's been fixed up, with blue and white tiles lining the edge. The furniture has been chosen for comfort. Plush sofas and oversized armchairs invite you to sink in and relax.

"How?" I splutter.

"Happy anniversary, little fox."

I spin around. "Joao, this is. . . amazing. This is the best surprise."

"And you haven't even seen it all yet. Come on, let's look around."

We climb up the stairs, and Joao throws a door open. "Our bedroom," he announces.

"I hardly recognize it without a tree sticking through the ceiling," I quip. I start to look around, but then my attention is caught by something in the back yard. I walk to the window and look down. "Joao, there's a tent in the garden."

"Huh," he says innocently, joining me at the window and brushing a kiss over my lips. "Yeah, you're right. Imagine that."

I'm not buying that tone—not even for an instant. "What have you planned?"

He takes my hand in his, his thumb stroking the plain golden band on my ring finger. "We never had the wedding of your dreams," he says quietly. "And you never complained, but I know you wanted one."

"Sure, but it doesn't matter." I never want Joao to feel like I lack for anything. "The trappings are fun, but a wedding is just a big party." I give him a tremulous smile.

"What's important is the marriage that follows, and I have the marriage of my dreams."

"There's nothing wrong with a big party," he replies. "So, I thought, how could I give you this, and then it struck me that we could have a renewal ceremony." He stares into my eyes, his expression serious, yet tender. "The odds of us making it to thirty were bleak, and yet, here we are. Not just alive, not just surviving, but thriving. Our bellies aren't empty. We have a roof over our head, and a house filled with laughter. We have a family now, Charlie, Christopher, and Magali. Don't you think that's worth celebrating?"

I swallow the lump in my throat and nod. "I do," I whisper. "I really do. A wedding renewal? Here?"

He smiles as brilliantly as the sun. "What better place?" he asks. He tugs me toward the closet and throws open the door. Three long white dresses hang there. "We spied—okay, Charlie spied—on your Pinterest board, but—"

Once again, my mouth falls open. "I only had a wedding Pinterest board to help Alina out," I mutter defensively.

"Of course," he says, biting back his smile. "Anyway, we weren't sure which style was your favorite, so Rosa made a version of all three."

My head snaps up. "How?" I ask, my voice faint. I know Rosa Tran because she's married to Leo, the mafia enforcer, but she's a famous fashion designer and she's booked up for years. "But her waitlist... How did she find time to do this?"

He shrugs. "Family," he says simply. His phone

The Hunter

buzzes, and he looks down at the screen. "And speaking of family, that's the convoy now."

It's one amazing surprise after another, and my head is spinning. "Convoy?"

"Come downstairs, and you'll see."

I rush downstairs, and just as I look out of the front window, a line of cars pulls into the driveway, and people start to get out. Charlie emerges from the first car, carrying a squirming Magali, a wide grin covering her face. Christopher gets out from the other side, wearing a tuxedo, his hair neatly combed.

Antonio, Lucia, and their daughter Anna-Teresa get out from the car behind them. Dante, Valentina, and Angelica aren't far behind, as are Tomas and Alina. Then there's Leo and Rosa, Daniel, Matteo, Ignazio, Paulina, Goran, and Marta.

And all the women are wearing dresses in shades of yellow...

Because it's my favorite color.

As much as I want to hold it together, I can't. I turn around in Joao's arms and hold him tight, tears rolling unchecked down my cheeks.

I'm tearing up because all of our Venice family is here, and I didn't realize it until now, but I've always wanted this. It's not the dress or the flowers or the cake—it's this feeling of standing up in front of your family and friends to declare that you've chosen each other, and you'll stand by each other for the rest of your life.

"You did this," I whisper, my voice trembling with all the emotion swelling in my heart. "How did you know this is what I've always wanted?"

He squeezes my hand. "Because I'm very clever," he says with a smirk. Then his expression turns serious, and his voice drops low. "And maybe because I've always wanted this too."

WE RENEW our vows in a flower-filled garden. Charlie, Christopher, and Magali walk down the aisle with me to give me away, and Daniel acts as our officiant.

Joao looks like he's on the verge of tearing up as he takes my hand in his. He's doing better than me—I'm straight up weeping.

When I was ten, I saw a nun pull a knife on a skinny kid. I'd seen him around the compound, and I knew his name was Joao. But I never talked to him. He wasn't my friend, after all. He was a *boy,* and they were mostly just annoying.

Helping him was the smartest thing I did.

Joao and I have been through hell and back in the twelve years of our marriage. And we're still here. Still in love. Together, standing back-to-back, us against the rest of the world.

And I know I'm going to love him forever.

The party that follows is loud and chaotic. Polish pop blares on the speakers, a sly nod to the Szczecin nightclub that makes me blush.

Magali and Anna-Teresa run around the garden like two riotous butterflies, trampling flowerbeds and stuffing

The Hunter

raspberries into their mouths, while Christopher and Angelica chase after them to minimize the chaos they leave in their wake. Magali's pretty party dress is already torn, of course, and Anna-Teresa's has a big mud stain down the front.

Lucia is looking at her daughter with resignation in her eyes. Rosa has her arm around Leo and is listening to something Ali is saying. Ignazio is in conversation with Matteo, but he keeps looking at Charlie when he thinks no one is watching. Charlie is pretending to ignore him, but she keeps sneaking glances at him too. Tomas and Matteo are laughing over a beer, and Daniel is, no surprise, reading something on his phone.

Joao comes over with a couple of bottles of beer. "I'm not going to lie: this beer is a little tasteless." He winks at me. "If you have any suggestions on how to fix that. . ."

Heat creeps up my cheeks, and I smile up at my husband. "I do." I glance at the chaos unfolding in the garden—Magali chasing Anna-Teresa with sticky raspberry fingers, Christopher valiantly trying to keep them out of trouble—and then back at Joao, and then I put my arm around his waist. "Let's go inside, and I'll show you. The bathroom door has a lock, doesn't it?"

A look of shock flits over his face, and then he starts to laugh. "The smartest thing I ever did was ask you to marry me," he says appreciatively, clinking the neck of his bottle against mine. "Let's go, little fox. Show me what you've got."

Thank you for reading The Hunter.

More Joao & Stefi?! If you can't get enough of our happy couple, I have a slew of bonus goodies. A great deleted scene where Joao goes on a murderous rampage to find his wife, a scene in which we finally find out why Cecelia d'Este has a file on Stefi, and more! *You're going to want this.*

Sign up to read it by scanning the QR code below or going to:
https://taracrescent.com/bonus-the-hunter/

Want more Venice mafia?
Lucia and Antonio fall in love in **The Thief,** which kicks off with Lucia stealing a painting from Antonio. Read this

mafia hero+art thief heroine romance with second chance vibes today!

Valentina and Dante banter, hack, and stab their way to love in The Broker. Enemies-to-lovers, with a mafia hero and a single mom hacker heroine? Yes please.

Leo and Rosa are forced to get married to save Rosa's brother. Love a broody hero, arranged marriages, and an age-gap romance? You're going to want to read The Fixer.

Alina and Tomas get off to a fiery start when Tomas buys a controlling share in Ali's gym. Find out how they fall in love in The Fighter.

The next book in the series features **Ignazio and Charlie.** My newsletter is the best way to find out when it goes live, so sign up by scanning the QR code above.

Turn the page for a preview of THE THIEF, Antonio & Lucia's story.

THE THIEF

**I stole from Venice's mafia boss...
But when I get home with his painting,
He's there in my bedroom, *waiting for me,*
And he says...
"Hello, little thief."**

In the dark and shadowy underworld of Venice, one man rules with an iron fist.
Powerful mafia boss. King of Venice. **Antonio Moretti.**
Ten years ago, he was the stranger who emerged from the shadows to protect me on the worst night of my life.
But when I return to Venice to steal a priceless painting from Antonio, intent on returning it to the museum it belongs to, I realize...
The king of Venice has set a trap for me, and this time, *he's not letting go.*

A PREVIEW OF THE THIEF

LUCIA

I am very drunk, and everything is hazy.

It's a dark night—cloudy, moonless, and foggy. I've been wandering for hours, not paying attention to where I'm going, and I've ended up in a neighborhood I don't recognize. Venice is a safe city, but this section of town is far from the tourist core. The boats aren't pleasure yachts; they're working fishing vessels. Warehouses dot the docks, and there are more rats than people this late at night.

A week ago, I was working on my senior thesis in Chicago. I didn't know my mother was dying of cancer because my parents had kept her illness a secret from me. Which meant I didn't know she'd gone into hospice either.

I never got the chance to say goodbye.

I lift the bottle of vodka I'm clutching like a lifeline to my mouth and take a healthy swig.

A Preview of The Thief

Three days ago, I got a call that destroyed me. My mother had succumbed to the cancer ravaging her body. My father, unable to contemplate life without his wife, put a bullet in his brain. One day, I was wondering if I could convince my art history professor to grant me an extension for my final paper. The next, I was flying back home to bury my parents.

A hint of movement jerks me to the present. Something rustles to my right. Before I have time to react, three bodies coalesce from the fog and surround me. One of them holds a knife to my throat. "Don't move, and don't shout, signorina," he growls. "I don't want to hurt you. Give me your purse."

I'm being robbed.

Numbly, I hold out my bright green bag. I bought it on Calle Larga XXII Marzo from a *vu compra* who'd set up shop opposite the Dolce and Gabbana store. Mama and I did a bunch of tourist things before I left for college: we visited St. Mark's Basilica, listened to musicians at the *piazza*, rode a gondola, and ate at a restaurant a stone's throw from the Ponte di Rialto. The vendor insisted that the bag was actually Prada, not a fake, and my mother laughed at him. "We're not tourists," she said and haggled with him for the next fifteen minutes.

I should have realized she was sick. She'd lost weight, and for the last couple of months, she wouldn't FaceTime me. "My cell phone broke," she said. "I have to go buy a new one."

I should have suspected that something was badly wrong.

One of the men snatches the imitation Prada bag

A Preview of The Thief

from my hand while another shines a flashlight in my face. "Your necklace too."

Things are moving too fast for me to process, but those words penetrate my drunken stupor. The necklace I'm wearing, a filigreed ruby pendant dangling on a gold chain, belonged to my mother. My father gave it to her as a wedding present, and she never took it off. She's gone now, and this is all I have left of her. It's my most cherished possession.

"No."

"Don't be stupid, signorina," the man with the knife snaps. "It's not worth your life. Take off the goddamn chain and hand it to me before you get hurt."

"Someone's coming," Flashlight Guy says, his voice nervous. "We're not authorized… We need to get out of here." He makes a lunge for my necklace. The chain digs into my neck, and I yelp in pain.

A tall, lean man glides out of the shadows, his face obscured by the brim of his hat. "Stop," he says, his cold voice slicing the moisture-laden air like a whip.

One word. Just one word, but the reaction is electrifying. The man holding my purse takes one look and bolts. "Fuck," the guy who made a grab for my chain swears. The knife clatters to the ground, and the thief who held it holds up his hands in a gesture of surrender. "I'm sorry," he says, his voice trembling. "I didn't mean to… I didn't know—"

"You didn't know I was here. But I'm always watching. You should remember that." My rescuer's voice is ice. "Leave."

The remaining two criminals flee.

A Preview of The Thief

The man turns in my direction. He studies me for what seems like an age, his gaze lingering on the side of my neck. "You're hurt."

"I am?" I reach up, and my skin stings where the necklace cut me. "Yeah, I guess." The pendant is safe, though, and that's all that counts. "It'll heal."

He moves closer, his breath warming my face, and he touches the cut with a feather-light touch. "Who did this to you? Which one of them?"

A shiver runs down my back. Once again, everything is moving with bewildering speed, events rushing past me like leaves in a windstorm. The vodka has scrambled my thoughts, and this man isn't helping. His voice and touch aren't supposed to permeate my numbness, but they are, and I don't know how to react.

"The guy holding the flashlight."

"Marco." My hero's voice promises death. His eyes settle on me again, and his tone softens. "You're cold, signorina." He pulls off his jacket and drapes it around my shoulders, and warmth descends over me like a blanket. "This isn't a good part of town to be in alone. Alone and drunk."

My gratitude evaporates in a rush. He's judging me? What the hell does he know about my life? "You shouldn't offer unsolicited advice either, but here we are." Okay, that's quite rude. Mama would be shocked. "But thank you for your help," I add grudgingly, turning to leave.

"You're welcome," he replies, falling in step with me.

"What are you doing?"

"Escorting you home," he says, as if it were obvious. "Like I said, this is a dangerous neighborhood, and I would hate for you to get hurt again."

Home is filled with memories I'm trying to obliterate with a bottle of vodka. "I don't want to go home," I mutter sullenly. "And I don't care if I get hurt."

There's a long pause. "But *I* care, signorina."

Why? "We're at an impasse, then." I take another deep drink of my vodka, and then, out of some strange impulse, I offer the bottle to him.

I expect him to turn it down. I'm even prepared for him to do something dramatic, like fling it into the canal. But shockingly, he does neither. He pries it gently from my fingers. His lips wrap around the mouth of the bottle, the way mine did a second earlier, and he drinks. Then he hands it back to me, his fingers brushing mine.

Heat blossoms in my chest.

We walk in the darkness, taking turns drinking from the emptying bottle, neither breaking the silence. "I buried my parents today," I finally blurt out.

He glances in my direction. "I'm sorry."

"I'm not sad." It's not exactly a lie. *Sad* is too simple an emotion to describe how my world has been shattered. "I'm angry. I'm *furious.* My mother was sick, but she hid it from me. And when she died, my father blew his brains out."

He doesn't say anything.

"It wasn't just my parents who lied," I continue. "They all did. My best friend didn't tell me either. Did they think they were protecting me?" I take another healthy swig.

A Preview of The Thief

"Because I don't feel protected." My voice comes out defiant, shrill, and bitter. "I feel abandoned. I *hate* them for that."

He remains silent, but this time, the silence prickles at me. "What are you thinking?" I demand. "Are you going to give me the same advice the priest did? Are you going to tell me to forgive them?"

"I would never presume to tell you how to feel."

I stumble over a coil of rope. I'm about to fall, but his arms are around me before I do. His touch feels. . . solid. Reassuring. *Shockingly male.* "So, what then?" I persist. He's a tall body in the darkness, a warm presence at my side. I still can't see his face, and maybe that's what loosens my tongue. Or maybe it's the vodka. "You don't have any advice for me?" I keep stabbing at the open, bleeding wound. "If you were me, if your parents abandoned you like mine, what would you do?"

"I didn't know my parents," he says without inflection. "I was left at a church as a baby."

Oh. *Oh.* "I'm so sorry."

"I don't need your sympathy, *tesoro.*" The easy, relaxed set of his shoulders is replaced by stiffness. This is clearly not a welcome topic, and it's obvious he'd much rather talk about my problems than his own.

"Give me advice, then," I breathe. "Tell me what to do. Tell me how to move forward from this."

He still has his arm around me, and I've made no effort to pull away. It's nice to be held. His touch is a portal into a fantasy world where I'm not suddenly alone. A world in which there's someone who cares for me. Someone who will catch me before I fall.

"Did your parents love you?"

I nod wordlessly. That's why their betrayal hurts so much.

"We don't make our best decisions under pressure," he says quietly. "When we are hurt, when we are in pain, we don't think. We hide, we lash out. I can't pretend to understand your parents' decision. Maybe they thought they were protecting you. Or maybe they didn't want your last memories of them to be filled with pain."

I make a scoffing sound, but he's not done.

"As for moving forward," he says softly. "You just do. You remember that you were loved, and you put one foot in front of the other. Until one day, you think about them without pain. The anger and grief will fade, *cara mia*, and you'll be left with the good memories."

We've been walking steadily toward civilization. The Ca'Pesaro looms before me, casting ornate shadows into the canal. I drain the rest of my vodka and fling the bottle into the water.

He tracks the angry movement. "Where are you staying?"

I cannot go to my parents' apartment. I just cannot. I can't be in the place where they died. I can't run into the neighbors, and I cannot cope with their sympathy and concern. "I don't know." I reach for my phone and realize it's in the bag the thieves took. "My purse is gone." I take a deep breath and fight the urge to burst into tears. "I have no money."

He puts his hand on the small of my back, a comforting gesture that tells me I'm not alone. "Come

A Preview of The Thief

with me, signorina. Let's get you settled for the night. We'll find your purse in the morning."

My rescuer takes me to a hotel. The lobby is brightly lit, and I turn to him to finally see what he looks like, but all that vodka has caused me to see double and triple of everything. I get the sense of a firm jaw and full lips, but that's it.

"A room," he says to the clerk behind the counter.

The man jumps to attention. "Si, Signor," he says. There was respect in his voice but also a trace of fear? Or am I imagining it? I can't tell.

A key is produced. The well-dressed stranger steers me to the ancient elevator. Can I really call him a stranger if I've spent the better part of the last hour pouring out my troubles to him? I slump against him, my bones turning to liquid. "You smell nice," I tell him. It seems important that he knows that. "Like the ocean." I sniff him again. "And something else. Pine, maybe? I like it."

He doesn't reply, but his grip on me tightens slightly. I like that too.

We reach the room, and he follows me in, heading to the bathroom. I collapse on the bed, feeling his absence like a loss. I hear water running, and he returns with a glass, motioning me to sit up. "Drink this," he orders. "It'll help with your hangover."

"I don't get hangovers."

He laughs shortly. "Oh, you will, *cara mia*." It's the second time he's called me that. He cups my cheek with his hand and looks deep into my eyes. "Go to sleep," he says, his voice gentle. "Things will look slightly less bleak in the morning."

A Preview of The Thief

He turns away from me. I stare blankly after him. Only when he's almost at the door do I realize he's leaving. "Stop!" I don't want him to go. "I don't want to be alone tonight." I grip the bedspread with my fingers and take a deep, shaky breath. "Please?"

He hesitates for a long moment, then he relents. "Okay." He turns off the lights, and the room plunges into comforting darkness. A minute later, the mattress sags with his weight as he gets into bed with me.

My eyes close. Sleep tugs me under, but I fight it. I want one more thing tonight. "I don't know your name."

"Antonio."

"Antonio." I try it on my tongue. "I'm Lucia."

"A lovely name for a lovely woman." The words feel trite, but the weight in his voice makes me believe him. "You're safe here. Sleep well, Lucia."

When I wake up the next morning, I'm alone. There's no sign that anyone was ever with me. In fact, if I wasn't in a strange hotel room, I'd be convinced I imagined the whole thing.

I get out of bed and wince. Antonio was right. My head feels like it's going to explode. This is what I get for drinking an entire bottle of vodka in one evening.

I go to the bathroom and splash some water on my face. The skin around my neck is abraded and raw where the thief tried to yank my chain off. I finger the pendant

A Preview of The Thief

absently, a complicated cocktail of emotions churning through me. Antonio's words from last night ring in my head. *The anger and grief will fade, and you'll be left with the good memories.*

There's a knock at the door. I open it to a staff member wheeling in a cart of food. "Breakfast, signorina."

I'm starving, but I have no money to pay for the food. I'm about to tell him I didn't order anything when he adds, "Also, this was left for you at the front desk."

The *this* in his hands is my bag. The green, imitation Prada bag my mother bought for me before I left for college. And it's untouched. My passport, money, and phone are all in there.

My gallant rescuer strikes again.

Tucked in a front pocket is a thick, cream-colored card.

A phone number is printed on the front, and there's a handwritten note on the back. *Call me.*

I stare at it for a very long time.

Last night, Antonio took care of me. Stayed with me, listened to me. He made sure I was safe. When everything around me was crumbling, when I desperately needed someone to lean on, he was there.

But safety is a myth. Your world can shatter in the blink of an eye. People betray you. They hide illness from you and die. They shoot their brains out and leave you bereft.

The last three days have taught me I can't afford to lean on anyone.

A Preview of The Thief

I take a deep breath and tuck the card back into the purse. "Can you call me a cab in an hour?" I ask the man.

"Of course, signorina. Where to?"

"The airport." There's nothing left for me in Venice. Not anymore.

Ten years later...

When you're a museum curator moonlighting as an art thief, having a hacker for a best friend is a pretty good deal. Especially when it's time to plan your next heist.

It's Friday evening. I pour myself a glass of cheap red wine, settle in front of my laptop, and call Valentina. I feel the familiar stirring of excitement as I wait for her to connect. My first art heist was a mad impulse, but recently, I've been targeting rich and powerful people who knowingly acquire stolen art. People who think their wealth provides them immunity. It gives me great satisfaction to steal from them and return the paintings to their original owners.

And I can't wait to kick off this year's project.

The last time Valentina and I talked, I presented her with a list of seven potential targets, compiled by scouting through news reports, auction listings, and talking to my parents' old fence, Alvisa Zanotti. Signora Zanotti might be retired, but she keeps her finger on the pulse of the art world and stays updated on the ins and outs of black-market art. Valentina promised to look into the seven and narrow it down for me.

Italy is six hours ahead of Boston, so it's midnight in Venice. When Valentina logs on, she looks exhausted. "Long day?" I ask sympathetically.

Valentina and I have been best friends since kindergarten. Growing up, we spent practically every waking hour together. Valentina often took refuge at our house because her parents fought constantly. Some of my fondest memories are of the two of us spending long afternoons doing homework at our battered kitchen table, my mother supplying an endless stream of snacks.

"You could say that." She fills her wine glass right to the brim. "Some of the other children have been bullying Angelica, so I pulled her out of school."

After the death of my parents, I didn't talk to Valentina for two years. I blamed her—unfairly—for the secrets my parents kept. But Valentina didn't give up. No matter how often I ignored her, she kept reaching out. Our friendship finally resumed when she sent me a picture of a newborn. "This is Angelica," she wrote. "My daughter. Will you be her godmother?"

Anger stirs in me now. "Why were they bullying her?"

Valentina shrugs wearily. "Because she doesn't have a father."

"Ah." She's never once talked about the guy. I asked about him once, and she shut me down. Since then, we've reached a tacit understanding that neither of us will talk about the past. She doesn't mention my parents, and I don't ask why Angelica's father doesn't play a role in his daughter's life.

"I'm sorry," I tell her, wishing I had something more helpful to say. Something I could do, something more useful than offering support from afar. "That sucks."

"Yeah." She drinks deeply from her glass. "I haven't had time to look at your list."

"Forget the list." Valentina looks like she's at the end of her tether. I can't blame her. It's been one thing after another the entire year. Angelica broke her ankle in January. Then Valentina was sick all summer, and to cap off a truly shitty year, her father died in August. The two of them weren't close, but even so, I know it's taken a toll on my friend. As for Angelica, she's been having nightmares ever since her grandfather died.

And now this. My poor friend.

"How's Angelica doing?" I lean forward. "How are *you* doing?"

"I'm fine," she lies. "I'm putting her in a different school. A more international, diverse one." She stares morosely into her glass. "I miss you. Sometimes, I wish you were closer—" She cuts off whatever she's about to say next. "How's the job hunt going?"

"Miserable." My employment troubles are nothing new. I'm trained as a curator, but museum funding is highly volatile, and permanent positions are few and far between. I've spent my adult life hopping from one short-term contract to another and lived in eight cities in the last ten years. My last contract ended a couple of weeks ago. I've sent out some feelers, but it's getting close to the end of the year, so hiring is slow.

But that's not what's bothering me now. It's Valentina's despondent expression. Her uncharacteristic melancholy.

She's never once complained about the physical distance between us. Never once expressed discontent that I hadn't met Angelica in person.

Both her parents are now dead. They weren't much, but they're gone now, and she's spending her first Christmas without them.

I remember my first Christmas alone. The crippling loneliness and aching sense of loss. I would never wish that on my worst enemy. How can I do that to my best friend?

On impulse, I look at job listings in Europe. Then I go perfectly still.

Because there's a job opening in Venice. A four-month contract at the Palazzo Ducale to digitize their catalog.

Speaks fluent Italian? *Check.*

In-depth knowledge of Italian art? *Check.*

The pay is... well, I won't starve. And most importantly, I'll be there for Valentina.

Can you do it? Can you go back to Venice, the city you fled ten years ago?

My heart starts to race. I take a deep breath and order myself to calm down. It's only four months. I'm not going to stay forever.

Out of sight of the camera, I open my purse and fish out the business card I've held onto for a decade. It's faded. Dog-eared. I run my thumb over the handwritten note.

A Preview of The Thief

Call me.

I wonder if the number still works.

I'm tempted to call. *So tempted.*

It's been ten years, Lucia. He's probably married with a handful of children by now.

I tuck the card away.

Valentina says, "Lucia?"

"Sorry. I got distracted by something on my phone." I'm more than qualified for the Palazzo Ducale role. I should be a shoo-in for the job. I won't tell Valentina until I know for sure, but after ten years away, it looks like I'm finally returning home.

ANTONIO

Venice is my city. I head up her mafia, run her casinos, and rule her underworld. I know every dark alley and every narrow canal. All her secrets are mine. I started life with nothing, and I've fought my way to the top. Everything I've ever wanted is within my grasp.

And still, lately, I've been so fucking *bored* with it all.

I walk into our weekly meeting a good twenty minutes late. My second-in-command, Dante, glances pointedly at his watch as I enter. He's the only one who dares. My other lieutenants—Joao, Tomas, and Leonardo—ignore my tardiness and greet me respectfully.

"Sorry I'm late," I say crisply. "Let's get started."

Joao delivers an update on our smuggling operations. Leo goes next, and then it's Tomas, our numbers guy. As usual, his presentation is detailed and thorough. I normally find his briefings fascinating, but today, I have to work hard at faking interest.

"We're flush with cash," Tomas finally finishes. "Business has never been better. I have identified some investment opportunities. Padrino, I recommend—"

"Send me an email with the options," I say, cutting him off before he gets into the weeds. "Is there anything else?"

Dante, who's been silent all meeting, nods. "We have a problem," he says grimly. "The bratva has been spotted in Bergamo."

I sit up. Bergamo is only a couple of hours away. Too close for comfort. "Who?"

"A couple of foot soldiers of the Gafur OPG. Should I reach out to the Verratti?"

Salvatore Verratti runs Bergamo, and I can't see him forming alliances with the Russians. As far as I know, the family's finances are in good shape, and even if they weren't, Federico, Salvatore's father and the former head of the crime family, loathes foreigners.

And yet my instincts urge me to proceed cautiously. "Not yet," I reply. "Not until I have a better sense of what's going on."

"You don't trust Salvatore?"

I give Dante a dry look. "I don't trust *anyone*, as you should know by now. Get Valentina to intercept their communications." Valentina Linari is my most talented hacker. If she can't keep the Russians under surveillance, no one can. "If the bratva makes contact with the Verratti family, I want to know immediately."

"Yes, *padrino*." My lieutenants look alert, almost excited by the prospect of a turf war. Not me. I just feel a headache coming on.

I look around the room. "Anything else?"

"One more thing." Dante opens the folder in front of him. Extracting a note, he pushes it in my direction. "You got a letter from Arthur Kirkland."

The name is vaguely familiar. I search my memory. "The art collector?"

"Yes."

That explains the letter. Arthur Kirkland is eighty and doesn't believe in computers. I scan the sheet of paper with a frown. "He's warning me about an art thief. Do you know what this is about?"

Dante has an answer, of course. He always does. My second-in-command is loyal, ruthless, and, above all, unfailingly competent. "Arthur Kirkland collects Italian art. Some of his collection has been acquired through dubious means."

"Most of his collection," I correct, remembering more of the details now. "The Third Reich looted Italy in 1943, and Kirkland's uncle, a Nazi sympathizer, mysteriously ended up with priceless paintings when the war ended." I glance at the letter again. "This mystery thief stole one of his pieces last year."

"I think I like this thief," Joao says. Dante glances at him, and he lifts his hands in an expressive gesture. "What? You expect me to feel bad for a Nazi looter?"

A Preview of The Thief

Can't say I disagree with Joao's sentiment. "Kirkland says his security people have put together a profile of the thief."

"Yes, there was a dossier enclosed with the letter." Dante reads from his file. "The thief's specialty is sixteenth-century Italian religious art. Ten major works have been stolen, all from that period. And all from private collectors. Interestingly, the targeted paintings were also all previously stolen." He pauses for effect. "And they've all been returned to their rightful owners."

That *is* interesting. "A thief who fancies himself a modern-day Robin Hood?"

"Herself," Dante corrects. "At least, that's what Kirkland's investigative team concluded."

"A woman?" A current of anticipation hums through me. "How did they determine that?"

Dante pushes forward a tablet. "One of the cameras from Kirkland's compound took this before it shorted out."

I play the video. The thief is wearing a faded sweatshirt, its hood obstructing her face. But it's definitely a woman. The baggy sweatshirt can't hide her curves.

There's something about the way she moves that tugs at my memory.

"Kirkland wants her caught, padrino," Dante finishes. "It feels personal. He's written to everyone who might be her next target."

"Has he now?" I have an extensive collection of Venetian art that was mostly bought in public auctions, but not all.

Not my Madonna.

A Preview of The Thief

Painted by Titian himself and valuable beyond measure, the *Madonna at Repose* was my first big job. I stole it from the Palazzo Ducale when I was sixteen. I should have fenced it immediately but couldn't bring myself to part with it. It currently hangs in my bedroom.

I play the five-second clip again. There's nothing here —nothing to identify the thief—and yet something continues to tickle the back of my mind. The way she moves feels familiar somehow.

Tomas is reading the file. "Weird," he says. "She targets people all over the world but always strikes between November and January. Every single time."

"Well, it *is* Christmas," Leo points out. "People are distracted during the holidays."

"You know what else is strange?" Tomas continues. "Look at her targets. Vecchio, il Giovane, Lorenzo Lotto... These are all Venetian painters. But she's never struck in Italy."

I look at him curiously. "I didn't realize you were interested in art."

Tomas flushes. "I like to paint, padrino. It's a hobby of mine."

Dante takes the file from Tomas and scans it with a frown. "You're right," he says. "That is strange. There's plenty of stolen art in Italy, but it's almost as if she's avoiding coming here. You want Valentina to look into this?"

The puzzle pieces finally connect. I pull up my tablet and run a search to confirm my hunch.

Teresa Petrucci, died the seventh of December.

Paolo Petrucci, died the seventh of December.

And now I know why the woman seems familiar.

Teresa and Paolo were art thieves. And Lucia Petrucci, their only child, wandered the wharfs the night after she buried her parents, clutching a bottle of vodka and nursing raw grief in her heart.

Lucia, who graduated from the University of Chicago with a master's degree in art history.

The timing matches up. The thief stole their first painting ten years ago on Christmas Day. That would have been only two weeks after Lucia's parents died.

She's been stealing a painting every year since her parents died. A way of remembering them, perhaps?

Beautiful, *reckless* Lucia. Where is she now? I run another search, and the Internet provides me answers. After stints worldwide and ten years away, she's finally coming home. She starts as an assistant curator at the Palazzo Ducale next week.

Ten years, and I still remember the bottle green of her eyes. Ten years, and I still remember the hitch in her voice as she asked me to stay with her. *Don't go,* she whispered, her lips quivering. *I don't want to be alone tonight.*

She didn't call me the next day, and when I stopped at the hotel after dealing with the trio who accosted her, she wasn't there. She'd left for the airport. Flown out of Venice and out of my life.

Now she's back.

And she's an art thief.

I can't wait to see her again.

Venice is my city. I head up her mafia. I rule her underworld. Nobody steals in my city without my permission.

A Preview of The Thief

"I know who she is." Sharp hunger fills me, a hunger I haven't felt in years. "Don't involve Valentina; she has plenty of other things to do. I'll take care of this thief personally."

Dante studies me thoughtfully, but whatever he's thinking, he keeps to himself. "Yes, padrino."

ABOUT TARA CRESCENT

Get a free story from Tara when you sign up to Tara's mailing list.

Tara Crescent writes steamy contemporary romances for readers who like hot, dominant heroes and strong, sassy heroines.

When she's not writing, she can be found curled up on a couch with a good book, often with a cat on her lap.

She lives in Toronto.

Tara also writes sci-fi romance as Lili Zander. Check her books out at http://www.lilizander.com

Find Tara on:
www.taracrescent.com
tara@taracrescent.com

ALSO BY TARA CRESCENT

CONTEMPORARY ROMANCE

Venice Mafia

The Thief

The Broker

The Fixer

The Fighter

The Hunter

Hard Wood

Hard Wood

Not You Again

The Drake Family Series

Temporary Wife

Fake Fiance

Spicy Holiday Treats

Running Into You

Waiting For You

Standalone Books

MAX: A Friends to Lovers Romance

WHY CHOOSE / MFM ROMANCE

The Club M series

Menage in Manhattan

The Dirty series

The Cocky series

Dirty X6

You can also keep track of my new releases by signing up for my mailing list!

Made in the USA
Las Vegas, NV
20 February 2025